ROGUE JUSTICE

4.11.26

For the orcas!

All best,

ROGUE JUSTICE

A NOVEL

WILLIAM NEAL

Published by Alucard, LLC, Playa del Rey, California

Book design by Insana Media
Typesetting by wordzworth.com

Excerpt from "Black Marsh Eclogue" by Sam Hamill. All rights
reserved. Used by permission.

Rogue Justice
First edition: January 2013

Library of Congress Control Number: 2012922817

ISBN 978-0-615-73739-3

Printed and Published in the United States of America.

For Mom and Dad

What is man without the beasts? If the beasts were gone, man would die from a great loneliness of the spirit. For whatever happens to the beasts, soon happens to man. All things are connected.

—Chief Seattle

Prologue

"MAYDAY-MAYDAY-MAYDAY! This is the fishing vessel *Diamond Lil*. Repeat – this is the fishing vessel *Diamond Lil*. Rogue wave...boat going down...crew abandoned ship. Repeat – crew abandoned ship...wearing life jackets...four of us...please hurry." The captain radioed position, speed, and bearing, repeated the coordinates, then he, too, plunged into the abyss.

Five miles away – anchored off the east coast of Alaska's Aleutian Islands – a statuesque, thirty-something woman stood at the helm of the *Dawn Quixote*, her torch-red hair glowing in the ethereal light of the radar screen. Captain Zora Flynn was no stranger to rogue waves, had faced their destructive power before. They were stealthy and struck without warning, like dreadful aftershocks rebounding through time. She listened to the distress call through a screech of static, and immediately notified Coast Guard authorities. Seconds later, she anchored up, steering her rugged long-liner on a southwesterly course. Less than forty minutes later, she arrived, first on the scene, the deck lights and portals all that were visible on the stricken vessel.

Zora and her three-man crew wasted no time. They rapidly scooped all but one of the half-frozen men from the icy Bering Sea waters, waters that could kill in under an hour. But the fourth man had suffered deep cuts on both hands, making it impossible for him to grasp the life ring. A posse of great whites cruising in the area homed in on his blood, their small, primitive brains instantly recognizing prey. Driven by instinct and an easy meal, the hungry predators closed fast, their dorsal fins breaking the water, tails thrashing violently back and forth.

Paralyzed by fear, the man was moments away from an unimaginable death when Zora did the unthinkable, seemingly *without* thinking: she grabbed a pistol from under her bunk, peeled off her poncho, and dove in after him. One of the sharks hastily changed course, hurtling past her just below the surface. The big fish made a sudden, sweeping turn, and, with one powerful thrust of its tail, was upon her. Seconds later, she took a bone-jarring hit from the big conical head, throwing her up and out of the water. Landing hard, she absorbed some of the impact with a nifty tuck and roll, but she was completely disoriented, not sure which way was up. Her eyes were burning like hot coals from the salt, the metallic smell of blood overpowering. Several panicky moments passed before she found her bearings. She kicked her way to daylight, gasping for air and coughing up seawater. Somehow she'd managed to hold onto the weapon.

Then...a frightening surge of pressure.

The shark was barreling straight toward her again, jaws agape, its big teeth fixed in a savage grin. In that instant, she locked eyes with nature's most perfect killing machine, felt the intensity of its cold, dead, expressionless stare. It was only for an instant, but time enough for everything to slow down. Time enough for Zora's *highly* advanced brain to comprehend the inevitable – she had just seconds to live.

The mind-numbing thought instantly galvanized her will.

In a desperate now-or-never move, she raised the weapon, lunged toward her aggressor, and fired off three quick rounds. The bullets traveled only a few feet, but her aim was remarkably straight and true, striking the shark directly between its eyes. Stunned by the unexpected volley, the big fish banked hard right, then disappeared into the inky darkness. The other sharks, confused and disoriented, began zigzagging in strange crossing patterns, running everywhere at once. Soon they too dropped below the surface and vanished from sight.

When it was all over and the terrified man safely on board, Zora collapsed in a heap on the aft deck. The harrowing rescue had taken less than ten minutes, but she had a dark premonition the consequences would last the rest of her life.

CHAPTER 1

SIX MONTHS LATER
28 March, 2:40 PM PDT
Puget Sound, Washington

THE SLEEK WHITE CRUISER was a custom-built Hatteras – and she was a beauty.

More like a floating palace than a yacht, the powerful vessel stretched a full sixty feet from bow to stern and could comfortably accommodate eight indulgent souls on the cruise of a lifetime. The Skye Deck, located aft of the high-tech flybridge, was equipped with a Bose sound system, hydrotherapy Jacuzzi, and plush lounge seating. Down below, the luxurious cabin was all leather and mahogany, with a full-beam master suite the size of a small vacation villa.

The big boat was anchored off the southern tip of Lopez Island, one of four large islands that made up the spectacular archipelago known as the San Juans. And the handsome couple on board could not have asked for a more pristine day. A high pressure system had parked over Puget Sound two days earlier, bringing light winds and unseasonably warm temperatures. The sky was brilliant blue and a bronze sun reflected off water that gleamed like polished steel.

The luxury motor yacht had cost Jason Taylor a bundle, but there was plenty more where that came from. Jason's small Seattle law firm had become rather infamous in legal circles after he and his wily partner had outsmarted and out-lawyered an army of silk-stocking Wall Street attorneys in a massive corporate fraud case. The "Big One" – as it was known in the tort world – involved thousands of duped employees, many of whom had lost their entire life savings. The company eventually agreed to pay more than $100 million to settle the class-action lawsuit.

After expenses, Taylor & Associates pocketed a cool $26 million.

Not bad for a thirty-one-year-old greenhorn from the sticks of Minnesota.

Jason had purchased the craft with a portion of the spoils, then enrolled in an intensive, hands-on training course. The only license required, it turned out, was for the VHF radio. He had christened her *Lois Lane* in honor of his fiancée, the lovely Jia-li Han. Her name meant "good and beautiful" and, of course, she was both of those things. She had high cheek bones, sparkling dark brown eyes, and flawless skin. She was also Seattle's most popular news anchor. And like the intrepid *Daily Planet* reporter who tamed Superman, Jia-li came with all the bells and whistles: Ivy League smarts, a marvelous pedigree, and talent to burn. She was a tenacious journalist too, with a Midas touch for digging up compelling stories. It had taken Jason some time to win her over – she called him the "blue-eyed lady killer" – but eventually his good heart and first-class mind had carried the day.

Exactly six months after meeting, they were engaged.

As they cuddled together in a lounge chair on the Skye Deck, Jason reached for her hand, an engagement ring the size of Rhode Island sparkling in the brilliant sunshine. "Okay," he said. "'Fess up, babe. Something's been bugging you all afternoon."

"It's nothing," Jia-li replied.

"C'mon, is it the yacht? I know you hate it. I'll unload the damn thing as soon as I can find a buyer."

"I don't hate it, Jason. It's just so...*pretentious*, that's all." He knew Jia-li was being coy, that in her mind, the big boat was much more than that. In fact, she saw it as downright obnoxious, not at all in line with the values of a small town girl from Castine, Maine.

"What then?" Jason asked.

"Oh, no biggie, just a little dust-up with Ned. We squared off in his office yesterday after that massive pile-up on I-5 I told you about."

"The police chase. Three people died, right?"

"Four. It was awful, looked like a war zone out there. Anyway...after the accident I talked with one of the victims' mothers. She seemed okay at first, then she suddenly freaked out, went absolutely ballistic. After I calmed her down a bit, she begged me not to broadcast the interview. I gave her my word I'd cut it from the piece, but Ned aired it anyway. He can be a real pain in the ass sometimes."

Ned Calkins was Jia-li's news director and Jason agreed – he *was* a pain in the ass. "If it bleeds, it leads, right?"

"Yeah, only that's so *wrong*, Jason. This ratings-at-all-cost mentality is nuts and I told him so." Jia-li took a deep breath, stretched her arms, and calmed down a bit. "Sorry for being such a slug."

"Hey, it's okay. Look, let's chill a bit longer before we head back to base, soak up a few more rays. You know what they say about people from Seattle, 'they don't tan, they rust.'"

Jia-li leaned in, smiled, kissed him on the cheek. "You know what, sweetie? You're right. It's absolutely heavenly out here."

And it was.

Brilliant sunshine cast two-tone hues on the Cascades and Olympics, the muscular, snowcapped mountain ranges that flanked Puget Sound. Mt. Rainier and Mt. Baker were both visible in the distance. Closer in, gnarled, ochre-colored madrona trees hugged the rocky shoreline of Lopez Island. The air smelled clean and ocean-fresh.

They lay that way for several minutes without speaking. Then, glancing at her watch, Jia-li said, "Listen, captain, we need to haul anchor soon. This landlubber reports for duty at 1800 hours, remember?"

"Sure. Another half hour, okay, babe?"

"Yeah, but that's it."

Jason hugged her tenderly, closed his eyes, and soon drifted off to sleep.

Jia-li eased her arm from under Jason's neck, slid off the lounge chair, and tiptoed over to the entertainment center. A pile of CDs sat on top. She shuffled through the stack until she found her favorite Mozart concerto – *The Marriage of Figaro* – and slipped the CD into the bottom slot. Knowing her fiancé could sleep through a Category 5 hurricane, she hit the play button, cranked up the volume, and stretched out on another chair.

Held in the embrace of soaring violins, Jia-li soon nodded off herself, oblivious to the muffled sound of twin Mercury engines approaching on the starboard side of the *Lois Lane*. Had the music been a little softer, maybe she would have felt the tiny hairs on the back of her neck stand up, a million years of evolution telling her to pay attention. Maybe she would have said something to Jason. And just maybe they would have smelled trouble and come up with a plan.

But none of that happened.

Instead, the twenty-six-foot Sundancer eased closer until the bow rested alongside the much larger vessel. A wiry, small-boned woman in her late twenties stood at the helm. She had wavy, surfer-white hair and wore baggy shorts, a pink T-shirt, and floppy socks. Whitey throttled down and pushed the handle into neutral. "Ahoy there," she hollered.

Jia-li woke with a start, jumped to her feet. She turned down the music then hurried to the rail. "Ahoy back. What's up? You need some help?"

The woman flashed a dazzling smile. "I'm afraid so. This is going to sound really stupid, but I completely lost track of time. Radio says there's a big storm rollin' in."

Jia-li glanced up, saw only big fluffy clouds soft as cotton floating across a sapphire blue sky. "Really?" she said. Then she caught the name on the side of the boat. It appeared to be freshly painted in big, bold, black letters: *Queen Anne's Revenge*. It nagged at her – that name – but she couldn't quite pin down why.

"Yeah, she's comin' on strong, they say. Listen, we could really use some fuel."

Jia-li scanned the cockpit of the boat. There appeared to be no one else on board. "We?" she said smiling. "You got a mouse in your pocket?"

"Nope," Whitey shouted, the charm now a million miles gone. "Just me and my rowdy friends."

A loud bang!

Seconds later, two behemoths burst from the shadows and scrambled aboard the *Lois Lane*, scaling the ladder to the Skye Deck like hungry mountain cats. Jia-li froze. She tried to cry out, but the words would not come, only hysterical thoughts. One of the bruisers sported a Mohawk. The other had a nasty, zipper-like scar on the left side of his face that arched from cheek bone to chin. Both men were dressed head-to-toe in combat black. Scarface moved quick and sure, grabbing Jia-li from behind in a paralyzing chokehold.

Jason, startled awake by the commotion, leaped to his feet. Mohawk charged at him, ramming a knee into his rib cage, sending him reeling across the deck. He landed hard, gasping for air. The next shot, an iron-like fist to the jaw, was paralyzing. Jason's head hit the deck hard, blood oozing from a gash on the bridge of his nose. He struggled to his knees, fell backwards with a heavy thud, and lost consciousness.

Then more trouble...in the shape of a fourth pirate. He seemed to come from nowhere. This one looked like a madman, with maniacal eyes, the eyes of a dictator. He walked to within inches of Jia-li, stared at her menacingly, then, in one violent motion, ripped off her cotton tank top. She felt violated and vulnerable, fought to cover her bare breasts. But the hulking bruiser only tightened his vice-like grip, the inside of his elbow nearly crushing her windpipe.

Finally, overtaken by exhaustion and fear, Jia-li slumped to her knees. She had one final, coherent thought before darkness closed in.

Queen Anne's Revenge was the name of Blackbeard's boat.

CHAPTER 2

TWENTY MILES SOUTHEAST of the *Lois Lane's* position, a very different tempest was brewing, and the anxious-looking man staring blankly out the smoked-glass window felt dangerously close to its epicenter. He shifted nervously from one foot to the other, squeezing the life out of a rubber exercise ball. His eyes were fixed on the dark, empty stadium below.

The office was large with stacks of folders neatly piled on the floor, clear evidence of a man juggling many things at once but staying one step ahead of the fray. He was average height, early forties, with short brown hair that matched the color of his wardrobe: brown suit, brown tie, brown shoes, brown everything. No one, in other words, would mistake him for a matinee idol.

In the world of theme parks, however, Colby Freeman was a marquee name.

Since taking over Kingdom of the Sea's flagship operation in Seattle five years earlier, his savvy marketing strategies and innovative guest relations programs had resulted in impressive revenue gains. Skeptics had warned that a "warm-weather" operation would never work in the sun-starved Northwest. But Freeman proved them all wrong, effectively tapping into a population base of more than seven million people who lived an easy drive away.

Still, it was his leadership role in rebranding all fifteen KOS oceanariums as places of "science and education" that had truly put the shine on Freeman's soaring corporate star. Private research, animal rescue, and species conservation had become the new buzz words at each of the company's parks, now spread across three continents and five countries.

The Seattle property occupied 160 lavishly landscaped acres of prime real estate ten miles northwest of the city on the shores of Puget Sound. The prized site had once been part of Golden Gardens Park, one of the area's most popular destinations. The shrewd land grab – negotiated nearly a decade earlier – had included an exclusive sales, marketing, and advertising deal with a private brewery owned by the city council president, a fact that had conveniently slipped under the radar where it had remained. Permits were granted and construction completed. In the end, fears by local conservationists that the wetlands would be destroyed turned out to be largely unfounded, and most area residents quickly embraced the beautifully conceived attraction.

Since then, annual attendance at the Seattle location had consistently topped the three million mark, surpassing even the Paris and Shanghai venues. Freeman's pride and joy generated nearly $400 million in annual revenues, about half of it from gate receipts. The other half came from parking, food, beverage, and merchandise sales – including posters, mugs, T-shirts, stuffed animals, and all manner of other premiums, all made in China, all marked up at least five hundred percent.

Together, attendance at all fifteen parks exceeded forty million customers annually – a $5.2 billion cash cow that made the Aquatic Theme Parks division the most profitable entity within the sprawling, multinational conglomerate known as Chandler Global Enterprises, or CGE.

As in each of its sister parks, guests in Seattle were treated to a lush, tropical-themed paradise with a unique, family-friendly face. Inside the gates, the lineup of shows, rides, and exhibits was also essentially the same, a cleverly conceived strategy designed to control costs and reduce overhead. It was a first-rate entertainment destination and the catchy tag line said it all.

COME TO ANOTHER WORLD – WHERE LAND AND SEA CONNECT.

The acrobatic dolphins, up-close shark encounters, and rollicking, thrill-a-second metal coasters were all part of the appeal. But the core attraction – the one that lured crowds and drove revenues – was the wildly entertaining killer whale act featuring a pair of magnificent orcas, Samson and Delilah. Kids of all ages delighted in the carefully choreographed routines of these powerful animals and their daredevil trainers. It was a form of staged magic designed to give the appearance the whales could practically fly, an extravaganza simply called...BEYOND!

The devil, so the saying went, was in the details: hire a low-wage, non-union workforce, put a sound management team in place, bring in professional trainers, and exploit the hell out of the world's apex predator, a mega-star performer with no equal, animal or human.

And that, to the letter, was the KOS blueprint.

Freeman applied the formula with great energy and enthusiasm while looking past the fact that animal rights groups cried foul, declaring the company's wide-ranging public relations efforts were nothing more than elaborate smoke screens designed to disguise the truth. The parks, the activists claimed, generated obscene profits by exploiting the big mammals, primarily killer whales, turning them into cruel "circus acts." Freeman contended this reasoning was not only misguided, it was flat-out wrong. He and his staff were doing good work here, something important, something valuable. They were educating and entertaining the masses.

What could possibly be wrong with that?

The whales performed four times daily, six times on weekends, in the audience-friendly confines of Samson Stadium. And every show sold out. As Freeman surveyed the 6,500 empty seats, however, he felt his whole world crumbling around him – and with it his promotion to vice president of the division, a job that included a substantial salary increase and a lot more clout.

For the past two weeks Samson had been lethargic and irritable. Delilah seemed to sense his distress and she too had become temperamental, forcing the cancellation of more than sixty performances. And there was no end in sight. The whales were simply too unpredictable, threatening the safety of everyone around them. Worse, attendance had taken a precarious nosedive. Freeman was losing the turnstile game, the only game that mattered in this business.

His other major quandary? The park's senior vet, James "Big Boy" Medlin, a good ole boy from Odessa, Texas. Big Boy was a likeable enough guy, but the recent death of his wife after a prolonged illness had sent him into a tailspin. He became deeply depressed and often missed work. When he did show up, he was usually strung out on Valium, Johnny Walker Red, or both. Mitchell Chandler – CGE's enigmatic founder and CEO – had made it clear, however, that firing Big Boy was not an option. The two had served together in Vietnam where Big Boy reportedly saved the boss's life by dragging him off a booby-trapped bridge. An instant later, it blew sky-high, killing five of their comrades.

Big Boy's diagnosis of Samson's condition – an acute viral infection – appeared sound in the beginning. So did the heavy-duty antibiotics he'd prescribed. But as the whale's condition deteriorated, Freeman was left with little choice. He needed a second opinion. After all, they were dealing with the company's most valuable asset here. Turned out Samson's head trainer, Leanne Bucaro, didn't agree with Big Boy's findings either. She suggested Freeman speak with a friend of hers, a marine biologist who lived in the area. It was risky going out of house – he knew that – but, after reviewing the woman's bio, he'd reluctantly agreed.

Freeman picked up the two-page document off his desk, stared at the glossy photo paper-clipped to it.

She's really quite pretty, he thought. *In a natural sort of way.*

He then read through her credentials again.

Dr. Katrina Kincaid was a graduate of the Marine Science program at the University of California, Santa Barbara, specializing in Evolution and Marine Biology. She had gained renown in her field as the youngest member of "Mission Blue," an ambitious three-year project designed to protect large mammals and save the world's oceans. Leading scientists from around the world lauded the group's findings and sensible approach to problem solving. After completing the assignment, she'd accepted the position of executive director at Orca Network, a mostly volunteer organization dedicated to connecting whales and people in the Pacific Northwest.

Dr. Kincaid was expected any moment now and Freeman hoped the pounding in his head would shut down first. It had been a long time since he'd craved a cigarette, but he sure as hell could use one now.

Yes, maybe just one...to calm his nerves.

Katrina Kincaid arrived a few minutes later. She entered Freeman's office with the easy swinging gait of an athlete, her dancing brown eyes clear and direct. Her honeyed hair had been pulled into a tight ponytail. She wore little makeup, making no attempt to hide the spray of freckles across her nose. Extending her hand she said, "Nice to meet you, Mr. Freeman."

They shook.

"Please, it's Colby," Freeman replied. "Thank you for coming, doctor. I really appreciate it. Can I get you anything?"

"No, thanks," Katrina said, all business.

He gestured toward a beige couch in the corner. She sat down. He took a seat across from her in a matching chair. A glass table separated them, several colorful KOS brochures stacked neatly on top. Samson was prominently featured on the covers.

"I read your bio," Freeman said. "Very impressive. You're quite the adventurer."

"Yeah, I guess you could say that."

"Good for you. Most of the marine biologists *I* know seem to spend their time in windowless labs, their eyes glued to a microscope."

Katrina nodded. "Charting the habits of microbes in a Petri dish, no doubt. It's important work too, but just not for me." She glanced down at the brochure, wondering if Samson had ever experienced the same wanderlust she'd been blessed with. Even as a young girl, she was bitten by the travel bug, meticulously mapping out journeys to exotic, far-off places. And the world's great oceans had always captured her imagination. After a long, awkward silence, she said, "I'm sure you're busy, so I'll get right to the point. As you know, I performed a blowhole exam on Samson yesterday and took some blood samples. The test results came back a few hours ago. I had a friend of mine review them for me, a vet over at the CRC in Olympia."

Cascadia Research Collective was a non-profit scientific and education organization involved in a variety of research initiatives, many focused on killer whales. Katrina had worked with the scientists there many times before and trusted them implicitly.

"Talented group," Freeman said. "They know their stuff. But I have a feeling the news isn't good."

"No, sir, it's not. Samson is sick, *very* sick. He has Hodgkin's disease."

Freeman reacted as if she'd just pulled a gun on him. "Hodgkin's disease! I had no idea whales could come down with such a thing."

"It's rare, but it happens. We're not sure why. One thing we do know is that, over the past two decades, there's been an alarming increase in the number of large mammals dying from metastatic cancer, sea lions mostly. We haven't identified all the causes, but industrial contaminants are clearly one of the main culprits."

"Pollution," Freeman said matter-of-factly.

"Yes, pollution. The oceans are overdosing on toxic compounds. Millions of tons are being washed into the sea every day from factories, fertilized crops, sewer pipes, you name it. Fish become contaminated, and the sea lions eat the fish. That means high concentrations of PCBs and DDTs in their blubber. These poisons get passed on from mothers to babies in the mothers' milk."

Freeman shook his head. "I had no idea it was this bad. What are the other causes, besides pollution, I mean?"

"One is related to the contaminants. Studies suggest PCBs can suppress the immune system. In the case of sea lions, it may increase their vulnerability to the herpes virus infection, a close relative of *human* herpes virus, the one that fosters Kaposi's skin cancer lesions in AIDS patients."

"Sounds dreadful."

Katrina nodded her agreement, continued. "The third piece of the puzzle is genetics. For some unknown reason, animals with cancer are more likely to be inbred than those without it, so bad genes are probably at work here as well. Again, the data are incomplete."

"But Samson's been with us since...since he was a baby. He's eleven now. How could –"

"Well, as you know, killer whales eat about three to four percent of their body weight every day. Samson's what, four tons?"

"Five," Freeman replied, like a proud father.

Katrina quickly did the math in her head. The whales were eating, on average, at least three hundred pounds of food every day. It was very likely that at least some of the fish Samson consumed had been contaminated. She ran the numbers past Freeman, then added, "Over time, healthy cells turn into cancerous cells, causing tumors. It's only a theory, but that's my guess."

Freeman's face went pale. "Samson is dying. Is that what you're telling me, doctor?"

"Yes, sir, he's dying."

CHAPTER 3

28 March, 3:50 PM PDT
Puget Sound, Washington

JIA-LI HAN CAME TO sometime later. How much later she wasn't sure. Everything was a blur. Her wrists were tightly bound with hemp rope that had been tethered to the starboard rail. Jason was tied up next to her, little more than an arm's length away. He was still unconscious. She craned her neck, slowly gaining focus, until her eyes locked on Madman. He was alone, pacing back and forth across the Skye Deck, eyeballing her like a cattle rancher judging a prize bull at auction. Jia-li could almost hear his brain clicking, and in that instant, she knew what she was up against. Thinking back, she'd known it the minute the thugs had stormed the boat.

The media machine labeled them "Pirates of the Pacific," a predictable play on the popular movie franchise, *Pirates of the Caribbean.* For two years they had played a cat-and-mouse game with authorities up and down the West Coast, committing ruthless acts of high-seas larceny, each more brazen than the last. And according to police reports, they were even more heartless than their infamous counterparts from Somalia.

The most recent attack – off the southern coast of British Columbia – had left a fifty-six-year-old bank vice-president paralyzed and on life support. Jia-li had covered the story, landing an exclusive sit-down with the victim's grieving wife. It was one of the toughest interviews she'd ever done. Now, crouching in the shadow of evil, she felt every bit as helpless, overcome with one of those pit-of-the-stomach feelings that something horrible was about to happen.

Madman stared at her for another long moment. Finally he spoke, his manner as chilling as his words. "You need to pay close attention to what I say here, snowflake, because I don't mince words, and I never repeat myself. Understand?"

Jia-li nodded, trying to impose a sense of control she did not feel.

"Okay, so here's the deal. My colleagues and I will take care of business, then we'll be on our way. As for you and your boyfriend, say one word to *anyone* and I promise I will hunt you down, I will put your arms where your legs are, and only *then* will I kill you. You got that?"

Jia-li was numb, trembling so hard she could barely speak. "Yes, yes," she stammered. "Take whatever you want and leave us alone."

"That's more like it," Madman said, his eyes firmly planted on her bare breasts. "Damn, you really *are* a gorgeous piece of meat. But then, you already know that, don't you? Your kind always does."

A long silence.

Footsteps broke the spell.

The other pirates climbed the ladder to the Skye Deck, loaded down with the bounty they'd lifted from below. Madman looked over the loot – a Movado watch, pearl earrings, two MacBooks, Czech crystal vase, a bundle of cash, and assorted other goodies. "Respectable haul," he said.

Whitey nodded. She then knelt down on one knee taking Jia-li's left hand in hers. "Yeah, but this, boys, *this* is the mother lode. What's it worth, sweetheart, two hundred grand? Three?"

Jia-li said nothing, tried to pull away, but her wrists were too tightly bound.

Whitey smiled a mischievous smile, then yanked off the engagement ring, a 5-carat Blue Nile stunner in a platinum setting. She stood up, handed it to Madman.

He examined the diamond with an experienced eye. "Well, well, your boyfriend's got good taste, I'll say that much for him."

Madman's next words were drowned out by an earsplitting crack of thunder.

Jia-li glanced up at the turbulent sky, now a cloudy mess of mustard yellow.

It was the birth of a storm. A big one!

"Okay, let's get the hell out of here," Madman barked.

The pirates moved to the ladder and began descending to the main deck, Whitey leading the way. Jia-li felt an overwhelming sense of relief...but it lasted only a fleeting moment. Mohawk hesitated at the top step, stopped, and slowly turned around. "Not so fast," he shouted, his eyes flying up and down her body. "I know this broad. She's on TV. One of them Seattle stations."

It was like getting punched in the gut. "Jason," Jia-li mumbled out of the side of her mouth. "Please come to. Please. Please!" Jason's eyes fluttered a few times, but remained closed.

The other thugs scrambled back up to the Skye Deck, gathered in a semicircle around Jai-li.

"Shit!" Madman screamed. "Are you sure?"

"Damn right, I'm sure. It's been bugging me ever since I laid eyes on her. News at Eleven, ain't that right, anchor lady?" He leaned down, groped Jai-li's breasts.

Shivering with rage, she lashed out with her right foot, landing a crushing blow to Mohawk's groin. He doubled over in pain. "Why, you little bitch, I'll –"

Whitey lurched forward, grabbed Mohawk by the scruff of the neck. "Get up, you moron," she screamed, pulling hard on his collar. He staggered backwards, squawking like an angry crow, arms wind-milling to keep his balance. "How the hell did we miss it?" she shouted. "The goddamn name is a dead giveaway – *Lois* fucking *Lane*."

"Hell if I know," Madman said, a look of cold detachment in his eyes. "But it's really not a problem." Holding the ring in his left hand, he pointed his right index finger at Jia-li's temple like he was holding a gun. Then he pulled an imaginary trigger. "Bling bling, bang bang!" he grumbled, turning to Scarface. "Tank, take care of Clark Kent over here and make it quick."

Jia-li felt a chill rush through her body.

Dropping a name, even a street name, could mean only one thing: certain death.

"No!" she screamed. "We won't say a thing. I swear. Please don't..."

Tank/Scarface ignored her pleas. He pulled a Ruger pistol from the lightweight holster strapped to his belt, worked the slide, and jacked a bullet into the cylinder. The clip held 15-rounds, far more ammunition than this job would require. He then took two angry strides toward Jason, raised the pistol, and took a steady aim.

Jia-li turned away, gasping in horror.

She held her breath, waiting for the explosion.

It never came.

Instead, there was a sudden change in the sea's rhythm, subtle yet unmistakable. Then, a deep rumble shook the air, followed by an uneasy silence. In that moment, the center of gravity shifted and the entire earth seemed to stop its spin.

The pirates froze, their eyes darting about nervously.

Jia-li caught some movement off the port bow, followed by a sharp, piercing sound, like nothing she'd ever heard before. She swiveled around, craning her neck, pain shooting through her arms and shoulders.

It took a few seconds to register.

A dorsal fin – an *immense* dorsal fin.

Then...in a wild, frenzied blur, a black beast shot out of the sea like a giant torpedo, twisting and spinning, towering above the yacht, blocking out the last sliver of sunlight. Fifty, seventy-five, one hundred feet it soared into the angry sky before its massive tail even cleared the water, before it came crashing back to the surface with a ferocious concussion. The big boat lurched violently to one side, began rocking like an amusement ride gone haywire.

Tank/Scarface spun around, his eyes wide in shock. His legs skidded out from under him. The gun flew from his hand, swallowed instantly by the sea. The other pirates scurried along the deck grabbing for anything they could hold onto. Just then a second monster streaked past the yacht, going so fast Jia-li could barely follow its path. It burst through the surface in a spectacular breach, its back impossibly arched, torrents of water cascading down like a giant waterfall. Moments later, a third monster appeared, then another, and finally a fifth creature. They converged from every direction, moving with military precision, their giant tail flukes slapping the water in an awesome display of mass and power.

Swish, swish – WHACK! Swish, swish – WHACK! Swish, swish – WHACK!

Jia-li watched in astonishment.

Mohawk was the first to go, smeared by two colliding waves. An instant later, the other three pirates were swept overboard, their arms flailing about in the roiling waters. The giant beasts soon thundered around them forming a feeding carousel. They moved slowly at first, then gradually picked up speed as if powerful turbo-thruster engines had just kicked in.

The wind growled, thunder crashed, deafening loud and very close, followed by sustained bursts of lightning. Heavy rain drops began pelting the deck in blinding, horizontal sheets. Mountainous waves whipped the ocean into a fury of foam.

The scene was bedlam.

The pirates were now fifty feet off the port bow in a loose circle, clawing their way up and down the rising swells, groping for outstretched hands. They rode one wave after another, reaching the crest only to plunge down the back side into a swirling whirlpool, their frantic screams quickly whipped away by the wind and rain.

In the next instant, the underwater assassins burst from the raging black sea, vocalizing in a series of high-frequency calls that sounded like a chorus of shrill whistles. The noise was deafening, a ferocious sound that nearly shattered Jia-li's eardrums. She turned her head, forcing herself to look at the terrifying scene.

That's when they struck…with homicidal ferocity.

Whitey screamed bloody murder as fierce, twelve-inch conical teeth – teeth designed to tear, not chew – tore through her upper body, ripping apart tendons and crushing bones. The huge black mass wrenched her out of the water, soaring skyward in a wild shower of spray. For a long moment, they hung there together, suspended in mid-air, the writhing woman so tiny in the mouth of the giant beast, she didn't seem real.

"Good God, Jason!" Jia-li cried, fighting back nausea. "Did you see that?" The creature had dropped its prey and thick chunks of flesh were now hanging from its mouth.

Jason groaned, his eyes fluttered open, but no words came out.

Then, a second monster exploded from the depths. Mohawk spun around, his eyes wild with fear, his face dead pale. It was over in seconds. His legs disappeared, severed at the hips. He barely had time to scream.

An instant later, a third creature burst from the water, Tank/Scarface squirming in its mouth. Red rain streamed from gaping wounds in his neck and abdomen, the flesh completely shredded. He let loose a hideous cry that seemed to come from some other world, a shriek beyond agony.

Jason finally stirred. "Jesus," he muttered. "His guts are falling out."

Tank/Scarface was dead before he hit the water.

As the monster crashed back to sea, a huge wave torpedoed the *Lois Lane*, nearly capsizing the big yacht. The boat rocked wildly to port, then to starboard, back and forth, like a cradle in the hands of an angry giant.

Loud thunder rumbled across the sky, followed by another wicked flash of lightning. The rain was coming harder now, so hard Jia-li could barely see. Her eyes stung. She tasted blood. The hurting cold cut to the bone. Then, amid the confusion and chaos, she spotted Madman. He was swimming hard and going nowhere. For an instant their eyes locked and, strangely, an image of Saddam Hussein flashed across her mind. She had reported on his execution in 2006, watched the pirated video of the hangman's noose tightening around his neck. Different fiend, same expression: defiant, yet panicked.

An instant later, the image of Hussein was gone and so was the other madman.

His corpse, hideous and ravaged, had disappeared into the gloom.

The queasiness rose again in the pit of Jia-li's stomach as another wall of water swept over the rail. "Jason, watch out," she yelled. The boat heaved wildly. There was a loud bang that sounded like a shotgun blast. Something had torn loose on the deck – she couldn't make out what it was – but the flying missile struck Jason on the forehead, knocking him unconscious again.

"Shit! Shit! Shit!" Jia-li roared in frustration, fighting desperately to loosen the rope binding her wrists, the skin now raw and bleeding. It was no use. The knots only pulled tighter. She looked up, pleading for help. The skies burst forth with one final torrent before the downpour finally stopped. An instant later, everything went quiet, spooky quiet – and for several minutes there was almost no sound, save for the water lapping against the boat's hull and the occasional squawk of a seabird.

Jia-li blinked her teary eyes, fighting with every breath to remain conscious. The slightest movement hurt like hell. As the temperature began to drop, she curled up into a ball, shivering uncontrollably, the cold penetrating so deeply into her bones, it felt as if someone had wrapped her body in a blanket of ice. She could already feel her systems beginning to shut down, the early stages of hypothermia setting in. Growing up in the Northeast, she had endured some of the harshest winters imaginable and recognized the symptoms – weakness, drowsiness, shallow breathing, loss of concentration, the constant shivering.

Anxious moments passed.

Then...the boat began to rock, gently at first, but soon more violently.

She sensed it before she saw it – an immense black mass slowly rising out of the water on the port side of the boat.

Time slowed to a crawl.

Jia-li felt a sickening fear.

Fear beyond anything imaginable.

She was staring into the fathomless black eye of a one-hundred-ton monster.

CHAPTER 4

28 March, 3:30 PM AKDT
Juneau, Alaska

THE FIERCE STORM pounding the coast of Washington had moved north and it kept getting worse. Waves were coming in seismic bursts of fury, tall as buildings, with sustained winds of more than 80 miles per hour. At the National Weather Service offices on Mendenhall Loop Road, meteorologists huddled around computers tracking what they called a "bomb" – a rare confluence of weather fronts fueled by a massive low-pressure system. Initial forecasts had called for winds of 40 to 50 miles per hour. They were wrong. In fact, the storm was moving faster, with far greater intensity, than anything on record. The barometer continued to drop, and no one seemed to have any idea what the storm would do next.

One hundred forty miles due west of Juneau, the *Dawn Quixote* was taking the full brunt of Mother Nature's wrath. For more than two hours, the sturdy, sixty-eight-foot wooden vessel had been hammered by mountainous seas, the waves stacking up as tall as California redwoods. Winds whipped through the riggings making a fearsome, screaming sound, and through that noise, the crashing torrents thundered down. The dizzying punch of the ocean came seconds later.

Sixty feet up, sixty feet down, WHAM!

Sixty feet up, sixty feet down, WHAM!

Captain Zora Flynn maintained a white-knuckle hold on the wheel, flexing her long, tendril-like fingers to keep the circulation flowing, alert searching eyes scanning the angry sea. The fiendish storm had wiped out all satellite signals, rendering the GPS useless. She was navigating on instinct, fighting hard to keep the ship afloat, fighting even harder to control her fear. Fear was the bogeyman as surely as the savage elements. Fear clouded judgment. And where there was fear, there was shame, a lesson her mother had taught her as a young girl.

Yet, this was a moment Zora had been preparing for since landing her first crew job six years earlier. She had signed on with the skipper of a lobster boat out of Hyannis, Massachusetts, working her way up from cook to first mate. She'd learned everything there was to know about gear, fuel, bait, radar, engineering, navigation, rigging, tying knots, splicing line, cleaning fish, managing the fish hold. She'd learned about compass error; that good seamanship was equal parts common sense and experience; and how to calculate revenue, expenses, profits, losses, and crew payments as reflected on the "settlement sheet."

It all came down to crew seniority and the size of the catch: no fish, no pay.

But this trip wasn't about fish or money. Not anymore.

This trip was about survival.

Ascending the liquid slopes took everything the tough, old seiner could handle. The descent was like dropping off the edge of the earth, the bow free-falling into the deep trough on the other side. Zora braced for another monstrous wave, shouted to the rugged-looking man standing next to her in the wheelhouse. "Jesus, Rico, we're getting the shit kicked out of us here. If I take my hands away for even a second, she rolls sideways. You ever see weather like this?"

"No, Skip, she's one mean motherfucker, all right." At thirty-seven, first mate Federico Lapenda was a year older than his captain and the most senior member of the crew. A master welder and exceptional mechanic, he had a lean, confident look that commanded respect.

But right now, his face was as white as an oyster.

They stared out the pilothouse windows into a tortured black sky. Seconds later, another giant swell crashed on the foredeck and their world lit up like the Fourth of July. The wave hit with such force, the boat groaned as if she were in agony, listing so far to starboard the mast nearly dipped into the water. The lights dimmed, flickered, came back up.

"The generator," Lapenda shouted. "I just checked the damn thing a minute ago."

"Don't worry about it now, Rico. Listen, are all the hatches and portholes dogged down?"

"Uh-huh."

"What about the decks and engine room?"

"Roger that too, Skip. Any gear not nailed down is either stowed or lashed. She's as ready as she'll ever be."

"Let's hope it's enough."

"Yeah," Lapenda said, staring out at the blistering tempest. "You know something, Skip? When I was a kid and things got really rough, momma always said we should turn to the Lord. She'd say, 'What would Jesus do?'"

"Yeah, so what *would* he do about now?"

"Damned if I know."

Zora threw him a penetrating look. "Well, maybe you should ask him."

"Yeah," Lapenda said, thoughtfully. "I guess maybe I should."

A long moment passed between them.

"All right, then," Zora said. "In the meantime, you better jump into your survival suit. Tell Cassidy and McCabe to do the same."

"You got it, Skip. Be back in a flash."

Zora watched Lapenda fight his way out the wheelhouse door, straining so hard the veins on his neck looked like they might explode. He was a good man. So were her two deck hands, Luke McCabe and Blake Cassidy. Cassidy was twenty-three, built like an NFL linebacker and every bit as tough. Give him a tool to grip and a broken valve to fix, and he was happy as a clam. McCabe was two years younger. Ex-army, fit and strong, he rolled his own cigarettes, and could spin a yarn with the best of them.

Zora had hired them on five consecutive runs now, probably some kind of record. Most young fishermen folded their tents after one or two trips, beaten down by the back-breaking, sleep-depriving, mind-numbing grind. She wondered how they were holding up in the cramped berthing compartment below. Dragon's Alley, they called it.

For the next twenty minutes, the furious assault continued. It seemed like twenty hours. The *Dawn Quixote* cleared some swells and punched through the crests of others. Then, with a sudden jolt, the boat dropped into another deep trough, vertical walls of water climbing both sides of the vessel like hungry predators. The wicked weather had pushed Zora's body past all limits of human endurance, and her mind began playing tricks. She closed her eyes, trying to shake the disturbing images that roared through her head.

In her vision, the dark gray mass had turned to stone. She was seven. She and her best friend, Callie, were horseback riding in the Idaho hills. It was getting dark. Zora knew a shortcut back home, double-dared Callie to go. She said she was too scared. Zora persisted. They rode into the narrow passage. Neither of them saw the rattlesnake, but Callie's chestnut gelding did. He reared up defiantly, then staggered sideways as his foreleg slipped over the edge of the cliff. One horrifying instant later, horse and rider disappeared into the abyss. Callie's chilling screams echoed off the granite walls, spooking Zora's Appaloosa. Zora reflexively wrenched in the reins, but couldn't hold on. She was catapulted out of the saddle. The next thing she remembered was waking up in a hospital bed, hooked to a bunch of machines, floating in and out of consciousness, the awful smell of antiseptic turning her stomach. She was surrounded by a legion of somber-faced strangers in blue scrubs, Callie's desperate cries still coursing through her head.

She heard those cries still, most every night, in fact.

Damn ghosts.

The flash to the past took only a few seconds, yet the haunting memories had a sobering effect. Zora swore she would not be responsible for any more death. Not on her watch. No way.

The maverick seas were now three times as high as the *Dawn Quixote*, the winds gusting out of the southeast at more than 100 miles per hour. It was like being mauled by a giant grizzly, only worse. Merely maintaining balance on the heaving bridge was exhausting, aching muscles stabbing at her like ice picks. She'd read somewhere that "pain was weakness leaving the body," but she couldn't get her head around it now.

Zora had already tuned the VHF and single-sideband radios to emergency channels – channel 16 on the VHF, 2182 megahertz on the SSB. She tried both frequencies again hoping to raise another boat, but got nothing but static. Then she issued an urgency alert. "Pan-Pan, Pan-Pan, Pan-Pan," she said in a sharp, measured tone. "Hello all stations, this is the fishing vessel *Dawn Quixote*. We are one hundred fifty miles west-northwest of Sitka, Alaska." She rattled off the coordinates. "We're taking on water, but the pumps are keeping up for now."

More static.

She repeated the call.

Still nothing.

An instant later, Lapenda burst through the wheelhouse door wearing his one-size-fits-all survival suit. The bulky orange get-up was made of neoprene and looked something like a space suit with its hood, feet, and mitten-shaped gloves. It was designed to delay hypothermia and keep its occupant afloat. How long they'd last in these seas, though, was anybody's guess.

"How are Cassidy and McCabe doing?" Zora asked.

"Hangin' in," Lapenda replied. "Cassidy said they tried playing a few hands of gin rummy, but the floor kept jumping up and swallowing the cards."

"I'm sure. Are they suited up?"

Lapenda nodded in the affirmative.

For a long moment, their eyes locked – and that's when fate intervened, in the form of a massive Norwegian tanker called the *Polar Seas*. In a heavily-accented voice, the ship's captain radioed that the vessel was en route to Valdez, and currently six miles from the *Dawn Quixote*'s position. He said he could be at her side in less than half an hour.

Zora decided then and there that the only way to save boat and crew was to successfully execute two back-to-back maneuvers, moves she knew would send shivers up the spines of even the most seasoned mariners. She felt them herself. The first – coming around in an angry sea – could cause the vessel to roll heavily and capsize. The second – hiding under a ship – was exactly that, and in this case it was a very *big* ship. The deck of the *Polar Seas* could swallow three football fields. From keel to flying bridge, she was as tall as a twelve-story building.

Some thirty minutes later, right on cue, the giant tanker approached to starboard, slowed to six knots, her course altered slightly to the northeast.

Zora then explained her hair-raising plan to a skeptical captain.

Finally, after a long pause, he said, "Roger, *Dawn Quixote*, we'll slow to nine knots." The voice was calm, reassuring. "You'll need to turn onto a parallel course with us. The winds are still out of the southeast. If you can keep position amidships, that's the sweet spot. We'll do our best to calm it down for you over there. Good luck, captain. Over."

"Roger that, *Polar Seas*. Over."

Then...an unsettling *bang*.

Seconds later, Cassidy and McCabe burst through the wheelhouse door, scrambling to maintain balance in their clumsy survival suits. "What the hell's going on down there?" Zora shouted.

Cassidy coughed hard, caught his breath, and gave her the news. "Overhead cable, Skip. The damn thing snapped, nearly took my head off. And that last wave sheared off the bolts on the galley porthole. Fuckety-fucked-shit-eating-weather."

"Take it easy, man, you'll blow a gasket," Zora shouted. "What else?"

McCabe said, "The anchor tore loose from the roller. We got ourselves two hundred pounds of forged steel jumping around out there like a wounded tiger."

"Jesus, that's all we need. Got any more good news, McCabe?"

"The engine room, Skip, it's flooding. We've been checking it every five minutes like you said, but –"

"You pumped out the bilges?"

"Yeah, it's no use. Water just keeps on coming. It's rockin' so bad down there, I can't find the goddamn leak. "

Zora glanced at the oil pressure and engine temperature gauges. Both were low, heightening the danger of fire or an explosion. Just then, the *Dawn Quixote* ploughed into the base of an immense wave. The force blew out a window panel on the port side, assaulting the crew with shards of glass and raging seawater, the smell of brine overwhelming. The pilothouse was now in shambles. Seconds later, the bilge alarm sounded, extremely loud and menacing.

The bottom of the boat was rapidly filling with water.

"I'll grab some plywood," Cassidy yelled.

Zora yanked him by the arm, her eyes burning from the spray. "Forget it. We go now or we go down." She cranked the helm hard to port, pushed the throttle full ahead.

Lapenda, Cassidy, and McCabe braced themselves against the bulkhead.

Zora took another deep breath, thinking what the others had to be thinking...

The margin of error here is zero.

She gritted her teeth, gave it heavy throttle, and held her breath. "Sweet Mary, here we go."

Up, up, up the vessel went, drifting broadside as she ascended the immense dark wall, creaking and moaning like some prehistoric monster that had just been awakened from a deep sleep. At the height of the swell, Zora wheeled harder to port and eased off on the throttle. Seconds later, the boat plunged down the backside of the big comber, propellers out of the water and spinning wildly. Then, at the precise moment the bow caught the base of the wave, she completed the impossibly difficult turn. The *Dawn Quixote* was now on the port side of the big ship, shielded from the ear-splitting winds.

Lapenda let loose a wild yelp, knuckle-smacking Cassidy and McCabe. "Halle-fucking-lujah, I don't believe it."

Zora froze them with a look. "Hold the bubbly, boys, now the fun *really* begins."

She slowly pushed the throttle forward again, inching the boat closer to the soaring dark hull of the tanker, one hundred feet of cold steel looming directly in front of her face. Finally, several agonizing minutes later, Zora brought the vessel bow-to-port, midship. The *Dawn Quixote* was now running parallel with the tanker, lying safely off the hull, matching her course and speed. The challenge now became staying close without getting crushed like an ant under a steamroller.

For the next half hour, Zora held her position, the smaller boat laying to the lee of the immense steel hull. It was exhausting just to keep her balance. Pain stabbed at every joint. Then, without so much as a hint of warning, she was blinded by a brilliant flash of light. The sun had broken through heavy layers of steel gray clouds, like a lightning bolt shot from heaven.

Next the sky opened up, the winds subsided, and the giant waves stopped cresting. So sudden was the change that captain and crew looked at one another with blank stares.

Lapenda shook his head in disbelief. "How weird is that? I've never seen waves spread out so fast in my life."

"Ten thousand cocksuckers!" Cassidy shouted.

Lapenda and McCabe looked at him sideways.

"My old man," Cassidy exclaimed. "He'd say that when there was nothing else to say."

Zora flashed a quick smile and continued holding firm to the wheel. Moments later, she backed off the throttle, slowly drifting away from the massive tanker. Before turning for home she instructed the crew to board-up the wheelhouse and inspect for leaks and hazards. They fixed the main leak, found a few other trouble spots and general seepage, but nothing the bilge pumps couldn't handle.

She then checked the radar. The front had turned sharply northeast.

There would be no more killer waves, not this day. Zora had brought boat and crew to the brink and back again. It wasn't pretty, but they were alive. Still, something gnawed at her gut, a sense of foreboding that seeped in like a poison. She'd dodged two bullets in less than six months – first the marauding sharks and now this wretched storm – and didn't bad things always come in threes? Shaking off the feeling, she reached for the mike, so bleary-eyed with exhaustion she could barely speak. "Captain, I owe you one. This is the *Dawn Quixote*. Clear and standing by on 16."

CHAPTER 5

28 March, 5:50 PM PDT
Kingdom of the Sea Oceanarium, Seattle, Washington

AFTER A LENGTHY MEETING with Leanne Bucaro and Big Boy Medlin, Katrina checked on the dying whale again. No change. He didn't have long to live, maybe a few days if that. She then returned to Colby Freeman's office. They sat in the same seats as before, only this time there were no pleasantries exchanged.

Katrina spoke first. "All due respect, sir, but your senior vet's a little past his prime. In my opinion, he found what he wanted to find…a viral infection. And the heavy-duty antibiotics he's administering are probably doing more harm than good right now."

"I'm sure that's true," Freeman said, slumping down in his chair. He looked like he'd just been hit with a load of buckshot. "But what I don't understand is how fast all this came on. I mean, Samson seemed perfectly fine up until a few weeks ago."

"I'm afraid he *wasn't* fine. Besides, most sick mammals don't linger for long, not when they lose the will to live. And I suspect that's the case here."

"So how long does he have?"

Katrina told him.

Freeman removed his glasses and began massaging his temples. "This can't be, doctor. Our entire operation's built around that animal. Hundreds of millions of dollars are at stake here, not to mention Samson's value as a stud. I can't even begin to estimate *that* number. He's fathered six calves already and he's still young. It's not like you just go out and buy another killer whale. They must be bred."

Katrina knew all about so-called breeding program, and it was fatally flawed. Females that typically did not produce calves until age fifteen or so in the wild were forced to conceive much younger than that in captivity. The result was a lot more miscarriages and higher rates of infant mortality. "Look," she said. "Why breed an animal that has demonstrated aggressive behavior, especially when you know its offspring will interact with humans? You're producing more whales, true, but without regard to their health, or the safety of those who work with them. That's exactly what happened in Japan three months ago."

The story had made headlines around the world. A veteran trainer at the KOS park in Osaka had been feeding an orca when the four-ton whale turned on her. She was repeatedly assaulted by the powerful animal, then dragged under water. She drowned before help arrived. The official report, crafted by attorneys and tweaked by publicists, tactfully implied the trainer had been "careless." In fact, three eyewitnesses claimed the whale attacked with aggression and purpose.

Freeman shook his head. "A terrible accident, that's what it was. I can assure you, the safety of our employees and guests is job one here in Seattle. Same goes for all of our parks. And you're completely overlooking the other benefits we offer."

Katrina had heard the arguments before, ad nauseum, about how the parks promote education, conservation, and protection. She didn't buy any of it. KOS was all about the bottom line, and much of what went on here she found morally reprehensible. "Orcas are unbelievably ill-suited to live their lives in captivity," she said. "It strips them of their heart and soul, turns them into nothing more than circus performers. As you well know, sir, these are social animals, acoustic animals, but, if all they get to do is stare at concrete walls all day, why use their echolocation, right? Not when there's no variety, no texture. So what happens? In a year or two they become completely bored, or neurotic, or both. And that makes them dangerous, *extremely* dangerous."

"So you're suggesting we let all the whales go, is that it? Okay, then how do we make people care if they never get to experience these animals up close? It all boils down to education. The more we learn about these animals, the better off they'll be. I know because I see the faces of the kids. They light up like it's Christmas morning when the orcas perform." Freeman paused, took a shallow breath. "And one more thing you need to understand..."

Katrina had heard enough. She stood up, but Freeman grabbed her arm, tugged it gently.

"Hear me out, doctor. Please."

Katrina hesitated, then gave a short nod and sat back down on the edge of the couch.

"Thank you," Freeman said. "Look, as you know, our organization spends well over a million dollars a year rehabilitating and releasing injured and stranded marine mammals. And where do you think that money comes from? Gate receipts! A one-day pass for a family of four is two hundred fifty bucks, plus parking, food, and premiums. Do you really think mom and dad shell out that kind of dough so their kids can look at some ugly old walrus? No! They want them to see dolphins and sharks, but most of all they want them to experience *Samson*."

"I get the attraction, sir, believe me I do. But that doesn't make it right."

"There's something else you need to understand," Freeman shot back. "There are people out there who will stop at nothing to shut us down, people with very liberal agendas. Certain animal rights groups, misguided members of the media, and the like. They'll make Samson their poster boy, use him to bring down an entire industry, everything we've built. And if you think I'm exaggerating here, doctor, I assure you that I am not."

Katrina held his gaze, but said nothing.

"Let me show you what I mean," Freeman added. He stood, retrieved a laptop from his desk, set it on the glass table. After punching in several keys, he turned the computer toward Katrina. The grainy video showed a rag-tag collection of men and women carrying protest signs and chanting, *"Free the Whales!"* "This is an outfit down in Portland, a loony bunch of aging hippies, trust-fund radicals, and Echo Boomers. Call themselves the Orca Crusaders and they're intolerant of anyone who disagrees with their far-left agenda."

Katrina nodded. "I'm aware of who they are."

"Then you know it's impossible to have a reasonable debate with these people, not when their battle cry is 'Attack! Attack! Never Defend!' Here, take a look at their web site." Freeman punched a few more keys on his computer. The image cut to an emaciated couple wearing black and white wet suits, lying in a partially-filled bathtub, arms chained to the wall. There was a caption scrawled in large blood-red letters at the bottom of the page.

IMAGINE LIVING YOUR LIFE IN A BATHTUB!

"I'm telling you, doctor, these extremists are serious, focused, and quite literally insane – and that makes them very, very dangerous."

"We both know the Orca Crusaders is a fringe group," Katrina said. "Most activists aren't like that, not at all. They care deeply for the animals, only want what's best for them. In any case, what's your point?"

"My point, doctor, is this. We employ a lot of people here. Jobs are on the line, *lots* of jobs." Freeman pressed his case like a seasoned defense attorney seeking acquittal for a guilty client. The extremists, he said, had been camping outside the park in Osaka since the accident, driving down attendance by more than forty percent. He claimed the numbers had also fallen sharply in Seattle, despite aggressive marketing efforts to keep the turnstiles turning, absent the park's star performer. "Look," he added, his lower lip trembling. "If these lunatics show up on *my* door, the game's over. I need to put 8,000 people through these turnstiles every day on average to make budget. And without the whales, there's no way in hell I do that. The rest of the animals are bit players. So it's not just about the money."

Katrina wasn't buying this argument either. "With all due respect, sir, it *is* about the money. And Samson's a license to print the stuff. He's the central spectacle here, your Mickey Mouse."

"Okay, look, what I need from you is a little time," Freeman said, lowering his eyes. "Is that too much to ask?"

Katrina thought about that. "How *much* time?"

"Forty-eight hours."

A long silence, then, "Samson may not live that long."

Freeman nodded demurely. "Let me be frank about something, okay? Leanne's daughter is quite ill, as I'm sure you know. If these pot-smoking lefties put us out of the killer whale business, then she's out of a job, which means no health coverage. I have two girls of my own, both headed off to college soon, and I can't imagine not having health insurance. So please, doctor, carefully consider what's at stake here."

Katrina didn't respond right away, wondering why Freeman hadn't reported Samson's illness to authorities two weeks earlier when he should have. It wasn't as if the Feds wouldn't find out. Then again, his request did not seem all that unreasonable. "Okay, forty-eight hours," she said. "And if Samson's still with us at that point, we'll need to talk about euthanizing him. He must be suffering terribly."

A hefty weight seemed to lift from Freeman's shoulders. "Absolutely. Thank you."

Katrina stood up again, only this time she headed for the door.

"Oh, one last thing," he said. "Samson's test results, I assume they're confidential?"

"The lab techs know there's a sick animal, but that's *all* they know."

Freeman smiled weakly. "Perfect! Again, I can't thank you enough, doctor."

At that, Katrina stiffened somewhat. "Good luck, Mr. Freeman. You're going to need it." She ignored his outstretched hand, marched out the door, and did not look back.

CHAPTER 6

28 March, 7:10 PM PDT
San Francisco, California

THE EVENING RUSH HOUR was winding down as the big black Town Car rolled along Lombard Street in light traffic. The lanky man sitting in the back seat stared mindlessly out the window. Mitchell Chandler loved this City by the Bay, yet he deplored its politics and despised the perpetual cold and fog. Like tonight, a thick gray soup. He was a people watcher, always had been, and spotting the locals was easy enough. They dressed for the weather. Most tourists did not, which often left them shivering in long lines to catch cable cars or squeezed together inside crowded, over-priced restaurants.

Chandler glanced at his watch, then tapped the hand of the striking brunette sitting on his right. Forty-six-year-old Savannah Sokolov was not only his lover and confidant, she also ran CGE's worldwide security operation out of the company's headquarters in Olympia, Washington. She'd held the job for nearly three years now, and they'd been an item for exactly half that time. Initially, of course, the talk was that Savannah had slept her way to the top. In fact, the relationship was built on mutual trust and respect. Those were feelings Chandler had never experienced before, certainly not with any of his gold-digging ex-wives, all three of them.

He turned to her and said, "Ten minutes, Savannah."

"What's that?" she asked.

"We're ten minutes late."

"You're the big tuna, Mitchell. They'll wait."

"I know. I feel like I'm running for the goddamn bus all the time, that's all."

Savannah wore a simple black wrap around her shoulders, her strapless red evening gown accentuating a cleavage so deep, it made Chandler shudder. "Then, let's make it a short night," she said, smiling flirtatiously.

This was a woman used to handling powerful men, even one *this* powerful. "Besides, I have a surprise waiting for you back at the house."

Chandler winked and said, "Now that's an offer no man in his right mind could refuse."

Savannah smiled. "It's a date, then."

The limo driver turned right on Van Ness and accelerated up the steep hill. A few minutes later he pulled in front of The Fairmont Hotel, its stylish facade shrouded in an amber-colored mist. He jumped out and opened the back door.

"Thanks, Rizzo," Chandler said. "You and the boys stay close. Got that?"

Rizzo was a hulking brute with a buzz cut and deep-set eyes. He nodded. "Of course, sir."

Chandler's three-man security detail never trailed more than a few car lengths behind, which was where they were tonight, riding in a dark green SUV with tinted windows and a souped-up engine. There were simply too many nefarious characters out there with warped agendas to take any chances, even at a swanky soiree such as this one.

The handsome couple slipped out of the vehicle, walked quickly up the red-carpeted steps, and moved inside. Savannah took it all in. "They sure don't build 'em like this anymore, do they, Mitchell?"

They entered the lobby. It was as busy as Grand Central Station and damn near as big. Moments later they passed through a crowded restaurant and into the elegant Venetian Room. Like everything else in this storied place, the ballroom had a fascinating history. Crooner Tony Bennett had first sung his signature song, "I Left My Heart in San Francisco," on the Venetian's compact stage.

Tonight, a shimmering, full-dress affair was in full swing. Soft string music played in the background and everyone appeared well-heeled, well-connected, or, at the very least, beautiful. The room had been transformed into an authentic Italian villa by two flamboyant party planners, affectionately known among their peers as the VIPs of RSVPs. And for this event, they'd somehow managed to wangle a dozen priceless paintings from a pair of enterprising museum curators, including works by Chagall, Rembrandt, Matisse, and Van Gogh.

Chandler looked around, admiring the impressive display. The Van Gogh, he mused, would probably fetch $10 million on the open market, which was precisely $10 million more than the tortured genius had earned while he was still alive, a fact most people didn't know. But Chandler did. That was because he belonged to an exclusive club, a rogues' gallery of eccentric art lovers, prepared to fork over millions of dollars for paintings they often stashed in attics or basements.

His art collection included more than two thousand pieces. Even he didn't know the exact number, or the value. But there was no mistaking his status among this crowd. He was the richest guy in a *roomful* of rich guys. Chandler's net worth was estimated at more than $20 billion, good enough to land him on Forbes' top-ten list of the wealthiest Americans. And on this festive occasion, he was being honored by the American Alliance of CEOs, or AAC, an invitation-only membership that included the most powerful names in business – investment bankers, hedge fund whizzes, high-tech gurus, oil barons, and other titans of industry. Collectively, they wielded enormous clout in a host of state capitals, and in the one place where it counted most, Washington, D.C.

The organization met twice a year, fall on the East Coast and spring on the West Coast.

Following cocktails and small talk, Chandler and Savannah took their seats at the head table. A sumptuous, five-course meal followed, after which AAC's president stepped to the dais. He cleared his throat, then gestured for quiet. "Ladies and gentlemen, as most of you know, Mitchell Chandler represents the quintessential American success story. He started modestly with a couple of small apartment buildings in Reno, Nevada. Today, Chandler Global Enterprises is a thriving conglomerate comprised of fifty-four companies – at last count – spanning the globe. And it's no secret Mitchell's rock-star lifestyle is catnip for the media. He does, dare I say, have an affinity for hiring beautiful women."

"Here, here!" one man shouted from the back. The room erupted in laughter and cat-calls.

Chandler smiled, threw Savannah an admiring look. With her radiant hair, porcelain skin, and gracious curves, she had always reminded him of the classic femme fatale from Hollywood's Golden Age – not the cagey former federal agent who knew more about art than he did. And that was saying something. He had lured her away at great expense from a booming Bay area high-tech firm, where she'd held a similar position in corporate security. She'd accepted that job after a somewhat controversial career in law enforcement, first as a criminal investigator in the Boston district attorney's office, and then with the FBI's renowned art-theft team. The small unit, established in 2004 following the looting of Iraq's Baghdad Museum, investigated all manner of stolen art, looted art, and art fraud on both national and international stages.

The speaker continued. "In just the past month alone, no less than five magazines have done feature stories on our distinguished guest of honor. Now, I took the liberty of lifting a few highlights from those articles. *Newsweek* calls him, 'Brilliant, aggressive, a steamroller with gold cuffs.' *Fortune* says, 'He makes waves other people ride.' Then, there's my personal favorite from *The Weekly Standard*, 'Mitchell Chandler is an alchemist when it comes to money. Nobody does it better.' As for Mitchell's enigmatic nature? I'm told he kept his latest acquisition so secretive that, when the announcement was finally made, someone said they saw white smoke coming from corporate headquarters: 'We have a deal!'"

"Domini Patris," someone bellowed, followed by a round of enthusiastic applause.

Chandler leaned in close to Savannah, whispered in her ear. "He left out megalomaniac, the Prince of Arrogance, and *my* personal favorite – he's got the ethics of an alley cat."

Savannah turned toward him, smiled, pressed two fingers against his lips.

"And now, ladies and gentlemen, please put your hands together for AAC's Executive of the Year, my good friend, Mr. Mitchell Chandler."

Stepping to the podium, Chandler was greeted by a standing ovation. With his chiseled features and tousled long, silver-gray hair, he looked every bit the swaggering deal maker. Born for the stage, as he'd often been told. He knew, however, that this acknowledgement, like the glad-handing during the cocktail hour, was mostly for show. A man in his position made plenty of enemies and the majority of people in this room landed solidly in that camp.

No matter, he would give them a performance to remember, anyway.

Chandler accepted the award with an appropriate degree of decorum, then immediately took off the gloves, unloading on government bureaucrats, the lunatic fringe, and a host of liberal causes, with the skill and passion of a seasoned politician.

After breathing fire for twenty minutes, he finished with a flourish.

"Today, more than ever before, this great country of ours is under siege from the far-left and from shadowy forces deep within our own government. Forces that threaten to systematically destroy the heart and soul of America. How we respond to these challenges will determine our future on the world stage. Will we continue as a beacon of freedom and hope, of economic security and independence? Or, will we slip into the abyss of socialism, the slow creep toward state control of practically everything that has swallowed large chunks of Europe? We must never forget, ladies and gentlemen, that knowledge is power *only* if we know how to use it. So I urge each and every one of you to take a stand. To make your voices heard. To fight back! And if we do that, if we can stop these raging liberals, then we will honor and protect all that has made this country great. It is time we reclaim our heart and soul – *America's* heart and soul."

Chandler took a moment, turned, and winked at Savannah.

He then stepped back from the podium to thunderous applause.

CHAPTER 7

28 March, 11:15 PM PDT
San Francisco, California

TWO HOURS LATER, following a lively performance by one of Oakland's top jazz ensembles, Chandler and Savannah said their goodbyes and slipped out of the still-crowded room. They jumped into the big limo and settled back for a short ride across the Bay.

Rizzo practically sideswiped a screeching cable car as he pulled away from the front entrance of the Fairmont. He dropped down the hill toward the Embarcadero and, within minutes, the Town Car was rumbling across the Golden Gate Bridge on Highway 101. The famous span had opened in 1937, linking two very different worlds – one, urban and congested; the other, rural and wide open.

Now, it was all congestion.

As they rolled into Marin County, Chandler felt a strange sense of unease. There was something about this place, this Mecca of wealthy liberals and New Age proselytizers, something that had always set his pulse racing. The home Savannah had purchased after taking the high-tech job, however, was located in much friendlier political territory. Once an island, the mega-rich enclave of Belvedere was connected to the mainland by two roads layered over sand bars. She had since moved to a penthouse apartment near CGE headquarters in Olympia, but still owned the charming home. It was a rather modest dwelling, certainly when compared to the regal estates that surrounded it.

Chandler recalled the first time they'd met, during an art auction at Sotheby's in Manhattan. Nearly five years ago now. He was there to bid on a 17th century masterpiece by Vermeer. She was following up on a tip involving a painting stolen from the Isabella Stewart Gardner Museum in

Boston. The brazen heist – orchestrated in 1990 by two armed men wearing police uniforms and dime-store mustaches – resulted in the loss of thirteen precious works of art, now estimated to be worth more than $300 million.

Entering the crowded room that rainy fall day, Savannah had held every eye, vivacious and confident, but without any trace of arrogance. In the end, the bad guys never surfaced, and Chandler decided to pass on the Vermeer. But he walked away from the event with something far more valuable, an introduction to one *very* remarkable woman. Yet, despite the attraction and numerous job offers, it had still taken him nearly two years to entice her to join the firm, and another eighteen months before things turned serious between them.

He was thinking about all that when his cell phone burred.

It was Colby Freeman.

Freeman apologized for the lateness of the call, then came right to the point. He recounted what Dr. Kincaid had said about Samson's condition, her analysis of the test results, and the dire prognosis.

"Jesus, Colby," Chandler said in an annoyed tone. "I thought Big Boy said it was a virus, something that could be treated with antibiotics?"

"Yes, sir, he did."

"And?"

A long pause.

"I'm afraid he was wrong."

Chandler considered that. He knew it had been a mistake to hire his old Vietnam buddy, but the guy had saved his life, for God's sake. And Big Boy was a damn good vet too, at least when he was clean and sober, which hadn't been all that often in recent months. "What about the marine biologist?" he asked, trying to focus on the crisis at hand. "Any chance *she* got it wrong, Colby?"

"No, I'm afraid not. The test results don't lie. I managed to buy us forty-eight hours…" Another long pause. "Make that forty hours now. I was going to call you earlier, but didn't want to mess up your evening. I guess I –"

"Never mind that. Just tell me what's going on."

Freeman then took several minutes to explain how he'd used the friendship between Dr. Katrina Kincaid and head trainer Leanne Bucaro – specifically Leanne's ill daughter – as a bargaining chip. He further explained that

Samson remained isolated in an enclosed sea-pen guarded round the clock. "Only a handful of employees know about his condition," he assured Chandler. "And they've all been sworn to silence."

Chandler said, "Okay, what are you proposing, Colby?"

"Well, sir, as you know, we've issued several press releases announcing new safety measures being implemented in the wake of that incident at our Osaka park. The work is scheduled to begin next week. So I plan to issue another release in the morning saying construction has been delayed. Happens all the time, no reason it should raise any red flags."

"And when the whale dies?"

There was a long silence.

"I don't know," Freeman said. "I'm doing the best I can here."

Chandler dialed down his angry tone a bit. "Okay, look, go ahead with the press release. Then sit tight. I need some time to think this through."

"Of course, sir, I'll get on it first thing."

Chandler clicked off, sat quietly holding the phone in his hand.

"What's going on?" Savannah asked.

He told her.

After several seconds of silence she said, "Jesus, Mitchell, why wasn't I told about this?"

"I had no idea the whale's condition was this serious," he snapped. "Goddamn Big Boy. I told him –"

"I'm afraid Big Boy might be the least of our problems," Savannah said, her eyes flaring. "What about the hordes of picketers lining up outside the parks? Their numbers are growing every day."

"Tell me about it. I'm constantly being hounded to shut down the whale exhibit in Japan. And if Osaka closes, the other fourteen parks will fall like fucking dominos." Chandler paused briefly, sighed. "They're demanding the orcas be set free, all thirty of them."

"Would they even be able to survive?"

"No. At least I don't think so. But the jury's still out on that one."

"Well, come to think of it, it's not such a bad idea, Mitchell, releasing the whales, I mean."

Silence.

After some contemplation, Chandler said, "Maybe someday, Savannah, but not now." He was thinking there was no way he could walk away from a $5 billion operation that threw off insane profits. Certainly not after the company's filmed entertainment division had just dropped one of the biggest box office bombs in movie history. In fact, thanks to the lousy global economy, four of the company's other five divisions were also bleeding red – Real Estate, Energy Management, Casinos, and Telecommunications. No, the lucrative Aquatic Theme Parks division must be protected at all costs.

Chandler leaned back in his seat, thinking hard. His mind worked like an intricate machine, especially under stress, and the wheels were already turning, channeling his anger and frustration into cold resolve. In that instant, he was suddenly struck with an idea. "Rizzo, hand me my bag, will you?"

Rizzo grabbed a well-worn leather attaché case off the passenger-side seat, passed it back to his boss. Chandler released the metal latch, reached inside, and pulled out a thick book. He knew Savannah was familiar with it – the book was required reading for all senior managers with CGE – yet he had never really explained its history to her...or anyone else for that matter. He wasn't sure why he decided to do so now, but he did, beginning at the beginning.

His late father, Harry Chandler, was a decorated World War II pilot, flying more than a hundred missions over the Philippine Sea in an F6F Hellcat. He racked up twenty-seven kills. Most flyboys, he said, were thrilled with one or two. After the war, Harry settled in Des Moines, married his high school sweetheart, and opened a successful tool and die shop. "I arrived in 1951," Chandler added. "My sister, Tess, came along three years after that. The old man was a tough guy, mentally and physically. Never did less than the best he knew how, expected the same from me. 'Son,' he'd say, 'the most pig-headed mistake beats the hell out of not trying.'"

"Pretty good advice, Mitchell."

"I guess so, but the man never let up. It all changed after the accident though." This part of the story Chandler had already told Savannah, the part about the humid summer day in the mid-sixties that changed everything. His mother and sister were returning home from the market when a drunk driver with three priors crossed the median and crashed head-on into their vehicle. He escaped with minor injuries. They were killed instantly. "Dad went into a deep depression after that, made life a living hell for me."

Savannah took Chandler's hand in hers. "So, you hit the road and became a street kid at, what, twelve years old?"

"Yeah. Dad gave me this book for my ninth birthday. I was hoping for a baseball mitt, read it anyway, several times in fact. It became my bible. So, when things at home got totally unbearable, I left. Nothing but the clothes on my back, ten bucks in my pocket, and my prized possession stuffed inside an old canvas bag."

"Then you bounced from one abusive foster home to another, right?"

"Right. But I grew up fast and I grew up smart. It made me what I am today." Chandler paused for several long moments. He then turned over the hand-tooled red leather book revealing a gold-embossed title, "The Art of War." It was written by a famous Chinese general named Sun Tzu. He'd been dead for more than 1,500 years.

Savannah said, "Hey I know you admire the man, but I'm not sure I see the fit here."

"His approach to warfare, Savannah. It was radically different from his contemporaries then and still relevant to this day, maybe more so. Here, let me show you." Chandler flipped to a couple of highlighted passages and began reading, "'Warfare is the Way – Tao – of deception. Attaining one hundred victories in one hundred battles is not the pinnacle of excellence. Subjugating the enemy's army without fighting is the true pinnacle of excellence.'" Pausing again, he added. "Look, we both know the goddamn activists will hit the war path if they get wind of Samson's death, right? One whale... that's all it will take to set them off."

"So what are you saying?"

"I'm saying...what if there's no war to *fight*?"

"Meaning?"

"I'm not sure yet, Savannah. I'm not sure."

CHAPTER 8

AN UNMARKED, BLACK Chevy Caprice pulled away from the front entrance of Harborview Medical Center, turned left, sped down the hill, then headed north on 4th Avenue. Seattle homicide Detective Cloyd Steiger was behind the wheel, Jia-li Han and Jason Taylor huddled together in the back seat. Jason looked like fifty miles of bad road. He sported purple welts under both eyes, a busted nose, and bandages covering a pair of stitched-up lacerations.

Jia-li was banged up, too, but mostly she looked exhausted.

Steiger had been assigned to track down the high-profile reporter and her fiancé after they were reported missing. It had taken some serious digging, but his investigation eventually led him to the Seattle Yacht Club where Jason docked his big cruiser. Two hours after that – with the able assistance of the U.S. Coast Guard – the couple was safely back on land, at the rescue opera-tion's headquarters on Pier 36, close to downtown. The mission, however, had hardly been a slam dunk. Puget Sound extended a hundred miles or so from Olympia, Washington in the south to beyond Deception Pass in the north, and was more than five miles wide in some places. But thanks to a bright moon and starry night, the *Lois Lane* was quickly spotted in calm waters by the USCG's workhorse helicopter, the MH-60J.

Moments after touching down, Jia-li and Jason were rushed by ambu-lance to the closest ER. In addition to treating cuts and bruises, doctors diagnosed mild cases of hypothermia and suggested they remain overnight for observation. Both refused.

"You two okay?" Steiger said, raising his voice over the constant chatter of the police radio.

Jia-li looked up, sighed wistfully. "Yeah, I think so. Still can't believe what happened out there."

"Me neither," Jason added. "If there's such a thing as a waking nightmare, we just lived it."

"Look, I need you both to tell me everything, top to bottom," Steiger said. "But it's got to be on the record, so hold those thoughts, okay?" Ideally their statements would be taken at headquarters, but he'd offered to conduct the interview at the TV station instead. It wasn't a big deal really. In fact, the familiar setting might prove advantageous. Experience had taught him to play every angle on every case. What might seem insignificant now could prove crucial later.

"I called my news director from the hospital," Jia-li said. "Brought him up to speed. He's on his way in to the station now. It'll give us all a jump on the story. So, thank you again."

"No problem," Steiger said, quickly calculating in his head the OT he'd clocked. Probably enough to cover the cost of a long overdue overhaul on his vintage Harley. "Listen," he added with a hearty laugh, "I get why you wanted to high-tail it out of the ER. I took a bullet in the shoulder last year chasing down a murder suspect. Nothing serious, but they admitted me anyway, department policy. Spent two days getting poked and prodded by Nurse Ratched. I swear the miserable old battle-ax had never cracked a smile in her life until she yanked me out of bed the first time. That seemed to get her juices flowing."

Jason nodded. "You're nobody till somebody shoots you, right, detective? I remember that line from some old movie. So, did you catch the guy?"

"Yeah, we aced him," Steiger replied. "Found the murder weapon stuffed under the back seat of his car. I mean, this dude knows he's royally screwed, right, so I give him my best Ricky Ricardo impression. I say, 'Son, you got some 'splainin' to do.'"

Jia-li and Jason laughed out loud.

"We got lucky on that one," Steiger added. "It happens sometimes, dunkers we call them. And speaking of luck, you two must have a touch of the Irish in ya, too. While you were getting checked out, I spoke with the chief petty officer, the guy who piloted the chopper. Good man, I've worked with him before. He told me he played a wild hunch, decided to search the waters around Lopez Island first. Sure enough, there you were."

"What's the saying?" Jia-li interjected. "Sometimes it's better to be lucky than good? In this case I'm sure it was a little of both. I can't say enough about him and those other guys, a solid bunch of pros. We owe them our lives. You too, detective. I don't see any way we could've made it through the night, not the way the temperatures were dropping."

"That's why they pay me the big bucks," Steiger said with a straight face.

Moments later, he pulled in front of a brick fortress on Dexter Avenue, home to King 5 TV. The windowless building was massive and occupied an entire city block. He inched up over the curb, parking the Chevy where he always parked in traffic-challenged Seattle – on the sidewalk.

The news director met them at the front door, vibrating like a tuning fork. Steiger could hear the feverish thrill in his voice, practically read his mind. This was what guys like Ned Calkins lived for, to blow the lid off the ratings pressure cooker, to break the *really* big one. He had probably created space already for all the Emmys and other prestigious awards his team would surely rack up.

But nothing was going to happen until Steiger had taken statements from his witnesses. He would then decide what facts, if any, should be held back from the public to protect the integrity of the case. A case that now allegedly included robbery, assault, attempted murder, four dead thugs, and a ravenous pack of sea monsters.

Jesus, he thought, *the only thing missing is the marching band and pom-pom girls.*

They walked through a cavernous lobby hung with images of the interconnected history between the station and its city, scaled a long flight of stairs, and entered a glass-encased conference room. It looked out on the bullpen, a large warren crowded with reporters' desks, most piled high with files and reports. Beyond that was the control room, the station's nerve center. At this hour, there were only a few people milling about.

Calkins made small talk, thanked the detective for rescuing his superstar anchor, and exited the room. When the door closed, Steiger gathered Jia-li and Jason around one end of the oval conference table. He then pulled a microcassette recorder from his coat pocket and set it in front of him. There were much fancier recording devices on the market – like smartphones – but he preferred his trusty Sony. He nodded toward the young couple and pushed the "record" button.

Following an awkward silence, Jia-li took a deep breath and began to speak. Her voice trailed off from time to time, and she choked up at certain points, but her account of their harrowing, eighteen-hour ordeal was remarkably lucid and undeniably riveting.

Steiger listened intently as she described in intimate detail the pirates' cold-blooded attack, the violent storm, and the colossal whales that saved the day, as surely as the cavalry did in the movies. He carefully observed her body language, too. Facts and evidence were crucial in any investigation, but it was often instinct that cracked a case. Forget polygraph machines or truth serum, too. He had his own BS meter and it didn't take much to set it off – a nervous twitch, subtle eye movement, or, his favorite, unconscious rubbing of the nose. If the lovely reporter even *thought* about stonewalling him, he would know.

As the incredible tale unfolded, however, his skepticism melted away.

He believed this woman.

When she finished her statement, Steiger glanced at his watch, realized he had barely blinked in the half hour it had taken her to tell her improbable tale. Thirty years as a cop, he mused. He thought he'd seen and heard it all … until now. "Anything to add, Mr. Taylor?"

Jason leaned forward, rubbed his swollen jaw. "Yeah, actually there is something, detective. Since my lovely fiancée here won't ever say it, I'd like the record to reflect how incredibly courageous she was through all of this. As God is my witness, those pirates were meaner than junkyard dogs. And the whales? Nuclear subs on steroids."

Jia-li wrapped her slender fingers around Jason's forearm, squeezed gently.

He smiled. "She's a hero in my book. And so are you, detective. Thank you."

Steiger gathered up his things. "No problem. Look, I'll likely have more questions later on, but that's it for now."

"Sure," Jia-li said. "Can I ask you something before you go?"

"Shoot."

"I know Ned talked to you about releasing the story – the timing, I mean. What are you thinking at this point?"

"Like I told him, Ms. Han, I need to run all this by the brass downtown. But unless those goofs masquerading as pirates come back from the dead,

I'd say bring it on. I'll call you later this morning with a definitive answer. Fair enough?"

They all stood, shook on it.

Five minutes later, Steiger walked out the front door of the building, jumped into his cruiser, turned the ignition, and rolled the vehicle off the sidewalk. Despite the long night, he was on his game, like the great athlete who throws down a 360 tomahawk jam at the buzzer to ice the championship. Easing into traffic, he snatched the mike and keyed it. "Dispatch," Steiger said with a satisfied grin. "This is 624. I'm on my way in."

CHAPTER 9

AFTER STOPPING FOR A DRINK at the Buckeye Roadhouse in Mill Valley, Chandler and Savannah were ready to call it a night. The pub was crowded and because of that, they'd tabled the distasteful discussion involving Samson. No telling who might be listening in. Instead they talked about Savannah's parents – both retired musicians living in Darien, Connecticut – and her 25th college reunion coming up in the fall.

She had graduated at the top of her class from Smith College with a degree in art history, added a master's degree a year later, and made plans to go into teaching. Law enforcement hadn't even been on her radar, but a police officer friend suggested she give it a shot. She did, found she liked the work, the challenge, the chase. Eventually, she was recruited by the FBI, her knowledge of the eccentric world of art giving her a leg up on most of her colleagues in the art-theft unit. Savannah quickly became drawn to a criminal enterprise with estimated losses running as high as $6 billion a year, making stolen art the third largest illegal trade, behind drug trafficking and arms smuggling. She was good at the job, too, though it had ended rather badly.

Twenty minutes after leaving the popular watering hole, Rizzo headed down Belvedere Avenue, negotiating a series of twists and hairpin turns over an impossibly narrow road. Swerving to miss a deer, he hung a left on Cliff Road, made another left at the bottom of the hill, then pulled up in front of a charming clapboard doll house. The home was nestled among tall trees and lush foliage that seemed, even in moonlight, to wrap it in a blanket of green.

Chandler gave Rizzo his marching orders for the following morning and followed Savannah inside. The décor of the home, like its owner, conveyed a sense of casual elegance and charm. They climbed two flights of stairs to a cozy loft with jaw-dropping views – Mount Tamalpais to the north; Golden Gate Bridge to the west; San Francisco to the south.

"I really should sell the place," Savannah said, her eyes fixed on the glittering skyline. "And I will, one of these days. But this view, Mitchell, it's heavenly. If ever there was a shining city on a hill, that's got to be it."

Chandler nodded. Savannah's lovely home had, in fact, fueled much of the controversy that swirled around her FBI career. According to an internal report never made public, she had befriended an odd collection of rogues and aristocrats known to populate the art underworld. She said they were recruited as snitches. Her boss accused her of helping them unload stolen goods – namely, a priceless Van Gogh cut from its frame in a Cairo museum – and snagging a piece of the action. The allegations were never proved and Savannah stubbornly refused to acknowledge that most of the money had come from a trust fund set up by her grandparents. But the incriminations lingered and she eventually resigned, moving into the corporate world. Chandler had never pushed her on the "real" story. One day he would. It intrigued the hell out him.

Savannah ambled over to a small, well-stocked bar. "Listen, how about a nightcap? Cognac okay?"

"Perfect, make mine a double." Chandler took off his jacket, loosened his tie, and stretched out his lean, six-foot-four-inch frame on the leather sofa. The recessed lighting threw a soft glow over the baby grand piano in the corner, reminding him of how beautifully his mother once played. On the far wall, a small library collection had been neatly arranged in a floor-to-ceiling bookcase. An original work by Monet hung above the marble fireplace, a gift he'd given Savannah on her forty-fifth birthday.

Savannah dropped in a CD and soon returned carrying two glasses, the soulful sounds of Kenny "Blues Boss" Wayne filling the room. She handed one snifter to Chandler, set hers on the end table next to the sofa. "I'm gonna freshen up a bit, slip into something more comfortable. Why don't you kick back, relax. We'll figure this thing out with Samson, okay?" She leaned down, gave him a lingering kiss on the lips, then disappeared down the stairs.

Chandler took a long pull of Cognac, set his glass down on the table. He began rubbing both temples to ease the grip of a gnawing headache. He leaned back and closed his eyes, soon lost in that netherworld between wakefulness and sleep. But his mind soon began spinning again and, when he sat back up, his gaze landed on the latest edition of *Vanity Fair*. Glancing at the striking woman on the cover, he did a double-take. She was sitting on the aft deck of a commercial fishing boat dressed in a khaki safari shirt, cut-off blue jeans, and no shoes. Her streaked red hair was short and spikey, her flashing green eyes the color of a tropical sea. They seemed almost luminescent. She had been blessed with a generous bust and her tanned, graceful legs seemed to go on forever. A tattoo of an Arctic wolf appeared prominently on her left forearm.

Intrigued, Chandler immediately flipped to the story. He began reading and couldn't stop.

COVER STORY

A Force of Nature
Hungry Sharks. Hostile Seas. A Man Overboard.
How a Courageous Boat Captain Pulled Off the Impossible.

By Lynda Wilding ◊ Photographs by David Samuels

Captain Zora Flynn. The name conjures up all kinds of images. Conventional is certainly not one of them. And her high-seas heroics – snatching a helpless fisherman from the jaws of death – can only be described as astonishing, a triumph of the human spirit, already the stuff of legend.

But does the myth match the reality?

Let's start by examining the facts, which are indisputable. The statuesque redhead did indeed save a man's life by diving into frigid Alaskan seas teeming with great white sharks. And she was armed only with a pistol, a weapon which had very limited range underwater – a few feet at most. It was, to be sure, an act of supreme heroism. But the question everybody seemed to be asking was why? Why would an apparently sane person perform such an insane act?

The answer, it turns out, is as complex as the woman herself.

Zora Flynn is a study in contrasts. Heads – she is strong, resolute, scary-smart, and impetuous. Tails – she is somewhat shy, aloof, restless, and emotionally vulnerable. Or, as her first mate described her, "Skip is Thelma and Louise rolled into one."

Zora's adventure begins in the mountains northwest of Boise in the spring of 1976...

Chandler scanned the rest of the story: *Grew up running the rivers of Idaho...parents fearless adventurers...vagabond lifestyle...fierce independent streak...loses father at young age...soldiers on with mother...graduates high school at age sixteen...awarded graduate degree from Stanford at twenty...backpacks around the world...befriends the Dalai Lama...establishes orphanage in Nepal.*

The woman's bold foray into the world of commercial fishing and her dramatic rescue in the Bering Sea played out in all their glory, clearly written by a journalist who knew her craft. But what really grabbed Chandler's attention was the captain's fascination with the Dalai Lama and his nineteen "instructions for life." She claimed that three of those instructions had profoundly impacted her own life: *One, be gentle with the earth. Two, great love and great achievements involve great risk. Three, learn the rules so you know how to break them properly.*

Chandler read over the short list several times, smiled, and lowered the magazine to his lap. He had always considered the Dalai Lama to be timid and weak, yet surprisingly the man's philosophies seemed to closely mirror those of the great Sun Tzu.

Leaning back on the sofa, he closed his eyes...and a plan began to take shape.

It was a good one, too.

Brilliant, audacious, imaginative – and risky as hell!

Just his style. He'd never been one to take the easy route. Tackling the seemingly impossible had always been a lot more fun and infinitely more rewarding.

But this was a whole new ball game.

CHAPTER 10

29 March, 2:30 AM PDT
Marin County, California

SAVANNAH SOON RETURNED, wearing slim-fitting, midnight black velour pants and matching hoodie. She sat down and curled up against the end of the sofa. Taking a sip from her drink, she said, "Hell of an article, isn't it? That woman – Zora what's her name – is either the bravest person on the planet, or the craziest, I'm not sure which."

"I agree," Chandler said, lifting the magazine, and scanning down the page. "I especially like the part where one of her crew says, 'She gets rammed by the biggest damn shark I'd ever seen, does this insane acrobatic flip, then comes firing with a freakin' pistol – and there *we* are standing on deck with our dicks in the wind and our jaws hanging open.'"

Savannah chuckled. "Yeah, nice imagery, don't you think?"

"The captain's a piece of work, all right. And she just might be our ticket out of this mess."

"How? What do you mean?"

Chandler understood Savannah's confusion. He spent the next twenty minutes fleshing out his plan, going over it this way, then that, as it took shape in his mind. She looked at him the entire time like his hair was on fire.

"Okay, let me see if I've got this straight, Mitchell," Savannah said. "The sick whale dies and you somehow convince the captain here to dispose of the body, then capture his replacement. I don't see that going particularly well, but let's say, for the sake of argument, she pulls it off. You then have someone train the new and improved Samson to perform just like the old one and hope no one notices. Is that about it?"

"Yeah, that's about it. Look, Savannah, killer whales are practically indistinguishable from one another, right? They're like penguins. Do you really think anyone will be able to tell the difference?"

"The average Joe? Maybe not. But what about Big Boy, the trainers, the marine biologist? They're gonna know."

"Our people will keep their mouths shut, and there are ways to deal with the scientist."

"Money and muscle."

"Powerful incentives, Savannah."

She took another sip of her drink, peered inquisitively over the top of her glass. "Look, Mitchell, if you're thinking about calling in Atwater, I would strongly advise against it."

Atwater was Darnell Atwater, the managing partner at Black Stallion, a private security outfit on retainer to CGE. A hard-nosed former Army ranger, Atwater used top-level connections at the Pentagon to secure billions in no-bid government war contracts, money he then used to grease the skids of his corporate juggernaut. Many considered his team of ex-special forces commandos nothing more than black-ops artists, gun-toting thugs, and money launderers.

Chandler cared only about results. "You don't like him," he said matter-of-factly.

"*Like* has nothing to do with it, Mitchell. The man's dangerous and so are his goons."

Silence.

"Look," Savannah added. "Before you make that call, why don't we explore some other options here, something that might buy us some time to think this through..." She stopped mid-sentence, seeming to recognize Chandler's impatience. "I assume bringing a whale in from another park is out of the question?"

"Damn right it is," Chandler said, thinking that a five-ton orca could not simply be dropped into the back of a pickup truck. It was a major production, moving a creature of that size and weight, one that required an army of people, heavy equipment, and police escorts. "We can't risk the exposure, Savannah. It used to take these activist crackpots at least two or three days, maybe a week, to establish a command post and get the word out. Now, thanks to tweeting and all the other crazy shit, they're up and running in a matter of minutes. And their cyber-attacks are vicious."

"Okay. What about talking to the Japanese or Russian whalers, then? They still hunt and capture killer whales, all perfectly legal far as I know."

"True. It's also true my dad spent three hellish years fighting the god-damn Japs. He would roll over in his grave if I even entertained the thought. I don't owe the man much, but I at least owe him *that*. Besides I don't trust the little bastards, should never have opened a park there."

"Yeah, well, that still leaves the Russians."

"I don't trust 'em any more than I do the Japs. But let's assume for a minute the Ruskies *were* an option? It's still no good."

"Why is that?"

"For starters, they'd need a permit to capture the whale and that means full disclosure – who, what, why, where, and when. That document gets filed with the International Whaling Commission, becomes part of the public record. So that doesn't work. And even if it did, we're talking weeks, not days. I just don't have that kind of time." Chandler gulped down the last of his drink. "There's always the black market, I guess, but then we'd be in bed with –"

"The Russian mob," Savannah interjected. "Don't even go there, Mitchell. I've seen their handiwork, some serious maniacs in that bunch. Those guys make the Sicilian mafia look like a bunch of country preachers at a church social. They'll want a pile of cash up front, more on the back end, and God knows how much down the road."

"I agree," Chandler said, leafing back through the *Vanity Fair* article. "Look, there's only one way to win this game and that is not to play...which means the captain here is our best option. Hell, she's our *only* option." He paused, flipped the page. "This bit about the Dalai Lama. Do you remember it?"

"Yes, but what does that have to do with anything?"

"Quite a bit, actually. He's got a lot in common with Sun Tzu."

"C'mon, you don't really believe the Dalai Lama would condone this half-baked plan of yours, do you?"

"No, but Sun Tzu would. He's the master of deception, remember?"

Savannah picked up the magazine, quickly read through the section featuring the Dalai Lama again. "I'm not sure I see it the same way you do, but I *can* tell you the captain here is not someone who is easily intimidated. So forget about using Atwater and his Black Stallion thugs. I don't see her being for sale either."

"Everyone has a price, Savannah."

"No, they don't, Mitchell. This woman is smart and tough. She's also fiercely independent, words people have used to describe me, I might add – though not always in the most flattering light. But that's not the point. The point is I can relate to her. And I assure you, women like us don't react like you men. You've got to think about pushing different buttons. And the dollar sign isn't one of them, certainly not with her."

"Okay, I'm listening."

Savannah pointed to a paragraph halfway down the page. "See this? There's a brief mention of a school she started in Nepal for orphaned kids. I can make some calls in the morning, find out exactly what the deal is. So if you're hell bent on moving forward, then use this as your carrot."

Chandler leaned back, the gears meshing now. He was not a man who believed in luck. He was methodical, logical, a planner. He also knew his instincts were right. The charity angle was a good one, but there would need to be a backup plan. There was *always* a backup plan.

The discussion then turned to Captain Zora Flynn, how best to approach her, and who should make contact. Savannah couldn't go for a whole host of reasons. She was in the direct employ of CGE; she had a prior commitment that might raise a red flag if canceled; and there was no way someone who looked like her could slip in and out of Sitka, Alaska without causing a stir. They'd already ruled out using a Black Stallion operative, which left only one other viable choice. Chandler would make that call at first light.

With that settled, what he needed now was to forget about whales and theme parks and goddamn activists and enjoy this ravishing woman. Bringing Savannah on board had been one of the smartest decisions he'd ever made, despite the challenges involved in making it happen. Besides her obvious traits – beauty, brains, and talent – Chandler also loved the fact that she cared nothing about his net worth or his high-powered friends. The truth of the matter was, she had plenty of money and influence in her own right. She liked him for him and, all in all, it was a damn good package. At sixty-two, he was in remarkable shape. He worked out at least three times a week, kept his weight in check, and could still hold his own on the racquetball court with men half his age. Then there was the brown belt in tae kwon do, something he wore with great pride.

"Hey, enough talk," Chandler said. "How about that little surprise you promised me earlier?"

It took Savannah a few moments to shift focus. But when she did, she smiled a lascivious smile and stood up. "Never thought you'd ask, lover boy." She then sashayed over to the window, began swaying back and forth in a rhythmic dance. "I watched an interview with a former stripper on cable the other night, quite the babe. She had some interesting tips on pleasing a man."

Chandler instantly perked up. He felt like he'd just been hit in the groin with a heat-seeking missile. "Like you need a tutorial, Savannah?"

"Hey, a girl can always use a new trick or two. Shall I demonstrate for you?"

It was a question that needed no answer.

Savannah stared at him for a long moment, then unzipped her hoodie in a long, steady pull, letting the soft material slide over her shoulders. She then strolled languidly back to the couch, slowly drawing the edge of a perfectly manicured red nail down Chandler's cheek. Her milky white breasts were now temptingly close to his face. She reached for his hand, whispered in a satiny voice, "Come, Mitchell, come along with me."

They moved arm-in-arm down a flight of carpeted stairs, entered her spacious bedroom. It smelled of jasmine and glowed from the flickering light of a dozen ornate candles. There were big, fluffy, pastel-colored pillows everywhere. Chandler pulled her to the bed, felt the trance-like movement of her hips, the burning desire in her lips. His breathing was fast now and his heart was pounding like a jackhammer. He buried his face in her hair, smelled the faint scent of apples, felt her teeth on his neck, biting gently.

"Relax, Mitchell," she said, slowly unbuttoning his shirt. "Let it go, unwind a little."

Later, they lay together silently on the bed. Her head was resting on his chest, his right arm draped over her back. He lifted her chin gently with his left hand, kissed her tenderly, and, in the golden flicker of candlelight, he saw a tear roll down her cheek.

CHAPTER 11

29 March, 5:10 PM AKDT
Sitka, Alaska

PRESTON TRADD ARRIVED at Rocky Gutierrez Airport tired and out of sorts. Less than twelve hours earlier, he'd been packing up his new Benz S-Class sedan for a spring skiing trip to California's Mammoth Mountain, a vacation he and his wife had been planning for months. It was going to be just the two of them, their eleven-year old son and six-year-old daughter having been dispatched to Grandma's house in Irvine, a short drive from their own home in Huntington Beach. Instead, he'd received an early morning phone call from headquarters, and now here he was, in the wilds of the Alaskan panhandle on a thoroughly disagreeable assignment.

Tradd walked through the lone terminal, curiously eyeing the stuffed heads of long-dead animals that adorned the hallways. They seemed to be staring back at him, as if he were personally responsible for their fate. He passed the Avis car-rental counter, shaking his head disgustedly at the small plastic sign displayed on the back wall: *"A cleaning fee may be charged due to fish smell or having animals in the car or trunk."* For someone who didn't know how to bait a hook or load a rifle – let alone actually kill something – this land of big game reels and double-barreled shotguns was indeed a strange land.

Truth be told, Preston Tradd was a product of privilege. He knew which fork to use and held his wineglass by the stem. He'd grown up in River Oaks, a swanky enclave in the geographic center of Houston, sailed through college, and graduated near the top of his class at Yale Law School. The next fifteen years were spent honing his litigation skills at a prestigious law firm in North Dallas. Now, just a few days shy of his forty-third birthday, he made seven figures as a full partner with Hannah & Associates, LLC.

Headquartered in Dallas, H&A was the most powerful law firm in America no one had ever heard of, its entire operation an enigma. There was no web site, an unlisted phone number, and a shadow client list which included the biggest names in oil, tobacco, insurance, pharmaceuticals, and transportation, among others. The rich and powerful paid healthy retainers to make distasteful, often unsavory problems go away.

And this was one of those.

The bumpy flight from Los Angeles had included stopovers in Seattle and Juneau, where it was delayed by a saucy old broad carrying a hunting crossbow, gold tip arrows, and high-powered scope. She insisted on bringing the weapon on board. Cops had other ideas, but the woman did not go quietly or quickly, causing a two-hour layover. Tradd had put the time to good use, however, downloading a stream of documents on his subject, including a couple of grainy photos. He marveled at the speed and efficiency with which his team of corporate sleuths had assembled such a detailed dossier.

A very fine piece of work.

Except for two nuns, the passengers on the final leg of the trip were all men, most of them wearing red suspenders and plaid shirts. Tradd – dressed in Chinos, loafers, and heavy wool sweater – was doing his best to look the part and fit in. His normal attire, custom made suits, silk shirts, and power ties, would make him stand out like a creature from the *Star Wars* bar scene. He already felt uncomfortable enough; drawing unwanted attention would only add to the misery. He'd had less than half an hour to review the documents, but with his near-photographic memory, the pieces quickly fell into place.

Now thinking back on those few moments, one thing towered above all else: he absolutely, positively had to get this job done right. His client, Mitchell Chandler, was not someone who tolerated anything less. Neither did his lovely, high maintenance wife, bless her heart. On top of that, there were private schools, plastic surgeons, two sets of braces, a new summer home on Lake Arrowhead, and various other financial obligations large and small, mostly large. All in, his monthly nut was more than many working stiffs made in a year. Sure, he could borrow from daddy, but he'd never had to play that card before. And he sure didn't intend to start now.

Tradd walked out of the terminal building into a light drizzle, a black trench coat cradled over one arm. Other than that, all he had with him was a carry-on bag containing his laptop, toiletries, and a change of clothes. Getting in and out of Sitka had been dreadful, leaving him no choice but to stay the night. He could only imagine what the Totem Square Inn must be like. He inhaled deeply, the fishy smell telling him everything he needed to know about America's last frontier.

Just then a Red Explorer pulled up, "Hank's Cab" painted in bold white letters on the side. The driver, a craggy-faced old graybeard, rolled down the window. "Where to, my friend?"

Tradd jumped in the back seat. "Pioneer Bar."

"Sure, the P-Bar. Kind of an institution around here," the driver said, pulling away from the curb. "Partial to Ernie's myself, but then that's just me. Say, bet you didn't know our little metropolis sits smack in the center of a temperate rainforest."

Tradd feigned interest. "You're right, I didn't know that."

"The Tongass, that's what she's called. So we get plenty of the wet stuff around here, if you know what I mean." The driver cleared his throat, coughing a smoker's cough. "Town ain't what she used to be, no sir, not since the big cruise ships started coming. Quarter-million people last year alone. Don't bother me none, good for business in fact. Can't say the same for the missus, though. She's not too fond of all them crowds. Gotta love the scenery though, right, Mister?"

Tradd craned his neck to see out the front window. The state's fourth largest city, population 9,000, was situated on the west side of Baranof Island, flanked by the Pacific Ocean on one side, coldly white-capped mountains on the other. And it was, indeed, spectacular.

Five minutes later, the Explorer pulled up in front of the P-Bar, a white, two-story stucco building in need of a major face-lift. The driver hopped out, opened the back door. Tradd exited next to the sidewalk. He peeled a twenty from a gold-plated money clip and handed over the bill. "Keep the change."

The driver flashed a gap-toothed grin. "Thanks, mister, mighty obliged." He hopped back into the van and drove off, leaving his fare standing in a puddle.

Tradd took a deep breath, tugged on the collar of his coat, and strode confidently toward the front door. Inside, he was met by the smell of stale beer and an assortment of colorful characters, most wearing oversized hoodies, or rain gear. Many of the regulars – at least he assumed they were regulars – hung by the bar marinating their mustaches in pints of Baranof Red Ale, their eyes glued to the Mariners-Blue Jays game playing on two wide-screen TVs. The boys of summer were still in spring training, the season of eternal optimism for baseball fans...especially those of the long-suffering Seattle variety.

Other patrons, further back, congregated around the pool table or dartboard, nearly hidden under thick halos of smoke. There was no law against lighting up in many of Sitka's watering holes, including this classic old place. It had a rustic 50s feel – bright lights, Formica tables, black-and-white-checkered linoleum floors. The walls were covered with framed pictures of local fishing boats and other maritime themes. The music was very loud and very country.

Tradd walked nonchalantly to the bar and ordered a Bud Light on tap, trying to remain as inconspicuous as possible. He took a long pull from the stein, reached into his bag, and grabbed one of the photos he had downloaded. After examining his subject, he darted a look down the long, wooden bar. Through a sea of bodies, he caught a glimpse of her.

And Captain Zora Flynn was truly a sight to behold.

Beautiful, he thought. *And surely dangerous if provoked.*

CHAPTER 12

ZORA HAD ARRIVED at the P-Bar a few minutes earlier. After greeting a few friends and politely declining a seat at the bar, she made her way to the back of the room. Thankfully, no one had mentioned the *Vanity Fair* piece, probably because they hadn't seen it yet, not that this crowd was likely to visit the website anyway. And the print version had just hit newsstands in the lower forty-eight. It would be another few days before the magazine arrived in Sitka. More than six months had now passed since her daring encounter with the marauding shark. The story had spread like jungle telegraph, bringing out the finest barroom performances in fishing villages on both coasts. And when the true champions were done spinning their outrageous tales, the great white had morphed into a beast grander than Moby Dick.

Her latest high-seas adventure had been no less stressful. Sixteen grueling hours after breaking free of the big Norwegian tanker, Zora and crew had arrived in port, exhausted and discouraged. Damage to the engine room, rudder, and aft deck had made it too risky to continue fishing. For the second time in three months, she'd returned to port with an empty fish hold. Adding up all the outlays for gear, fuel, bait, and other fixed costs made the math real simple.

Expenses: forty grand.

Income: zero.

No money, of course, meant no "settling up." She had given the men the day off and completed a few odd jobs on the boat before heading home and collapsing into bed. A few hours later, the phone rang, snapping her out of a deep sleep. The caller refused to identify himself, explain where he'd gotten her number, or how he even knew she was in town. He said only that it was urgent they meet in person and that he would be arriving in Sitka in a matter of hours. She asked from where. He wouldn't say. She asked why. Same response. Her next instinct had been to hang up, but there was something in the man's voice that tugged hard at her gut. And her gut was almost always right. After running through several other options, none of which seemed particularly appealing, she'd finally agreed. She told him to meet her here.

Zora now sat at a small table tucked into an out-of-the-way nook in back, nursing a beer, her stomach doing back-flips. Why, she wasn't exactly sure, yet for some reason she felt strangely alone in this very public place, her mood darker than an Alaskan winter night. Moments later, she saw him, a self-absorbed little peacock weaving his way through the boisterous crowd. With his casual attire and Gordon Gekko haircut, the man looked like he just stepped out of a J. Crew catalog.

The guy's obviously trying to fit in, she thought, *and failing miserably.*

His progress was momentarily halted by members of the Seattle Fire-fighters Pipes and Drums in town for the annual Sitka Cancer Survivors charity auction. Zora had already done her part, buying a lovely hand-quilted bedspread crafted by a neighbor who'd recently undergone six grueling weeks of radiation for breast cancer. The bagpipers finished their warm-up and the team's lone female informed patrons their performance would be starting in twenty minutes.

The short, wafer-thin man swam through the maze of bodies and approached her table. "Ms. Flynn," he said. "I'm late, I apologize." He pulled up a chair and set his coat and bag on the floor. Flashing a counterfeit smile, he then explained why his flight had been delayed. "Never seen anything like it in my life," he added. "The old gal was armed to the teeth."

"Yeah, imagine that," Zora replied in a surly tone. "Listen, I don't have a lot of time. You said it was urgent, so why don't you tell me who you are and what this is all about."

"Well, I need to remain anonymous for reasons that will become clear, and yes, it is most definitely urgent. Rather delicate too. It would be much better if we talked privately. Shall we take a little walk?"

Zora threw him a withering look. "No. We talk here or we don't talk at all."

The man nodded, clasped his hands together on the table. "Okay, have it your way, captain. You see, it's real simple. I'm here to make you a business proposition."

"Yeah? And what might that be?"

"I want to hire you and your crew. And I'm willing to pay you a lot of money for your trouble, over half a million dollars in fact."

"Half a *million*. You must be joking."

"Do I look like I'm joking? "

Zora took a sip of beer. She felt a slow rage building inside her, but said nothing.

"Let me spell it out for you. First, there's a cash payment, one hundred fifty grand, half up front, the other half upon completion of the assignment. Second, I'll cover the cost of your one-time fishing license, the IFQ, I believe you call it. That would be another three hundred thousand, if I'm not mistaken."

Jesus, what's with this guy?

The Independent Fishing Quota ran her ten dollars a pound for a thirty thousand pound quota. There was no way he could have known that number without greasing some palms at NOAA, the National Oceanic and Atmospheric Administration.

And how did he get to them?

"On top of that," he added. "I'll pay off the note on your boat, get the bankers off your back. I understand things have been rather tough up here lately, for you and everybody else."

Zora shifted uncomfortably in her chair. He was right again. She'd hauled in less than a ton of herring on her last run, nowhere near her allotment. "How the *hell* do you know all this?"

"Let's just say the people I work for are very good at what they do," the man said, preening a bit. He then reached for his brief case, opened it, and pulled out a green folder. "During my layover in Juneau, I downloaded this dossier on you. Rather impressive, wouldn't you say? There was so little time to pull it together."

Zora's face flushed red with anger. She tried to process this, reign in her emotions, hold off from decking the guy. "Look, I don't know what your game is, mister, but I don't like it. *Nobody* shells out that kind of cash to go sport fishing. So, the only other thing this can be about is smuggling dope, which means you've got yourself the wrong girl. I don't *do* drugs. I don't *deal* drugs. And I sure as hell don't *smuggle* drugs."

"No, I can assure you it has nothing to do with anything of the kind."

Zora took another long pull from the stein, never lifted her eyes off him. "Okay, you've got sixty seconds."

"They warned me you were a handful."

"Fifty."

"Okay, look, here's the deal. I need you to capture a whale."

"Excuse me?"

"You heard me. A *killer* whale, to be precise. Big one, at least five tons."

Zora threw him an incredulous look and for several moments they sat unmoving, like enemies glaring across the battlefield. Then she pulled a twenty dollar bill from her pocket and slapped it on the table. "Sorry, pal, you've *still* got the wrong girl. But let me give you a little advice, okay?" She slammed her elbows down, flashing her middle finger. "Number one, you don't go out and capture an orca for sport, like you would, say, a marlin or a sword." Next, she held up an index finger. "Number two, it's not only illegal, it's immoral. And even if it wasn't, you do not mess with an animal that powerful. Killer whales eat great whites for breakfast. I don't suppose *that* was part of your dossier?"

The man held her gaze but remained quiet.

"Didn't think so. You might try talking to the Japanese whalers, though. The words moral and illegal aren't in their goddamn playbook."

"I appreciate the tip, captain, but that option's already been ruled out. Same goes for the Russians. Now I need an answer."

Zora felt a wave of anger roll through her body.

What part of "no" doesn't this idiot get?

"We're done here," she said, pushing back hard from the table.

The man reached out, grabbed her forearm.

Zora instantly jumped to her feet, yanked her arm free. "Try that again, asshole, and I'll knock you into yesterday." The sudden commotion caught the eye of two bad-boy dart players who seemed ready to pounce on the stranger. Zora waved them off.

"Look," he said, straitening his collar. "I get that you're not for sale, captain. I respect that. I really do. But what about those poor orphans? Are you telling me they don't need the money?"

Zora threw him another fierce look, inched back into her seat. "What did you say?"

He leafed through the file, pulled out a sheet of paper. "It's all right here. Says you went to Nepal in 1998, at which time you met the Dalai Lama. A few years later, one of the villages you visited became overrun by Maoist insurgents. Terrible slaughter, lots of children orphaned. So you returned, befriended a young girl named Nasha. Like many of her friends, the little urchin was living on the streets, scavenging for food. No chance of ever getting an education, of course." The man hiked an eyebrow. "How am I doing so far?"

Zora gave him a cold stare, her heart thundering in her chest. Getting to the Feds was one thing – their hands were always out – but how in hell did he ever find out about her charity work? She'd been told that that information was strictly confidential, kept under lock and key.

"So you vowed to build a children's home, provide all the basic needs – food, clothing, books, healthcare, and the like. The price tag was one hundred fifty grand, enough to cover the architectural, construction, and start-up costs. You had absolutely no idea where the money would come from but then fate intervened. Or, should I say the publisher at *Vanity Fair*? He agreed to cover all those costs and then some, in exchange for exclusive rights to that high-seas adventure of yours. And the stunning photo spread, of course. Very noble of you, captain."

Zora shook her head, disgusted. She was going to mention that the transaction had been executed anonymously, through a private trust, but figured why waste her breath. He already knew that.

"Everybody came out a winner, right?" he added, seeming to enjoy the moment. "The building got built, and the magazine scored a fabulous scoop."

"You're one sick son of a bitch, you know that?"

The man narrowed his eyes, stiffened his spine. "Look, if you don't want the money, think of what it could do for the *kids*?"

"We'll manage without the likes of you. Now, I really need to go." Zora stared at the man for a long moment, caught something different in his eyes, something she hadn't noticed before. Disappointment? Resignation? A bit of empathy, maybe? It was hard to say.

"I'm afraid not, captain." He leaned closer and lowered his voice. He then pulled another sheet of paper from the bottom of the stack, slid it across the table like it was a dinner menu.

Zora took one look and was immediately welded to her chair, a stab of terror coursing through her body. "My *mother*. What the –"

"Don't worry, she's fine, for the time being anyway."

"You fucking bastard!"

"Look," he said, leaning hard on the table. "I don't like this any more than you do, okay? I really don't. Now why don't we go for that walk, work this thing out civilly."

Zora heard the man's words, but they didn't register, not really. Her world had suddenly taken a dizzying, dark turn that felt heavy, suffocating. She sat for a long moment, her eyes on fire. Then she jumped to her feet, grabbed her poncho from the chair, and bolted for the front door. As she left the building, the kilted firefighters launched into a lively rendition of *Scotland the Brave*.

CHAPTER 13

29 March, 6:15 PM AKDT
Sitka, Alaska

ZORA MOVED BRISKLY down Katlian Street, the town's main drag, the buttery smell of popcorn wafting up from a rolling food cart parked on the corner. The busy road twisted along the waterfront, a ramshackle collection of shops, canneries, and warehouses that had once been the heart of Sitka's thriving commercial fishing industry. Those heady times were long gone, though at the end of the day, most everyone's attention still turned to the sea, out where the fishing boats finished their work and began the tedious journey home.

A block north of the bar, she stopped in front of a rusted-out old building, its faded metal sign hanging precariously by one hinge. It made an annoying, high-pitched squeaking sound, like fingernails raked over a chalkboard. A few other hardy souls wandered by, braving the heavy drizzle. Otherwise, the sidewalks were empty.

Zora felt dead inside, wasn't exactly sure how to play this. She thought about her mother, how two years earlier, a vibrant, youthful woman of seventy-two began misplacing things. Answers to simple questions could no longer be brushed aside as "senior moments." Over time, Stella Flynn became a helpless prisoner to memories lost, her mind a terrible tangle of confusion, her past a mystery.

A battery of behavioral assessments and cognitive tests had followed.

The diagnosis: "Primary degenerative dementia of the Alzheimer's type."

There was no cure.

Zora arranged for live-in help, even moved in with her mother for a while. Some days, Stella would tease with a twinkle and a wry comeback, but mostly she remained a complete stranger. The disease eventually progressed beyond the moderate stage with no way to avoid the inevitable – an assisted living residence. Tranquility Manor was pleasant enough, the staff compassionate and professional. The location, in central Utah, was similar to the scenic mountainous terrain of Stella's beloved Idaho. And that was fine too. Yet for Zora, the picture that had formed in her mind was dark and absent all hope. Burning with shame and guilt, she had sobbed for hours after leaving her bewildered mother behind at the home. It was the final stop on a tortured journey.

All that came back to her now as the man approached.

Zora turned to him with fire in her eyes. "Okay, what do you want?"

"Is that question really necessary, captain? What I *want* is an answer."

Zora clenched her teeth, shot daggers into his eyes. She felt a flash of rage unlike anything she'd ever experienced before. Something deep inside her seemed to snap like a piano wire. "Listen, you hurt my mother in any way and I swear it's the last goddamn thing you'll ever do. I'm telling you – " She caught herself, refusing to give in to her anger, or fear.

"I can assure you, captain, no harm will come to your mother. Certainly not if you agree to our proposal."

There was that look again, not exactly an apology but something that seemed close. She wasn't sure what to make of it.

The man continued. "Listen, I read about the facility where your mother is living. From what I can tell, it seems like a rather pleasant little community."

"It's not a community, it's a home," Zora said, toning down her anger a bit. "And Mother's in the assisted living program." She flashed to better times, on the wonderful stories her mother used to tell about her younger days, back when her name was Stella Featherstone, long before her name became Flynn, long before she became mom. Then reality slammed that door shut. "Living *hell*, if you ask me."

"Yes, terrible disease, that Alzheimer's," the man noted. "She's quite a lady, your mother, at least she was in her younger days, anyway."

Zora began moving again, quickening the pace. The man hustled to keep up. "Yeah, I'm sure you know all about *her*, too."

He shifted a bit uncomfortably. "Yes, captain, I do my homework." Then he proceeded to tell just how well he'd done it. "Her name is Stella. She's a retired English teacher, seventy-four years old. Quite the athlete at one time, wasn't she? Among her many accomplishments, she was one of the first women to navigate the Colorado River through the Grand Canyon." He hesitated as if undecided about what to say next. "Your father was no slouch either. *His* name was Zach, a gentleman farmer and Idaho river runner."

Zora closed her eyes, felt a suffocating pressure, like she was being sucked into a black hole. She wanted to cut the man's throat, bit her lower lip instead.

The man continued. "You came along rather late in the game, excelled at everything you did. Life was good in the Idaho hills, a nice little slice of Norman Rockwell. Then one day, Zach left and never came back, tore the family apart, broke your heart. You were eight at the time, as I recall. He moved to some hick town in Missouri, not the end of the world but close, found himself another woman."

Zora was vibrating now, her face red with fury. She remembered hearing the news, remembered that day like it was yesterday. And every birthday, every holiday after that, she would run down to the mail box, hoping her father had sent a card, maybe even a gift. He never did. She kept reaching out to him anyway, hoping things would change. When she was eleven, she saved up all her allowance and bought him an expensive cardigan sweater for Christmas, wrapped it up nice and neat. She found his address in Mother's appointment book, rode into town, and sent it first-class mail. It came back ten days later, unopened. A year later, he shot himself in the chest.

The man took a deep breath and spread his hands, palms up. "Curious how most of this got left out of the *Vanity Fair* story, isn't it? Same goes for the unfortunate accident with your young friend, must have been terrible watching her and her horse disappear into that ravine."

"Give it a fucking rest, already," Zora snapped. "And leave my father out of this. He's burning in some dark corner of hell, which is exactly where he belongs." She tugged on the hood of her yellow poncho, took a deep breath. Just then, two bald eagles swooped down, soared above a broken-down old building, and disappeared over the harbor. Looking up she wished she could sprout wings and fly, too, get as far away as possible from this man and this nightmare.

A contrite look came over his face. He nodded and said, "You know what? I hear you. My old man's not exactly a candidate for sainthood either. He, uh, well he –"

Zora shot him a give-me-a-break look. "Remind me to bring my violin next time."

"Listen," the man said. "I've got no ax to grind here. I really don't. Personally, I hope your mother lives to be a hundred and nine. But there's something you need to understand, captain. The people in this game do not play by the rules. They *are* the rules. Think of the nastiest thing imaginable, the most despicable thing one human being can do to another, and they are capable of it. As cold and as cruel as all this must sound, I'm just trying to be honest with you."

Zora felt sick to her stomach, trapped in a dark tunnel with no way out. She stared at him in fury, then after a long pause, said, "Okay, so why me? I don't know a damn thing about killer whales. I catch fish for a living."

"Asked and answered. Other options were considered and ruled out, as I said before. I have no doubt you'll get the job done. Can't be any worse than playing Russian roulette with a man-eating shark, right?"

Zora ignored the reference. "Okay, let's say I *do* manage to pull this off somehow. What proof do I have that you'll leave my mother and me alone?"

"You don't. You'll have to take it on faith, captain. It's the best you're gonna do."

Zora threw him a cold stare. She was in complete free-fall now. "Fuck you and the horse you rode in on."

They stood toe-to-toe for several long moments, staring one another down.

Then the man slowly backed away. Glancing at his watch, he remaining maddeningly composed. "I'm sorry you feel that way." He pulled a card from his coat pocket and handed it to Zora. There was a number on it, nothing else. "This is a private number, untraceable. You have until midnight to call me with an answer. That's less than six hours from now. If I don't hear from you, or you decide not to accept our generous offer, then you'll just have to live with the consequences. Oh, and don't even think about calling the cops. We'll know before you hang up the phone. Goodbye, captain, and good luck."

Seconds later, the man vanished into the night mist.

Zora watched after him, her heart cold and heavy. She walked on another block to a wooden landing that looked out over the gloomy, wind-swept harbor. In the amber light of a streetlamp, a lone gull swooped in looking for scraps, found none, and flew off. She sat down on a stone bench, boiling mad, her mind racing. Not even tough Zora, the one she relied on, the one her crew relied on, could hold it together now. She felt achingly alone, a loneliness that settled on her like a second skin. She leaned forward, cradling her head in her hands, searching for answers.

None came.

But the tears did, pouring out so hard, her whole body shook.

What should I do, Mom, what the hell should I do?

CHAPTER 14

30 March, 10:30 AM PDT
Kingdom of the Sea Oceanarium, Seattle, Washington

COLBY FREEMAN PACED back and forth in his office like a caged animal, all dark circles and nervous energy. A smoldering headache pressed hard on his temples. He'd already popped four ibuprofens to dull the pain, but so far the pills hadn't kicked in. Nearly two hours had now passed since he'd learned of Samson's death. The news was hardly unexpected, yet still it hit with dizzying force.

Freeman thought about the steps he'd taken in the past twenty-four hours to contain the inevitable, satisfied that his actions had been quick and decisive. After moving Samson to a heavily-guarded sea-pen sealed off from the rest of the property, he'd then temporarily reassigned the entire orca team, except for Leanne and Big Boy. This was no small task. It took nearly three dozen pros alone, most working behind the scenes, to keep the whales healthy and the popular exhibit humming. And every one of them knew Samson was the glue that held the entire operation together, the gift that kept on giving.

Finally, he'd issued a carefully crafted press release, touting more safety measures in the wake of the Osaka incident. Employees around the world were fed essentially the same message, a message entirely consistent with CGE's unwritten policy. Known simply as "The Chandler Way," it said without saying that the company's position on employees discussing business matters with outsiders was one of zero tolerance. Those who disregarded the mandate quickly found themselves in the unemployment line, a place nobody wanted to be, especially in these tough times. The global outreach was no small task either. The KOS empire employed thousands of people divided into dozens of departments filled with specialists, from traffic flow engineers to designers to animal behaviorists to guest relations.

But Freeman had not pulled any punches with the two colleagues standing a few feet from him now, talking in hushed tones. Samson's death had changed everything and he told them so. Savannah Sokolov had flown in earlier that morning aboard a CGE corporate jet, and she too seemed taken aback by the news. On Savannah's right stood Darnell Atwater, managing partner at Black Stallion. He'd taken a commercial flight the night before from his headquarters in Denver. A former Army Ranger, Atwater was gym-rat fit with hard-boiled eyes, a poker face, and a nose that had been broken one too many times. His birth certificate put him at fifty-nine. He looked at least ten years younger.

They were staring at a photo.

Savannah turned to Freeman. "Okay, so you're telling us that, as of late yesterday afternoon, Dr. Kincaid here gave us forty-eight hours to notify the Feds, right?"

Freeman nodded.

Atwater said, "By Feds, you mean the National Marine Fisheries Service?"

Freeman nodded again.

NMFS was a division of the National Oceanic and Atmospheric Administration, the government agency responsible for carrying out more than three dozen federal statutes designed to protect fish stocks from depletion and marine mammals from extinction.

"She'll want a necropsy done too," Freeman added. "To understand how and why Samson contracted this fatal disease. And a proper burial, of course."

Savannah set the photo down on Freeman's desk, her displeasure with the entire affair written all over her face. "Yeah, well, given this plan Mitchell's cooked up, we need to persuade her otherwise, don't we?" She glanced at her watch. "And there's no time to waste. We've got less than thirty hours left, not nearly enough to get done what needs to get done."

Freeman stared at his feet. "I'm just saying ... "

Atwater spoke up. "So, who else knows about the whale's death, Colby?"

"Our senior vet and Samson's head trainer, Leanne. That's it."

"And they're not talking, right?"

"Not a chance," Freeman said. "The vet's actually an ex-marine buddy of Mitchell's. Long story short, let's just say I *inherited* old Big Boy and leave it at that. He's as loyal as a sheepdog though, so no worries there. Now Leanne, she –"

"She's a friend of Dr. Kincaid's," Savannah interrupted, her voice icy cold. "Which means they talked. It's what girls do. They love to talk. Unlike you men who sit around shooting the shit...and saying nothing."

Freeman jumped in, ignoring the dig. "Actually, I've already spoken with Leanne. She gave me her word she wouldn't tell a soul, including the doc."

"And you believe her?"

"Yes. Her daughter's ill and the treatments cost a fortune. No way she can possibly afford them without good health coverage."

"I can appreciate that," Savannah replied. "Even so, we're running out of time."

"Then let's pay the good doctor a visit," Atwater said, tongue-in-cheek. "Suggest to her, in a nice way of course, that she needs to back away from all this, give us some breathing room. And I know just the man for the job."

Savannah threw him a look. "Let me guess, the same guy you sent to San Diego last summer to keep that cocky journalist quiet. What's his name?"

"Iago," Atwater replied.

Freeman was hardly a Shakespearean scholar, but he knew Iago was one of the Bard's more sinister knaves, a soldier and close confidant of Othello. "What am I missing here?" he asked.

Atwater explained. He said he'd grown up in Ashland, Oregon, the only child of two company actors with the town's famed Shakespeare Festival. In deference to his parents, he'd code-named all Black Stallion operatives after prominent characters from Shakespeare's plays, adding, "Iago's got the fiercest eyes I've ever seen and I swear he's got ice water running through his veins. Navy man, recruited back in the first Gulf War to be part of a secretive counterterrorist unit known as Seal Team Six. It's a quick-strike team with a single-minded mission – kill terrorists and rescue hostages. Same bunch that took down Bin Laden, they're that good. After leaving the Navy, he was recruited by a clandestine CIA unit and trained as an assassin. He's been with us for over three years now."

Freeman felt a small knot form in the pit of his stomach. He'd been raised in a white-collar suburb north of Chicago, the only son of a soft-spoken jeweler and an elementary school principal. He knew nothing of the dark world of mercenaries, men who trained in the shadows and jumped out of airplanes in the middle of some godforsaken jungle. His mind was now catapulting from one looming disaster to another. "C'mon, how much muscle do we need? I mean the woman's a marine biologist, not some bomb throwing maniac from al Qaeda."

"Relax, Colby," Atwater said with a perfect poker face. "Nobody's going to get hurt. The guy's a real pro. He'll be in and out and make his point before the woman has time to think."

The knot grew larger. Freeman glanced at the picture of his wife and daughters sitting on his desk. His future flashed before his eyes: arrest...trial...conviction...firing squad! What would his family think? Who would take care of them after he was gone? He took a deep breath, trying to keep the panic out of his voice. "Look, I still don't –"

"He's right," Savannah said tersely. "Now let's make sure we're all on the same page here. This woman is *not* to be harmed in any way. Understood?"

Atwater grimaced. "Look, I get paid to deliver results. And that's exactly what I intend to do. But yes, message received loud and clear."

"Okay, good," Savannah said, turning back to Freeman. "What about Samson? What's going on with him right now?"

"He's in the sea-pen under lock and key," he said. "The water's cold enough to slow decomposition so we should be okay there for now. It's guarded 24/7 and nobody can get within two hundred yards of the place without my permission." Freeman wiped away tiny beads of perspiration that had formed on his brow. The old cliché, "caught between a rock and a hard place," came to mind, but he managed to dismiss the thought. "I'll tell you this, though," he added. "If Dr. Kincaid *does* find out Samson's dead, the Feds will storm in here like it's D-Day."

"It better not come to that," Savannah said.

Freeman nodded. "Yeah, good God, let's hope not."

CHAPTER 15

30 March, 11:30 AM PDT
King 5 TV, Seattle, Washington

THE STATION'S MAKEUP ROOM was located down the hall and around the corner from the studio control center, deep in the bowels of the building. Jia-li Han sat on a padded stool in the second bay, squinting into a brightly-lit mirror. She barely recognized the image staring back. Her face was scratched and bruised, her hair a fright. Dark puffs crowded bloodshot eyes. She took a deep breath, opened the black vinyl make-up kit lying in front of her and began by applying the dry mineral base. There was a time when the station employed a hair and makeup artist, but the job had been eliminated during the latest round of budget cuts. Jia-li didn't mind, not really. She had always done her own makeup, preferring a simple, classic look.

Typically, it took her about ten minutes, start to finish.

Today would take a little longer.

She'd been forced to sit on this incredible story for more than a day now, something to do with the police needing to wrap up some loose ends on the pirates' investigation. So far, their identities still remained a mystery. Predictably, the frustrating delay had set off the usual tug of war between the media and cops – the one involving the public's right to know versus the department's need to withhold information. Jia-li's bosses and the chief of police had finally settled on noon today. It wasn't her usual time slot, but this story couldn't wait a minute longer.

Surprisingly, there had been no other reported sightings of the colossal whales, at least so far, creating a rather curious dilemma. On one hand, there was the "exclusivity factor," the stuff big stories were made of, stories that won awards, important awards, maybe even the granddaddy of them all, the Pulitzer Prize. On the other was the "credibility issue." Would Jia-li's adoring public believe her? She wouldn't be the first reporter to exaggerate the facts of a story for personal gain. And Jason Taylor hardly qualified as an ideal witness, not with two black marks against him: fiancé and tort lawyer. Her news director, Ned Calkins, had expressed his own brand of skepticism, although he came around rather quickly after conferring with Detective Cloyd Steiger. The fact that Jia-li had convinced a grizzled Seattle homicide detective she was telling the truth seemed to put Calkins at ease, at least enough to give her the green-light.

Jia-li glanced over at the clock. 11:53. She remembered her first live report a dozen years earlier, and the thousand-yard stare she'd seen in the mirror moments before airtime. Now, despite all she'd been through on the boat, she felt confident, poised, prepared. Seconds later, there was a knock on the door. Calkins poked his head inside.

"Ready to roll?" he asked. It was the same question Ned *always* asked before each newscast. And Jia-li answered the way she *always* answered. "Good to go, chief."

"Great," Calkins said, smiling. "Listen, we go live at noon with your report; then at six tonight, we'll bring in the marine biologist for an extended interview. Unless –"

"Unless *what?*" she asked, knowing Calkins would backpedal fast if her story didn't connect with viewers, if she didn't come across as completely legit.

"Nothing," he replied, sheepishly. "I'll send a chopper to pick up Dr. Kincaid in a bit."

Jia-li's face flushed red, but this was no time to argue the point. "Okay, Ned, that sounds good."

Shortly before noon, Jia-li entered the spacious studio. She said hello to the stage manager and took her usual seat behind the news desk, the distinctive King 5 logo affixed to its glossy face. She checked her watch – two minutes to air. Closing her eyes, she was back on the big yacht, each image building on the last in a logical pattern. Then her mind began playing tricks, those same images now coming to her in a disjointed series of flashbacks. She fought off panic as she desperately tried to reconnect the dots, to regain the snapshot clarity that had been there just moments ago.

"Twenty seconds," a voice shouted from the dark.

Jia-li looked deep into the camera, took several quick breaths.

"Four, three, two… go, Jia-li."

And right then, everything came together.

"Good afternoon, Seattle. Welcome to King 5 News at Noon. I'm Jia-li Han and I have a story to tell. It began the day before yesterday with a fateful decision to…"

Over the next twenty minutes, Jia-li recounted her improbable tale with all the passion and professionalism that had become her trademark. She held nothing back, save for her strange encounter with one of the mighty creatures sometime after the initial attack. There had been no time to even process those feelings, let alone comprehend their meaning.

She wrapped the story with an intriguing tease, guaranteed to pull in an even larger audience. "So, where did these colossal whales come from? And what does it all mean? Stay tuned, there's more to come on the news at six when you'll meet a renowned expert on killer whales. You won't want to miss *that* interview. I'm Jia-li Han...and I'll see you right back here at six."

The lights dimmed, but there wasn't a sound in the studio.

In fact, no one moved a muscle.

Even the hardcore union workers remained frozen, shaking their heads in disbelief.

CHAPTER 16

30 March, 5:30 PM PDT
King 5 TV, Seattle, Washington

AFTER SPENDING MUCH of the afternoon researching killer whales, Jia-li now turned her attention to her famous guest. She had interviewed Katrina Kincaid before on the subject and the woman knew her stuff. They'd spoken early that morning. After hearing Jia-li describe her harrowing encounter with the colossal beasts, Dr. Kincaid had agreed to appear as a guest, seemingly undeterred by opinions the skeptics – and some of her own colleagues – would surely express. And indeed, the naysayers had come out in full force, popping up on cable news networks soon after the noon report had aired, most claiming the story was either a hoax or a gross exaggeration.

But all that had changed – at precisely 3:30 p.m.

It was then that jaw-dropping images of the mighty orcas were uploaded to the Web. Within minutes, killer whales were all the rage, easily topping the list of most popular subjects on every major search engine. The dazzling photos had been taken by a thrill-seeking couple who'd ventured into Puget Sound in a powerful speedboat hoping to catch a glimpse of history. Ted and Jenny Lagrange weren't alone – hundreds of other curiosity seekers had come up with the same idea – but only the Lagranges were lucky enough to strike gold.

And from what Jia-li could see, it was a spectacular show.

Shortly after four o'clock, Jia-li, news director Ned Calkins, and the station's general manager huddled together in a small conference room plotting strategy. Calkins, it turned out, knew the mayor of Port Angeles, the town the Lagranges called home. He agreed to contact the family, and twenty minutes later King TV's vice president for business affairs was headed for the North Olympic Coast to negotiate a deal with the local couple. It included a dozen photos and an exclusive interview.

Jia-li suggested she leave for Port Angeles immediately after her interview with Dr. Kincaid, but the GM nixed the idea after learning that the Coast Guard had banned all non-commercial traffic in Puget Sound, citing safety concerns. Instead, he directed Calkins to begin an aggressive promotional campaign built around a momentous event airing "live at five" the following afternoon. The ban, the GM reasoned, would all but eliminate any chance of additional sightings – at least during the next twenty-four hours – while providing him with sufficient time to assemble a worldwide grid of television networks to carry the feed.

This was the story of a lifetime, he said, and needed to be treated accordingly.

Jia-li felt like she was on an express train to some distant galaxy. Right now, however, she needed to keep her feet firmly planted on earth, prepare for the moment at hand: the 6:00 p.m. interview with Dr. Kincaid, an interview that had just taken on immeasurably greater significance. Jia-li shut off her iPhone and sequestered herself in an empty edit bay down the hall from the studio to review her research notes.

As a reporter, she'd always believed in doing her homework, a lesson firmly implanted in her head during four years at Columbia's School of Journalism. The key to a great interview, her favorite professor liked to say, was to make the subject open up, become a co-conspirator. Seek light, not heat. That meant being prepared, knowing the topic intimately, and asking good questions. And who could ever forget his oft-repeated mantra, *"If your mother says she loves you, get a second source."*

What Jia-li had learned about killer whales was eye-opening. She found the creatures to be at once fascinating and incredibly complex. Perhaps most compelling of all was their history. Killer whales, she'd learned, weren't really whales at all. In fact they were the largest member of the dolphin family. Official name: Orcinus orca. Orcus was a mythological Roman god of the netherworld; orca, Latin for "the shape of a barrel," which approximated the whale's body shape.

The name "killer" reportedly traced its origin to an ancient Roman scholar named Pliny the Elder, who cited the whale's enormous mass and savage teeth. Over the centuries, their fierce reputation only seemed to grow, causing them to be mercilessly hunted. Between 1950 and 1980 alone, commercial whalers from Russia and Japan took more than two thousand orcas, some of them captured live and sold to aquatic theme parks. Many didn't survive the journey, others died within the first few years of captivity. The practice of hunting orcas included a rather ugly history in North America as well, though the practice had long since been outlawed.

Not so in other parts of the world.

Their exploitation, it seemed, knew few boundaries.

As Jia-li jotted down an exhaustive list of questions, her thoughts were interrupted by a knock on the door. It swung open to reveal Ned Calkins, smiling like the proverbial cat who ate the canary. "Hey, the chopper landed a few minutes ago. I personally escorted Dr. Kincaid to the Green Room, made her comfortable. I gotta say she looks more like a grad student than a famous scientist, but what the hell, I'm sure she'll be great. And so will you. Go get 'em, tiger."

Jia-li buttoned her silk, navy jacket, walked into the studio, and greeted her guest with a warm smile and big "thank you." They then settled into a cozy living-room set some thirty feet from the news desk. The backdrop was a spectacular skyline shot of Seattle, the famous Space Needle front and center.

The stage manager adjusted their microphones, and, as he stepped away, three robotic cameras shuttled into position.

"Okay, ten seconds," a voice shouted. "Everybody settle." Then, "Three, two...go, Jia-li."

"Hello again," she said, smiling "And welcome to this special edition of King 5 News at Six. Joining me now is one of the world's most renowned experts on killer whales, Dr. Katrina Kincaid." Jia-li formally thanked Katrina for coming, quickly established her academic and professional credentials, and then said, "As you know, doctor, a lot has happened in just the past couple of hours. Much of the world has now seen the enormous creatures I spoke about earlier today. Please, give us your thoughts."

"First off, this is all very exciting," Katrina replied. "And after looking at the photos I'm convinced your initial impressions were right. These are definitely killer whales, though clearly they belong to some super species, probably gifted with some sort of mysterious genetic coding we've never seen before. But that shouldn't come as a big surprise, not when you consider over two-thirds of the earth's surface is covered with water and less than five per cent of the deep oceans have ever been explored. I mean we're talking about a great scientific blank space down there. Truth is, we know a lot more about distant galaxies than what lies below our own seas."

"In other words, almost *anything* could be lurking down there?"

"Exactly," Katrina said. "And through the ages, killer whales have survived and thrived, masters of their realm. And for good reason. Orcas are apex predators with a pack mentality; it's why they're often called 'wolves of the sea.' And they sit alone at the top of the food chain; no other animal even comes close."

"Including the ferocious great white shark we see on TV all the time?"

Katrina chuckled. "No contest. Put a killer whale and a great white in the same ring and it's not a fight, it's an execution. Nevertheless, I think it's highly unlikely this new species would even bother with a shark."

"Why is that?" Jia-li asked.

"Sharks are fish. And I'm guessing these are transients."

"Transients?"

Katrina nodded. She went on to describe the two primary types of orcas – residents and transients – with the single biggest distinguishing factor being diet. Residents, she said, ate fish, primarily salmon, *Chinook* salmon being their preferred dish. Transients, on the other hand, preferred warm-blooded prey – sea lions, seals, and porpoises mainly. Occasionally they hunted other whales, much *larger* whales, grays mostly. "And diet shapes all aspects of the transient lifestyle," she added. "Behavior, social structure, acoustics, everything. They also travel in much smaller groups, six or less, compared with ten to thirty, which is typical for a resident pod. So we know a lot less about transients. The two groups hunt the same waters, but feed on different prey. And they stay out of each other's way. It's quite remarkable, really, like nothing else in nature."

Jia-li asked, "Okay, any other major differences?"

"Well, transients are also very stealthy compared to residents, but they both produce a dazzling array of similar underwater sounds – clicks, burst-pulsed signals, and whistles. Some calls are as loud as sirens, and the clicks are used for echolocation."

"Like sonar on a submarine," Jia-li said matter-of-factly.

"Exactly," Katrina noted. "The clicks bounce off objects and come back forming a 'sound picture' in the brain. Again, it's a remarkable survival mechanism."

Jia-li nodded. "Okay, so how long do killer whales typically live?"

"Females average about fifty years, males around thirty. But killer whales have been under assault for years by commercial whalers, and now our own Navy is killing and maiming thousands of whales and dolphins through the use of high frequency sound testing." Katrina paused, rubbed her hands together. "Don't get me started on that stuff, though, or we'll be here all night."

"Fair enough," Jia-li said. And on that note she broke for commercial.

During the break, Jia-li reviewed her notes, thinking how well the interview was going. Katrina Kincaid was smart, articulate, and easy on the eyes – the trifecta when it came to the fickle world of television. A production assistant then handed her a stack of phone messages, requests for *her* to appear as a guest. There were calls from the network morning shows, evening news anchors, and most of the cable mouthpieces, not to mention Katie Couric, Tom Brokaw, and Oprah Winfrey. It was all a bit overwhelming. Now, however, she had a job to do. Following two minutes of commercials, she welcomed back viewers and picked up the thread with Dr. Kincaid.

"Okay, let's talk specifically about these mega-creatures, if we can. First, their coloring. The killer whales we've grown to know and love have distinctive black and white markings, with some touches of gray. These giants are jet black except for what appears to be a metallic gold slash running down the sides of their bodies. Any explanation?"

"Not really," Katrina said. "Except that there are albino orcas. So why not solid *black* orcas? Think about it. The animals could approach prey without being heard *or* seen, so it probably has something to do with their eating habits."

"Makes sense. So, why show up now?"

"That's an easy one. Food! It stands to reason they came down from the polar region. Killer whales thrive in cold water, tough for anything to penetrate those three-to-four-inch-thick coats of blubber. My colleagues and I have identified several pods living close to the polar ice cap. Maybe the rogues were up there too, perhaps even beyond the limits of the fast ice."

"But they have to breathe, right? How could they survive in that environment?"

"It's just a theory," Katrina replied. "Even in the coldest regions there are patches of ocean that never freeze, but the truth is, I just can't say. Nobody can. And considering the size of their dorsal fins, it's especially baffling. The thing is, there's so much we *don't* know about killer whales. But this much we do: they're on the move because their *prey* is moving. Look, I've been to that region on research expeditions three times over the past five years, and what I saw was downright scary. The climate is on *steroids*."

"Can you give us some examples?" Jia-li asked.

"Sure. Glaciers are shrinking and flexing and creeping in completely unpredictable ways. You'd swear they're almost alive. And the signs are everywhere up there. Longer summers, warmer winters, more intense storms, thinning salmon runs, bears that have stopped hibernating. I could go on and on. And it's getting worse." Katrina leaned forward, formed a steeple with her fingers. "You know, there are scientists who will tell you that nature is fragile. Well, that's flat out wrong. Nature is strong and packs an enormous counter-punch."

Jia-li nodded, glanced down at her notes. "But not everyone agrees, right? I recently read a report from an eminent scientist who claims the sun is the root of our climate problems, not man. He says if you really want to know what will happen when CO2 rises or temperatures change, look at the history of the planet. How do you respond, Dr. Kincaid?"

"I say nature's calling the bet. Look, man has been tampering with the terrestrial thermostat for far too long. But don't take my word for it. Ask the natives. Climate change is happening before their very eyes, in real time. What scientists see from satellites, they see up close. As one elder told me during my last trip, *'The Arctic is screaming, and no one is listening.'*"

Jia-li let that sink in, then said, "Okay, final question, doctor, one I'm sure is on the minds of every person in our viewing audience. What about the sheer size of these creatures?"

"Well, the blue whale is still larger – some weigh as much as 150 tons – but when it comes to pure predators, nothing else in the history of the planet even comes close."

"Right," Jia-li said. "Let's do a few comparisons then." She glanced quickly in the direction of the stage manager. He gave her the thumbs up, meaning they were ready in the control booth. "First, what I'll call a 'normal' killer whale."

The picture cut to dramatic footage of an orca exploding out of the water, cleanly snagging an unsuspecting seal right off the shore. The speed and power were almost incomprehensible. Then a tight shot and freeze frame on the whale, its dimensions graphically displayed on the screen. Length: 22-24 feet. Weight: 4-5 tons.

"What you're looking at here is a mature male," Katrina added. "Females are somewhat smaller. Awesome, isn't it?"

Jia-li nodded.

Another cut. This time to an artist's rendition of *megalodon*, a fierce looking shark with razor-like teeth, fossils of which had been discovered by scientists just decades earlier. Its stats were also listed. *Length: 50 feet. Weight: 52 tons.*

"Now this is probably the most infamous carnivore of all," Katrina said. "The tyrant lizard known as Tyrannosaurus Rex." A movie clip from *Jurassic Park* showed T-Rex in all its ferocious might. Again a graphic flashed on the screen. *Length: 40 feet. Weight: 6-7 tons.*

Finally, the picture cut to an image taken just hours earlier by the couple in the boat on Puget Sound. Jia-li's heart began to race, the terror of her ordeal still raw and deeply intense. The sleek, glossy black giant had been captured in a spectacular breach, its immense body soaring out of the water like a solid booster rocket lifting off from Cape Canaveral. In the brilliant sunshine the metallic gold slash that ran from its eye to beyond its dorsal fin seemed to glow.

"*This* is leviathan," Katrina exclaimed. "The largest predator the world has ever known."

An instant later the mind-numbing stats appeared on the monitor. *Length: 120 feet. Weight: 100 tons.*

CHAPTER 17

30 March, 7:15 PM PDT
Olympia, Washington

THAT SAME EVENING, Mitchell Chandler sat alone in his study, perusing a thick black binder. The room was large but comfortable, with floor-to-ceiling bookcases along the north wall. Two of the shelves were filled with first editions, many of them among the world's most treasured works of non-fiction. The more contemporary manuscripts were also first editions, every one of them signed. There was an ornately carved cherrywood desk in one corner and opposite it, an impressive ivory sculpture framed by two Van Goghs. Cantilevered bay windows looked out on a diamond-shaped swimming pool bathed in soft underground lighting. Beethoven's Symphony No. 7 played quietly in the background.

Several hours earlier, Chandler had ordered a member of his inner circle to dig up everything she could find on killer whales, and it had nothing to do with the colossal creatures raising hell in Puget Sound. He reviewed those materials now, zeroing in on the history and controversy surrounding live captures of killer whales, back when such activities were legal. He'd heard of the two main players, of course, but knew almost nothing about them.

Their names were Ted Griffin and Don Goldsberry and their controversial tale began in the mid-sixties with the capture of an orca Griffin named Namu. He'd purchased the whale for $8,000 from a British Columbia fisherman after the animal became trapped in his nets. The whale was then dragged in a floating cage for public display at a Seattle aquarium, long before KOS appeared on the scene. Griffin trained Namu, rode him, and sold plenty of tickets to audiences anxious to see him perform. Almost overnight, the reputation of the killer whale changed from feared and hated "man-eater" into goodwill ambassador.

Chandler flipped through a series of newspaper headlines and photos. The story had made front page news around the world. So did Namu's death a year later. According to several articles, Griffin and Goldsberry had then gone into the whale hunting business full time, plying the waters of Puget Sound and the coast of British Columbia. Reportedly, they'd paid $1,000 for each permit with no limit on the number of captures. And there appeared to be no shortage of buyers. Turning the page, Chandler landed on another photo. This one featured a crowd of well-dressed men standing on a floating dock literally waving bundles of cash in the air. The going rate for each whale, the caption read, was between $20,000 and $30,000.

Jesus, what a gold mine.

Reading on, Chandler discovered that, over the next several years, the two men had captured and sold more than thirty whales, many purchased by SeaWorld. By the early seventies, however, the partnership had soured and Griffin got out, reportedly because of death threats from animal rights groups.

The activists had denied the charges, yet made no bones about their position. They accused Griffin and Goldsberry of employing cruel and inhumane tactics by playing on the whales' weak points, mostly the family instinct. The thinking went that if one whale was captured, the others would stick around to lend support. Simply put, that meant there were a lot more animals to choose from. Perhaps most damning of all, however, were claims that many of the whales had become trapped during capture. Some drowned, others died in transport, or from improper care and handling. Most within two years. Those that lived longer, the activists had alleged, lasted only about eight or nine years on average as opposed to at least three times that long in the wild.

Chandler scanned one last story about how Don Goldsberry had moved his act to Iceland following the passage of the U.S. Marine Mammal Protection Act in 1972. The article went on to say that, over the next several years, demand by SeaWorld and other aquariums around the globe had increased exponentially, with the price for a healthy killer whale soaring to between $150,000 and $300,000.

Hell, if it was legal today that number would be well north of a million.

Chandler closed the binder and clamped his arms across his chest, thinking about all this. He was about to step outside for some fresh air when his cell phone burred.

It was one of his assistants at the office.

Preston Tradd's phone vibrated at precisely the same moment, waking him with a start. He'd fallen asleep soon after being picked up at Sea-Tac airport, the return trip from Sitka every bit as brutal as getting there. It took a moment for him to orient himself, but he quickly recognized his surroundings as the plush leather and teak interior of a hand-crafted Rolls-Royce Phantom. His father drove the same model and swore by these whisper-quiet, half-million-dollar driving machines. For a just a second, Tradd was a kid again headed to lacrosse practice in Laguna Beach, not far from where he and his family now resided.

He checked the caller ID, picked up, and was instantly transported back to real time by the voice of his exasperated wife. She wasn't happy about the stop-over in Seattle, and it took some doing to convince her that he would be home later that evening. He said they'd leave the following morning for their long-overdue ski vacation. After a brief exchange, she calmed down. He told her he loved her, clicked off, and pocketed the phone.

A few minutes later, the driver turned onto a smooth ribbon of asphalt that snaked up to a spectacular hilltop manor. Tradd had seen some lofty estates in his day, but this was the Holy Grail. The gates were huge, the walls high, the setting breathtaking. The compound sat gloriously on fifty manicured acres, with drop-dead views of Puget Sound and the Olympic Mountains. Even through a gray mist, the dome of the Washington state capitol building glowed in the distance.

"Nice digs," Tradd said.

The driver nodded. "Yes sir, the boss does it right. Helipad's over there behind the waterfall. Par-three golf course down the hill. Tennis courts out back. 'Wimbledon-inspired,' I'm told, whatever that means."

"I didn't think the *boss* even played tennis. Golf either, for that matter."

"True, but many of our visitors do. The guest house can accommodate a dozen people, give or take, and the garage holds enough cars for every one of 'em to drive their own vehicle."

"And what's your story?" Tradd asked. "I take it you weren't a mall cop in a former life."

The driver laughed. "No, sir, special ops, Marine Force Recon, same as the other guys in the unit here. Actually I'm filling in for Mr. Chandler's regular driver tonight. It's his day off."

"Well, I appreciate the lift. Feel safer already."

"You're in good hands, sir. Just like the commercial says."

Moments later, the Rolls pulled in front of the mansion. The driver explained that the main house was thirty-five thousand square feet. It included a climate-control wine cellar, art deco 3-D home theater with Dolby Surround Sound, yoga studio, fitness center, nine bedrooms...and more bathrooms than he could count.

"Like I said, quite the pad," Tradd noted. "Listen, thanks for the ride. This shouldn't take long. I need to catch the last flight out of Sea-Tac tonight for LA, leaves a little after nine."

And this time tomorrow night, I'll be relaxing in a comfy chateau at Mammoth Mountain.

Tradd couldn't remember his last vacation, something his wife constantly reminded him of. Maybe this time away, this escape from the kids, would help mend a marriage badly frayed around the edges.

"Yes, sir, no problem. Standing by."

Tradd slid out of the vehicle and was greeted at the front door by a polished-looking older gent wearing a crisp white shirt and dark slacks.

"Mr. Chandler is expecting you, sir. He's in his study. Right this way."

They walked down a long, wide marble-floored corridor, their footsteps echoing off the fortress-like walls. Mitchell Chandler was dressed casually, stretched out in a recliner, speaking into a cell phone. He was bigger than Tradd had expected and everything about him communicated a single message: absolute and total control. Tradd took a deep breath, reminded himself of something he already knew.

This is not a man you want to disappoint.

Chandler looked up, waved Tradd in, and covered the phone. "Have a seat. I'll just be a minute." He then motioned him to a heavy burgundy sofa.

Tradd strolled across the room and, as he sat down, he adjusted the knot on his $300 tie, unbuttoned the jacket of his $4,000 Armani suit. Despite his overall uneasiness with this assignment, he felt much more at ease in these surroundings than in some honky-tonk bar in the Land of the Midnight Sun.

Chandler's phone conversation was brief, less than a minute. "Hello, Tradd," he said, after clicking off. He didn't bother to stand or shake hands.

"Listen, I got your message earlier, about the flight delays. A real bitch. I'd rather walk through a snake-infested swamp than fly commercial." He then reached for a crystal Waterford decanter sitting on the oak table next to his chair, poured three fingers of Hennessy X.O into a pair of snifters, handed a glass to Tradd. "Here, this will take the edge off."

"Thank you," Tradd said, glancing outside. He repeated the remark he'd made to the driver about the estate.

Chandler nodded, sipped his brandy. "Well, it's home, my one and only these days. Fortunately, I was able to keep my ex-wife's mitts off the property. You married, Tradd?"

"Yes, sir, seventeen years."

Chandler raised his glass. "Well, here's to seventeen more. Listen, I have a conference call in twenty minutes, so why don't you tell me what you've got, starting with the infamous Ms. Flynn. I'm guessing she's a Hall of Fame ball-buster. Am I right?"

Tradd sat up straight. He felt good about what he'd accomplished up in Alaska, though he regretted having to resort to the unseemly tactics. "Well, let's just say the woman's alpha all the way, sir, a real man-eater."

"Can't say as I'm surprised, not after reading the dossier your people put together. The most thorough goddamn piece of work I've ever seen, especially on such short notice. Good job."

"I'm just the messenger. You can thank our team of investigators for that. All former big-city homicide cops, as you know. L.A., mostly. Hollywood Division."

Chandler nodded. "Well, now, Hollywood is precisely where our talented captain belongs one day. If she plays her cards right, that is. I understand she's on board."

"Yes," Tradd said, his neck flushing hot. "But, umm, things didn't go exactly as planned."

"You said. What happened?"

"For starters, she refused your generous cash offer, didn't bat an eye in fact."

Chandler shifted in his chair. "No surprise there, either, right? What about the charity angle?"

"I'm afraid the response was the same, and believe me, I pushed her hard. She left me no choice but to go with the backup plan."

"Shit! The mother," Chandler barked. "I was hoping to avoid that unpleasant bit of business. How did she react?"

"Not well, sir." Beads of perspiration the size of tiny pearls now formed on Tradd's brow. And the room was cool. "To be honest with you, I thought she was going to come across the table and break my neck. She could've done it, too, in a heartbeat. Anyway...I managed to calm her down. Assured her no one would hurt her mother if our terms were met."

"And no one *will* hurt dear old mom, assuming our captain gets the job done. And keeps her mouth shut, of course."

"I made that very clear."

And God help me if I didn't.

"What about the money transfers?" Chandler asked.

Tradd finished his drink with one gulp, set it down on the table in front of him. "The account is under one of our corporate shells. No way can it be traced back to us, *or* you. But here's the thing – Ms. Flynn's only taking enough cash to cover expenses. She refused the rest, even for her girls' home in Nepal."

"Well, now, that's interesting, isn't it?"

Tradd smiled. He thought he might score a few points with that one.

"So at this juncture, she knows nothing about the dead whale?"

"No, sir," Tradd said. "I explained that further instructions would be forthcoming as soon as she put everything in place. I checked in with her an hour ago, right after my plane landed. She said things are already in motion. Some bush pilot friend is flying her down to Port Angeles. She plans to rent a big fishing boat there. I had to Google the place, it's–"

"I know where it is, Tradd. When is she leaving Sitka?"

"Tomorrow morning."

"Okay, good. Did she say anything else?"

"Like what, sir?"

"Like how she intends to pull this off."

"No, but then I don't see how we could expect her to –"

"Look," Chandler interrupted. "Obviously, this is not going to be easy, but what I *don't* want is a repeat of the goddamn tactics used back in the day when it was legal to capture killer whales."

"In the early sixties to mid-seventies, you mean?" Tradd had downloaded and absorbed reams of information on killer whales while biding his time in that miserable little motel room in Sitka. He'd known almost nothing about the powerful creatures before making the trip. Now he qualified as a quasi-expert.

"Precisely," Chandler said. He leaned down, picked up the binder sitting on the floor, and tapped the hard plastic cover repeatedly. "Inside this file is everything you need to know about two enterprising characters named Ted Griffin and Don Goldsberry. These guys essentially created the entire killer whale industry and made a bundle doing it. They also made a lot of enemies along the way."

Griffin and Goldsberry. The names rang a bell. Tradd remembered reading about their brutal tactics, how they spent most of their time chasing down the whales. After making contact, they'd buzz them with helicopters and powerboats. The idea was to confuse the big animals, get them to crowd together in bunches. If that didn't work, seal bombs were deployed, nasty little suckers that looked like miniature sticks of dynamite. Once the orcas were contained, the men would drop big mesh corrals into the water, trap them inside, then lasso them like cowboys roping steers.

Chandler took a long pull from his drink. "It was a circus sideshow, Tradd, something we've got to avoid at all costs. Understood?"

And Tradd did. But what could all this possibly have to do with him? All he wanted now was to catch a ride back to the airport and fly home. Hell, he'd done his job and done it well, which was why Chandler's next words came out of left field.

"I need you to stick around for a few days, make sure our captain takes a more, shall we say, *subtle* approach."

Tradd nearly choked.

A few more days? Son of a bitch!

His wife was going to kill him.

Chandler seemed to pick up on his discomfort. "Is that a problem, Tradd?"

"No, sir, of course not," he lied.

"Good man. Normally I would offer you the guest house out back, but under the circumstances, that's not going to work. That was my assistant on the phone when you came in. She made arrangements for you to stay at a nice little B&B down on Budd Inlet. You'll find it quite comfortable there."

Hell, maybe he'd move in. It would beat going home to face the wrath of Khan. "Thank you, sir. Mind if I ask a question before we wrap up?"

"Sure, make it quick," Chandler replied, glancing at his watch.

"I was just wondering about Griffin and Goldsberry. They're a little long in the tooth by now. Is that why you didn't recruit them for this assignment?"

"That's part of it, Tradd. Of greater concern was the fact that those two yahoos stirred up so much shit in their day they'd *still* stink up the place. We just can't afford that kind of risk."

Tradd stood to leave, cleared his throat. "I understand. Oh, one last thing. What about those monster whales everyone's talking about? I mean, they're all over the news...the Internet too."

"Yes, I know. But look at it this way. They'll provide valuable cover, distract any reporters who might otherwise come snooping around."

"And if they don't, sir?"

Chandler cut him a piercing look. "Goodnight, Tradd. Get some rest."

CHAPTER 18

AFTER AN ARDUOUS eight-hour flight from Sitka, the four-seat de Havilland bush plane banked over Ediz Hook, turned east into an unforgiving headwind, and set down in choppy waters a mile from town. As the pilot taxied to a small marina, his passenger prepared to deplane. Zora Flynn grabbed her bag, handed the man a thick wad of hundred dollar bills, and stepped onto the small wooden dock. Their eyes locked for an anxious moment, then Zora's trusted friend, Tanner Lockhart, pulled the door shut, throttled up, and taxied back out to sea.

Five minutes later, he lifted off into overcast skies.

Zora cabbed to a local car-rental agency and was soon zipping east along Highway 101 in a sporty red coupe. She'd asked for something less conspicuous, but the fast-talking mosquito behind the counter said it was the only vehicle available. Traffic was light and Zora's thoughts turned once again to her mother, a woman so unfairly robbed of mind and memory. What did she see when she stared into the mirror? Did she even know who she was? Did she wrack her brain searching for remnants of the past and dreading the future? Zora had asked herself those same questions a thousand times over the past two days, playing and replaying in her mind the disturbing conversation with the man in Sitka.

For the briefest of moments, she had considered letting her mother go, allowing these monsters to lift her out of the fog. Maybe she would find something truly beautiful on the other side? Maybe there really was a place of infinite serenity somewhere? Zora had never been a particularly religious person, yet who could say for certain what death held in store? Whatever it was would surely trump the nothingness of Alzheimer's. But that had been Zora's own dark side talking. In her heart and in her head she knew she could never allow that to happen. She must do everything in her power to protect her mother, preserve whatever intellectual and emotional threads still remained grounded in reality, no matter how murky that reality may be.

And that would take near flawless execution of a plan that was still a work in progress.

The pieces, however, seemed to be falling into place.

Before leaving Alaska, Zora had checked her bank statement and, as expected, $75,000 had been deposited into her account via a wire transfer. It was drawn on an offshore bank, a bank undoubtedly beyond the scope of any U.S. regulators. Soon after confirming the transaction, she got a call from Katrina Kincaid. She couldn't wait to see her, she said. That left her crew, convincing them to put their lives on the line. They were good men, had always followed Zora's simple, sea-faring rules to the letter – no booze, no drugs, no guns. And they worked damn hard, too. But this was going above and beyond. This was asking a lot.

Even so, that conversation had gone well, too. Lapenda, Cassidy, and McCabe had each expressed genuine concern for Zora's mother, the health of the whale, and their own safety. Yes, they were fishermen and fishermen liked to talk, but they also understood the gravity of the situation and each had sworn an oath of silence. The promise of a healthy paycheck – twenty grand each – sealed the deal. Zora had then booked them on a commercial flight into Seattle. From there, they would rent a car and meet her in Port Angeles.

A few miles past Sequim, oncoming traffic began backing up, as one brightly colored media truck after another rolled by in a seemingly endless parade. She wondered what that was all about.

Maintaining her speed, Zora rounded a sharp curve, and made a left turn onto a gravel road that rolled through long stretches of deep woods. She slowed as she approached a small gathering of reporters and camera crews huddled behind a police barricade. After adjusting her sunglasses, she pulled the bill of her baseball cap low over her forehead. She had to admit it wasn't much of a disguise, but then she really didn't expect to recognized, at least not around here. Ironically, fame wasn't something she either envied or pursued. She much preferred her privacy to some trumped-up image crafted by phony, self-important spin doctors and their clients who found no shame in anything, as evidenced by the depraved state of reality TV.

Zora had agreed to the *Vanity Fair* piece only after the magazine's editor had pledged to double the hefty fee he'd already proposed, the entire amount to be earmarked for her children's home in Nepal. The money would not only secure the future of the operation, it would also provide food, clothing, education – and most important of all, self-respect – for an additional two hundred kids. All the stuff that moron in Sitka wasn't supposed to know, but did.

The beaming faces of those kids were still on Zora's mind as she stopped the car and rolled down the window. Two state troopers approached. They were wearing trademark campaign hats, aviator sunglasses, and snappy blue uniforms so crisp they looked like they could stand on their own.

The older trooper stepped forward, clipboard in hand. He was tall, stocky, his manner brisk and business-like. "Afternoon, ma'am. Live in the neighborhood, do you?"

"No, I'm a friend of Dr. Kincaid's. She's expecting me."

"Your name, ma'am?"

"Zora. Zora Flynn."

"ID please."

Zora produced a driver's license from her bag, handed it to the trooper. He examined the card for a long moment, tilted his head to one side, and peered suspiciously over the top of his glasses. "You're a long way from home, Ms. Flynn."

"Very observant of you," she replied, glancing at his nametag. "Is that a problem, Trooper Miles?"

He smirked, handed back the license, and checked off her name. "No ma'am, no problem at all. Appreciate your cooperation. You have yourself a nice afternoon, now."

The younger trooper tipped his hat and moved the stanchion. Zora slowly drove past a half-dozen reporters, attracting a few sidelong glances. But the group quickly went back to being bored. Katrina lived in Port Townsend, but had set up her lab twenty minutes west of town at her parents' place. She had forewarned Zora about the greeting party, explaining that reporters had camped out at her home immediately after she'd returned from the interview in Seattle. They might follow her here, she'd said. But why the troopers? What were they doing here? And where were all the other newshounds she'd seen on the highway headed?

After another mile or so of twists and turns, Zora reached the house at the end of Old Gardiner Road. She'd been here once before to help celebrate Allan and Dorothy Kincaid's golden wedding anniversary. That had been over a year ago. At the time, their charming Victorian home was being torn apart from top to bottom. Now, fully restored to its original splendor, it lay nestled like a sleeping cat amid a deep green forest of hemlocks and firs. The house was painted eggshell white and consisted of three levels – a porch, veranda, and balcony, all supported by monumental columns.

Zora pulled up in front of a two-story garage, stepped out of the car, and looked around. The grounds, like the home, were postcard perfect and surrounded by perennial gardens. The grass smelled fresh, like it had just been cut. And everywhere there were birds flitting about, chirping like it was the first day of spring. A vast rolling lawn sloped down to the tree line, beyond which the Strait of Juan de Fuca could be seen. She followed a narrow path that curled around an ornate octagon tower to the backyard.

A voice startled her. "Hey, girlfriend! Here, on the deck."

Zora looked up, craning her neck, "Oh, hi, Katrina. Great to see you."

"You, too. Come on up."

Zora climbed a dozen steps to the landing and hugged her friend. "It's been a long time."

"I know, sweetie," Katrina said. "*Too* long."

"Say, what's with the cops? I know you mentioned there might be reporters, but –"

"Yeah, sorry about that. I drove over earlier this afternoon to get some work done. The reporters followed. I was told the old biddy down the street filed a complaint, something about her flower garden being trampled on. Next thing you know we're looking at 'Checkpoint Charlie.'"

It was odd, Zora thought, that something so innocuous as a few cops could feel so unsettling.

Katrina then told her about the couple from Port Angeles and the remarkable photos they'd captured of the colossal whales, adding, "Jia-li Han is interviewing them over at the marina at five o'clock. It's a huge deal around here, so I'm not surprised by all the hype."

"I liked how she handled *your* interview, Katrina. And you did a great job. I caught a replay on CNN last night. Incredible stuff."

"Yeah, this is a real game-changer, all right. I'll fill you in over a glass of wine, okay? And I want to hear more about your shark experience, too. You only told me half the story last fall. I had no idea. I mean nobody in their right mind dives into those freezing waters, let alone with a bunch of hungry whites lurking around. And with a freakin' pistol, no less?"

"I know. I reacted, that's all. It was either that, or watch the poor guy get eaten alive. To tell you the truth, I thought the bullets would travel farther underwater. I lucked out."

Katrina rolled her eyes, smiled, and opened the screen door. "I'll say. C'mon, check out my new digs. I've added a bunch of new equipment since you were here last. It's pretty cool."

CHAPTER 19

ZORA STEPPED INSIDE the lab and looked around. It *was* cool, in a mad scientist sort of way. The large, windowless room was strewn with books, books piled high on the floor, shelves full of them. A long metal shelf ran along the far wall. Several microscopes equipped for state-of-the-art optical analyses sat on top. Other sophisticated-looking scientific instruments were scattered about. There were stacks of paper everywhere. A TV monitor, video equipment, and two laptops occupied a pair of marred-up old wooden tables.

"Not exactly Woods Hole," Katrina said. "But it works for me. Besides, the price is right. Mom and dad won't take any rent, and, for a girl on a small government grant, that's a big help."

The grant, Katrina explained, provided partial funding for "The Orca Project," a wide-ranging initiative designed to ensure the survival of killer whales by raising awareness, studying threats they faced in the wild, and creating comprehensive strategies to address those threats. The program got its start several years earlier, she said, following the discovery of a dead orca on a low-lying sandbar near Port Townsend. Tests revealed the young female carried one of the highest loads of toxic chemicals ever recorded in a marine mammal.

Zora shook her head. "Yeah, it's pathetic. I see tons of junk floating around in places you'd never expect, like the Bering Sea. Nothing like that garbage patch out in the Pacific, though. It's the size of Texas, mostly plastic, too."

"I know," Katrina said. "Will we *ever* learn that nature is calling the shots, that we can't upstage the main act no matter how hard we try?"

"Amen to that," Zora replied. After a long pause she asked, "So tell me, how are your parents doing?"

Katrina said, "Slowing down a bit, but otherwise fine. Both retired now and seem to be enjoying it, though I think dad's going a bit stir-crazy. He finished renovating the old place last month and now he pokes around up here way too much. I'm afraid he's gonna blow something up. Anyway, right now they're on a safari in Kenya. 'Wild and remote,' the brochure promised."

"Good for them. What about that handsome brother of yours?"

"Mickey's great, keeping busy. He helped dad with the house, which was interesting to watch. They're quite a pair, yapping at one another all the time about lord knows what. But if two better carpenters exist on the planet, I'd like to meet them. I told Mick you were stopping by. He asked about getting together for dinner, maybe tomorrow night if you're around?"

Zora nodded, but didn't say anything.

"Listen, give me a sec, okay?" Katrina said. "I need to make a couple of notations in the Sound Log before I forget. Then I want to show you something that totally blew me away."

Katrina then moved quickly to a worktable, sat down, and adjusted a couple of dials on the recording device. Zora stepped back nervously, her mind doing backflips, wondering how best to approach this fiasco. It wasn't in her makeup to ask for help, not from anyone. If she couldn't solve a problem herself, it just wasn't solvable. She noticed a glossy wall chart pinned to the back of the door. Scanning the categories, she made a mental note of each one.

<u>Taxonomy</u>

Kingdom – ANIMALIA
Class – Mammalia
Order – Cetacea
Suborder – ODONTOCETI
Family - Delphinidae
Genus – Orcinus
Species – orca
Common Names: Killer Whale, orca, blackfish

Zora stared mindlessly at the chart for several moments, then turned back to Katrina. She loved the woman's passion and devotion to her work. There was nothing the least bit phony or pretentious about her. She had met Katrina two years earlier during a brief vacation on the Galapagos Islands. They had teamed up to save a stranded sea lion and quickly struck up a friendship over dinner and several bottles of wine, a friendship that had only strengthened with time. Katrina phoned and e-mailed regularly, and she'd been a tower of strength during Zora's darkest hours, times when she felt as if she could no longer cope with her mother's illness.

After scribbling a few more notes, Katrina slipped off the headset and waved Zora over. She pulled up a stool on the opposite side of the table and sat down.

Katrina seemed lost in thought. "Hey, do you remember me mentioning a Canadian scientist named Michael Bigg last time you were here? *Dr. Mike*, we called him."

"Vaguely," Zora said. "What about him?"

"Back in 1970, he devised a new technique to study killer whales called photographic identity. He matched the photos of some three hundred fifty orcas and found that he could distinguish them by the shape of their dorsal fins and gray saddle patches. It was – and still is – our most important research tool in the field. Led to passage of the Marine Mammal Protection Act two years later. And that put an end to orca captures in U.S. waters. Prohibited their importation, too. It's because of Dr. Mike's foresight that we understand so much about killer whale biology today."

"Now I remember," Zora said. "He died quite young, didn't he?"

"Yes, fifty-one, leukemia. I was in high school at the time, but had been lucky enough to land an internship with him the summer before he died. Anyway, I got a call earlier this morning from a guy I interned with. He's now working for Nat Geo. They're planning a documentary on the evolution of killer whales and he wants to hire me as a consultant."

"That's great, Katrina."

"Uh-huh. That's not why I mentioned it, though. We got to reminiscing about Dr. Mike's memorial service. He had asked that his ashes be scattered over Johnstone Strait and..." Katrina looked off for a moment, her eyes moist. "Sorry. I always lose it when I talk about this."

"It's okay," Zora said. "What happened?"

"Well, it was the fall of 1990, early afternoon, gorgeous day. I'll never forget it. We all gathered on a cliff above the shore, huge turnout from all over the world. Then, just as the ceremony was about to begin, this pod of orcas showed up. Maybe thirty or so. The most amazing thing I've ever seen. And the whales stayed in that exact same spot for the entire service. When it ended, they circled Dr. Mike's ashes, then dropped out of sight and disappeared, just like that."

Zora smiled. "Wow! That *is* amazing."

"Yeah, their powers of cognition are extremely complex. And this colossal new species takes that complexity to a whole new level. If we humans weren't playing second fiddle on the evolutionary scale *before*, we sure are *now*. I guess that phone call was a reminder." Katrina grabbed the headset off the table, handed it to Zora, and fiddled with a few knobs on the recording device. "And then there's this," she said. "I've been monitoring cameras and hydrophones strategically situated throughout Puget Sound as part of my work. Here, give a listen."

Zora placed the headset over her ears and concentrated, trying to makes sense of what she was hearing. Nothing but static. Then…an explosion of sound that nearly knocked her off the stool. It was like stepping into an opera house with everyone singing at once. She listened for several moments before removing the headset. "Jesus! That's really intense. What's going on?"

"To be honest, it's baffling," Katrina said. "Like I stated in the TV interview, I'm almost certain the rogue whales are transients, not residents. And transients are expert stalkers, masters of stealth."

"So that's what you think is going on? They're chasing down dinner?"

"Exactly, only here's the thing. Both residents and transients possess laser-beam echolocation, but transients *rarely* vocalize while hunting. Instead, they use a sophisticated call and counter-call system to lock on to prey, and typically hide their vocalizations in the general ocean noise."

"Okay," Zora replied, a bit unsure of where this was all going.

"Here, take a look at the camera feed." Katrina hit a button on the monitor, did the same with the remote.

Murky gray waters…then movement.

"What you're looking at is a school of dolphins. Now, watch what happens when I switch to the surface camera."

Zora leaned forward to get a better look. The noisy images coalesced into a landscape of jagged bluffs rooted in algae-slick rocks. An instant later, it was mass chaos. The dolphins began hurling themselves onto the rocks in a noisy, suicidal frenzy. "They're freaking out," she said, her ears still ringing.

Katrina hit the "pause" button on the remote. "I've watched that tape at least twenty times and I still don't believe it. Dolphins instinctively flee from orcas but not like this. Their behavior is completely out of character."

"Any sign of the whales when you switched back to the underwater cameras?"

"No," Katrina replied. "But it explains the piercing sounds. These animals are so friggin' powerful, they don't *need* to stalk their prey. They take what they want when they want it. I'd say at least half a ton of food every day, probably more. And you know something else?"

Zora stared into Katrina's unblinking brown eyes. "What's that?"

"I think the whales *knew* we were watching. I feel it right here," Katrina said, tapping her chest with a clenched fist. "And if I'm right, we're not only dealing with the largest predator *ever*, we're also dealing with the most intelligent. Man *or* animal."

There were several seconds of silence as they both thought about that.

Zora finally said, "I believe it. Look, I've been out of the loop most of the day. Have there been any more sightings since all that activity yesterday?"

"No," Katrina said. "Not that I know of. But the whales are obviously still out there, so it's only a matter of time." She glanced at her watch. "Hey, time flies…it's almost four-thirty. Why don't we go over to the house where it's more comfortable? I picked up a nice bottle of wine on the way over. It's got your name on it."

Zora hesitated, reached for Katrina's arm, squeezed gently. She wasn't exactly sure what to say next, except that she needed to choose her words carefully. "Hey, before we go I need to tell you something, okay?"

Katrina looked expectantly at her.

"I wasn't entirely honest with you on the phone last night," Zora added. "Not my style. I'm sorry. The thing is, I didn't just *happen* to be in the area. A friend flew me down in his float plane. We left early this morning."

"All the way from Sitka?"

"Yeah…all the way from Sitka."

CHAPTER 20

31 March, 4:40 PM PDT
Sequim Bay, Washington

IN THE NINETY SECONDS after King 5 TV's helicopter set down in a roped-off area next to John Wayne Marina, Jia-li Han had applied her makeup, revised a list of questions, and spoken to her boss, Ned, back at the station. Her producer and two-person crew had arrived an hour earlier in a mobile news van. They were already setting up for the heavily-promoted interview with Ted and Jenny Lagrange.

Jia-li didn't know a lot about the iconic actor whose name graced the two-story concrete structure in front of her, but after learning he was one of Ted's heroes she'd conducted a quick Internet search. It revealed that "The Duke" once frequented this spectacular bay aboard his yacht, the *Wild Goose*. Reportedly, he became so enamored with the area that he envisioned a marina on the site, and after his death, the family donated twenty-two acres of land to realize his dream. Built in 1985, the property included permanent and guest moorage, a popular seafood restaurant called the Dockside Grill, public beach access, and picnic areas. More importantly, it was from this location that the Lagranges had launched their speedboat the previous afternoon, later capturing the remarkable photos that were about to make them household names.

Nothing like returning to the scene of the crime to amp up ratings.

Before exiting the chopper, Jia-li checked her Facebook and Twitter accounts and raced around the Internet. Her story on the colossal orcas continued to generate an endless stream of postings all over the globe. Friends had shared with friends who shared with other friends, the numbers growing exponentially by the minute. It was truly one of those defining events that changed everything, like the death of JFK or 9/11.

Scientists, politicians, and philosophers weighed in on its significance and every pundit from Chris Matthews to Bill O'Reilly to Rachel Maddow to Rush Limbaugh talked about little else. *Dateline, 20/20,* and *60 Minutes* were all running promos for upcoming stories. And so it was with blogs, chat rooms, and cybercafés on every continent. Imminent scholars were calling the colossal killer whales "the greatest discovery in the history of mankind." Even the Pope issued a statement asking for calm, assuring his billion-plus flock that this was not the rapture, as some religious leaders had alleged.

Not to be denied, the fringe element also jumped in.

A Stockholm-based group called The Luminous Society issued an immediate e-blast to its small but devoted membership. The group believed spiritual elders from other worlds, known as "Celestial Masters of the Universe," had sent the giant beasts as emissaries. Several other UFO-inspired organizations quickly joined the party as well, including Captain Cody and his Cosmic Commandos. From his home base in Tuscaloosa, Alabama, the captain had ordered his followers to establish "Alien Viewing Sites" on several islands in Puget Sound. Fans of the Loch Ness monster also sounded the trumpets, asserting that they'd finally been vindicated. The beasts, they proclaimed, must surely be closely related to Scotland's notorious "Nessie."

Jia-li had spoken briefly with Jenny Lagrange earlier in the day. Jenny could hardly contain herself, explaining that she and her husband were huge fans, that they trusted Jia-li like a friend, adding that they'd turned down a king's ransom from media outlets as far away as Australia to sign a modest deal with King TV. The contract called for exclusive rights to their story so long as Jia-li conducted the interview.

The trust factor was huge, something Jia-li had been careful never to betray throughout her career. In fact, trust was the lifeblood of any reputable news-gathering organization, the link to inside sources, people who could tell the story behind the story, those who could separate fact from fiction, hype, and innuendo.

Every reporter's success depended on those contacts.

Shining a light on the truth, she called it.

Now she was moments away from sharing the Lagranges' improbable story with the world, an All-American family perfectly suited for the job.

Jenny was a stay-at-home mom to two young kids. She helped out at the local soup kitchen and never missed a PTA meeting. Ted was a foreman at the local Nippon Paper Mill, an avid hunter and sportsman.

Jia-li stepped from the van into a scene that verged on hysteria, fueled by an avalanche of news and speculation. It was Barnum & Bailey without the elephants or trapeze artists. A fleet of satellite trucks – their electronic masts pointed to the heavens – covered both marina parking lots. There were cops everywhere, state troopers mostly, attempting to ride herd over a flash mob of photographers, reporters, and looky-loos crowded behind a cluster of barricades. Overhead in the now-cloudless sky, a trio of helicopters hovered low and annoyingly loud. Reporters from the cable news networks, BBC, NHK, and Asian Television Network were all providing "live" updates on the festivities. Even Al Jazeera got in on the action.

Moments later, Jia-li felt a surge of bodies shouting out questions so fast, they became little more than gibberish. And judging from some of the accents, it was clear many foreign reporters had already staked their claims. As she waded through the noisy throng, she spotted her producer, Jan, standing in front of the boat launch area. She was huddled beside a perky, bottle-blonde woman and a burly chap with short hair and a Fu-Manchu mustache.

The Lagranges were in their early forties and appeared to be a bit shell-shocked by the hubbub. Jia-li had insisted on doing the interview on location. Her news director preferred the controlled atmosphere of the studio, but had reluctantly agreed.

Ned, she had to admit, was probably right for a change.

Jia-li flashed her ID to a fleshy sheriff's deputy who didn't look old enough to shave. He immediately led her into a cordoned-off area where she was warmly greeted by the star-struck couple. She chatted them up as the crew made last-minute camera and lighting adjustments. Stepping away for a moment, Jia-li applied a final dusting of powder to her forehead, acutely aware that the King 5 feed would be picked up by the other networks and beamed to the world.

Grand opera on a global stage. Truly it was.

Then, at precisely five o'clock PDT, the interview began. Within seconds, the incessant babble around them stopped, and the massive crowd went pin-drop quiet.

Jia-li first tossed a couple of softball questions at Ted before asking him to set the scene. His face blushed scarlet as he explained how he'd broken away from hundreds of other boaters to search out the immense creatures. "We were about half an hour out and –"

"You, Jenny, and your two kids, right – Michael and Molly?"

"Yeah, the whole crew. Anyway, that's when we ran into a pod of gray whales, probably migrating to their summer feeding grounds up north. There were a dozen of them, maybe more, including two calves." Ted paused, took a deep breath, cleared his throat. "One of the bulls – I guess he thought we were going after the 'babies' – suddenly charged the boat. We were toast, I mean seconds away from being completely annihilated. Then the rogue whales showed up...and all hell broke loose."

For the next five minutes, Ted rambled on about his version of purgatory.

Jia-li waited for the right moment, then wrested back control of the mike. "Amazing," she said, while thinking...

Ted, you idiot, you almost got your entire family killed.

"Yet with all that going on," Jia-li added, calmly, "You somehow managed to keep your wits about you and capture some great shots on your cell phone."

Three of the pictures, in fact, turned out to be remarkably clear and in focus.

"Beginner's luck," Ted replied, avoiding Jenny's glare.

As the now-famous photos flashed on the screen, Ted recounted what happened next. He explained that the rogue whales had isolated the attacking gray, later estimated to weigh thirty-five tons, then closed in for the kill – first by delivering a series of thundering body blows; next by covering its blowhole to cut off air supply; and finally by ripping open the skin with a barrage of precision, ax-like cuts. Ted equated the blistering noise to the crack of a thousand rapid-fire gunshots.

"And the speed and power?" Jia-li asked.

"Mind-blowing," Ted said. "Those beasts were moving so fast they looked like huge streaking shadows, big as the freakin' space shuttle. I know, I saw one up close."

Jia-li remembered the same frightening sights and sounds as she replayed in her mind the gruesome attack on the pirates just three days earlier. And Ted was right about the space shuttle. She too had stood next to one of those complex machines, in 2011, while covering Endeavour's final mission into space. It was huge, weighing more than eighty tons. Yet even something that massive did not compare to the monster orcas.

Ted continued. "The kids were screaming, Jenny was screaming, hell, *I* was screaming."

Jia-li glanced over at Jenny who had remained silent the entire time, letting Ted do the talking. A sullen look in her deep, blue eyes told Jia-li that she still harbored deep-rooted fears. Still, when it was her turn to speak, she described the final, excruciating moments of their ordeal with surprising clarity.

"I remember reciting the words to the Twenty-Third Psalm," Jenny said. "The boat was getting tossed around like a toothpick in a tornado and I just kept saying those blessed words over and over, 'The Lord is my Shepherd, I shall not want...The Lord is my Shepherd...' Anyway, it all happened so fast. And when it was over, the seas suddenly went calm."

"Really. And then what happened?"

"A miracle," Jenny said, her eyes clouding up. "I absolutely believe that. One of the giant killer whales surfaced maybe twenty feet from the boat. I mean it was looking right through Ted and me. The kids too. It was terrifying...yet incredibly peaceful at the same time. I can't begin to..." Jenny paused, tears now streaming down her cheeks. She tried to continue, but couldn't find the words.

"I understand," Jia-li said, glancing down at the monitor. But did she really? As the picture cut to an extreme close-up of the whale's piercing black eye, she stared straight ahead unmoving. She knew she was fighting off her own emotional meltdown. After several anxious moments, she wrapped the interview, thanking the Lagranges for their courage and candor. Jia-li then tossed the feed back to the station. Her mind was reeling now and, despite the heat generated by the TV lights, she felt cold and clammy. She too had experienced an eerily similar encounter with the rogue whales, her own life up for grabs.

What did it all mean? What message were they trying to convey?

CHAPTER 21

31 March, 5:30 PM PDT
Sequim, Washington

A FEW MILES EAST of the media circus, Zora arrived back at the Kincaid's lovely Victorian home after taking a long walk along the shore. She'd needed some time to clear her head and Katrina had happily given her the space. They sat down at a wicker table on the wrap-around back porch, their faces warmed by the soft afternoon sun slanting across the lawn. The sound of lazy waves lapping against the pebbled beach was almost hypnotic. Katrina poured two glasses of Chianti from a bottle labeled Ruffino Riserva Classico and offered a toast.

"To friendship, in good times and not-so-good times," Katrina said.

They clinked glasses.

Then, with a sense of urgency, she added, "So talk to me, girl. What's going on?"

Zora fingered her wine glass, taking a moment to gather her thoughts. "Okay, look. I don't mean to be melodramatic here, but I'm in a hell of a jam."

"No kidding," Katrina said. "It's written all over your face. What kind of jam?"

Zora paused for a long moment then repeated the entire convoluted story, leaving nothing out, virtually word for word as she'd told it to Tanner Lockhart the day before. After hearing her out, he'd immediately cancelled a lucrative charter into one of the remotest fishing outposts on the planet, agreeing to fly Zora south instead. And for that she would be forever grateful.

Katrina now responded much as Lockhart had, with shock and surprise. She hiked her eyebrows and cocked her head. "The killer whale, is it male or female?"

"Male."

"How big?"

"Five tons," Zora replied. The thought sent shivers up her spine. She had wrestled with plenty of ornery swordfish in her day, including a few four hundred pounders, but this was very different.

Katrina threw her a curious look. "Wow! That's a huge animal, Zora."

"Tell me about it."

"I don't suppose this guy gave you a name, told you who he worked for, why he wanted the whale?"

"No, no, and no."

"Did he say where you were to drop it off?"

Zora shook her head. "Nope, nothing about any of that. He gave me an untraceable number to call once I pull everything together. He said I'd be given the specifics then."

"Okay, what am I missing here, Zora? I know damn well you'd never do this for the money, so it's gotta be something else."

Zora reached into her back pocket, pulled out a sheet of paper, unfolded it, and held it up.

Katrina stared at the photo for a long moment, reacted with a start. "Jesus...your mother. Don't tell me these monsters kidnapped her?"

"No, but I was told if I didn't play along, I'd never see her alive again. Not in so many words, but that was clearly the message."

"I don't believe it. Who *are* these people, Zora?"

"No idea. They play for keeps, though, I can tell you that."

"I'll say. I take it you haven't called the cops?"

"No. There's not a damn thing they can do. It's like those domestic violence cases you read about. Some lunatic becomes obsessed with his ex, threatens to kill her if she doesn't take him back. She knows he's trouble with a capital T, but the police can't arrest him until he actually commits a crime. By then, it's usually too late." Zora cringed at the thought of her mother – confused, alone, and scared out of her mind – being hauled off in the night by a couple of heartless thugs. And who would be there to stop them? Certainly not the security guards at the nursing home. They earned ten bucks an hour, carried no weapons, and looked like a collection of floats in the Macy's Day Parade.

"Okay, makes sense," Katrina said. "What about a private eye, somebody like that? Maybe he could sneak your mother out of the home, take her somewhere safe until all this blows over?"

"I thought about that too, Katrina, but the place is being watched around the clock. The man said if I even so much as *contact* her there, they'll know. I believe him."

Silence.

Zora looked up a second later, maybe two. Katrina's face was so ashen she looked anemic. "What is it, what's wrong?"

More silence.

Finally, Katrina spoke. There was just the slightest hesitation in her voice. "You're not going to believe this, but I think I know what's going on here."

Zora leaned forward, both elbows on the table, her hands trembling. "You do?"

Katrina took another moment then explained all that had happened at KOS-Seattle beginning with Samson's illness, his all-but-certain fate, and finally the forty-eight hour window of time she'd reluctantly granted Colby Freeman.

"Holy shit!" Zora exclaimed, suddenly riding a wave of adrenaline. "That can only mean these greedy bastards –"

Katrina nodded. "Yeah, after Samson dies, they're planning to secretly dispose of the body and replace him with another orca. That's gotta be it – and it's *insane.*"

"But possible," Zora said.

"I don't know, I guess so. If it all happened at night. Listen, you mentioned the capture part, but did the guy up in Sitka say anything about dealing with a deceased whale?"

"No. Like I said, he told me I'd be given further instructions as soon as I made all the arrangements."

"When will that be?"

"Soon, I hope. My crew is flying down tonight, and I'm meeting another friend in an hour in Port Angeles. His seiner's in dry dock at the moment. If I can negotiate a short-term lease, we'll be good to go."

"You know you're playing with fire here, Zora," Katrina said, her voice barely above whisper. "These are incredibly powerful animals, like I have to tell *you* that."

"Believe me, I get it. But that creep I met the other night knew everything about me except for the goddamn brand of underwear I had on. And maybe he knew that too. So, no matter how you cut it, Katrina, it all comes back to one thing. These people are capable of anything, and that includes hurting my mother, maybe worse."

Katrina shook her head. "What about this? What if I call the reporter in Seattle? She could expose these monsters for who they are and –"

Zora cut in. "They, Katrina? Who are *they*? Right now there's no proof these two situations are related, none at all. So who exactly would we be exposing? Besides, that's a risk I just can't take. Would you if it were your mother?"

Katrina thought about that. "No, no I wouldn't."

They sat for several minutes without speaking. Then Zora slumped down in her chair, frustrated and angry. She drained the last of her wine and said, "You know something? Maybe this isn't such a good idea. I could be implicating you in a serious crime. It could ruin your career, everything you've worked for. Maybe I should –"

Katrina held up a hand. "Don't even go there, Zora. Listen, I break one law or another in just about every field study I go on. If I didn't, I would never get anything done, what with all the government regulations. So, if capturing a five-ton killer whale is our only option, then that's our only option. Let's just make certain you, your crew, and the animal aren't harmed in the process."

"Are you sure?"

"Damn right I'm sure. And if we play our cards right, nothing happens to your mother and we expose these people for who they really are."

Zora had no reason to doubt Katrina's resolve, had watched her chew out a couple of obnoxious tourists who impeded their efforts to save the injured sea lion off the Galapagos Islands. When it came to justice and fair play, this mild-mannered scientist could be a pit bull.

"You heard about the horrible accident in Japan, right?" Katrina asked. "Involving the killer whale and his trainer?"

Zora nodded.

"Well, I gotta believe it's the driving force behind all this."

"What do you mean?"

"I mean one more incident with a sick or dying animal would be a lightning rod, maybe force these morons to stop exploiting captive whales altogether, even release them back into the wild."

"KOS owns parks all over the world, right?" Zora said. "So we're not just talking about one location then."

"Exactly. Which explains the heavy-handed tactics, and why the GM in Seattle hasn't called. His deadline passed a couple of hours ago. I had no problem cutting him some slack, but now –"

Zora stood up and walked to the edge of the patio. Her whole world was closing in around her, yet she felt helpless to stop it. "I'm flying blind here, Katrina. I catch fish for a living. I'm not sure where to even *find* a killer whale, let alone capture one."

"Well, this is your lucky day, girlfriend," Katrina said, sidling up to Zora. "Because it just so happens I know someone who does."

Zora felt her pulse quicken. She turned to face her friend. "Seriously?"

"Seriously! His name's Houdini. I met him during a hiking trip last summer up on Vancouver Island."

Zora considered that. "Okay, I give. The only Houdini I know of was named Harry, and he's been dead a really long time."

"Well, it's safe to say *this* Houdini wields his own brand of magic. He's a shaman, actually, which might sound a bit far out. I thought so too at first. But he's the real deal. He has this amazing connection to killer whales. I've seen it, Zora. I watched him paddle out in his kayak, maybe a hundred yards from shore, and within minutes, he'd be surrounded by orcas. Sometimes they'd hang around for half an hour or more." Katrina leaned in, her voice dropping. "Here's the other thing. Typically it takes forty, fifty years to acquire the wisdom and knowledge needed to become a shaman, so most are well into middle-age, if not older. But Houdini is something special. He's all of thirty-five, if that."

"And what makes you think he'll even *consider* getting involved in something like this?"

"I don't, not for sure," Katrina said. "But I can come up with three good reasons why he will. First of all, he's a Makah Indian. His people have suffered terribly, so he knows all about threats and coercion. He's seen the destruction of an entire way of life – broken treaties, forced relocation, and worse. Second, his parents are not well. He'll relate to this awful situation with your mother. Lastly, he'll see the potential here, the potential to free all those tormented orcas trapped in theme parks."

Zora shook her head, unconvinced.

"Look, Zora, scientists like me know a collection of facts about orcas. We believe they're armed with telepathic sensors, that their discrete calls constitute a language. We also believe they communicate as we do, only better. But there's so much we *don't* know, so much we can learn from someone like Houdini. He knows orcas...relates to them...thinks like them. He told me once how very humbling it was to be in their presence, how it taught him about listening, about respect, about the mysteries of the universe. I totally get it. I've been there myself. So yes, if he really believes there's a chance to make their world better, I think he'll be open to it."

"Would you trust him with your mother's life, Katrina?"

"Yes, absolutely."

Zora gazed into Katrina's eyes, squeezed her hand, and took a deep breath. "Okay, I believe you. But is he even around? We don't have much time here."

"I know. Houdini's usually off in the wilds of Alaska somewhere, but I just spoke with him the other day. He's visiting his parents over in Neah Bay. I'll call him in a bit. And remind me to give you his number before you leave so you have it too."

"Okay, fingers crossed," Zora said. Her mind then immediately shifted to Mack Bowen. If she couldn't convince him to lease his seiner, the rest of this wild scheme didn't really matter.

"So I'll see you back at my place later on," Katrina said. "The spare room's all made up."

Zora sighed, hugged her friend. "Yeah, sounds good. And thanks, Katrina. This means more to me than you will ever know."

CHAPTER 22

31 March, 6:15 PM PDT
Kiotlah Point, Olympic Peninsula, Washington

ONE HUNDRED MILES to the west, a lean, ruggedly handsome young man with long, raven hair traversed a steep wilderness trail. It was a fine trail as trails went and he knew it well. He'd been coming here since he was a boy, to the top of this jagged ridge, to a lone cabin tucked away in a mature grove of hemlocks, alders, and stories-tall cedars.

A forest so green, it shimmered.

The young man stopped in a small meadow, breathing deeply of the age-less cedar and rich organic soil, listening to the sounds of the wild. His eyes missed nothing. He felt at home here. He was part of this place. Moments later, he was moving again, traversing the downsloping switchback with Zen-like efficiency and all the confidence of a jungle cat. The trail soon narrowed, then turned back on itself. To the north and far below him raged the furious waters of the Strait of Juan de Fuca, a ninety-five-mile-long channel that connected the Georgia Strait and Puget Sound to the open Pacific. Twenty minutes after that, he approached his destination, overcome as he always was by a deep sense of reverence, for the individual he loved and respected more than any other on earth called this place home.

They called him the Old One. And for as long as anyone could re-member, he had served as elder statesman of the Makah Tribe, a proud and ancient People who had once held vast areas of inland and coastal territories on the Olympic Peninsula. Days that had long since been buried in a painful past. It was said that the wise old sage had one foot in this world, the other in the otherworld. And while the young man had just turned ten when they'd first met, he quickly came to understand why everyone sought his counsel.

After rounding a sharp bend in the trail, the Old One's cedar cabin came into view. A green wave of mountains was visible above the tree line behind it, their jagged peaks glistening white with snow. North of the property, a fast-moving stream cut through the deep woods, and to the south, an eagle stood guard on a wooden fence post. The cabin itself was small and tidy, and it occurred to the young man that the place had aged as well as its occupant. The front porch was weathered but solid, with firewood piled high on one end. A few feet away, two fan-backed chairs framed a large picture window.

As he crossed the sturdy footbridge, the young man could smell smoke curling up from a splendid stone chimney. He walked briskly to the front door and before he had a chance to knock, it opened. As was his custom, the Old One greeted him with a warm embrace. After a long moment, he took a step back and placed his right hand flat over his friend's heart. Only then did he speak, in a voice that was richly accented, strong, and resonant.

"My son, it is so nice to see you. It has been far too long."

"Thank you, Old One, it's good to be back."

He never changes, the young man thought as he stared into his mentor's intense brown eyes.

The Old One was small and sinewy with workingman's hands and long stringy white hair. His face, though still strikingly handsome, looked as if it had been sandblasted, his high cheekbones the reddish brown of the clay. He wore a denim jacket, faded jeans, and weathered cowboy boots. The years had slowed his step, but his mind was as bright and clear as it had been half-a-lifetime ago.

"You look well," the young man said.

"Well enough. My eyes are failing me, and my appetite isn't what it used to be. I eat mostly salmon, buckskin bread, and a few huckleberries. I don't need much more. Long walks, my pipe, and my books, they keep me going."

As they turned to go inside, a small bird landed on the porch railing and skittered toward them, singing its heart out. The Old One acknowledged his colorful, feathered friend with a wave and a smile. "He's a plucky little critter, that one. Comes and goes on a whim, much like you, my son. Where have your travels taken you this time?"

"Spent most of the winter on Vancouver Island, up in Nitinat Lake," the young man said, flashing a happy-go-lucky grin. "Bought me a new camera, captured some great shots. For some reason, I can find just the right light, in the right place, at the right time up there. Even got myself an agent. She works exclusively in nature photography, sells to select magazines and some stock photo houses. But I've been really bad about e-mailing digital files, so I don't think she's real happy with me right now. Not sure where I'm off to next. Somewhere wild, I guess."

The Old One frowned, the deep wrinkles on his forehead forming a tight knot. "I am afraid modern technology has passed me by, my son, but this I *do* know – you are well suited for the path you have chosen."

"Yes," the young man agreed. "I like to think so." For more than a decade he'd been kayaking up and down the coasts of British Columbia and southern Alaska, spending months on end in parts unknown. He would disappear in the wink of an eye, then reappear in a shadow, seemingly out of nowhere. It was how he'd earned his nickname: Houdini. Some in Indian country considered him to be mischievous and rambunctious, traits of the oft-maligned Coyote Trickster.

Others called him a visionary, mostly for his insight into nature and his love of books. He quoted everything from Homer's *Odyssey* to *Forrest Gump* and carried the bible of counterculture cool with him everywhere, Jack Kerouac's *On the Road*. Some said he was too handsome for his own good, but he never saw himself that way. When cash ran short, as it often did, he had no trouble scaring up jobs. He had acquired an arsenal of useful skills over the years and often found work on commercial fishing boats.

"Is it your father's stroke that brings you back to us this time, my son?"

Houdini nodded, a pained expression on his face. "He spends most days chained to a wheel chair. His arms and legs are useless, and I can barely understand a word he says. He's a broken man."

"And your mother?"

"She's struggling too, arthritis in both hands. It's all she can do to get Dad to the doctor. I told her I'd move back home, help her take care of him, but she wanted none of that. She told me to follow my heart and my dreams. Theirs were over, she said."

"This troubles me deeply. They are fine people, your mother and father."

Houdini sighed. "I'm not sure what to do about it, Old One."

"Sometimes the answer is asking harder questions. And how we ask those questions will often affect the answers. You must always remember that a change in perspective changes everything. Come, we have much to talk about."

Moving inside the cabin, Houdini was instantly struck by the incense-like aroma of Turkish tobacco. The smell permeated every nook and cranny of the sparsely furnished home. The Old One had a fine collection of pipes, but his brand had never changed.

Neither did their routine, not since Houdini's first visit more than two decades earlier. He began by making a pot of herbal tea in the neat, well-stocked kitchen. Next he would build a blazing fire in the stone hearth and sit for hours, spellbound, while the Old One read works by the Masters – Dickens, Melville, Steinbeck, Faulkner, Stegner, and other literary giants. He took their stories, lifted them off the pages, and gave them a sense of time and place. He gave them a soul. It was here that Houdini had also learned about his brothers and sisters in other Native tribes and the ways of his own People. He learned of ancient traditions, not recorded in some holy text, but rather passed down orally from one generation to the next.

And the Makah had a rich, vibrant history.

For centuries, the Tribe had adapted, survived, and flourished, ever serving as faithful guardians to both land and sea. As mariners they had few equals, their navigational skills the envy of fishermen the world over. Yet the Tribe's greatest source of pride was its long tradition of whaling. The hunt was considered life-affirming and spiritual. Prayers were offered to both whalers and whale with thanks given to the animal for its sacrifice and to free its spirit for passage to the other side.

"I hear a lot of talk around town," Houdini said. "People are divided on many issues."

"Yes, my son, it is true. There are those among us determined to return to the old ways. They fail to understand that life is a river that flows in both directions at once. Language and culture – they define us in so many ways, and it is important that we honor our past. Yet we must also look to the future. We must build new schools, libraries, museums, and other places of community. Our survival depends on such things, not on some long-ago treaty that stole our land and destroyed our identity."

It was known as the Treaty of Neah Bay, ratified by Congress in 1859. In exchange for the right to continue hunting gray whales, the Makah had ceded title to thousands of acres of land to the U.S. government, land they had called home for centuries. Some sixty years later, however, commercial whalers had all but annihilated the gray whale population, and the Tribe had voluntarily agreed to suspend its whaling rights.

There had been only one exception – in the spring of 1999 – a controversial hunt that took place just off the coast of Neah Bay. Houdini had been recruited to participate, a decision he later regretted with all his heart and soul. Just twenty at the time, he'd been trained to use a uniquely designed .50 caliber rifle to fire the fatal shot. The vet had assured him it was far more humane than the traditional 'killing lance,' which usually took several blows to bring down the whale. In this case, a forty *ton* whale. But Houdini could not pull the trigger. One of the other whalers did.

Houdini sighed. "When he fired that gun, a part of me died, too, Old One."

"A tough lesson, my son, but one you learned well. I am proud of you. It is why I called you here today. You see, I have a story of my own to tell… a very *personal* story."

Houdini hiked an eyebrow. The Old One had rarely shared anything about himself. In fact no one even knew his real name, or his age. "Older than the hills" was all he would ever say. Rumor had it he'd been born on April 15, 1912, the same date the unsinkable RMS *Titanic* sank, but it remained just that…a rumor.

The Old One slowly sipped his tea before speaking. "When I was a young buck, I lived for a time with the Haida, a proud and fierce people who settled many centuries ago on the northern coast of British Columbia. The Tribal Chief was named Raven Claw. He was much older than me and very wise. He communed often with the orcas, blackfish, he called them. He spoke to them and they spoke back, with their eyes. It was as if he could see into their souls and they into his. Sometimes he took me with him. He taught me to open my heart to these sacred animals, to feel the very essence of life that flows through each of us from the wild. It is something we cannot see, or measure, or explain, but it is the very essence of who and what we are."

Houdini leaned in close. "And the blackfish knew this."

"Yes, my son, for they are blessed with a level of intelligence far superior and infinitely more enduring than our own. They hear our every thought, understand our every word. They do not speak our language, but they communicate with something far stronger: their spirit."

A long pause, then, "I think I get it now," Houdini said.

"What is that, my son?"

"Why you taught me such respect for the orcas."

"Yes, it is true. Allow me to explain. In his final days, Raven Claw had fallen ill, but before becoming bedridden, he paddled out one last time to greet a pod of blackfish, to say his goodbyes. But they did not come. Instead he was surrounded by a family of *immense* creatures, creatures the likes of which he had never before seen. And he sensed in their thoughts a great sadness for they came bearing a message, one of unspeakable evil about to befall mankind."

"What kind of evil?" Houdini asked.

"I cannot say, my son. These things you must discover on your own, as Raven Claw did from his ancestors and I from mine. You must remember that we are all related to everything else, to the elements, to the earth and seas, to all animal life. It is the Native way, the way of the Great Spirit. When the time is right, you will know, through dreams and visions, powers all shamans receive from their ties with the spirit world."

"Chief Raven Claw must have *done* something, right?"

"Yes. He tried to warn the white man, but his words fell on deaf ears. A crazy old Indian who drank too much and told tall tales, at least that's what they thought. In truth, the great Chief had never touched a drop of alcohol in his life."

"Did he ever see the creatures again?"

"No, he did not. But I was with him when he passed on, when he reunited with the Great Spirit. And before he breathed his final breath, something extraordinary passed between us."

Houdini could feel his heart beating wildly, sensing that something extraordinary was about to pass between him and his mentor too. "He gave you his special powers, didn't he?"

"Yes. And soon those powers will be yours, my son. But I must tell you the rest of the story, so you will understand." The Old One paused for a long moment before continuing. "You see many years later, after I too had become an old man, the blackfish returned. This time they brought another warning, in many ways more frightening than the last. And like Raven Claw, I attempted to communicate with people in power, people in Washington, D.C. I even traveled there. I spoke of the mighty creatures, my visions, and those of Raven Claw before me."

Houdini swept a hand through his long hair. "And no one listened to another crazy old Indian, right?"

"*One* man did," the Old One said, his voice now a whisper. "He understood Native culture and he asked many good questions. But sadly, the result was the same. He could not convince his superiors of the horrors that lay ahead."

There was a prolonged silence.

Houdini stood and slowly paced the floor, dancing flames from the roaring fire mirroring his inner thoughts. Another minute passed, then two. He walked back to the Old One, bent down on one knee, gazed deeply into his expressive eyes. "The mighty blackfish, Old One, they are back."

The old man leaned forward in his chair, taking hold of his young protégé's hands. Houdini winced at the still powerful grip, felt a charge of electricity shoot through his body. "Yes, I sense their presence. But it is up to you, my son, to figure out why they have come."

CHAPTER 23

31 March, 7:00 PM PDT
Port Angeles, Washington

THE BLUE METAL BUILDING on North Cedar Street loomed large, six stories tall, with more than thirty thousand square feet of production floor space. The facility was owned by Platypus Marine and included full mechanical, paint, and fabrication shops, radiant heated floors, five webcams, and a fifty-ton mobile crane. A gigantic Travelift, used to transport large vessels from dock to shop, sat like a giant albatross on the property's fenced-in back lot.

At the moment, inside crews were working overtime to complete routine maintenance and driveline repairs – shafts, props, and bearings – on a commercial fishing rig called the *Northern Star*. She was a 58-foot Delta, arguably the toughest class of boats ever built. The big seiner had made her first run in 1984 and had continually been in service ever since. Over the years, she'd been meticulously maintained, undergoing a major retrofitting program in the late 1990's, then again in 2003, with rolling chocks added in 2009 for better stability.

It was tricky work, making the new fit with the old and having everything match, but the experienced team at Platypus had carved out a profitable niche doing exactly that. Elevated on heavy steel davits, the boat now sat ghost-like, shrouded in heavy plastic awaiting a long-delayed paint job.

Zora drove down a gravel road that ran along the east side of the building and stopped next to an aging, gun-metal gray maintenance building. As she sat there thinking, a sharp tap on the window made her jump. She forced a smile, stepped out of the sporty rental car, and gave the captain of the *Northern Star* a big hug. MacKenzie "Mack" Bowen was a throwback to wooden boats and iron men. He was powerfully built with barn-broad shoulders, a square head, and a neck like a bull. His arms were as big as most men's thighs.

Mack's wife had befriended Zora soon after she arrived in Sitka. Most everyone else in town had given her the cold shoulder, or were downright nasty. The really superstitious fishermen said she was nothing but bad luck – a Jonah – while a hornet's nest of gossipy wives tossed around labels like "Vixen" and "Evil Seductress." But that had all changed following Zora's encounter with the great white sharks. Turned out the man she'd rescued from the hungry predators was married to one of the catty women, and she was pregnant with their first child.

Mack Bowen was something of a legend in Sitka, but lately life had not been so kind to him. His lovely wife was battling breast cancer, his teenage daughter had run off with a local rapper, and he'd had a string of bad runs. The result was a woeful lack of fish and way too many bills.

Zora and Mack sat down on a work bench in front of the maintenance building. She could hear the pounding of the ocean just over the rise and smell the salt water, but, other than a flock of squawking seabirds, they were alone. "Listen, Mack," she said. "Sorry for the cloak and dagger stuff last night, but I couldn't go into this over the phone."

"Okay, no problem. You sounded really stressed, though. What the hell's going on?"

Zora turned to face him, her hands tightly clasped together. "Yeah, like I said when we spoke I need your absolute discretion on this, okay? Not a word to anyone."

Mack placed an iron grip on her wrist and nodded. He barely moved in the twenty minutes it took Zora to tell her incredible tale, though she purposely left out the part about KOS and Samson. Information he did not need to know. When she'd finished, he looked at her like he'd just been jabbed with a cattle prod. "So you're saying they'll kill your mother if you don't play ball, is that the bottom line?"

"Yeah, that's the bottom line."

Mack took a deep breath, stared off into space. "I'm really sorry, Zora. And I sympathize, I really do. Look, my mother's eighty-four, lives in Oakland. I call her every Sunday, but…"

"But *what*, Mack?"

"You're shadowboxing with the devil here. I'd like to help, believe me I would, but, to be perfectly honest with you, I'm not sure I –"

Zora shifted uncomfortably. She tried to think of all the things that must be running through his head. *Why not use her own boat?* There wasn't time. Even running hard, it would have taken her four days to make the trip from Sitka to Port Angeles. *What about damage to his boat?* Seiners were practically bullet proof, but she would pull back if things got too crazy. *What if things go to shit and the Coast Guard rolls in?*

Mack answered the last question himself. "Look, if things go south, I'll be looking at a big fine, maybe even jail time. I'm too damn old to be making license plates, Zora."

"I understand," Zora said. "And in that case, this conversation never happened. You met with another fisherman who wanted to lease your boat. We agreed on a price and signed the papers, end of story. It happens all the time. I have a draft contract in the car, pulled it off a legal website last night. We can make it all official with the stroke of a pen. No matter how this goes down, Mack, you stay clean and pocket the money."

"I don't know. What's your time frame?"

"Day after tomorrow... I think."

Bowen stroked his chin and thought about that. "Damn, that soon, huh? Well, I'd have to postpone the paint job for now, but that's no biggie. And I'd be lying through my teeth if I said I didn't need the cash. Believe it or not, I've been thinking about selling the old girl. She'd probably fetch seven hundred grand, maybe more. But what on God's good earth would I do then? Fishing is all I know."

Zora leaned in closer. "I get it, Mack, I do. Like I told you on the phone, the fee is substantial."

A long silence. She could see that he was thinking.

"Okay, you got a number to throw at me?"

"How does thirty grand strike you? For three days, four max. I'll even kick in an extra ten grand so you can pay your crew to go raise hell, stimulate the local economy a bit."

Bowen cracked his jaw, sighed. "Jesus, you weren't kidding, were you? About the money I mean."

Zora had done the math many times in her head, could tell Bowen was working through the same calculations. Even in good times, it would take him two or three solid runs to net that kind of cash. And solid runs had been in short supply of late.

They sat without speaking for several minutes. The wind whipped up and it was getting colder. Bowen tugged on his collar, rubbed his hands together, and said, "Well, captain, like the country song says, 'We all bleed red.' And right now, I'm hemorrhaging. Where do I sign?"

CHAPTER 24

31 March, 7:30 PM PDT
Port Townsend, Washington

THE LEAN, GRACEFUL WOMAN moved deer-like over a steep, winding trail that led to the highest point at Fort Worden State Park. Katrina Kincaid didn't jog, she ran, and this was a runner's paradise – an ever-green wonderland of towering fir trees and thick underbrush that gave way to breathtaking views of the Strait of Juan de Fuca.

Built in the early 1900s, the former Army outpost had once provided the first-line of defense for Puget Sound, its long-range guns concealed in a warren of cavernous, concrete bunkers. Predictably, the men in command had named the spectacular stretch of heavily fortified land Artillery Hill. But the guns had long since been silenced, and by the 1970s, the 443-acre site had been converted into a popular recreational, artistic, and educational retreat.

Katrina loved to sweat, loved what an exhilarating workout did for her mind, body, and spirit. She picked up the pace as she made her way to the top of the bluff, feeling stronger with every stride. From all around she could hear the sounds of the forest and the critters that lived there. A gentle wind danced among the tree tops, leaving only soft whispers behind. There was a scent of resin in the fine mist. The trail soon narrowed and turned back south where Katrina was greeted by a battalion of chattering squirrels and two wily raccoons.

She stopped briefly to commiserate with the animals, then moved on.

Five minutes later, she broke into a small clearing, an area known as Memory's Vault. It was here in the deep forest where plans for the Fort's gun batteries had originally been kept. All but one of the original structures was gone, replaced by seven Stonehenge-like concrete pillars inscribed with the works of poet Sam Hamill. This place where men had gathered generations ago, making plans for war, now stood as a testament to peace. For a moment, Katrina stood quietly, reflecting on the irony. Sometimes she dreamed she was the great blue heron from her favorite Hamill poem, *Black Marsh Eclogue*. She whispered the final stanzas to herself.

> *But when at last he flies,*
> *his great wings cover the darkening sky,*
> *and slowly,*
> *as though praying,*
> *he lifts*
> *almost motionless*
> *as he pushes the world away.*

Katrina took several more deep breaths, murmured a few words of thanks, then headed back down the hill. Twenty minutes later, she stepped through the back door of her two-story Craftsman cottage on Castellano Way. She sat on the stairs and pulled off her new racing flats. Despite feeling energized, she couldn't shake the ominous thoughts rattling through her head – Samson's dire condition and the blackmail scheme involving Zora. The connection seemed obvious, but the question was what to do next? She sat down at her computer, typed in a few notes, and tried reaching Colby Freeman. The call went to voicemail. She left a brief message, not tipping her hand one way or the other. She then tried her friend, Leanne. No luck there either. This time, she decided not to leave a message. Leanne had enough on her mind dealing with her daughter's illness.

After showering, Katrina pulled on a sweatshirt and jeans, and grabbed *The New York Times*. She then curled up on the living room sofa with her best friend, a sweet marble gray tabby named Vera. Flames from an antique-looking gas stove licked at the walls, giving the room a soft, golden glow. As she finished reading the front section of the paper, the weather took a sudden turn. A driving rain began drumming the windows and gusty winds set in motion a Japanese wind chime hanging from the porch. The entrancing sound made her wistful, sleepy. She leaned her head back, lowered the newspaper, and closed her eyes. Vera quickly nuzzled in under her arm.

Sometime later, a high-pitched squeaking sound woke her with a start. Before she could react, the room went black. Out of the corner of her eye, she saw a fleeting shadow. Vera shrieked like a wounded mountain lion and bolted from her lap, sending an antique lamp crashing to the floor. Katrina scrambled off the couch, slipped on the throw rug, and lost her balance. In the next instant, the intruder exploded out of the darkness, grabbing her from behind. A meaty, gloved hand covered her mouth, muffling another scream. She could smell the latex, feel the smooth rubber on the inside of her mouth. Jerking backward, she caught a glimpse of her attacker. He was dressed in black, wore a balaclava, and door-busting combat boots.

And he had animal strength.

He leaned into her ear, a dangerous glint in his eyes. "I am not here to hurt you," he said in a cracked, reedy voice. "Do you understand, Katrina?"

She cringed at the sound of her name, overcome by a feeling of cold dread. The room pulsed darker, the temperature seemed to drop, and the rain picked up.

"Listen to me and listen *good*. I said do...you...understand?"

He was squeezing her neck and she couldn't speak. She nodded.

"Okay, now we're going to have a friendly chat here and it's important you listen carefully. Because if you don't, there will be consequences. *Serious* consequences."

Katrina felt a choking panic as the man leaned closer, his lips now directly against her ear.

"Are we clear on that too?"

She nodded again.

The man inched his hand away from her mouth. "Let me hear you say it."

Katrina squirmed.

"*Say* it!"

"I get it," she mumbled. "Stop hurting me."

He loosened his grip. "See how easy this is? Now the message here is easy and simple. You need to forget you ever laid eyes on Samson. I repeat, forget you ever laid eyes on that whale. See what I mean? Real simple. You can do that, right, Katrina?"

She blinked, hesitated.

"*Right*, Katrina!" he barked.

"Yeah, but a lot of people know I've been treating Samson," she lied. "What about them? You can't shut us all up."

"The others are not your concern," the man said. "Now, I need your files. Everything you've got on the sick whale."

"They're in my office, upstairs."

"Let's go."

The intruder grabbed her elbow, pulled her to her feet, nudged her toward the stairs. He then followed her up to the landing. Katrina clicked on a desk lamp and opened the top drawer of her desk. She pulled out two green folders, handed them over. "Here, that's it."

"You sure?"

"Positive."

"Good," he said, tucking the folders under his arm. "Now the computer."

"You have everything. There's nothing *on* the computer."

"I don't believe you. Turn it on."

"I told you –"

"*I said turn it on!*"

Katrina booted up the laptop. The man leaned over her shoulder, scanning each of the icons on her desk top. None was labeled, "Samson."

"Pull up the Documents file," he said.

She did. Nothing there either.

The man seemed satisfied. She quickly logged off and moments later they were back in the living room. Just then, something in his eyes, his manner, sent chills up her spine.

Jesus, he's going to rape me.

It had happened to her once before – when she was fifteen – and she swore...never again.

With a sudden burst of energy, Katrina drove her elbow into the man's gut. It was like hitting a block of concrete, yet the blow landed with enough force to knock him off balance. She broke loose, bit hard into his wrist, and made a run for it.

"Fuck!" he shouted, clenching his arm. An instant later the man gave chase, moving like a coiled spring. Katrina was ten feet from the front door and freedom when her legs flew out from underneath her. She careened across the hardwood floor, crashing head first into the dining room table. Her attacker was on top of her before she could move. He then grabbed a handful of hair and wrenched her up like a rag-doll. "You're one stupid bitch, you know that?"

"And you're a useless piece of shit," she fired back. Then she spit in his eye. The big man lost it. He grabbed Katrina's wrists with his left hand pinning them to her chest. An instant later, a flattened, rigid right hand lashed out and crushed her cheekbone. She rocketed backwards, falling hard, her head striking something sharp and unmovable. Katrina felt a piercing stab at the base of her skull, but didn't hear the sickening thud. There was no sensation of pain, only the suffocating darkness that closed around her like a shroud.

The room lost color, turned to black and white.

Then...only black.

The man yanked off his hood, revealing the menacing, lantern-jawed face of the Black Stallion operative known as Iago. He pulled a penlight from his coat pocket, swept it back and forth over Katrina's face. Her mouth was slightly parted, her right ear oozed red, and her dark, green eyes were fixed wide, staring at the ceiling. Kneeling down, he gently lifted the hair away from her neck, pressed two fingers against the carotid artery.

Just as he thought, no pulse.

Shit! Shit! Shit!

Iago stood, took an unsteady step back, staring at the body in disbelief. His blood was boiling, his heart pounding. He thought back to the "evade and escape" training during his days as a Navy SEAL, how he had learned to control his breathing, slow his whole system down. It took only a moment to get there. Another deep breath and his heavy chest muscles began to relax. But nothing could change what had gone down here. He'd taken many lives before, yet the names and faces had meant nothing to him. It was kill or be killed. This was different. This woman did not deserve to die. He looked closer, a cold sweat glistening on his brow.

She's beautiful, even now. Why did she have to be so fucking stupid?

His next thought went to the man who called the shots at Black Stallion, Darnell Atwater. Atwater was defined and obsessed by perfection. He demanded the same of his men and Iago knew this pathetic effort had fallen far short of the mark. Every member of the team was expendable. He knew that, too. Damage control was the best he could do now.

He looked around. The place was a mess.

Iago moved stealthily into the kitchen, found a roll of industrial strength garbage bags under the sink, and a broom and dustpan in the small utility closet. Methodically, he went to work, sweeping the floor of broken glass and cleaning up the blood. He was especially careful to wipe down the edge of the propane stove where the woman had hit her head. Twenty minutes later, the job was done. The house looked neat as a pin. If the cops came snooping around, they would find no sign of a struggle, no incriminating evidence. He wrapped a plastic tie around the garbage bag and set it next to the door.

The question now became what to do with the body. The answer, he soon discovered, was lying on the kitchen table – a single sheet of paper with a map of Fort Worden State Park on one side, a description of the old gun batteries on the other. There were several designated running trails, one that had been highlighted in yellow.

That's it. The woman loved to run. And runners have accidents, especially in bad weather.

Iago dug through a few folders on the bookcase next to the stove and came up with a map of Port Townsend. The Fort was less than two miles away, an easy jog back to his rental vehicle. He had parked the blue sedan behind a storage building at the far end of the small complex. He then hurried up to the woman's bedroom. Inside a large walk-in closet were four wooden shelves piled high with outdoor gear. He quickly pulled together an all-weather ensemble: fleece jacket, turtle-neck sweater, underwear, long pants, and thermal socks. There were two pairs of running shoes sitting on a mat next to the back door. He grabbed the first pair.

Back in the living room, Iago carefully removed Katrina's clothes and dressed her in the running gear. He found a money clip on the counter with a few bills wrapped around a driver's license. He stuffed it into her pocket, checked his watch. It was nearly eight thirty and dark outside, *unnaturally* dark. He then moved to the front window, peered through the shutters. The rain continued its steady thrum and he saw no one moving about. He noticed a Volvo SUV parked on the street a stone's throw from the house. He searched around and soon found a set of car keys lying next to the phone. Stepping onto the front porch, he pressed the unlock button. There was a shrill chirp, the power lock released, and the inside light popped on.

He had the right vehicle.

Iago grabbed the garbage bag, threw it in the cargo bay, and came back for the body. He then jumped into the driver's seat and drove off, making a right turn on San Juan Avenue, another right on Admiralty. He passed Fort Worden Military Cemetery and reached the front gate of the park seconds later. According to the guide map, there was a paved road that skirted the trailhead. He turned off the headlights, drove slowly past the parade ground and old barracks, and up the narrow road. He parked the SUV next to a sign marked "Battery Tolles," tossed the plastic bag in a garbage receptacle and then slung the corpse over his shoulder.

As he trudged up the steep trail, he shifted the body from one shoulder to the other. The steady rain would wash away any footprints, and he was thankful for that much at least. But the going was tough, mostly because of the uneven terrain and gurgling darkness. Ten grueling minutes later, he looped along the edge of a bluff that plunged steeply to the rocky shore below. The distance was impossible to determine, though he guessed it to be at least a hundred feet, probably more. He gently laid Katrina's body next to a crooked wooden fence that separated the trail from the edge of the bluff. A sign affixed to one of the posts read...

Caution: Falling Can Be Deadly.

Jesus, ain't that the truth.

The authorities, he knew, would figure out soon enough that the woman's death was no accident. Then again, he might get lucky a second time. Small-town cops often bungled cases because of incompetence, inexperience, or both. Either way, he hoped to buy himself a little breathing room.

Iago took a deep breath, lifted the body, and finished the job.

It was the toughest thing he'd ever done in his life.

CHAPTER 25

31 March, 8:45 PM PDT
Port Angeles, Washington

ZORA AND MACK BOWEN sat in a corner booth at the Pho New Saigon Restaurant, just east of downtown. The location wasn't exactly ideal, wedged as it was between an automotive repair shop and an adult book store, but the food was fresh, the servings generous, and the prices reasonable. Bowen said he'd been turned onto the place by a supervisor at Platypus Marine and judging from the spicy, pungent soup, he'd made a good call. For their entrees, they ordered crab sticks and fried wonton from a demure Vietnamese waitress, then quietly reviewed the terms of their agreement. Bowen made one tiny change to the language before signing the two-page document.

Later, after they'd finished eating, Zora dropped Bowen off at his car and jumped back on the road for Port Townsend. She checked the time. It was ten past ten. She reached for her phone and punched in Katrina's number, but the call immediately went to voice mail. The mysterious shaman was the final piece of this very twisted puzzle, and Zora was anxious to find out if she'd made contact with him.

For the next half hour she listened to talk radio, non-stop chatter about the so-called "rogue whales." One moron suggested mounting a full-scale operation to capture one of the creatures, "for scientific purposes."

They tried that little trick with King Kong, she mused. *And it didn't work out so well.*

Zora shut off the endless blabber and rode on in silence. A minute or so later, her phone rang. She didn't bother to check the number, assuming it was Katrina. "Hey, I just … "

"Zora, it's Mickey."

"Mickey!" She was surprised to hear from him and said so. "Hey, how are you?"

"Not so good." There was gravity in his voice.

Zora had a really bad feeling, and hesitated before asking, "What is it?"

"Katrina...she's dead."

Her body numb, Zora stared at the road in horror, Mickey's words hanging there like a heavy, black cloud. "No, that's not possible. I mean I –"

"It's true," he said. "I just got off the phone with the DA. A couple walking their dog on the beach out by Point Wilson found her body a few minutes ago...at the bottom of a steep cliff."

"I don't know what to say, Mickey. I was just with her, at your folks' place. Are you sure it's not some kind of terrible mistake?"

"I thought the same thing at first. But Kat was carrying her driver's license. They found her car too. It was parked near a running trail at a park north of town." Mickey paused, his voice cracking. "The sheriff thinks she went for a run, slipped in the mud, and fell. An accident."

"You're not buying it, I can tell."

"No. She would never be that careless, Zora. *Never.*"

Zora wanted to say something, but couldn't find the words. Finally, she asked, "What can I do?"

Mickey hesitated, and said, "Mom and dad are out of town and I could really use a friend. I'm meeting the DA at the Courthouse in a few minutes. Can you be there? It's on Jefferson Street. You can't miss it."

"Of course," she said. "I was actually driving to...never mind, I'll see you shortly."

Zora clicked off, pounded her fists on the wheel, then stomped on the accelerator. She blew past everything in sight, horns blaring at her as she weaved in and out of traffic. A few miles up the road, she turned onto Highway 20, a thousand conflicting thoughts pin-balling through her head. Ever since she could remember, she'd always been able to figure things out – from her gentle way with horses, to solving thorny calculus problems, to cheating death by staring down a great white shark. But this was uncharted territory and she didn't like it, not at all. She'd just lost a dear friend. Was her mother next? And what, if anything, should she tell the DA?

Shortly before eleven o'clock, she pulled in front of the Jefferson County Courthouse, a marvelous red brick and sandstone structure built in the early 1890s. The architectural wonder stood three stories tall and covered an entire city block. Its soaring clock tower could be seen from just about anywhere in town. As she scaled the concrete steps leading to the entrance, the bell's hammer struck the hour, clanging so loud the building seemed to shift on its foundation. At that same moment, two heavy oak doors opened and a tall, distinguished man stepped out.

"I'm Scott Rosekrans, Prosecuting Attorney," he said. "Sorry we have to meet under these circumstances. Mickey told me you were coming. He just got here himself."

The DA, Zora guessed, was in his early sixties. He had a head full of soft white hair and the sort of affable face that made everyone feel at ease. She liked him right away. His handshake was firm and he spoke with calm authority. They made their way up three flights of stairs, walked down a wide hallway to a cluttered, communal work space.

Stepping inside, Rosekrans motioned toward a door in the far corner of the room. "My office is over there," he said. "Word to the wise, though, this area of the Courthouse was once the juvenile detention center. Somebody decided to keep the graffiti on the walls for old time's sake. My wife says it reminds her of something out of a gangster movie. I tend to agree."

They moved slowly into the brightly-lit office. As advertised, the whitewashed stucco walls still showed plenty of character. There was a staircase in one corner that appeared to lead to the clock tower. A large, half-moon window looked out on Port Townsend Bay. Mickey Kincaid was leaning against an antique oak desk the size of an aircraft carrier, his hands in his pockets, staring off into space. He was solid, rangy, with a photogenic face, brooding eyes, and short black hair. He wore jeans and a dark sweatshirt.

And he was African-American.

Zora had spent a little time with Mickey during her previous visit. She learned then that he'd been adopted by Al and Dorothy Kincaid when he was very young. No further explanation, or background information, was offered and Zora never asked. She embraced him now, fighting back tears. "I'm so sorry, Mickey. This is horrible."

"Yeah, I know. Thanks for coming, Zora. I really appreciate it." Fighting back his own tears, he turned to the DA. "So what's the latest from the police?"

"Chief Garcia is still investigating," Rosekrans said. "He's got both of his detectives on the case, but if your sister's death turns out to be a homicide, it's a little out of their league. As you probably know, Mickey, most of the crime around here is petty stuff."

"Meaning?" Zora asked, unsure if she was overstepping her bounds.

"Meaning, I'll bring in Seattle PD. I've done it before. We had a double homicide down in Quilcene awhile back. Drifter robbed and beat an elderly couple, then torched the place. I put in a call to the chief. He sent me two of his best detectives and a forensics team. A week later we had our man, put him away for life."

"Then you might as well make the call right now," Mickey said. "Because there's no way Kat's death is an accident."

Zora looked for some kind of tell in the DA's eyes, but he gave nothing away, saying only, "We should probably head over to the funeral home now."

"Yeah, I know," Mickey replied, sniffling. "Give me a minute to try my folks again, okay? I haven't been able to reach them yet."

The DA and Zora stepped into the outer office.

"Mickey's parents are on safari somewhere in Kenya," she said. "It might take a while."

"Yeah, he told me. That flight back is going to be horrendous, whenever it happens."

An awkward moment of silence passed between them.

Zora said, "You mentioned the funeral home. What's that all about?"

"Sheriff's deputies took the body there. We only do about twenty autopsies a year around here, so we can't justify the expense of a morgue. And you're looking at the coroner."

"Really," Zora said curiously.

Rosekrans nodded, explaining that in counties with less than forty thousand people, the Prosecuting Attorney wore both hats. He said he'd been certified in the medical aspects of death investigation by the state Coroners Association, adding, "I was a big city cop in a former life too, so that helps, which is a long-winded way of saying I'll be conducting the prelim exam."

Zora picked up on Rosekrans's acerbic response, thinking he probably missed the juice of urban crime. Prosecuting shoplifters, drunk drivers, and small-time burglars had to get a bit stale after a while. "And you'll be looking for *what* exactly?" she asked.

"Any signs of foul play, that kind of thing. Of course, the autopsy will give us the complete story. We contract that work out to a pathologist from Tacoma. I spoke with him a few minutes ago. Normally he would drive over in the morning, but under the circumstances, I thought he should get it done tonight. It'll take him awhile to get here, though."

"Makes sense," Zora said. "You said you were a cop?"

"Yeah, Houston PD. The brass offered me a homicide shield, but I decided to give law school a go instead, went to work for the DA there after graduation. My wife and I moved to Port Townsend about six years ago, to escape the big city and all that good stuff."

"So what's the cop in you think?" she asked.

Rosekrans considered that. "There was a lot of trauma to the body which suggests Katrina may have fallen from the top of the bluff. The trail runs past one of the old artillery batteries only a few feet from the edge and it's a helluva drop. Down below, the terrain is extreme. Sand looks like coarsely ground salt and pepper, lots of big boulders, seaweed. She was partially hidden by a pile of driftwood. The couple who called 9-1-1 said their dog went a little crazy and actually discovered the body. Otherwise, it might have taken us days to find her."

"I still can't believe it," Zora said, shaking her head.

"Yeah, it's tough. Listen, Mickey mentioned that you left Katrina's lab at, what, six or so?"

"Yeah, I met another friend for dinner. He's a fisherman from up my way. His boat's in dry dock over in Port Angeles."

"Mind if I ask the nature of your business?"

"Shop talk," Zora lied. Part of her wanted to tell this man everything. She ran through the different scenarios again and again in her mind, decided the smart thing to do now was remain silent.

Rosekrans said, "Okay, so she died sometime between six and eight-thirty when her body was found. Did she say anything about going for a jog?"

"No. She said she needed to wrap up a few things at the lab before heading home. I planned to meet her back there later and spend the night."

"It's all very strange," Rosekrans noted, stroking his chin. "Look, did you –"

He never finished the thought as Mickey appeared in the doorway. He pocketed his cell and said, "No luck. Supposedly the guide over there has a satellite phone, but he's not picking up for some reason. Jesus, I hope something hasn't happened to them, too."

Zora was thinking the same thing, but said nothing.

Rosekrans pulled his gray, four-door sedan away from the front of the Courthouse, Zora riding shotgun. Mickey sat in the back seat. The DA turned right off Jefferson and headed west. The sun had long since set and a light drizzle began to fall, seeming to capture the somber mood inside.

At the bottom of Sims Way, the vehicle was met by two police cruisers and escorted up the winding hill. At its crest, a small lawn sign on the corner read: "Kosec Funeral Home & Life Tribute Center." The nondescript, single-story structure occupied a half-acre of land in a quiet residential neighborhood. A posse of baying reporters had already arrived, establishing base camp in the parking lot. Gathering crowds of locals looked on from across the street and from every other vantage point they could find. Four deputies assigned to control the mob were doing their level best, but clearly losing the battle. What was already a chaotic scene then became worse when four news choppers swooped in from the south, the deafening thud of their engines making the misty air reverberate.

"Jesus," Mickey said. "This is nuts. How did the press find out so fast?"

"Radio scanners," Zora said matter-of-factly. She knew the drill all too well. After word had spread about her daredevil encounter with the sharks, she'd been forced into hiding by eager television producers stalking her like bloodhounds in a prison-break movie.

Rosekrans added, "Thing is, since the story broke on those monster whales, we've had reporters crawling all over the place. It's been absolutely crazy around here. The whole town's going bonkers."

A squat, pudgy deputy moved two stanchions allowing both cruisers and Rosekrans's sedan to proceed up the circular driveway to the front entrance of the building. Moments later, a pair of double glass doors swung open revealing a fit-looking, dark-haired man with a boyish face. He wore wire-framed glasses and was dressed in slacks, cable-knit sweater, and beige jacket.

"The owner," Rosekrans said. "Real Robles is his name. Good man, knows his stuff. He doubles as my Deputy Coroner."

As they stepped inside, the doors closed behind them, muffling the shouts of the screaming reporters. Zora lingered in the foyer, looking around. The interior of the building looked much like the exterior – nondescript – and smelled of yesterday's roses.

It took several moments before the trembling began, her breaths now coming in short gasps. As quick as the back turn of a page, she was twelve-years-old, staring into her father's coffin, looking down at a man she both loved and loathed. Then the memories came flooding back in a torrent of emotion, the somber faces, the disapproving looks, the cruel innuendos. What could possibly compel a man to take his own life, they whispered? How could he leave behind such a charming little girl and her lovely mother? Zora felt like screaming. A comforting hand touched her arm. She looked up, startled.

"You all right?" Mickey asked.

"Huh? Yeah, sure," she said, glancing over his shoulder at Rosekrans and Robles. She wished she could wave a magic wand and make this all go away, for both Mickey and her.

Rosekrans approached. "Listen," he said quietly. "I need Mickey to make a positive ID, okay? We'll be right back."

Zora nodded, watched after them. They moved slowly down a narrow hallway to a door marked "Private." Robles punched in a four-digit code into the keypad and the lock clicked open. Mickey looked back mournfully then disappeared inside with the others.

He and the DA returned less than a minute later. All color had drained from Mickey's face. Zora slid over beside him, took a hand in hers and squeezed gently. There simply were no words for times like these.

Rosekrans looked at Mickey with narrowed eyes. "I'll do my best to find some answers tonight. I should know something one way or another in half an hour or so...maybe less."

CHAPTER 26

31 March, 11:30 PM PDT
Port Townsend, Washington

MINUTES LATER, the DA-turned-coroner was back inside the prep room, the awful smell unmistakable. Once experienced, he'd often said, it was never, ever, forgotten. The windowless room was twelve feet by twenty feet and illuminated by stark fluorescent lighting. The floor was gray linoleum with a drain in the middle. A body hoist, dressing table, and several rows of cabinets took up the near and far walls. Two poster-sized anatomy charts hung on an otherwise bare side wall. There was a small sink in one corner, a red Craftsman six-drawer tool chest in the other, and beside that, a rolling cart with two open boxes of protective gloves sitting on top.

Katrina's body lay on a stainless-steel table in the center of the room, a PERK – Physical Evidence Recovery Kit – next to her left arm. She was covered with a white sheet, her head supported by a rubber block. An embalming pump, aspirator, organ scale, overhead spray hoses, and various other instruments of death were neatly arranged on a shelf directly behind the table. Next to all that was a larger sink.

Robles handed Rosekrans a disposable blue gown, plastic face shield, and shoe covers. He suited up then pulled on a pair of latex gloves. Next he pulled back the sheet and began the examination, slowly circling the body, leaning in, looking close. Katrina was still dressed, arms straight by her sides, fingers slightly curled, her limbs still somewhat supple. Rigor mortis, he observed, had only begun to set it, noting that it typically commenced anywhere from two to six hours after death. Rosekrans estimated Katrina been dead for something less than that. Upon further examination, he saw no obvious signs of sexual assault, nor did he find any visible knife wounds or bullet holes. He then checked the pockets of her warm-up jacket. One was empty. In the other he found a driver's license and four twenties tucked into a money clip.

Rosekrans held it up. "Well, Real, if we *do* find evidence of foul play, this effectively rules out robbery as a motive, wouldn't you say?" The DA trusted the funeral director's instincts even more than his own. He'd asked Robles once what attracted him to the business of death. He said it was all he ever wanted to do, even as a young kid. Something about growing up watching *Quincy, M.E.,* a popular TV series that ran for seven seasons beginning in the mid-70s.

Robles answered the question with a nod.

Rosekrans then examined the victim's hands, front and back, checking for broken finger nails, lacerations, or any trace evidence that might indicate a struggle. There were more cuts and bruises, including a shattered left wrist bone that protruded an inch through the skin. "Take a look at this, Real. Probably the result of the fall, but it looks like she was already dead at the time. What do you think?"

Robles moved closer, inspecting the blanched skin. "I agree, Scott. There would obviously be redness if she'd been alive."

"Exactly," Rosekrans said. He didn't need to be Quincy to differentiate antemortem injuries from the postmortem variety. The key was bleeding. Broken skin around an injury sustained *before* death appeared red in color because the heart was still pumping blood. If the same injury occurred *after* the heart had stopped, it looked pale, blanched. "Let me check something else." He picked up a lens and examined Katrina's face. It was a web of bruises and lacerations, dirt and debris embedded in the deeper cuts. He gently lifted her head with both hands, turning it from side to side. It was then that he noticed a gash at the base of her neck. Some of the skin had peeled away and the color was reddish brown, noticeably different from the other wounds.

"Looks like a burn," Robles noted. "First or second degree, I'd say."

Rosekrans nodded. "Yeah, and she was still alive when she suffered that injury. Real, my friend, we've got a murder on our hands."

Zora and Mickey paced nervously in a small waiting room, sipping hot tea. Zora fiddled with her phone and wandered out into the hallway. She had tried reaching the shaman twice already, only to have both calls kicked to voice mail. This time she left a message. "Hi, my name is Zora Flynn. I'm a commercial fisherman, a friend of Katrina Kincaid. I *really* need to speak with you, so please get back to me as soon as you can." She left her number, the time of the call, and continued pacing.

As Zora pocketed her cell, Rosekrans turned the corner at the far end of the hall.

Jesus, she thought. *He might as well have the word "murder" stamped on his forehead.*

Mickey saw him coming, too, and rushed out of the waiting room.

"Well, unfortunately, your instincts were right," he said. "This was definitely not an accident. I'm really sorry, Mickey. The ME will need to make it official, but I believe he'll concur."

Mickey stared ahead blankly.

"We found a deep cut on the back of her neck," Rosekrans added. "And there appear to be burn marks on the skin. Can you think of anything that might have caused that type of injury?"

"Not offhand, no," Mickey said. "Is that what killed her?"

"I think so. Again, we'll know more after the post."

Mickey shook his head, his voice hushed. "Kat didn't have an enemy in the world. I can't believe anyone would want to hurt her."

Rosekrans seemed to feel his pain. He put a hand on Mickey's shoulder. "Look, I can't bring your sister back, but I promise you we'll find whoever did this to her. I put in a call to Seattle PD right after I completed the exam. Dispatch is trying to reach the chief as we speak."

Zora listened without saying a word, not exactly sure what to do next. She turned to comfort Mickey, but he had already retreated to the waiting room.

Moments later, Rosekrans's phone buzzed. He excused himself, and ambled back down the hall to the foyer.

Zora stared silently at the floor for a long moment, her mind spinning in a hundred different directions at once. That's when she heard the DA's voice ratchet up a notch. He began walking in tight circles, a puzzled look on his face. He then snapped the phone shut, signaled her over with a nod of his head.

"What's going on?" she asked, hurrying up to him.

"There's been a change in plans."

"What kind of change?"

"Let's just say that call wasn't from Seattle's police chief."

"Who was it?"

Rosekrans's face blushed red, the veins popping on his forehead. "I'm not at liberty to say, except that the case has been turned over to a special unit operating out of the governor's office."

"The *governor's* office. What does that mean?"

"It means I'm persona non grata," Rosekrans hissed. "At least as far as the investigation goes. They're sending a team up here tomorrow, CSI, the whole nine. Until then, I've been told to secure the victim's home, like I wouldn't have done that already."

The DA's words hung in the air and Zora suddenly felt like Alice looking down the rabbit hole. She stared at her hands as she thought about what to say. Finally, she looked up with trusting eyes and said, "Can I tell you something off the record?"

Rosekrans hesitated. "That depends."

"On what?" she asked.

"Whether or not it involves criminal activity."

"Fair enough, I'll let you decide." As Zora told her story, the details came tumbling out just as she'd rehearsed them over the past hour or so. It was, without question, a monumental mess, that now included murder. What she didn't say, of course, was that plans were already in motion to actually *go after* an orca...and soon.

Rosekrans took a deep breath. "Okay, let me see if I've got this straight. You're saying Dr. Kincaid told the GM in Seattle his killer whale was dying and gave him forty-eight hours to inform the Feds. The next day, some nefarious stranger threatens to harm your mother unless you go out and *capture* a killer whale. Then, Katrina ends up at the bottom of a cliff, the victim of foul play. And now this phone call out of the blue from the governor's office."

Zora's anxiety deepened. "I don't believe in coincidences, do you?"

"No, I sure as hell don't," Rosekrans replied, stiffening noticeably. "Never have, never will. And I don't like what's going on here, not one bit."

"Okay, so what now?" Zora said, urging him on.

"To be honest with you, Ms. Flynn, I'm not exactly sure." He pulled a pen and business card from his pocket, jotted something down on the back of the card. "But since my hands are clearly tied at the moment, I suggest you call this number. It belongs to a Seattle detective. He just might be able to help *both* of us."

Zora looked at him skeptically. "I don't know, I –"

"Look," Rosekrans said, his tone a bit harder. "Most cops I know have a bag of tricks. This guy's got a whole arsenal. And he can be trusted. Clean and mean as we like to say in law enforcement. But just remember, you didn't get this from me."

Zora nodded, took the card, and moved slowly back down the hall. She was a bit bewildered by the curious exchange, but thoroughly convinced that the threats to her mother and the murder of her friend *had* to be linked. And she felt confident the DA knew it, too. Now, it was time to tell Mickey. His sister was dead, after all. He had a right to know. Besides, she remembered he had experience in such matters. Try as she may, though, she couldn't remember what it was. She straightened her shoulders, walked purposefully into the waiting room ... and began talking.

CHAPTER 27

31 March, 11:55 PM PDT
Olympia, Washington

INSIDE MITCHELL CHANDLER'S STUDY, Savannah Sokolov, Colby Freeman, Preston Tradd, and Darnell Atwater were pondering many of the same things. They had gathered around a crackling fire, but there was nothing warm or cozy about this midnight rendezvous. In fact, the mood was tense, the fatigue palpable, everyone grim-faced. No one spoke.

Atwater was about to say something when Chandler burst into the room. He flopped down in his favorite chair, noticeably on edge, outrage etched into his face. Leaning forward on his elbows, he clasped his hands together so tightly his knuckles turned white. He drilled Atwater with a piercing look and barked, "What the fuck happened, Darnell?"

Atwater stiffened, stared straight ahead. "I don't know, Mitchell. I've never had a problem with any of my operatives before. Iago's record is impeccable, he –"

"Not anymore, it's not," Chandler hissed.

"An unfortunate accident," Atwater countered, attempting to make a case for what he'd coldly referred to earlier in the evening as collateral damage. "Iago said the woman went ballistic, shouting rape or some goddamn thing. Then, she started scratching at his face, spit on him. He pushed back and she fell, hit her head. It just happened, that's all."

Chandler glanced at Savannah, saw the fury boiling in her eyes. They'd been enjoying a quiet dinner when Atwater called with the shocking news about Katrina Kincaid. Reluctantly, Chandler had then passed on the news to Savannah. She'd reacted angrily, ripping into him like a woman possessed. She said she'd given Atwater explicit instructions that Katrina was to be treated with kid gloves. Instead, she was now dead.

Agreeing it was a royal clusterfuck, Chandler decided his only recourse was to cash in a formidable chip with Governor Spencer Ryan, one he'd been holding for just such an occasion – namely the governor's affinity for playing the ponies, or any other game of chance, for that matter. Over the past year, Ryan had run up a huge debt which Chandler had covered with a check drawn on the same offshore account used to pay off Zora Flynn. Now it was time to square things, with help from the governor's own private security force. After a rather heated phone conversation, Ryan agreed to make the call.

Clusterfuck, indeed, Chandler thought.

"Now before we go any further, I want everyone in this room to understand why there can be no more screwups. And I mean *none.*" Chandler paused, looking hard at each face. Savannah had been on the receiving end of this rant before, but it was essential the others heard it now. "When I was chasing Charlie all over Nam, the prospect of dealing with whining, paper-pushing bureaucrats drove me up the fucking wall, what with their goddamn statistical models and shit. Of course, they had absolutely no concept of what war was really all about. War is one continual series of fuckups, which means there's no such *thing* as a 'statistical model.' I lost a lot of good men because of those clipboard-carrying assholes. You with me so far?"

Affirming nods all around, except from Savannah. She stared into the fire, unblinking.

Chandler continued. "So, I survived that sorry chapter in our country's history and what do I do for an encore? I get into the movie business. Now, making movies is even *more* fucked up than war, if you can believe that. The egos are immense and it's a bottomless money pit. What I'm getting at here, people, is that theme parks seemed like the antithesis of all that crap. Theme parks are happy places, right? Our guests have fun. They learn things. They leave with smiles on their faces. 'We bring the kid out in you,' that's our motto. On top of all that, we employ a lot of people. What are our summer numbers up to now, Colby?"

Freeman opened a thick folder in front of him, his hands trembling just a bit. "We peak at right around twenty-one hundred here in Seattle, sir." He then rifled through several pages before stopping. "Let's see, here it is. Corporate-wide, we're talking about thirty thousand."

"Thirty thousand," Chandler repeated. "Now that's a lot of goddamn jobs, isn't it? And I *care* about jobs. I really do. We give back to the communities in other ways, too. We support local charities, dish out truckloads of free tickets, and provide good homes for the animals. Marine mammal parks are a good thing, right, people?" Another long pause. "Wrong! Because I've got myself a dead whale, a dead woman, and a million hungry fire ants waiting to crawl up my ass. *Activists* they call themselves. Well, they're like the fucking gooks. They don't work from checklists and they don't operate by any rules. Are we getting what's wrong with this picture?"

"We get it," Savannah said coolly.

Chandler's grim expression softened. "Very well, then. Darnell..."

"Sir."

"You said your man left no evidence behind. Are you absolutely certain of that?"

"Positive. The cops are chasing shadows here."

"By cops, you mean Port Townsend PD?" Savannah asked.

"Yes, small force, couple of detectives."

Chandler managed a smile. "So we're dealing with Barney fucking Fife and Goober then?"

Atwater nodded.

Chandler said, "Okay, good. They'll be no match for the governor's boys. What about the woman's files? Anything incriminating there?"

"Mostly research documents and medical reports," Atwater replied. "Nothing to indicate she was doing anything other than treating the sick whale. And from what I understand, that was no secret."

"What about her computer?"

"Iago checked. It was clean."

Chandler turned to Freeman. "You must have had phone calls and e-mail exchanges with her."

"Yes, of course, sir," he said. "In fact, I got a message from her just before..." Freeman glanced over at Atwater. "Before Darnell's man paid her a visit, that is. I didn't call her back, though, so there's no way she could have known about Samson's death. And she didn't hear it from the head trainer, either. I checked with her."

Savannah shot Chandler a disdainful look, a volcano poised to erupt.

"Then, they've got nothing," he said, attempting to diffuse Savannah's rage. "But it doesn't change the fact that we need to dispose of the whale's body right away and bring in his replacement. What's the latest with our boat captain, Tradd?"

Tradd snapped forward in his chair. "Well, sir, she flew down from Sitka this morning as planned. So far all systems are go."

"And she still knows none of the details at this point."

"Right, sir. She said it will take her a couple of days to pull everything together, get her crew here, line up the boat, all of that. She'll be given final instructions then."

Savannah threw Chandler one of her all-knowing looks this time, flipping the script on him. "Look, Mitchell, you're asking a lot of this woman, you must know that. Disposing of Samson's body is one thing, but capturing another whale, then delivering it safely to the park...it's a *hell* of a lot to ask."

Chandler did not like having his authority or his ideas questioned, but he had to concede the point. Nothing new there. Savannah was almost always right. "Maybe so," he said. "But if anyone can pull it off, *she* can. Thelma and Louise rolled into one, remember?"

"Yeah, and we both know what happened to them." Savannah left unsaid the fact that the legendary movie outlaws had soared off a cliff in a blaze of glory.

There was a long silence.

Atwater then waded in. "There's something else you need to know, Mitchell."

"Jesus, what now?" Chandler said.

"We put a tail on Flynn, like you asked. One of my men picked up her trail at a car rental agency in Port Angeles. Turns out she's a friend of the deceased."

"Son of a bitch," Chandler screamed, glaring at Tradd. "Did your people not know that?"

Tradd shook his head slowly, stared down at his hands as if he were comatose.

"Forget Barney Fife," Chandler shouted, the anger rising inside him. "I've got the goddamn Keystone Cops on my payroll. Where is Flynn now?"

"She spent a couple of hours at Dr. Kincaid's lab near Sequim," Atwater replied. "She left around six o'clock and headed back to Port Angeles. There, she met up with a man we assume to be the other boat captain. They had dinner together, then she retraced her route. I'm guessing she was planning to stay at her friend's house in Port Townsend, but ended up at the Courthouse instead. Right now, she's at a local funeral home. Sheriff's deputies took the body there."

"How did she find out about the Kincaid woman?" Chandler asked.

"No idea. Somebody obviously called her. She took off like a bat out of hell at the turnoff."

Savannah added, "Look, if the two women were friends, then Zora Flynn knows about Samson, at least that he was dying. Trust me on that one. And for sure she'll connect the dots, figure out where the captured whale is going and why."

"Maybe so, Savannah," Atwater said evenly. "But it doesn't change anything, not really. Look, it makes sense that Flynn would seek out a killer whale expert, right? Friend or no friend. And there's not a shred of evidence linking Kincaid's death with her treatment of the whale."

Chandler thought long and hard before saying, "Then you better make damn sure you keep close tabs on the mother."

"Twenty-four-seven," Atwater replied confidently. "Trust me, Mitchell, we're all over it."

Savannah's face twisted in sudden fury, then she exploded off the couch, her hands firmly planted on her hips, her eyes on fire. "What in God's name does Zora Flynn's *mother* have to do with any of this?"

Chandler flinched at a stab of pain that struck his temples. Savannah's reaction was precisely the reason he hadn't mentioned this part of the plan to her, one that relied on another of Sun Tzu's cunning strategies: *If the goal is to make your adversaries listen, first seize something that they love.* And Zora Flynn, he knew, dearly loved her mother. So he'd danced around the truth, attributing the captain's cooperative nature to the sizeable donation made to her charity in Nepal, which of course had been Savannah's idea to begin with. But Chandler knew the real story would come out, sooner or later.

And now the jig was up.

Chandler took a deep breath, slapped his hands on his thighs, and stood up. Now facing Savannah, he explained that, yes, they were using

Stella Flynn as bait, that another Black Stallion operative had snuck into her room at the nursing home in Utah and captured a camera-phone photo. A short time later, he said, Tradd snagged the image from a secure web site during his layover in Juneau. The blackmail scheme followed from there. When he'd finished speaking, the room went silent. No one wanted to antagonize the woman further, including Chandler. Only once before had he seen her this livid...and once was enough.

Savannah stood frozen in place, glaring at Chandler with accusing eyes. Then she spun around, thundered out of the room, and slammed the door so hard a stack of first-edition books toppled off the top shelf from one of the bookcases. The volumes crashed noisily to the floor, seeming to make a statement of their own.

Chandler calmly gathered up the irreplaceable works, put them back in their proper place, and then strolled over to the window. He stood motionless staring outside, hands stuffed in his pockets, thinking about his next move. Part of his motivation in not telling Savannah the full story was to limit her exposure, keep her out of the dicey blackmail business altogether. It had been tough enough convincing her to go along with the charity angle. After initially agreeing to the plan, she'd changed her mind, took him to the mat on it. He now turned back, scanning the anxious faces of Atwater, Freeman, and Tradd.

"So what now, Mitchell?" Atwater asked tentatively.

For several moments Chandler said nothing. Then it hit him, *another* valuable lesson he'd learned in Vietnam: the most effective way to take down Charlie was to back-door him, come up with something completely unexpected. "Look," he said. "We all agree the cops are going to figure out the Kincaid woman was treating Samson, right? Even SIU won't be able to cover those tracks. So our job, gentlemen, is to essentially canonize the good doctor, show the world that, thanks to her fine care, our beloved whale made a full and complete recovery."

Atwater, Freeman, and Tradd nodded their agreement.

Chandler then sharpened his gaze on Freeman. "Here's what I want you to do, Colby. Once the whales are switched out, you invite a few of our media friends to stop by, people who don't drink the activists' Kool-Aid. Wine and dine them at Tulio's, then bring them over to the park, have them check out progress on the stadium. After that drop by the sea-pen so they can visit our star performer, tell them he's fit as a fucking fiddle. They'll never know the difference."

The blood seemed to drain from Freeman's face, but he nodded his consent.

"Now let's make this happen, people," Chandler said defiantly. "The clock is ticking."

CHAPTER 28

WHEN ZORA FINISHED telling Mickey everything she knew and didn't know about the events that had transpired over the past few days, the funeral director ushered them out a side door to his waiting car. The DA still had a long night ahead of him – the ME hadn't yet arrived – and he suggested the maneuver as a way for them to dodge the media stampede. Rosekrans had promised to call the Seattle detective immediately following the autopsy, fill him in on what was going on, and arrange for Zora to meet him for lunch. If all went according to plan, that was less than twelve hours from now. The thought sent an icy chill through her body.

No one spoke during the short trip back to the Courthouse, giving Zora time to ponder her next moves. The DA, of course, had no idea where they were headed next, something she assumed he would prefer *not* to know. Less than ten minutes later, she was hunkered down in the cab of Mickey's black F-150 pickup truck. He was racing toward his sister's house on the north side of town, clocking three times the posted speed limit. A heavy drizzle beat steadily against the windshield, the wipers throwing intermittent shadows across their faces. Zora killed the music – *Gypsy Biker* from the Boss's *Magic* album – and glanced over at Mickey. "Your brain's in spin cycle, I can tell. Care to share?"

"The DA," he said. "I can't figure out why he gave you the cop's number. From everything I've heard about Rosekrans, he plays things close to the vest, a belt-and-suspenders kind of guy."

"All I know is, whoever made that call really pissed him off."

Mickey nodded, his eyes fixed on the road ahead.

After a long silence, Zora said, "I know *you* know what you're doing here, Mickey, which is a damn good thing because it's way out of my league."

"Yeah, I guess you could say that."

"I don't remember the details, though. Military?"

"No, but close." Mickey replied. "I played some ball at Stanford, went fairly high in the draft even though I was small by NFL standards. You just don't see many six-one, two hundred pound linebackers playing at that level. None in fact. Anyway, I made the Jets practice squad but blew out my knee before the season even started. Just like that, my football career was over. Really bummed me out, so after mending from surgery I decided to chuck it all and see the world. I was broke, though, and signed on with this big international shipping company out of Denmark to make ends meet. A year or so into the job, terrorists bombed the USS *Cole* in Yemen. Security was ratcheted up on all vessels moving in and out of the region, so me and eleven other guys got tapped to be part of an internal strike force. 'The Dirty Dozen' they called us. Not very original, but it stuck. We ended up taking an intensive six-week course run by a couple of former Mossad agents, husband-and-wife team, real bad-asses those two, especially the woman."

"I like her already. So, how long did you stay on the job?"

"Eighteen months, give or take. Got out in the spring of 2002. As a kid I always enjoyed problem solving, puzzles, working with my hands, so I decided to give the home building business a shot. Besides, what else do you do with a degree in philosophy?" Mickey slid forward in his seat, pointed out the window. "That's Kat's place up ahead there on the right, the red two-story on the corner."

Zora nodded. "Looks like we've got some company."

A police cruiser was parked on 33rd, the street that ran alongside Katrina's house. Two officers stood outside the vehicle engaged in an animated conversation. Mickey drove on another block, turned right into a small lot at the end of the complex, parked the truck, and opened the center console. He grabbed a penlight, then pulled two pairs of latex gloves from his jacket pocket. "Here, put these on. I took them from a box at the funeral home as we were leaving. My fingerprints are no problem, but yours would raise some gnarly questions."

"Good thinking," Zora said. She took the gloves and stepped out of the truck.

Aided by the light of a bright moon, Zora and Mickey scaled a tall wooden fence that ran along San Juan Avenue. They dropped to the ground on the other side, squatting low. A murmur of wind through the fir trees wrapped them in a silent, eerie embrace. Moving stealthily, they slipped between a pocket of shrub beds and across a large cedar deck to the back door. There were strips of yellow police-line-do-not-cross tape crisscrossing the frame.

Zora hesitated. "What about a security alarm?"

"There isn't one," Mickey said. "Not a big priority around here." He pulled a key from another pocket, held it in the glow of a streetlight, adding, "Spare. Kat had one to my place, too." He then keyed the lock, pushed open the door, and motioned Zora inside.

She ducked under the tape, stepped into the foyer, and waited a moment while her eyes adjusted to the dark. "You okay?" she asked, sensing Mickey's distress.

"Jesus, this is tougher than I thought it would be."

"Maybe we should go."

"No, I'll be fine."

"You sure?"

"Yeah, it's okay." He checked the door. "No sign of forced entry. So either Kat knew her killer or he got in some other way. And I say *he* because whoever hauled her up to the top of that bluff had to be one strong son of a bitch."

"I agree," Zora said, glancing at the staircase to her right. "What's up there?"

"Kat's office and bedroom. I can't deal with that right now. Let's start down here, okay?"

They moved along a narrow hallway into the kitchen. Mickey turned on the penlight, holding it low to the floor. The kitchen and dining room were neat, orderly. He checked the front door. It was locked, no sign of forced entry there either. They then moved into the living room. It was cozy, artsy, the furnishings simple but elegant. There were two built-in bookcases on the far wall with an old fashioned looking cast-iron stove in between. A modernist painting hung above the sofa. They moved around the room in a slow circuit, careful not to disturb anything.

"What do you think?" Zora said.

"Looks clean to me. No sign of Vera either."

"Vera?"

"Kat's cat. We always laughed at the alliteration..." Mickey's voice fell off. "Anyway, V's an outdoor girl mostly, so she should be okay. I'll come back for her tomorrow."

Zora rubbed his forearm gently.

Mickey said, "I feel like Kat's going to come strolling in here any minute now wondering what the hell we're doing."

"Yeah, I know this is hard."

They were about to move on when they heard a soft "poof" sound. A flame then ignited behind the thick glass doors of the stove, illuminating the room in soft amber light.

"The thermostat controls the heat," Mickey said, pointing to a wall unit. "Opening the door must have..." He suddenly stiffened. "Holy shit, that's gotta be it."

"What?" Zora said.

Kneeling down, Mickey carefully touched the side of the stove. "Here, take a look at this." He focused the light on a sharp ridge beneath the doors. "Be careful, it's hot."

Zora leaned in close. "The burn mark on Katrina's neck," she said.

Mickey directed the beam up, down, and around the unit. "Yeah, I don't see any blood, though. No sign of a struggle either."

"But you're thinking this is where Katrina died, right?"

"That's *exactly* what I'm thinking."

Mickey offered up a theory, his voice coldly analytical now. "Kat was raped when she was like fourteen or fifteen. So if some guy broke in here and surprised her, she'd fight him with everything she had. Maybe in the process she got knocked down or fell, hit her head on the stove. Then the sick son of a bitch found her running gear, put two and two together, and tried to cover his tracks by hauling her up to Fort Worden."

Zora shuddered at the thought. "As horrible as that sounds, it seems totally plausible."

"Except for one thing," Mickey said, shaking his head. "It doesn't add up. If the motive was rape, or robbery, the place would never be this clean.

Look around, it's spotless. Whoever murdered Kat was methodical. He knew exactly what he was doing."

"You're saying it was a pro?" Zora said, feeling another shock run through her body.

"Yeah, but if that's the case something else doesn't make sense."

"What's that?"

"The coroner. He could easily figure out this was no accident. A hit man would know that."

Zora nodded. "Okay, so where does that leave us?"

"I'm not sure, but there's no question Kat's murder and the threat to your mother are connected."

Zora thought about that. "Yeah, now all we have to do is prove it."

"C'mon, let's check upstairs," Mickey said. "Maybe we'll find something there."

They moved back through the kitchen and down the hall. Mickey stumbled over a pair of running shoes lying near the back door. He picked up the shoes, played the beam over the brand name: Saucony.

"What is it?" Zora said.

He handed her the penlight. "Here, you go on up. I need to make a call."

"I have no idea what I'm looking for."

"It'll only take me a minute."

Zora blinked several times then moved cautiously up the carpeted staircase to a tidy, rectangular loft area. There was a gray, two-drawer filing cabinet in one corner. A mesh eyeshade lamp, laptop computer, and desktop printer sat on the desk, several green file folders stacked neatly off to one side. A slice of moonlight cut through a skylight directly above the desk. She thumbed through a couple of folders then stepped into the bedroom.

It was large, with an A-frame roof, queen-size bed, and private bath. Zora walked across the room to a set of French doors that opened onto a large balcony. She unlatched the door and stepped outside, careful to stay hidden from the patrol officers. Unit six was one of ten artisan cottages facing each other in two neat rows, each with a square of front yard separated by a rustic fence. She breathed deeply of the crisp night air, then retraced her steps back to Katrina's desk. Sifting through the files, she found a compendium of research reports on everything from environmental studies to marine pollution to hydrocarbons found in sperm whales. Nothing about Samson, at least that she could see.

Mickey startled her as he came bounding up the stairs, running shoes in hand.

"What's going on?" Zora asked.

"I just spoke to the DA."

"Jesus, he knows we're here?"

"No, he thinks we're at a bar downtown. I asked him to check the shoes Kat had on. He did, said they were Nike's."

Zora threw him a curious look. "Okay."

"Kat was a competitive runner, a cardio-junkie. And the Nike's gave her blisters. She only wore them once, that's it."

"How do you know?"

"I gave them to her last month, for her birthday. When she told me they didn't fit right, I wrote her a check to buy these Sauconys. Never got around to taking the other pair back."

"So her killer grabbed the wrong shoes."

"Exactly. C'mon, let's see if we can find anything on her computer that might help. I like to think I learned a trick or two from those ex-Mossad agents. We got into some really sophisticated shit. I swear those two could crack the nuclear launch codes in no time flat."

Mickey pulled up another chair, sat down, and booted up the machine. The screen jumped to life. "Okay, Kat, what is it? What's your password?" An instant later there was a password prompt. Mickey punched in several different names, all the usual suspects, but nothing took. The computer then displayed a "Password Hint."

Zora leaned in close, read the question out loud. "What was the name of your first dog?"

Mickey bolted upright. "That's it! Dad bought Kat a big black Alaskan malamute for Christmas one year. She was crazy about that animal, took him running every day." He typed in the word "wolfen." The screen jumped to life.

"You're in, Mickey. Good job."

He clicked on "My Computer." For the next several minutes they scanned the folders – videos, photos, research reports, scientific essays, and the like. The largest folder contained several files labeled, "Sea Change in Attitude."

"Looks like Kat's kind of thing," Mickey said. "What do you think?"

Zora nodded.

"Let's check the hard drive then." Mickey clicked on an icon, leaned back in the chair, shaking his head. "Look," he said. "Right here, under 'Details.' Kat's computer has 40 gigabytes of storage, but the numbers don't add up. There are at least 8 gigs unaccounted for, which is really strange."

"Any idea why?" Zora asked, not really tracking with any of this.

Mickey stared at the monitor for a long moment. "There, in the bottom left corner." He pointed to an icon with a pixilated white key on a blue background.

Zora still didn't get it.

"Something called TrueCrypt," Mickey said. "It's encryption software for establishing and maintaining an on-the-fly-encrypted disk. The program is super sophisticated, uses something like eleven algorithms, but basically it translates data into secret code which is stored as encrypted files. To read the files you need a secret password."

"So whatever's on that disk no one else is supposed to see."

"That's the plan."

"But you just said it takes a secret password to gain access?"

Mickey stood, tried to clear his head. "Right. And if the computer gods are smiling on us, Kat used the same one. It's a bad idea but a lot of people do it. I'm guilty myself sometimes."

He sat back down, typed in the word "wolfen" again. And again the machine responded. The program immediately began to whirr, scanning gigabytes, loading the encrypted section of the drive. He looked at "My Computer" a second time, noticed that another drive had also been mounted on the system. He clicked on the icon. There were just two folders in the drive, one labeled "DARK TIDES," the other "KOS." He double-clicked on the first folder. It contained several files with ominous sounding names – "Alien Species," "Venomous Weed," "Red Tides," and "Threatened & Endangered Species."

"Scary sounding stuff," Zora said.

Mickey nodded then clicked on "KOS." There were several files inside, all labeled "Samson," each with a subtitle and date attached.

Zora felt an icy shiver shoot up her spine.

The first document was a feature story from *The Journal of Comparative Pathology* titled "Hodgkin's Disease in Killer Whales," written by a veterinarian with the Wakayama Medical School in Japan. Mickey tried reading the opening paragraph, "*Generalized lymphadenopathy and spleno-megaly were noted at necropsy and the histopathological examination re-vealed*...blah, blah, blah. Shit! I can't even pronounce the words, let alone tell you what they mean."

"Dammit," Zora said. "Me neither. See if there's anything else?"

Mickey scrolled through a few more passages of medical mumbo jum-bo. None of it made any sense to either of them. He closed the document and clicked on one labeled "Samson: Treatment Beginning 3/21." There were a number of notations over a period of several days. He stopped on the final entry, checked the date and time it was input – 8:10 p.m., on 3/30, just hours before Katrina had been killed.

Zora and Mickey stared long and hard at the final chilling words.

Samson death imminent...Freeman evasive...COVER-UP!!!

CHAPTER 29

1 April, 6:15 AM PDT
Port Townsend, Washington

ZORA WOKE IN MICKEY'S guest room following a tortured, fitful sleep. She lay for a short while listening to the birds chatter in the tall cedars. The sun beat a blazing track through the bedroom window, making the room feel bright and airy, but the burst of light did little to help her dark mood. She felt sad and tired and angry and every one of those emotions was there in her face. She finally dragged herself out of bed and stepped into the shower.

As the steaming hot water cascaded over her body, she closed her eyes and ran through the previous night's events in her head. After printing out the last page of Katrina's disturbing computer report, she and Mickey had quietly retraced their steps back to his truck and driven here. But before turning in they'd gone online to research KOS-Seattle. There was no mention of a sick whale. A series of press releases cited progress on Samson Stadium which, according to the park's GM, was closed for construction. He claimed it was scheduled to reopen in the near future although no specific date had been mentioned.

The park, they'd discovered, was part of a multi-billion-dollar conglomerate owned by one Mitchell Chandler. A Google search generated thousands of hits. It was impossible to get their heads around the size and scope of Chandler's empire, but he was clearly a man accustomed to getting what he wanted. And there was no doubt about his political leanings. He was in the habit of writing big checks to his favorite politicians, including Governor Spencer Ryan of Washington. And it was all legal as far as they could tell. In fact, the world headquarters of Chandler Global Enterprises was located in Olympia, a few blocks from the state capitol.

A second search, this one on Detective Cloyd Steiger, turned up a recent story in the *Seattle Times*. He was described as *"a cop's cop of almost mythic proportions – old school, former "SWAT dog," with an iron will, titanium fists, and a nose for sniffing out trouble...a little rough around the edges, maybe, but capable of cajoling the most belligerent suspect into singing like the proverbial canary."*

Zora was still thinking about that as she stepped out of the shower. As she toweled off, her phone rang. The call from the DA lasted less than sixty seconds. Rosekrans said he'd spoken with the detective in Seattle and had arranged the lunch meeting as promised. She thanked him and hung up. Five minutes later, dressed in a pair of tailored black jeans and white turtleneck sweater, she strolled through Mickey's modest ranch house. It was a collection of good taste in every sense: Santa Fe motif, minimalist theme, black and white photos on the wall. Zora opened the screen door and wandered across the back porch, stopping long enough to feel the cool breeze on her face.

The home sat on an uneven bluff above the bend in a swift-moving creek that emptied into a large pond. A centuries-old alder tree draped in moss angled over the water like a giant bird of prey. Near the rear of the property, a whitewashed barn backed up to a thick grove of firs, beyond which she could make out a dirt road that angled up a steep hill.

There was no sign of Mickey and, except for the birds, only silence.

Zora took a moment to enjoy the peaceful setting, then headed down a winding path toward the barn. She was running on empty. It was an effort just to put one foot in front of the other. As she came around the side of the building, she noticed the door was open, heard rustling sounds. She stepped inside. The two-story structure had been completely remodeled and converted into a large work space. Hammers, saws, nail punches, putty knives, levels, and an assortment of other carpenter's tools hung neatly along one wall. Two oval windows at each end and a large skylight in the roof provided plenty of illumination. The floor was spotless, the air heavy with smells of cedar and varnish.

Zora didn't see Mickey at first. He was partially hidden by a support beam and leaning over a makeshift table, a large sheet of plywood stretched between two saw horses. A stack of blueprints lay on top. As she watched him work, she took in his strong shoulders and handsome face, his lean body accented in blue jeans and gray sweatshirt. She cleared her throat. "Hi there, I hope I'm not disturbing you."

Mickey looked up, smiled. "Oh, hey Zora, come on in."

"You're up early," she said.

"Couldn't sleep. Decided to go over the plans for a remodel I'm working on down in Gig Harbor. Doing something normal helps take my mind off things. It's surreal, you know? Never in a million years did I think I'd be arranging for Kat's..." His voice trailed off.

"I know, it's awful, I'm sorry. Didn't get much shut-eye myself."

"Yeah, well, you've got your own problems to deal with. Listen, how about some coffee? Good stuff, straight from the farmer's market here in town."

"Perfect."

Mickey poured two mugs. "No cream or sugar, sorry."

"This is fine," Zora said, taking a sip. The coffee smelled wonderful and tasted even better. It had a rich, earthy flavor. She told him about the call from the DA and her scheduled lunch meeting with the detective, then said, "Any luck reaching your folks?"

"Not yet. I tried again right after I woke up. They signed on with a local Kenyan guide, not one of those luxury operations, so there's no telling where they are right now." Mickey's lower lip began to tremble. "They're the salt of the earth, those two, the only parents I've ever known. This is *really* going to hit them hard."

"Yeah, no doubt," Zora said. "They adopted you when you were, what, five years old?"

"Four," Mickey said, setting down his pencil and slide ruler. "My biological father owned a successful tool and die shop near Detroit, but he smoked two packs of Camels a day and worked way too many hours. He had a stroke driving home late one night, died a week later. Ma did the best she could after that, but she had some demons of her own. One night neighbors found her wandering the street barefoot in a prom dress. She was carrying a knife and looking for John the Baptist. She said some guy named Jamie had sent her. He claimed that killing the Baptist would delay Armageddon and save humanity. A shrink put her in a mental hospital, pumped her full of pills. She never left. I was adopted the next year. Chosen, not abandoned, that's what Al and Dorothy Kincaid said to me, over and over, until it sunk in. I've never forgotten those words."

Zora said, "Special people, for sure."

"Yeah, and I learned everything I know about carpentry from dad. 'Big Al,' that's what his friends call him. The man's part artist, part Zen master. Ornery as an alley cat sometimes, but he'll build you anything you want as long as you're not in a hurry for it. He hates to be rushed." Mickey flipped over the blueprints, a not-so-subtle signal that he wanted to change the subject. "Hey, listen, enough about me. Your turn now. Kat told me a bit about your high-seas antics. I gotta say they make some of my adventures look awfully damn tame."

Zora took a sip of coffee, leaned awkwardly against a wooden post. She did not like talking about herself, but this man had such a comfortable way about him, it put her at ease. "Guess I come by it naturally," she said. "My parents were real adventurers, but they were gone a lot of the time, so I learned to fend for myself. Didn't think much of it, figured that's just the way it was. Besides I loved the outdoors, rode my horse everywhere. It was a great life until it wasn't."

"Yeah, how so?"

After taking a deep breath, Zora forced herself to reach back into memories three decades old. Even after all this time she could still feel the terror of that awful day. She told Mickey about Callie: how she'd dared her to ride into the dark ravine...the rattlesnake...the spooked horses...the deadly fall...the horrifying screams...waking up in the hospital. "They kept me in that awful place for three weeks," she said. "Busted tibia, bad head injury. The leg healed okay, not the head. I developed something called post-concussion syndrome. The headaches were relentless, drained my will to live for a long time. I was losing whole parts of myself until it became a landslide that nearly swept me away."

"How long did that last?"

"Depression comes and goes. My drug of choice is adrenaline. It keeps me from looking too hard at myself."

Mickey motioned Zora to sit on the staircase steps, inched in beside her. "What about the screams?" he asked.

"Awful. They get their claws into you and they just rip. When I don't hear them, it's usually because I haven't slept, which is more often than not." She hoped he wouldn't ask about her parents, about her father running off, then taking his own life. He didn't. Instead, Mickey gently brushed her cheek with his finger and remained quiet.

The silence lasted a full minute, their thoughts rapped around the magnitude of the events swirling around them.

"This stuff with your mother," he said. "It's going to be okay."

"I hope so, Mickey," Zora replied, momentarily forgetting all that happened over the past seventy-two hours. Their gazes locked then she felt the light touch of his other hand on her back, sending sparks of electricity jumping through her body. "Anyway, I should let you get back to work. Besides, I have a date with a homicide detective, remember? Twelve noon sharp."

Mickey removed his hand from her back. She wished he hadn't. It felt good to be touched.

After a long pause, he said, "I really should be going with you."

"No, it's okay. You need to track down your folks, make the arrangements for Katrina."

Another long pause.

"Yeah, I guess you're right."

Zora bent her face to his. They hugged a soft, tentative hug.

There was so much to say...and yet so little.

Mickey insisted on making breakfast and, after devouring a batch of whole grain flapjacks, yogurt, and raspberries, Zora hit the road. It was 8:45 a.m. Traffic was light, the sky overcast. As the miles rolled past, she kept one eye on the highway, the other glued to her rear view mirror. No sign of any tail, though she felt sure someone had to be following her. A dark blue sedan stayed close for several miles before turning off just after crossing Hood Canal. She tuned in a classic rock station for a while, but even her favorite Eagles song, *Desperado*, couldn't dislodge the dark thoughts smothering her mind.

Around 9:30, Zora stopped at Espresso Gardens, one of the many roadside coffee shacks that dotted the route. She ordered a double latte and a slice of homemade banana bread. It smelled heavenly. The caffeine jolt helped lighten her mood a bit too. So did the sign above the takeout window.

I DON'T REPEAT GOSSIP. SO LISTEN CAREFULLY.

An hour after that, she arrived at the Bainbridge Island dock. The trip to Seattle took another thirty-five minutes. As the big ferry sliced through Elliott Bay, the sun began to peek through a gray slate of low-hanging clouds, turning the city's skyline into a brilliant sheen of glass. After disembarking, Zora drove up Columbia, turned right on Fifth Avenue, then pulled into the multi-level parking structure directly behind police headquarters. The home of Seattle's finest was located in an uninspiring ten story building on the corner of Fifth and James. The Municipal Court was next door, the Correctional Facility across the street.

Zora parked the car, walked inside, and collected a visitor's pass from an old timer manning the security desk. She then rode the elevator to the seventh floor.

It seemed to take forever.

CHAPTER 30

1 April, 11:50 AM PDT
Seattle, Washington

AS THE ELEVATOR DOORS OPENED, Zora was greeted by the disarming smile of Detective Cloyd Steiger. She recognized him immediately from the photo that had run with the *Seattle Times* story. He was stocky, taller than she'd expected, with a bristly mustache, tufts of unruly white hair, and whimsical dark eyes that glinted with a sense of the absurd. He was dressed in a crewneck T-shirt, blue jeans, and brown loafers.

"Ms. Flynn," he said, in a big commanding voice. "Cloyd Steiger. If there's one thing this screwed-up old world of ours needs, it's more heroes. I'm truly honored to meet one of them."

"I appreciate that," Zora replied, stepping out of the elevator. She shook his meaty outstretched hand, thinking he wasn't the *Vanity Fair* type. She noticed a simple gold wedding band on his left ring finger.

Maybe his wife subscribed?

Steiger led her down a wide, carpeted corridor. Daylight poured through a wall of windows that looked out on the city. From here she could see the piers that jutted out into the blue expanse of the bay and beyond that, to the west, snow-covered mountain peaks. The homicide unit was a large, open area divided into several functional work spaces with identical government-issue desks and swivel chairs. Radios, files, three-ring binders, and other trappings of the police trade covered most of a communications desk in the center of the room. There were two flat-screen TV monitors suspended from the ceiling near the side and back walls. Both were blank.

The place was mostly deserted.

"Most of the guys took an early lunch," Steiger said, directing Zora to a chair that faced his cubbyhole. "Can I get you anything? Coffee, water?"

"Water would be great."

"You got it. Be right back."

Zora felt tense. She sat down, taking in her surroundings. The detective's desk appeared neat and organized. A couple of family photos were perched on one side, a large gold-embossed plaque on the other. The caption read: "The Proverbs According to Steiger." Zora couldn't help but smile as she scanned the list.

1 We will solve no crime before overtime.
2 The simplest explanation is the most likely.
3 Assume nothing.
4 The answer is always evidence.
5 Plea is a four-letter word.
6 Shit happens.
7 Everybody lies.

Steiger returned a few minutes later with a mug in one hand, a plastic bottle in the other. He handed Zora the water, sat down, and took a sip of coffee.

"Nice," she said, nodding toward the plaque.

"Yup, that about sums up three decades in this racket." Steiger set the mug on his desk and leaned back in his chair, fingers locked behind his neck. "It all comes down to those seven proverbs and a little sleight of hand, smoke and mirrors, if you will. See, I view my job as basically that of a glorified salesman peddling time shares at Walla Walla and other fine institutions in the Washington State penal system. That means convincing bad guys to say things they don't want to say … to someone they don't want to talk to … and do it voluntarily."

"From what I read in the paper you do okay."

"Yeah, I hold my own, I guess." And for the next fifteen minutes, the affable detective explained why. He also talked about his family – married thirty-one years to the same woman, two sons on the force, a third son in college studying, what else, Criminal Justice. He then expounded on some of his more unconventional interrogation techniques, like the time he tricked a murder suspect into identifying his victim. With a robust laugh he added, "Besides me and my partner, the goof was the only other person who knew her identity. Man, you should have seen the look on his face. Talk about your Master Card moment. It was priceless."

The more he talked, the more Zora was able to relax. The DA said she could trust this man and now she knew why. She stared at the detective, looking for answers on his face.

"Listen," Steiger said. "I thought it would be easier to meet here, parking and all, but this place will get real crowded real fast. Why don't we go grab some lunch? My treat."

"Sure, whatever works."

The First Hill Bar & Grill was located on the corner of Ninth and Madison, a short drive from the station house. Zora was only mildly surprised when Steiger rolled his Caprice onto the sidewalk, just steps from the front door. Parking in Seattle, he explained, was worse than Manhattan. Moments later, they strolled inside and grabbed a table near the back. Zora picked up her napkin and surveyed the room. There were several men sitting alone, none of whom seemed to fit the profile of a tail, whatever that was. The owner of the establishment, a plucky little terrier named Laurie, promptly arrived with menus and water.

Steiger gave her a big bear hug and ordered the special, souvlaki chicken with Greek salad.

Zora made it two. "So, how long have you known the DA?" she asked after Laurie left.

"Let's see, I met Scott Rosekrans about two years ago now. We helped him out on a couple of homicides up there in Jefferson County. He's a good man, plays by the rules even when the deck is stacked against him."

"And you don't," Zora said matter-of-factly.

Steiger feigned surprise. "Let's just say I've been known to wander off the reservation from time to time."

Zora laughed dryly. "Uh-huh, right. So when the DA talked about bringing in Seattle PD to investigate Katrina's murder, he meant *you*?"

"Guilty as charged."

"Okay, makes sense. What I'm having a tough time with, though, is why he gave me your number to begin with. I've been trying to figure that one out since last night."

"To tell you the truth, it caught me off guard too ... at first."

"What do you mean?"

"I knew why the call from the governor's office pissed him off, but it took me a little longer to figure out the other, the part about your mother and the killer whale, I mean."

Zora sat ramrod straight in her chair, eyes boring in on Steiger. "I'm not following you."

"Why don't we tackle 'em one at a time," he said, leaning in close. "Starting with that phone call to the DA."

Zora nodded.

"I don't suppose you've ever heard of SIU?"

"No, what's that?"

"Special Investigation Unit. A bunch of hacks who report directly to Governor Ryan." Steiger explained that the unit had been formed back in the early eighties to help hunt down Gary Ridgway, the so-called Green River Killer. Ridgway was convicted of murdering forty-nine women, mostly prostitutes and runaways, eventually confessing to nearly twice that many crimes."

"I remember reading about him," Zora said.

"Yeah, tough case," Steiger added, sipping on his water. "Took a huge task force of federal, state, and local cops over two decades to collar the guy. SIU didn't contribute a goddamn thing, but of course nabbed most of the credit. Governors have come and gone since then, but the unit is still around, probably hiding under some bogus counterterrorism façade."

"So who called the DA then?"

"The guy who runs the unit now, a hatchet man named Jake Towers. He spends most of his time digging up dirt on Ryan's political opponents, that or providing cover for his allies. I mean this guy blows smoke up his *own* ass. Anyway, he played the executive privilege card, something about the governor being a fan of the Kincaid woman. It's all bullshit."

"Why do you say that?"

"Ryan leans to the right of Attila the Hun. He'd probably go off and capture that killer whale of yours himself if he had the balls for it."

Zora looked at him sideways.

"That's the plan, right? To track down a whale?"

After a long pause, she replied, "Yes, that's the plan."

"And you didn't tell the DA."

"It's a felony, detective. To be honest it scares the hell out of me telling *you*."

"Fair enough. But here's the thing you need to know about Scott Rosekrans. He's been scorched by that grease-ball Towers before."

"How so?"

"Long story short, one of the governor's cronies lured a fifteen-year-old girl onto his sailboat over in Port Ludlow, tied her up, and raped her repeatedly over two days. The case was a lock until SIU reared its butt-ugly head. Then, poof, like magic, it all went away. Meanwhile the kid was all messed up, I mean real bad. She's been in and out of psychiatric hospitals ever since, going on three years now. Scott took it personal, can't say as I blame him."

"Me neither," Zora said with obvious contempt. "It's sick."

They sat silently as Laurie approached. She dropped off two heaping plates of food, topped off their water glasses, and quickly retreated to the kitchen. Steiger tore a hunk of chicken off the skewer, popped it into his mouth.

"Okay, so what about my mother and the orca?" Zora asked, eyeing him expectantly.

Steiger made a sour face. "Two words: Mitchell Chandler."

"What about him?" Zora asked, already going there in her own mind. She was certain Chandler was pulling all the strings, though so far she had no way of proving it. And even if she did, what good would it do? One wrong move could prove fatal for her mother.

"Let's just say he and I have a history, too." Steiger wiped the corners of his mouth with his napkin, took another bite of chicken. "It involves my ex-partner, guy by the name of Eddie Rice. We worked together for fifteen years. Damn good cop, last of a line, too. His father and four uncles were part of the brotherhood, true-blue believers every last one of them. And Eddie was the smartest of the bunch. He was really going places, would probably be chief by now if it wasn't for Chandler."

Steiger stopped, stared out the window. Zora sensed that beneath the gruff exterior this man had a heart of gold, that whatever happened with his former partner had shaped him more than anyone knew.

He continued. "Eddie loved playing golf. He attacked a course the way a tiger goes after a zebra. Two summers ago he signed up for the annual MDA charity event at his local club and by some fluke ended up in the same foursome as Chandler. Now you need to understand something about Eddie. He didn't pull punches with anybody, and he'd had some really bad dealings with this character in the past. So we're talking about a goddamn accident waiting to happen here."

Steiger then described what went down at the fifth hole, how Chandler had breached one of golf's time-honored rules of etiquette: the player with the best score has the "honor" of teeing off first at the next hole. "So Chandler hits out of turn and storms off down the fairway. By the time the others reach the green the idiot's already holed out. Well, Eddie rips him a new one, right? And what does Chandler do? He grabs a nine iron from his bag and shoves it right in my partner's face. Bad idea! Eddie was carrying heat. He pulls his pistol and shoots the club clean out of Chandler's hands."

Zora's jaw dropped. "That got his attention, I bet."

"Damn right. Back at the clubhouse, Chandler's fat-cat friends had a good laugh at his expense. But there were no grins the next day after Eddie landed in the hot seat. He was demoted to desk duty, a horseshit job in IA of all places."

"IA?"

"Internal Affairs, cops who investigate other cops. We call it the rat squad. Now I'm talking about a stand-up guy who had no use for those shit-for-brains bureaucrats, so that was a real boot in the ass. Chief back then said the decision had to do with a police brutality complaint, but we all knew the real story. Even the union played dead."

"What about your partner? How did he react?"

Steiger hesitated. Zora watched him do a slow burn.

"Like clipping the wings of an eagle. He was frustrated, pissed off, his self-esteem shot to hell. Jack and Coke became his best friends. He wouldn't talk to anybody, including me. His wife ended up throwing him out of the house, refused to let him see their eleven-year-old daughter. Eddie adored that kid. A week later we found him in this real shit hole of an apartment in Pioneer Square. Blew his brains out with his own service revolver."

Zora drew a quick breath as the face of her father flashed in front of her. "That's horrible. I'm really sorry."

Steiger's demeanor softened. Just a bit.

"Yeah, I've probably worked a thousand crime scenes and never had a single nightmare. All that changed when I found Eddie lying there in his own blood. I used to follow *him* through doors and there he was, eyes open, the light completely gone. Finest cop I ever knew and it ended like that. Damn shame. I should have done more. Tough to live with that."

Zora now understood why the DA had sent her to see this man. And she said so, adding, "But you can't blame yourself."

Steiger spoke slowly, deliberately. "Yeah...I'm working on it."

Yet even as they exchanged those words, Zora knew there was a false note here, knew she would never be able to forgive herself if something happened to her mother. She tried to process all this, but now was not the time. Instead, she found a way to shove it aside and recalibrate her focus. The answer to her next question she already knew. She asked it anyway. "So the governor and Chandler are tight then?"

"*Tight* would be an understatement," Steiger said. "Problem is, from where I sit there's not a shred of evidence linking Chandler to the Kincaid murder, or to the blackmail scheme involving your mother and the whale either. Which means there's no way to connect the dots. And SIU will make goddamn sure it stays that way."

"What if I told you there *was* some evidence."

Steiger tilted his head, cracked his knuckles. "You'd have my undivided attention."

Zora pulled a folded sheet of paper from her jacket pocket, handed it to Steiger like it was about to catch fire. He opened it slowly and mouthed the words, "Samson death imminent... Freeman evasive... cover-up!"

"Freeman's the General Manager at Chandler's Seattle park," Zora said.

"Yeah, I know the name. Where'd you get this?"

She told him.

"When was that?"

There was a long gap in the conversation as Zora reflected on what to say next. "Last night. The entry was made shortly before Katrina died."

Steiger thought about that, handed back the paper. "You obviously didn't tell this to the DA either, or he would have mentioned it to me on the phone."

Zora's mind raced. She thought about the antique stove and Katrina's running shoes, but decided to hold off revealing that information, at least for now. "It's that felony thing, remember, detective?"

Steiger did not respond. Zora took his silence as restrained consent.

"Okay, look," he said. "This information might not directly implicate Chandler, but there's no way any of this goes down without his say-so. There's something else here, too."

Zora felt her pulse quicken. "What's that?" she asked, leaning across the table.

"SIU might be able to cover up any physical evidence found at the crime scene, but Towers doesn't have his own geek squad to dig into the computer. For that he'll need the state crime lab and those young guns will find every file Ms. Kincaid ever created, saved, downloaded, sent, or even deleted, including the information on that sheet of paper you just showed me. If we're lucky, we might just stumble on a trail that *does* lead us to the promised land. Unfortunately, that could take some time."

"And *time* is a luxury I don't have, detective," Zora said emphatically. "I need to capture that whale in the next few days, or say goodbye to my mother. It's a choice I'd rather not have to make, but when you get right down to it, it's not really a choice at all, is it?"

"No, I guess not," Steiger replied.

They both went quiet. Zora looked away, feeling the tension build inside her.

He added, "Listen, I'll do everything I can to help, okay?"

She reached across the table, squeezed his hand. "I appreciate that, detective, I do. And I know your reputation, going off the reservation and all, but this is..." Her words trailed off.

Steiger held up a hand. "Look," he said. "I'm edging away from sixty, long past the time most cops retire. My record is clean, no skeletons in the closet, solid pension locked up. There's only one piece of unfinished business on my plate and that's avenging Eddie's death. Nothing would make me happier than knocking on Mitchell Chandler's door in the middle of the night with an arrest warrant, slapping on the bracelets, and then dragging him downtown in his goddamn skivvies. I'll make sure every TV station in town knows about it, too, so they can film the perp walk." He paused, a twisted grin on his face. "The icing on the asshole cake as it were. And that, as they say, is *that*. Now eat up. Best grub in town."

CHAPTER 31

HOUDINI CROUCHED BESIDE a giant stone arch, scanning the turbulent waters of Juan de Fuca Strait through a pair of powerful, range-finding Steiner binoculars. The ancient rock had been transformed by time and the relentless pounding of the sea into a towering work of art, its mass and sweep so severe it seemed to defy the laws of gravity. He closed his eyes, lowered the glasses, and breathed deeply of the invigorating ocean air. The rhythmic sound of the waves and a flock of screeching gulls combined to create a stirring soundtrack.

He had arrived at this sacred spot shortly after sunrise, the Old One's words still echoing in his ears: *Sometimes the answer is asking harder questions.* He'd been asking *himself* hard questions most of a sleepless night, but no answers had come, nothing that even hinted at why the mighty killer whales had returned. And thus far, his vigil had been a bust. No sign of the orcas. In fact, there wasn't much to see at all, save for the endless rolling gray swells. With the ban on all non-commercial vessels still in effect, traffic through the shipping lanes had been relatively light, limited to some large tankers, a few freighters, and a couple of cruise ships.

Houdini scanned the waters for another fifteen minutes, and decided to call it a day. He'd gathered up most of his gear when he heard the sound. It was faint at first but soon grew louder and stronger, a piercing, high-pitched tone that reminded him of a police siren. His pulse quickened. He raised the binoculars again and adjusted the focus, straining to see beyond the ranging distance of sixteen hundred meters. Anxious minutes passed before a mighty cloud of white mist exploded into the air. An instant later, there was a second blow, soon followed in quick succession by three more.

Set against a mist-shrouded sun, the powerful blasts created a stunning rainbow effect.

Then...the mighty whales appeared on the horizon.

Houdini had tried to visualize in his mind what that first image would be like, as any good photographer would do, yet the reality was beyond anything his imagination could comprehend. The creatures resembled giant gloss-black torpedoes and they were moving fast. *Really* fast. He watched in awe, unable to grasp the towering height of the dorsal fins, the sheer size of their bodies, or their mind-bending speed. A killer whale, he knew, typically traveled at five to six miles per hour, occasionally making a spectacular dash of up to thirty miles per hour when pursuing elusive prey. But these leviathans were moving at more than *twice* that top speed, faster even than the cheetah, the world's swiftest animal, land or sea.

It didn't seem possible.

Houdini had only seconds to capture this ultimate wild world thrill. He unzipped his sling pack, removed his Nikon D3X, and adjusted the 300mm lens. The high-end digital camera was designed for continuous shooting and he was about to test its limits.

Aim, focus, *click, click, click!*

Repeat – aim, focus, *click, click, click!*

His heart was beating so fast, he thought it would jump out of his chest. The wind suddenly picked up and shifted to the north, whipping fine needles of spray into his face. He buttoned his rain gear, pulled up the hood of his sweatshirt, and inched toward water's edge. The whales were closer now, no more than one hundred yards away, their cries and whistles so loud, the granite walls surrounding him seemed to vibrate.

Houdini raised the camera again and, as he took aim, something even more extraordinary happened. The creatures slowed their blistering pace and came to a sudden stop, sending a massive wave of water hurtling toward him. He dove for cover, barely avoiding the thundering crash. The ice-cold spray took his breath away.

He waited for a second mountainous wave to hit before repositioning himself. And what he saw next was glorious. The whales executed a stunning spy hop, their sleek heads bursting from the water, their mighty flippers thrusting back and forth like gigantic water wings. These were orcas all right, Houdini could see that clearly now, yet they did not bear the familiar markings: the great patches of white, the deep gray saddle behind the dorsal fin. These exquisitely streamlined creatures were black from head to tail – black as black velvet – with a diamond blaze of gold where the eye-patch would normally be.

The orcas hung there for several seconds, looking around as if to orient themselves. Houdini zoomed in, capturing one breathtaking image after another. He paused, his index finger poised above the shutter button. In that moment, he locked eyes with one of the creatures. It was only for an instant, but long enough. The whale seemed to acknowledge his presence.

Then, in one synchronized motion, they revved their mighty engines and dove beneath the surface, the water churning violently in their wake. Houdini watched after them, his body trembling with excitement. Only after the seas had calmed did he check his camera. He slid the mode switch to playback, shuttling back and forth between images. He could not believe what he was seeing, reminding him of just how powerful photographs could be – a few snatched seconds of time captured for *all* time. The creatures were now completely backlit by the sun, their shimmering black bodies rising majestically from the sea.

As he advanced through the photos, he recalled a quote he'd read once from Ansel Adams, "*Sometimes I get to places when God is ready to have someone click the shutter.*"

This was one of those times.

For the next several minutes there was no sign of the whales. The creatures remained hidden below dark, rolling waves. Houdini tucked the camera back inside his sling pack and lifted the binoculars still hanging from a cord around his neck. Nothing but deep gray. Then, off in the distance, he spotted several shotgun-blast blows. The whales were speeding for three barren rock islets that rose like jagged fortresses from the sea. He adjusted focus and quickly figured out why. The area was swarming with Steller sea lions, huge mammals, some of them ten feet long and weighing close to one thousand pounds.

In the wild, the hunted always know the hunter, and they were ready for all-out war.

Seconds later, a wall of white water erupted near a concentrated cluster of rocks. The giant predators soared to extraordinary heights then arched to one side, their backs curving down, down, down before crashing to the surface with extraordinary force.

It sounded like a volley of cannons going off.

A double breach. Impossible!

Now abreast in a single line, the whales closed in with frightening speed. They ran headlong into the terrified sea lions, hammering them with their giant tail flukes. Dozens of outmanned mammals went porpoising across the surface in a desperate effort to escape. Others huddled together, barking and snarling, exposed teeth slashing viciously at the monster orcas. They never had a chance. The water soon became a boiling cauldron of red as one sea lion after another was ripped apart, their still-squirming bodies turned into bite-sized chunks of flesh.

Houdini was overwhelmed by the sheer power and sudden fury of the attack. He'd seen transient killers target sea lions before, and the orcas always prevailed. But it had routinely taken them an hour or more to finish the job. This lopsided contest was over in less than five minutes, and other than a few bits of flesh left drifting on the water there was little evidence of the kill.

Then, as quickly as the whales had come, they were gone.

Houdini stood motionless for several minutes, waiting and watching, hoping for one more look. It wasn't to be. Finally, he gave up the search, unzipped his sling pack, and pulled out a waterproof pad. He then began scribbling notes like a madman.

Zora, meanwhile, was speeding northwest along Highway 104 heading back to Port Townsend. So far the ride back had been uneventful. There was no one on the ferry who looked even vaguely familiar, and she'd kept one eye in the rear view mirror just as she had on the drive over. The man in Sitka had explicitly warned her about talking to the cops, and she tried not to think about what would happen if she was being followed, or if one of Chandler's henchmen picked up the trail of the detective.

She turned her attention instead to the other key player in this bizarre cat and mouse game, the mysterious shaman known as Houdini. She'd left two more messages for him and still had not heard back. Reaching for her cell, Zora tried him again, willing him to pick up this time. She snapped upright in her seat when he did. "Houdini, this is Zora Flynn. I'm a commercial fisherman. I've been trying to get in touch with you since yesterday. I'm a friend of Katrina's and –"

"Yeah, I know who you are," he interrupted. "I've worked on a boat or two up your way. Sorry about not getting back to you. I took off on a canoeing trip last night, camped out in the deep woods near Cape Flattery. Cell phone reception is really crappy out there."

Zora had only heard the shaman speak a few cryptic words on his voicemail, and expected him to sound different in person. He didn't, and it was somehow comforting. The phrase "speak softly and carry a big stick" came to mind. She dreaded having to finish her thought, to tell him about Katrina's death, but of course she had no choice. He reacted, not unexpectedly, with a mixture of shock and anger. After a long silence, Zora told him what she knew, answered his questions as best she could, and filled him in on the blackmail scheme involving her mother. Then she went for broke, laying out the reasons why Katrina thought he would help – the injustices done to his people...the struggle with his own parents...and the possibility of freeing captive orcas around the world.

There was another long silence, after which Houdini said, "Katrina got it right, bless her heart, right up to the end. So tell me, what can I do?"

Zora had no idea how he'd respond, and breathed a sigh of relief. "Katrina mentioned something else too. She said you talk to orcas, that you see into their souls."

"Not exactly. Truth is, *they* see into *my* soul. Most people have a tough time with that."

"Well, I'm not most people," Zora said a bit more coarsely than she intended. "And believe me, I get it." She went on to describe an incident that had occurred during a run the previous fall in Alaska's Glacier Bay. Both generators had gone down in a thick fog, leaving the *Dawn Quixote* without radar and totally blind. "I knew we were in a shipping lane, but I had absolutely no idea which direction to go," she added. "We were helpless, totally without power. That's when a pod of orcas showed up, like messengers from beyond or something. So I followed their lead and you know what? Less than five minutes later, a giant ocean liner steamed by. If it hadn't been for those whales, my boat would've been crushed to kindling."

"I had a similar experience not too long ago," Houdini said. "Orcas are incredibly perceptive and smart as hell. But listen, I'm not all that surprised at what's going on here."

"Really?" Zora replied incredulously.

"Yeah, ever hear the phrase, 'Gone to Ohio?'"

"No, what's that?"

"Well, years ago, captive whales were often moved around, transferred from cold weather parks in the winter – like the one near Cleveland – and then returned in the spring. Nobody paid much attention to any of that, so if a whale became sick or too tough to handle, no big deal. Same when one of the animals died. It just got lost in the shuffle."

"Gone to Ohio," Zora said. "But I'm not sure what –"

"It's just that it's very different now," Houdini interjected. "The animal rights crowd monitors every park, so it's impossible to move the whales in or out without someone noticing. Seattle's no exception. What's going on with the whales there now, do you know?"

Zora tensed a bit, filled in the gaps of her conversation with Katrina, then told him about the research she and Mickey had done. She explained that Samson stadium had been closed for repairs, with no firm date given as to when it would reopen.

"PR spin," Houdini said. "An obvious cover-up. But at least it will keep the extreme activist element out of our hair. They're anti-establishment, for sure, but they operate much like the military. The generals send the troops where they can do the most good, or raise the most hell, depending. So, it's unlikely they'll be hanging around the park with the stadium shut down."

Zora recalled Katrina's words, about the terrible accident in Japan and how it would only take a single spark to ignite the debate on killer whales in captivity. She also thought about Houdini and the untenable position she'd be putting him in. Then, there was the money. Would it matter? She didn't think so, but still felt compelled to toss out a number. Again, his reaction was hardly unexpected.

"I appreciate the offer," Houdini said. "But this isn't about a paycheck. It's about doing the right thing – for Katrina, your mother, and the captive whales. Look, Zora, I know your reputation, okay? You shoot straight and play fair. That's all I ask, all me and my People have *ever* asked."

"Thank you for that," Zora replied. "So where do we go from here?"

"We want to stay away from the transients – they're too damn unpredictable – so we need to track down one of the resident pods." Houdini then gave Zora a quick tutorial on resident orcas in Puget Sound. They numbered about ninety, he said, and traveled in three separate communities, designated for identification purposes as J, K, and L. He added, "They spend roughly half their time foraging for food, so the most likely place to track down one of the pods is in a shallow inlet. I have some ideas, but we'll need a big boat, a *really* big boat. Five tons is a lot of animal."

"I've got that one covered," Zora said. "Delta seiner. Leasing it from a friend."

"Good call. What about your crew? How many?"

"Three. You'll like them, Houdini. They're flying down from Sitka, should be arriving in Port Angeles right about now in fact. Can you meet us there for breakfast tomorrow morning? We'll have a few hours in the afternoon to pull everything together...then we go."

"I'll have to juggle a few things around," he said, seemingly unfazed. "But I'll be ready."

Zora nodded to herself, quietly arranging the pieces of this bizarre puzzle in her head. "Great. I'll call you back with a time and place." Then she paused, adding, "Oh, one other thing."

"Yeah?"

"Bring your A game, Houdini. We're gonna need it."

CHAPTER 32

1 April, 4:30 PM PDT
Port Townsend, Washington

AFTER CLICKING OFF, Zora attempted to reach Mickey a couple of times, but he didn't pick up. He had offered his guest room again and she'd accepted, maybe a bit too quickly. Even so, she was thinking how good it would be to see him once more, even under these dreadful circumstances. Check that, *especially* under these dreadful circumstances. But first, she wanted to buy him dinner, see how he was doing, update him on her conversations with the detective and shaman. When he didn't answer on the third try, she drove to the town's library, another historic old treasure built not long after the Courthouse in the late 19th Century. Located in the Uptown area, it featured the simple, classical design favored by its benefactor, philanthropist Andrew Carnegie – one of more than 2,500 similar gems built with his considerable fortune.

Stepping inside, she felt as if she'd just entered a time capsule. The crowded shelves and musty smell of old books reminded her of the regular trips she'd made with her mother into the small town library near their Idaho home. She would give anything now to be that kid again. Making her way up the stairs to the second floor, she was directed to the Maritime section and soon found herself filtering through every book she could find on Delta seiners. The vessel was indeed a tough customer. With its powerful diesel engine and a fish hold capable of handling up to 50,000 pounds, the boat could easily accommodate a five-ton killer whale on deck.

Now all she had to do was go out and capture one.

Shortly before closing, Zora packed up her things and left the library. She then strolled down the block toward Sweet Laurette's, a charming French bistro she'd just discovered online. The reviews were excellent, boasting of locally grown, organic food prepared from scratch. As she crossed the street, she kept an observant eye on her surroundings. There was a fine mist in the air, making it feel colder than it was. She surveyed the parked cars and scanned the mostly deserted streets. No one suspicious. Zora had only picked at her lunch and wasn't all that hungry now, but knew she needed to keep her strength up. If these past few days were any indication, the days ahead would be positively brutal. After grabbing a table near the back, she ordered grilled Alaskan salmon and a glass of Chardonnay. The wine had a crisp, clean taste and she finally began to unwind a bit.

Reflecting back on the day, it had been a good one, all in all. The shaman, at least from what she could pick up over the phone, was smart, level-headed, and surprisingly down-to-earth. And the detective was solid as granite. Who better than an unconventional cop named Cloyd to exact justice? Of course, justice was hardly guaranteed when dealing with the likes of Mitchell Chandler – a man with unlimited resources and an army of high-priced lawyers at his disposal.

Precisely why I need a backup plan.

At the moment, however, Zora had no idea what that plan would be. After much thought, she ended up long on questions and short on answers. Then dinner arrived. It looked and smelled almost too good to eat, but eat she did, savoring every bite.

Less than an hour later, she was back in her car. Still no sign of any suspicious characters. After a short drive, she turned right off Hastings Avenue and headed west on Cape George Road. It was now eight thirty. The sun had set, and she wasn't sure she could find Mickey's place in the dark. The house was tucked into a secluded wedge of land down a long dirt road near Discovery Bay. At least that much she remembered. She slowed as the winding road turned sharply south, an area that now seemed oddly familiar.

Did I travel this stretch when I left early this morning?

The next two-track road looked familiar and she took it. Moments later she happened upon Mickey's place, more from sheer luck than any innate navigational skills. She saw no sign of his truck and the house was dark except for a night light burning in the foyer. A curve of moon provided the only other illumination, bathing the area in an eerie blue-white glow. She pulled onto the asphalt siding next to the driveway and stepped out of the car, bracing herself against gusty winds that rattled around, making the giant fir trees appear to come alive. Walking to the front door, she reached inside her leather bag, fumbling for the spare key Mickey had given her. The temperature had dropped and her breath fogged the air as she looked down.

Then movement…a blur of motion…and powerful arms around her chest.

An instant later, she was dragged to the side of the garage, the cold steel of a pistol pressed firmly to her temple. She froze at the click of the hammer.

"Don't move and don't turn around," the man said.

"Who are you, what do you want?" Zora snapped.

"The *who* is none of your concern," he said. "The *what* is easy. I need to know the nature of your discussion with the cop in Seattle. So happens I was there during your little luncheon get-together. On the other side of the room. You were probably looking for someone a bit younger, a goon the size of an armoire maybe?"

Zora closed her eyes, flashed back on the lunch crowd, but the faces all blended together. Her next thought was to retaliate. The man stood directly behind her at six o'clock. She thought about spinning around and unleashing a kick to the groin, maybe the knee. Yes, the knee, that intricate web of ligaments, muscles, and tendons most susceptible to a swift, direct strike. But even if she did gain the upper hand, it wouldn't change anything. Her mother would still be in grave danger. Instead, she tried to breathe normally and go along.

The man loosened his hold a bit. "You were told not to go anywhere near the police, but obviously that warning did not register. So here's what happens now. I'm going to ask you some questions. Your job is to answer them. And don't even think about lying. If you do, believe me you'll regret it." He shoved her toward the garage.

Zora stumbled, nearly fell, regained her balance. "Jesus," she said. "Take it easy."

The man barely took a breath. "First question: what's the nature of your relationship with the Kincaid woman?"

This had better be good, she thought. *If I screw up Mother will pay with her life.*

Zora inhaled deeply and started at the beginning, telling him how she and Katrina had met, about their meeting, and the awful phone call from

Mickey a few hours later.

"Why go to her lab in the first place?" he asked.

"C'mon. You know goddamn *well* why."

A sudden shift…then an arced elbow to the ribs. It caught Zora totally by surprise. She buckled over, fighting off the fierce pain, her heart pumping furiously.

"Lose the fucking attitude," he said. "Now answer the question."

Zora winced, took a few moments to catch her breath. She could feel the man's probing eyes on the back of her head. "To talk about killer whales, what else?"

"And you said nothing about your little assignment?"

Zora hesitated. "No," she lied.

"Bullshit. Did your friend happen to mention a whale named Samson?"

There was no playbook here. Zora had only one choice: wing it. She lied again, this time without hesitating. "I don't know what you're talking about."

A long silence.

"The hell you don't," the man barked, breathing hard. He was so close to her now she could feel his body shift. "So after the brother calls, you meet him at the Courthouse. Then what?"

"Look, if you already know…"

This time Zora felt the gun at the base of her neck.

"Jesus, woman, you do *not* want to mess with me anymore. You got that?"

"Yeah, yeah," she snarled. "Then we drove to the funeral home, okay? The DA examined the body. He said he could tell from Katrina's wounds that she'd been murdered."

"Brilliant fucking deduction. And after that, you and the brother go to her house. Why?"

"His sister was *dead*. He wanted some answers."

"And you just happened to tag along? Now wasn't that convenient."

Zora remained silent, a slow rage burning through her.

"So you parked down the street, dodged a couple of cops, and started snooping around inside. What exactly did you find?"

Zora hesitated again then quickly decided to give the man another dose of truth serum. She told him about finding Katrina's running shoes…about Mickey's theory that she'd been murdered right in her own home…that the killer had dressed her up in workout gear to cover up the crime.

"Well, now, Columbo would be right fucking proud of you two."

"You asked what we found. I told you."

"That's it? What about files, reports, things like that?"

He can't possibly know about the hidden computer files.

Time for the third big lie.

"No, we were afraid of getting busted. There were officers stationed right outside the front door, you just said so yourself."

"Look," the man said sarcastically. "My patience is running out here, so let's cut to the chase. Talk to me about the cop in Seattle."

Zora stiffened. To make her meeting with the detective seem even halfway plausible, she needed to buy some time, come up with something that made sense. She reverted back to the truth, how could she go wrong with that? "The DA didn't think the local sheriff could handle the case. He said he wanted to bring in a couple of experienced detectives from Seattle instead. Then someone called from the governor's office, and –"

The man cut her off. "Why would the DA tell *you* that?"

"I don't know. You'll have to ask him."

"The detective's name. What is it?"

"Steiger, Cloyd Steiger. I made a mental note of it at the time. He and the DA had worked together before."

"You know something, lady? I was born at night but not last night."

"It's the truth."

And once again it was the truth, more or less.

"Okay, so you call this detective out of the fucking blue?"

Think, Zora, think!

She felt a growing sense of panic, thought her knees were going to buckle. And then it came to her. "Look, I made up a story, okay? I told him a friend of mine was in serious trouble, that she was being harassed by her ex-husband, and that he'd threatened to kill her."

Lie number four, with number five waiting on deck.

"Let me guess. You didn't mention anything about your mother?"

"No."

Silence.

"And what did the detective say?"

"Exactly what I *thought* he would say. Cops hate domestic abuse cases.

They can talk to the guy, warn him to stay away, maybe issue a restraining order. That's about it."

A longer silence.

Then the voice turned ice-cold. "More bullshit. Your fucking stories don't add up, lady. You don't talk for damn near an hour about wife beaters."

"So shoot me," Zora hissed. And for one second, one fraction of a breath, she thought he would.

"You better believe I'm goddamn tempted, but that doesn't serve either of us now, does it? So here's what you do. You stand right where you are for the next sixty seconds. I mean, don't even blink an eye. Then, tomorrow, you go out and capture a killer whale, a *big* fucker. If you deviate at all from that plan, or if the Seattle cop surfaces again, I'll be back. *Count on it!*"

Then, like a silent rush of wind, her assailant was gone.

Zora snatched a glance of the man over her shoulder, quickly counted off the numbers, and found the key. When she stepped inside her hands were trembling, but her mind was more focused than ever.

I'll take down this son of a bitch and everyone else involved – if it's the last thing I ever do.

CHAPTER 33

2 April, 9:20 AM PDT
Port Townsend, Washington

AFTER ANOTHER RESTLESS NIGHT, it had been a busy morning. Zora left Mickey's place around eight-thirty after filling him in on her meeting with Detective Steiger and the phone conversation with Houdini. She didn't mention the frightening incident from the night before, thinking he had enough on his plate dealing with Katrina's arrangements. And he still hadn't tracked down his parents. Then, there was the phone call that had awakened her at the crack of dawn. She didn't tell Mickey about that either. It was the creep from Sitka with more information and the ultimate delivery destination for the captured whale.

Seattle came as no surprise.

But what the man said next surely did. He told her that since their meeting a few days earlier, there had been some "complications," that the job now involved disposing of a dead whale first...and *then* capturing his replacement. Zora knew Samson's death was imminent, yet oddly she hadn't even considered having to deal with his body. She was still reeling from that bombshell when she arrived in Port Angeles forty-five minutes later. By the time she met her crew at a downtown diner, however, she'd managed to calm down a bit.

Zora had called Houdini as promised and he showed up right on schedule. He was everything she expected him to be. The sun seemed to follow this man. He had a windburned face, cool, steady eyes, and a distinctive hawk-like nose. His shimmering black hair was loosely tied at the back of his neck. His dress matched his appearance – sweatshirt, sandals, and bleached jeans with holes in the knees. He wore a bright orange leather bracelet on his left wrist.

His manner was casual, yet direct.

Zora liked him right away. So did her crew. Huddled together in a small, private room off the main dining area, they ate and talked strategy. First mate Rico Lapenda had worked up a list of gear and special equipment that would be needed, dishing out assignments to the other crew members, Cassidy and McCabe. They would have less than four hours to pull everything together, assuming the local hardware stores carried all the goods. Lapenda was confident they did. Houdini then explained that he'd brought along a duffel bag full of paraphernalia, plus his most prized possession: a 13-foot carbon hulled kayak.

Satisfied with the plan, Zora left to meet Mack Bowen and take control of his seiner.

Shortly after 3:00 p.m., the *Northern Star* motored slowly away from the dock at Platypus Marine out past the jetty and into the Strait of Juan de Fuca. From there she steamed eastward through a low mist, long, gentle swells rolling beneath her hull. The boat was now on autopilot, the wheel moving itself, the bow of the powerful steel-hulled vessel smoothly parting the chop. The skies were overcast with gentle winds blowing offshore from the northwest. It was forty-eight degrees. The fog bank reduced visibility to less than a quarter mile.

Zora stood at the helm, sipping green tea, thinking the conditions were ideal for a mission best carried out as covertly as possible. She stared mindlessly into the void, barely able to distinguish between sea and sky. She could feel the smooth chug of the engine and opened up to ten knots, top speed for this 550 HP workhorse. The current was flowing with them and if it continued to hold, they'd reach their destination before midnight.

Every now and then, she glanced at the computer. There was little radio chatter and no cruise ships, tankers, or freighters in the vicinity. She thought that odd, not at all consistent with one of the busiest shipping lanes in the world. In fact, more than ten thousand vessels moved in and out of these waters annually. The heavy traffic spawned plenty of contentious debates between pro-nature and pro-commerce advocates.

Beauty versus the beast on a grand scale.

And the beast always wins.

Zora listened to the marine weather report which promised lighter winds to the south and a heavier layer of mist. She wondered if it was accurate. It would sure help if it was. As her hands played over the wheel, she angrily fought back tears, overcome by reflections of a young girl playing word games with her mother in front of the fireplace. The memory of those happy days in their small Idaho ranch house swept over her like the soft brush of a feather.

I will not let anything happen to her. I...will...not!

A short time later Houdini stepped through the wheelhouse door. As expected, he'd meshed well with the rest of the crew and for that she felt thankful. On this run there was simply no margin for error. Everyone must pull together as a unit.

"Fair winds and following seas, captain," he said.

Zora nodded. Indeed the weather gods seemed to be rolling right along with them. Even Point Wilson north of Port Townsend remained relatively calm. Normally, it was a place where winds, currents, and tides conspired to create the kind of hellish conditions area fishermen called *bad, real bad, or awful.* "So what's going on down below?" she asked.

Houdini flashed his megawatt smile. "McCabe's quite the cook. Pea soup, meat loaf, broccoli, and mashed potatoes topped off with a cherry cobbler. Good stuff."

Zora wasn't hungry and had passed on the hearty meal. "Now, let me guess, they're watching *Fargo* for the forty-ninth time." Movies broke up the grinding discipline aboard shipboard life, and she knew the black comedy was Cassidy's favorite film.

"Yup," Houdini said, smiling. "Listen, I spent some time with Lapenda before dinner. Interesting guy."

"Yeah, they call him, 'The Professor.' He's got a wild imagination, devours books like a kid eats candy. Classics mostly. Just don't ask him about Charles Dickens, though. I made that mistake once and he talked my ear off for an hour."

"I'll remember that," Houdini said, chuckling. "He's a good man. So are the others."

Zora nodded.

"Hey, is that your mother?" Houdini asked, pointing to a framed photo sitting on the window sill. "She's beautiful. So much of her good looks in you." It was a simple statement of fact, with no other meaning implied.

"Thanks. It's my favorite picture of her. She was about thirty then. My aunt Bonnie used to say Mother was the sort of woman poets write about."

Houdini picked up the plain black frame, cupped it in his hands like a piece of fine china. "Well, she sure as hell nailed that one."

Indeed, Stella Flynn looked radiant, smiling out to the world, her long reddish-brown hair falling gently on strong shoulders. She was dressed in a flowing white peasant dress, gold necklace, and lace-up leather boots. Zora brought the photo with her on every run, usually kept it in a drawer next to her bunk.

This trip was different.

"Rico told me about her condition," Houdini said. "Must be really tough, seeing her gradually slip away from you like that."

"Yeah, *really* tough. Every time we talk, another part of me gets ripped to pieces. I keep trying though, grabbing onto whatever bit of hope I can find. She was so vital, you know? I guess that's the saddest part. I'm telling you that woman could run whitewater rapids with the best of 'em. Class *five* rapids, Houdini. Pure adrenaline rush. Anyway, on good days she sometimes remembers things. I see a flash of recognition there. And you know what? Twenty years falls from her face when she smiles that dazzling smile of hers." Zora paused, lowered her eyes. "But most of the time, she's mired in a thick fog, with no idea what's going on."

"I'm sorry," Houdini said, handing back the photo. "Listen, we'll make this work, okay? I promise."

Zora sighed, thinking it *had* to work. She checked the computer again. It was set on three mile range and this time the vessel monitoring system picked up some activity. Crossing the shipping lane could be dangerous, even deadly, and she would be careful not to make that mistake. She sat down, then turned to Houdini. "Let's go over your game plan again, okay? To be honest I've been a little preoccupied since breakfast. Mack had second thoughts, nearly backed out on me."

"No problem," Houdini said. "So here's the deal. We give Samson a proper send-off to the other side, then head up to Whidbey Island, a place called Penn Cove."

"Penn Cove. Why does that ring a bell?"

"Ever hear of Ted Griffin and Don Goldsberry?"

Zora confirmed this with a nod. "Yeah, but I don't know much about them."

Houdini filled her in on the history of the two men, then provided details of the debacle that made them famous, or rather infamous. It was the summer of 1970. Griffin and Goldsberry had brought together a small army of whalers in the Cove. Using boats, helicopters, and explosive devices, they chased dozens of orcas to the point of exhaustion inside three acres of purse seine nets. Several whales were eventually corralled with long gaffs used to slip ropes over their fins. "It took several days to finish the job," Houdini added. "The locals said that at night the squeals and splashing flukes could be heard for miles. Rumor had it that the tavern cat at Captain Whidbey Inn became so freaked out, he went berserk."

"No kidding," Zora said. "How many whales?"

"Nobody knew at the time. Griffin later said there were over ninety."

Zora was now shivering with rage. "Ninety. Holy shit!"

"There was no shortage of buyers, either, mostly looking for weaned juveniles. Easier to train and posed less risk during transportation." Houdini went on to explain that, by the end of the week, Griffin and Goldsberry had sold seven young orcas, pocketing big bucks in the process. During the capture, however, four whales had become tangled in the nets and drowned. Two months later, their bodies washed ashore and the scam was exposed. "After that, Goldsberry went solo, played a cat and mouse game with reporters for years, but eventually copped to what he'd done."

"What about the captured whales?" Zora asked.

"Only Lolita is alive, still being held prisoner in a small tank at the Miami Seaquarium. Whale lovers have tried for years to get her released, but so far no luck."

"It's criminal," Zora said. "Absolutely criminal."

"Yup. And for decades after that disaster, the whales stayed away. That all changed a few years ago when the salmon runs further north became hit and miss. The residents started coming back again, mostly in the spring. They much prefer their Chinook, but sometimes feed on the clams and mussels around here. Best in the world."

Zora shook her head. "Well, here's to not scaring them off for *another* forty years."

CHAPTER 34

3 April, 12:10 AM PDT
Seattle, Washington

THE REMAINDER OF THE TRIP went smoothly. Kingdom of the Sea Oceanarium was located on Puget Sound in northwest Seattle, and the *Northern Star* arrived right on schedule. Zora throttled back to three knots and skillfully steered the boat into a narrow, man-made channel that dead-ended at a small wooden dock just off Puget Sound. Using the bulbous bow thrusters, she eased the vessel in sideways and gently made contact with the tyre fenders. Five minutes later, she stepped off the boat, Houdini at her side. She looked warily at the man standing on the dock, a man she instantly recognized from her meeting in Sitka. She still did not know his name, but given his role in all this, Sewer Rat seemed to work just fine.

Zora threw him a withering look. "Jesus, they left *you* in charge? Where's the GM?"

"I'm afraid my colleague is indisposed at the moment."

"My lucky day," Zora said.

The man smiled, but did not respond.

Straight ahead, Zora could see two massive panels of black tarpaulin, ten feet high and set thirty feet apart, panels that ran from the channel to a large prefabricated metal building. It was a distance of about fifty yards, most of it uphill. A pair of heavily armed guards stood watch at the entrance. As Zora, Houdini, and Sewer Rat approached, one of the guards stepped forward smartly, slid open a pair of heavy steel doors.

Zora shivered when she stepped inside. The structure was refrigerated by a portable, industrial-strength cooling unit. Samson's bloated carcass lay on a sweep of thick plastic sheeting and despite the freezing temperature the smell of decomposing whale was nauseating. Sewer Rat explained that the body had been moved earlier in the day from an enclosed sea-pen.

"He's all yours, captain," he said.

Zora looked at Houdini. He clenched his teeth, pivoted on his heels, and stalked off.

"So when might we expect our new arrival?" Sewer Rat asked. "My people are rather anxious to know the details. Here, take a look, the arrangements have all been made." He stepped to the near wall, lifted a blind covering one of the windows. "Hard to make out in the dark, but that sea-pen I mentioned a moment ago is just down the hill. That's where your captured whale will be housed and trained."

Zora cut him dead, her eyes on fire.

Trained, my ass!

She then stormed outside, hustled to catch up with Houdini, and to-gether they retraced their steps back to the *Northern Star.*

Lapenda had rigged the boat's hydraulic power block with a special pulley and heavy, industrial-gauge rope. Houdini, Cassidy, and McCabe hauled out a padded rubber harness, pulled it up the hill, and tied it to Samson's peduncle just forward of his flukes. The big animal was then gently towed out of the building, down the incline, and dragged into channel waters. Despite the thick padding, the rope still bit deeply into the whale's rotting flesh.

It's got to hold, Zora thought. *It has to.*

Ten minutes later, the powerful seiner pulled away from the dock and eased her way back into Puget Sound. Three hours after that, shortly before five o'clock in the morning, Zora steamed into view of Whidbey Island some thirty miles north of Seattle. She slowed the boat, and the rope attached to Samson's body went slack. A cool mist settled over the water as the crew dropped anchor. Zora then stepped out of the wheelhouse, signaled Lapenda, Cassidy, and McCabe to go below, and joined the shaman on the aft deck.

Houdini was dressed in traditional Makah regalia – feather-soft red cloak woven from cedar bark, cedar braided bands on his forehead and arms, deer-hoof bracelets on his ankles. A soft white ermine pelt swung loosely from a colorful headpiece, his long braided hair falling to the middle of his back. In his left hand he held a small rattle.

"Thank you for your life and the gifts you have given," Houdini said, slowly shaking the rattle. "Your time on this earth was far too short, made intolerable by conditions no animal should ever have to endure. You were stolen from the sea, deprived of your independence, and denied the most precious thing in your world – your family." Tears welled up in Houdini's eyes. Zora could tell the words were now coming with great difficulty as the ritual continued. "For that, and many other indignities, I apologize. And I humbly ask you to forgive man, for he does not realize the destructiveness of his ways. I wish you well and bless you on your next journey. Go in peace, great orca, and may you enjoy your new-found freedom."

Zora fought off a wave of emotion as Houdini leaned down, grabbed a nine-inch fillet knife from the deck, and cleanly sliced the rope attached to Samson's tail flukes. Just then the wind shifted to the south, lifting the fog, and unleashing a million dazzling stars. More stars than she had ever seen, shining white and all-knowing in the black sky. An instant later, a flaming red meteor streaked across the horizon in a spectacular show of celestial might. The seas went flat calm. With a profound sense of sadness, Zora and Houdini watched the mighty whale slowly drift away from the boat and disappear beneath the surface, finally at peace in his natural home.

Bloated carcasses float, Zora thought. *Yet this one did not.*

They stood side by side in silence for several long moments. Then Zora returned to the wheelhouse. She set the vessel on a northerly course at seven knots, barely avoiding a giant wedge of driftwood bobbing up and down like a prehistoric crocodile. As the boat passed between Camano and Whidbey Islands, the wind picked up again, making a whistling sound as it whipped through the riggings. The seas began to churn.

But as the sky blushed with the first streaks of dawn, the *Northern Star* slipped out of the chop and inside Penn Cove, sheltered by the rain shadow of the Olympics. From here, Zora could see the lights from the small waterfront community of Coupeville twinkling in the distance. She'd visited there once, remembered it as a quaint little town that billed itself as "a Mecca for artists and artisans of all stripes." And now she could practically hear the whispers of the old timers talking about the merciless capture of 1970 as if it had happened only yesterday, hoping she would not be the cause of even more grief.

Just minutes after the crew dropped anchor, a dense fog began drifting over the shore and soon the boat was draped in primeval mist, like the icy fingers of some malevolent, unseen force. But was it a force for good...or evil?

Zora would know soon enough. For here they would wait until dark.

Wait for the killer whales.

CHAPTER 35

3 April, 5:00 PM PDT
Kingdom of the Sea Oceanarium, Seattle, Washington

COLBY FREEMAN WALKED down a narrow concrete tunnel that led directly from his office into Samson Stadium. The magnificent whale that had brought so much joy to so many, had been gone for nearly eighteen hours now and Freeman still felt sick about his death. He'd watched from a safe distance as Preston Tradd had capably handled the removal of the body, thinking it foolish to risk a face-to-face encounter with the boat captain.

Standing silently at the entrance, Freeman wavered slightly, leaning back against a concrete pillar to keep his balance. His eyes were bloodshot from lack of sleep and nervous tension. Still, he couldn't help but feel humbled by this marvel of corporate ingenuity. In addition to the 6,500 bleacher-style seats, there were five deep-blue pools filled with eight million gallons of specially treated seawater. The "main stage" tank was comparable in size to a hockey rink, though curved on one side rather than rectangular. The depth was thirty-six feet. The two "backstage" pools where the whales actually lived were smaller and less than twenty feet deep. The other tanks – smaller still – were used for primarily for animal husbandry procedures.

A fifty-foot-square LED screen on the far side of the main pool loomed over a wide concrete "beach." During shows, the multi-million-dollar electronic marvel came alive, every dazzling move of the whales exploding in a riotous display of colors and nonstop action. The spectacle was accompanied by a masterful music score from an Oscar-winning composer, providing meaning and emotion to the motion. It was all carefully orchestrated, nothing left to chance.

But now the big screen – like the rest of the stadium – was blank, foreboding, silent.

Freeman heard a shuffling noise, glanced over his shoulder, and greeted Samson's trainer, Leanne Bucaro. She wore jeans and a silk blouse. There was no need for a jacket. The temperature had ticked up over the past hour, part of a strange weather pattern that had settled back over the Sound. They sat on the bleachers a few rows up from water's edge, a section known as the "splash zone." The final show of the day would normally be starting about now, filling these same seats with kids of all ages, eager to be drenched by the acrobatic killer whales.

Not today. This area too was empty and eerily quiet.

Humans were genetically engineered to fear the unknown, Freeman had once read, and that instinct – the crawling dread of things unseen – was tugging at him now. The past six days had been stressful as hell, leaving him feeling like the sole survivor of a ship wreck. But he did find some consolation in the masterful cover-up of Samson's death. Thanks to his shrewd penmanship, most of the world, including the media, believed the big orca was happily at play in the enclosed sea-pen adjacent to the park, or as happy as any captive animal could be. Only a handful of people knew Samson was no longer there, fewer still that he was dead. And a team of heavily armed Black Stallion guards remained behind to make sure it stayed that way.

There was nothing remotely consoling, however, about the tragedy that had befallen Katrina Kincaid. Accidental or not, it was stupid and senseless, and he, Colby Freeman, was an accomplice in that. How could things that had seemed so right just three weeks ago have gone so terribly wrong? He knew Katrina's death had left Leanne shaken and scared, that she was going along to get along because of her daughter's illness. It was only a matter of time before she came unglued and exposed the entire charade. Those thoughts he kept to himself.

Freeman slid forward on the bench, elbows resting on his knees, and turned to her. "Listen, Leanne, I'm really sorry about your friend, Dr. Kincaid. I know you two were like sisters."

"Yeah, I've got a hole in my heart the size of Texas. Miss her like crazy already."

"Well, look, if there's anything I can do, you let me know, okay?" Freeman thought about asking how Leanne's daughter was doing, but decided it best to avoid yet another delicate topic.

Instead, they sat side by side in silence.

Then... footsteps.

Mitchell Chandler's footsteps.

"Ms. Bucaro," Chandler said, taking a seat on the opposite side of her. "I appreciate you coming. Thought it might be nice to meet outside, enjoy this great weather."

Leanne nodded, fiddled with a pen she was holding, her head down.

"I know Dr. Kincaid's death is very upsetting," he added, patting her gently on the arm like a doting father. "It's been a shock to all of us, of course. But rest assured we're doing everything we can to help find the person responsible."

"That would be good, sir."

Leanne's eyes, Freeman observed, were darting about like a trapped animal looking for an escape. He couldn't help but think of the irony in that, or the fact that he shared the exact same feelings. If Chandler noticed, he didn't let on.

"Listen," Chandler said. "I've only got a few minutes, so let me start by stating the obvious. We have one core product at KOS and his name is Samson. He's our logo, our mascot, our trademark, the magic bullet that pulls everything together. But there's a much bigger picture to consider here. These parks are just plain good for business. Now, admittedly, we catch a lot of flak over our pricing – seventy-five bucks for an adult ticket on top of fifteen bucks to park. It's a lot of bread. And you know how I respond to that criticism, Ms. Bucaro?"

Leanne shook her head.

"I say, okay, maybe the price of admission *is* a little steep, but we sure as hell keep the riff-raff out, don't we? And isn't it true you get what you pay for? Besides who else caters to the educated and affluent audience anymore. Where can a nice, white suburban family go these days without feeling like they're a minority? Right here, that's where. The only way we keep this machine humming is to sell people's dreams back to them. Does that make sense?"

Leanne nodded this time.

Freeman stared off at the crowds milling about beyond the fenced-in stadium, crowds that continued to shrink by the day. He suddenly felt like the concrete walls around him were closing in, every cell in his body screaming to get out of there. But of course he could not. And he knew what was coming next, thought Leanne probably did too, but they both listened with virgin ears.

Chandler continued. "It's all about image. And every message we send supports and enhances that image. Lose it and you don't get it back. By associating Chandler Global Enterprises with animals and kids, not to mention the environment and family entertainment, it shows that we're socially responsible, that we have a heart, that we're *green*. This is my ace in the hole when the regulators start sniffing around at some of our other operations, those that might be considered, well, *less* nature oriented. Am I making myself clear, Leanne?"

In fact, Freeman thought, peel back the layers and this corporate-wide view of nature was worth billions in tax breaks and deregulation. Of course he would never say that to Chandler...and didn't.

Leanne replied, "Yes, sir." Then, in a measured tone, she expressed some of her own views, about educating the public on the uniqueness and importance of orcas; about the need for intimate study, that observations in the wild were not enough; that it was critical to understand how the whales reproduced, to learn what worked and what didn't work with breeding programs.

Freeman jumped in. "So unlike your friend, Dr. Kincaid, you see captivity as crucial to the whales' survival."

A tear welled up in Leanne's eye. "Katrina is...*was* brilliant," she said, correcting herself. "We both agreed that when kids learn about nature and the outdoors they learn about themselves. And that's the bottom line here. We just differed on the approach, that's all. But I certainly respected her opinion."

"I'm sure the feeling was mutual," Chandler said, his tone somewhat condescending. "Now tell me, Ms. Bucaro, what kind of time are we looking at to train our new whale? Colby here says two to three weeks. Do you agree?"

"Yeah, pretty much. It depends on several factors, though. Size and temperament for starters. Like most animals, whales learn by watching and mimicking other whales, but we're talking about a whole new set of rules here. The brain anatomy of whales is as complex as our own, so they're incredibly intelligent. That's the good news. The truth is, I just don't know.

I mean we're obviously dealing with an adult whale. It might be impossible to gain his trust and without that, nothing else matters."

"I get that," Chandler said, his stare as unyielding as a cat's. "Look, this timeline seems reasonable, but I'd like to get a better handle on what all's involved here. Why don't you run me through the basics?"

Leanne seemed a bit perplexed by the request. "Now?" she asked.

Freeman gave her a *yes-now* nod, thinking how long it had been since he'd seen any of the trainers in action himself, other than watching an occasional performance.

"Okay," she said. "First we make sure the whale is properly rewarded for desired behaviors." Leanne went down the list that included food, playing games, scratching their backs, adding, "But sometimes the best reward of all is a big old hug."

Chandler nodded for her to go on.

"The real magic happens with what's called the underwater cueing system. Essentially it's a series of computer codes based on calls recorded from killer whales in the wild. The whale responds to hand signals that correspond to a learned behavior, so eventually the tone becomes the stimulus for the behavior. When that happens, I stop using the hand signals altogether. What we're going for here is precision – it's everything – especially when you understand how complex some of these behaviors are, like getting the whale to leap completely out of the water."

Freeman added, "The breach is a show stopper, all right. Still gives me the chills every time I see it. Puts the *killer* back in killer whale, I like to say."

"I guess so," Leanne said, her voice sinking to a whisper. "Oh, and one other thing I can't stress enough. We need to make sure the audience doesn't think we're manipulating the whale, or trying to dominate him. That's really important."

"Agreed," Chandler noted, turning to Freeman. "Can we live with three more weeks?"

"Shouldn't be a problem, sir," Freeman said, with all the confidence he could muster. He'd spent the past few hours crafting a press release intended to squeeze out at least *two* more weeks.

After that all bets were off.

"Very well then," Chandler said, glancing at his watch. "Now before I go, Ms. Bucaro, let's be clear on one other thing. It is absolutely essential that you work alone here. Colby can provide all the tools you'll need, *except* additional people. Do you understand?"

"I do. I could use the help of at least one animal behaviorist, but I'll get it done."

Chandler stood, clamped his left hand firmly on Leanne's shoulder. "Good to have you on board. You'll find a sizeable bonus added to your next check. And another in three weeks, assuming our new whale is ready for prime time, of course."

"I appreciate that, sir. But this isn't about the money. It's –"

"*Everything* is about the money, young lady. Right, Colby?"

Freeman felt his blood freeze. "Yes, sir, I suppose it is."

CHAPTER 36

3 April, 8:35 PM PDT
Penn Cove, Washington

AS DARKNESS DESCENDED over the *Northern Star,* Houdini and Zora stepped out of the wheelhouse. They stood quietly side by side, listening to the sounds of night. Off the port bow, two seagulls announced their presence, dipping and slicing through the moist night air. Down below, a sea otter rushed by, checked out the vessel, and quickly moved on. The heavy patches of fog had begun to lift, giving way to a yellow-red sky that quickly faded to purple.

Soon it would be black.

And still, there was no sign of the whales.

It had been a long wait, more than fifteen hours now, and the tension was palpable. More time passed in silence, then Houdini cocked his head to one side, nodded to Zora. "Listen," he whispered. "Did you hear that? They're out there, they're coming. It's time."

An instant later, Houdini clambered down the steel ladder to the deck, alerted Lapenda, Cassidy, and McCabe to get busy in the hold. The men dragged Houdini's kayak on deck, lowered it carefully over the starboard side. He slipped inside, pushed off, and paddled effortlessly, moving body and boat through calm waters with smooth, easy strokes. It wasn't long before he lifted the oars and drifted to a stop. The sober stillness of night closed in around him, the only sound coming from water lapping against the hull of his boat. The air soon became thick again, a chilling patchwork of rain and mist. Somewhere, off in the distance, a foghorn blasted.

The wait was excruciating.

He wanted this over.

The thought of sentencing one more magnificent creature to a life of endless monotony tore at Houdini's gut. He lowered his head to his chin, drifted into a deep, meditative state, then began murmuring a prayer. "Oh Great Spirit, I humbly ask your forgiveness for what I am about to do, this unspeakable act of deception. May you grant me strength to see it through and, in your infinite wisdom, the courage to right this terrible wrong."

The great tribes of the Arctic and Northwest coast had many names for the mighty killer whale. Names the whales understood. Names the Old One had taught him to recite. Houdini repeated them now in a slow, rhythmic chant: "*Axlot... Agliuk... Polossatik... Skana... Mahk e-nuk... Qaqawun.*" As his words drifted across the still night air, two bald eagles swooped in from the north. They hovered directly above him, floating effortlessly on the wind, hardly a motion in their wings. Eagles, like wolves and orcas, were revered in Indian country.

It was a sign, Houdini thought. *Yes, a sign.*

The sacred chant went on for some time with little sound or movement. Then the waters became dead calm. The stirrings were faint at first, one animal, somewhere distant, vocalizing in two- or three-second riffs. Then, a second call, followed by a chorus of loud clicks, rising and falling in hypnotic patterns that were almost humanlike. Steady and repetitive.

Orcas!

The shaman caught a glimpse of what looked like a shadow in the mist. Moments later, a massive current of water rolled in. In its wake, no more than twenty yards away, a big black body emerged like a surfacing submarine. The whale spouted three times, floating there, watching him with penetrating dark eyes.

Houdini took a deep breath, allowing his mind to slip back through that familiar cottage door, if only for an instant, back to one of his most memorable encounters with the Old One. The great sage had spoken of fate and destiny that day, how they often appeared in the coincidences that weren't coincidental, how one thing could turn into another in order to reveal the wonder and mystery of life.

And what could possibly hold greater mystery than this?

The extraordinary encounter had barely registered when a second orca broke the surface, followed by a third, and then a fourth. Houdini soon found himself surrounded by the entire pod, whales everywhere, too many to count. Thirty? Forty? He couldn't tell for sure.

Yet, something was wrong. *Very* wrong!

Houdini could feel it, sense it. He should have known the whales would instinctively recognize they'd been lured into a trap. Within seconds, the kayak became a roller coaster. It was all he could do to hold on, his heart pounding so hard he could feel it in his throat. Houdini began paddling feverishly toward the big seiner. "*Light*," he shouted to Zora. "Throw me some light." She didn't hear him at first. He repeated the request, screaming louder this time.

"Hold on," she hollered back, reaching for the pistol-grip spotlight on the roof. Zora flipped the switch and flashed the beam on the boiling waters. The orcas were now circling the kayak in a synchronized ballet – breathing together, vocalizing together, their giant flukes moving rhythmically in a mesmerizing display of power and fury.

Houdini then shouted to McCabe. "Luke, haul out the net."

McCabe dashed to the stern of the vessel and jumped into the skiff, a powerful flat-hulled boat used to pull out and position the heavy seine net. Lapenda and Cassidy worked the winches and pulleys, lowering the craft into the water. McCabe quickly settled in, easing away from the mother ship in a sweeping clockwise motion, stretching the net between the two boats. Houdini and the large pod of whales were now contained by a fenced-in half-circle some fifty yards in diameter formed by the buoyed and weighted sides of the net.

The orcas began hammering the surface with their tail flukes, creating a riotous noise. Houdini knew they could crash through the polypropylene nets with little effort, yet they seemed confused and made no attempt to escape. Plumes of mist exploded from every direction, accompanied by loud, piercing cries of distress. The sea foamed white as several orcas burst from the water, their backs impossibly arched, hanging in the hazy orange glow of the boat's spotlight. Seconds later, they crashed back to the surface in a series of thunderous claps that nearly swamped the kayak.

Now fearing for his life, Houdini paddled harder and quickly reached the perimeter of the net. He positioned the kayak parallel to the surface floats, then executed a tricky roll that propelled him out of the kayak and over the top of the net. The shock of icy water took his breath away. He felt like he'd been shot, a million raw nerve endings singing opera. *Swim! Swim! Swim!* Seconds later his head popped up just feet from the port bow of the boat. Cassidy and Lapenda hoisted him on board. He was shivering uncontrollably, his clothes as heavy as lead.

But there was no time to change. Not now.

"The gaff," Houdini shouted. "Where's the gaff?"

Lapenda pointed to the power block. "Over there."

Houdini grabbed the long wooden pole, adjusted the heavy nylon noose attached to the end, and leaned over the starboard gunwale. The water was now a boiling cauldron of fins and foam as the tightly bunched whales surfaced and dove in all directions. He cringed with every scream and click, wanted the madness to stop. "Zora," he shouted. "Bring the spot closer to the boat."

She adjusted the light.

Cassidy turned to Houdini. "How the hell do you tell them apart? They're like icebergs, right? Most of their bulk is underwater."

"It's not that tough, really. The males have much larger dorsal fins."

"Ten thousand cocksuckers!"

Houdini gazed stonily at him. "What the hell's that supposed to mean?"

"Nothin' man. This whole thing's a fucking crapshoot."

"Tell me something I don't know, Cassidy."

An instant later, one of whales broke away from the rest of the pod, pumping its tail up and down in an even, rhythmic pattern, propelling it closer to the stern of the boat.

"It's a bull," Houdini shouted. "A big one."

"Jesus," Lapenda gasped. "That tail's gotta be ten feet wide."

Houdini nodded and readied the gaff. The whale disappeared beneath the surface, but only for a moment. It then shot straight up next to the boat in a spectacular spyhop. For a long moment, the giant orca hung there, vertical in the water. Houdini lunged forward, slipping the lasso over the whale's rostrum. "Okay, boys, here we go. Give me everything you've got."

They pulled the rope taut, bracing for a violent reaction. Instead the orca dropped back to the surface and rolled onto its side, rocking slowly back and forth using its pectoral fins as stabilizers. Lapenda then made his move. He'd rigged the steel boom with two padded leather slings, each twenty-five feet long, "D" rings affixed to both ends. One end of each sling snapped into a hook supported by a heavy steel block. The other end of each sling hung loose. While Lapenda and Cassidy released the boom, Houdini signaled to McCabe.

He was still in the skiff.

McCabe revved up the boat's outboard engine, reversed direction, and gathered in the seine net. The other orcas, now released from their floating prison, slapped their tails mightily against the water and disappeared into the heavy mist. The whales had been trapped for less than ten minutes.

Back on the *Northern Star* Cassidy activated the power block. As he hauled in the seine net, Lapenda swung the heavy boom out over the starboard gunwale, lowering the dual slings into the choppy seas. Houdini handed off the gaff to Cassidy, then jumped overboard. He came up shivering, every muscle rigid, cold shooting through him again like tiny daggers.

"Where's the sling?" he shouted, shaking his head furiously. "I don't see it."

"Next to the whale," Lapenda yelled back. "Over this way."

Silence, then, "Okay, got it." Houdini clawed his way through the frigid black and grabbed hold of one of the slings. The animal was now floating motionless a few feet from the hull, puffing occasionally through its blowhole. Houdini dove beneath him, surfacing on the other side. He positioned the sling behind the whale's eye patch and just forward of its flippers. Even so, there was almost no movement. Next he pulled the hoisting block close, snapping the ring into the hook. He took a moment to catch his breath and yelled to Cassidy, "Okay, let him go."

Cassidy released the noose and lowered the gaff.

Houdini reached for the second sling and repeated the maneuver, this time wrapping it around the whale's mid-section just behind the dorsal fin. Again, he snapped the ring into the big hook.

Did I get it right? Were the lifting rings over the center of gravity? Would they hold?

Houdini then swam free of the big mammal, shouting to Lapenda. "Okay, bring him up slow...slow and easy. Try not to spook him."

Lapenda threw the winch in reverse wrenching the straps taut to the whale's body. Zora scrambled down the wheelhouse ladder and stepped in beside him, wrestling with the hoist cable to keep it from rubbing against the side of the boat and snapping. The twenty foot boom jerked and shuddered as they slowly lifted the orca from the inky waters. Its body had almost cleared the surface when the boom unexpectedly lurched hard to port.

"Jesus!" Zora shrieked.

Lapenda braced himself against the railing. "What the hell happened?"

Zora grabbed the line, looked closer. "The hoist," she shouted. "It's not spooling on the winch right. I don't know why...too dark to see."

Cassidy jumped in between Lapenda and Zora. There were now three pairs of gloved hands pulling on the hoist cable.

Another violent lurch.

Zora stiffened, grabbed hold of the railing. She could feel the heat from the cable, smell it.

The winch screeched as the whale dipped to a dangerous angle, its rostrum now angled down toward the sea. McCabe tied off the skiff and helped Houdini back on board.

Two more sets of hands.

"You okay?" Zora shouted.

"Yeah," Houdini said, shaking the water out of his hair. "What can I do?"

"Grab the...wait!" she yelled, as the cable suddenly jerked. "Rico, hold on a minute."

Lapenda jammed the winch into the stop position. For a long moment the whale hung there suspended in its sling, swinging slowly back and forth, five tons of raw power perilously close to breaking free.

Zora checked the line, noticed a burr. There wasn't much time. If one strand snapped the whole thing would unravel. "Go!" she shouted.

Again, Lapenda shoved the hoist in gear.

Again, the whale began to rise.

The winch screeched louder, the leather straps popping like fire crackers as they pulled tighter around the whale's massive body. But the cables held. Cassidy and McCabe then climbed down into the hold, hauled up a thick foam rubber mattress, and positioned it on the aft deck.

Several tense moments later the animal was lowered onto it.

The boat lurched and rolled under the shifting weight.

A loud scream!

McCabe was stretched out on the deck, clutching his left wrist and writhing in pain. The whale's thrashing fluke had sent him reeling against the capstan. Houdini crawled past the power block and over to the injured man.

"How bad is it?"

"It's crushed, man," McCabe shrieked. "Fucking burns like hell."

"You hurt anywhere else?"

"I'm not sure. C'mon let's get the hell out of here."

Houdini helped McCabe to his knees. They crab walked arm-in-arm toward the cabin, barely squeezing past the angry whale, now thrashing wildly on the deck.

"Shit," Zora screamed. "He's going to destroy the goddamn boat."

Houdini shouted back, "No, he's not. I'll talk to him."

She threw him a look, "Are you crazy?"

"No, trust me on this, Zora." Houdini took baby steps toward the big orca, softly chanting the sacred song he'd sung earlier. The thrashing subsided almost immediately, picked up for several seconds then stopped altogether. Looking into the whale's upturned eye Houdini was overcome with awe and a deep sense of sadness. Moving nearer to its rostrum he realized this was the same creature he had just encountered at sea, the first one to surface.

This time, however, there was no malice…only acceptance.

Houdini shifted slightly to his left, motioned for Zora to join him. She hesitated at first, then inched her way closer until she was standing an arm's length from the whale. She stroked him gently, tentatively, looked into its eye for a long moment, and turned back to Houdini. "I'll be damned. If I hadn't seen this myself, I wouldn't believe it."

Houdini nodded and smiled. Speaking in whispers, he said, "Thank you, mighty orca. We are honored by your sacrifice. And I vow before my ancient ancestors that I will stop at nothing to set you free." He then turned back to Zora. "Please, captain, do him the honor of repeating this sacred pledge."

Zora did, word for word.

The rest of the crew looked on in silence. They too seemed dumbfounded by what they'd just witnessed. For the next several minutes, Houdini didn't move. He barely breathed. Finally, he said to Lapenda. "Okay, let's get the blankets. We've got to keep him cool and wet."

A dozen heavy wool blankets had been stored on ice in the hold. The three men dragged them on deck while Zora helped McCabe into the wheelhouse. In the time it took her to splint his shattered wrist, most of the whale had been covered. Houdini then pulled the washdown hose through the access hole in the forward bulkhead and began pumping salt water over its body.

Thirty minutes later – after hauling Houdini's overturned kayak on board – the *Northern Star* was steaming her way south at nine knots through the swirling curtain of fog. The crew, tired to the point of delirium, knew they still had a long night ahead of them.

What they didn't know was that they had company.

CHAPTER 37

4 April, 4:20 AM PDT
Seattle, Washington

COLBY FREEMAN HAD left the office and gone home, soon after his meeting with Mitchell Chandler and Leanne Bucaro had ended the previous evening. He'd tried napping, but he was a bundle of nerves and sleep would not come. Then, around 2:00 a.m., Freeman had received a call from Preston Tradd, with the words he'd been waiting to hear. "The package will arrive in a couple of hours."

Returning to the office, Freeman decided to catch up on some work. Before his life had gone careening off the rails, he'd been developing several new marketing initiatives, most notably, one that would lengthen the average stay of each KOS visitor from six point two hours to nearly seven hours. The logic was simple: first and foremost, this was a place where people spent money, and more time in the park translated directly into increased spending, higher profits, and a bigger bonus.

Yes, he thought, *keeping the guests around longer was a very good thing.*

But try as he may, he found it impossible to concentrate. He felt like a punch-drunk fighter struggling to survive the final round, the burning sense of guilt over Katrina Kincaid's death and the thoroughly disagreeable business with the whales eating away at him like a cancer. He took a deep breath, stood up, and stretched. The muscles in his aching back were now screaming for relief that only sleep could bring. The loud jingle of his cell phone caused him to jump.

He picked up.

It was Preston Tradd calling again, this time from dockside.

The captured orca was just minutes away.

Freeman grabbed his coat, slipped out a side door, and walked around the back of Samson Stadium. The large arena sat high on a hill, providing a spectacular vantage point from which to view the entire park, an all-encompassing vision of marine nature at its best. He felt proud to be part of a safe, clean, family-oriented environment that placed science, conservation, and education above even the animal shows. Except, of course, for the star performer.

The thought of losing all this made him physically ill.

Freeman turned up his collar, unlocked a metal gate marked "Authorized Personnel Only," and followed a gravel path along the backside of the hill. There was a heavy mist in the air. It began to sprinkle rain. He then headed down the curved, graded slope.

The maintenance building that had temporarily housed Samson's body was on his left, the man-made channel off to his right. The sea-pen had been sliced out of a valuable spit of land that ran along Puget Sound adjacent to the park. The pen was covered by a domed, three-story clear-span structure made of stainless steel and heavy canvas. The pool itself was one hundred feet long, fifty feet wide, and sixteen feet deep with concrete walls. A hinged sluice gate on the west end of the pen controlled the flow of water in and out of the Sound.

Tradd was standing beside a truck-mounted crane that idled nearby, its stabilizing outriggers firmly planted on a patch of gravel road. The driver, a hulking former pro wrestler everybody called Rhino, had worked at the park since day one, his loyalty never in question. He'd successfully moved Samson under the cloak of darkness soon after the whale's death. And now he was being called into action again.

Freeman stopped, nodded toward the big crane, then said to a waiting Tradd, "Where's the boat?"

"She just called," Tradd replied. "Be here in a jiffy."

Straining to see through the thick soup, Freeman thought about how all this would play out. So many things could go wrong he'd lost count, yet the crazy scheme seemed to be working. Now came the really dicey part, transferring a wild, perfectly healthy killer whale to the same sea-pen Samson had recently vacated. As he juggled these things in his mind, the *Northern Star* steamed into view and dropped anchor in choppy waters about twenty-five yards offshore. Freeman could see the captured orca breathing laboriously on the aft of the vessel, yet the heavy layer of fog

offered ample cover. No one aboard that boat could possibly identify him
– God forbid it ever came to that.

The crew then removed the heavy, water-soaked blankets and made
preparations for the transfer.

Zora stepped slowly out of the wheelhouse, closed the door, and
leaned over the rail.

Inching closer to water's edge, Tradd shouted, "I see the trip was a re-
sounding success, captain."

"We've got your whale if that's what you mean."

"How big is he?"

"Big enough," Zora snapped. "Now I need to get him off here before
somebody gets killed."

Freeman signaled the crane operator, and the big engine roared to life.
He maneuvered the telescopic boom out over the sound until it hovered
about six feet above the deck. Lapenda and Cassidy connected the slings to
a hoisting hook, and moments later the whale was airborne. The huge
animal began swaying pendulously back and forth, its blunt face poking out
one end, its tail flukes the other. Several anxious minutes later, he was
lowered through an opening in the roof of the massive steel and canvas
enclosure. There was a collective sigh of relief when the sling went slack
and Rhino flashed the thumbs up sign.

Tradd turned back to the boat. "Nice doing business with you, captain."

Zora said nothing, disappeared back inside the wheelhouse.

Freeman winced at the sound of the door slamming, then he and
Tradd watched the Northern Star steam out of the narrow channel, turn
north into Puget Sound, and disappear again into the swirling mist. In that
same moment, the wind picked up, the rain stopped, and the sky began to
lighten with the first hint of dawn.

"So far, so good," Freeman said, his body beginning to relax a little.
"C'mon, Tradd, there's a viewing window on the far side of the enclosure.
Let's go have a look."

They moved cautiously along a wooden walkway that circled the perimeter of the sea-pen, and soon were peering through a small plastic
window that had been cut into the heavy fabric. The orca was circling at a
slow, relentless pace, its dorsal fin creating a smooth rolling swell.

Tradd leaned in. "Holy shit! I've never been this close to one of these damn things before. It's *huge*."

"Yeah, looks to be all of five tons," Freeman noted. "We'll give him a day or two to get acclimated to his new surroundings, then begin the training regimen. He'll adjust soon enough. There are social and biological issues that need to be addressed, but they aren't insurmountable."

"So, how long before you move him to the main stage?" Tradd asked.

"Three weeks, maybe a little less if all goes well."

"Wow! That fast, huh?"

Freeman sighed, a bone-weary look on his face. "I hope so. Look, I'm bushed. Why don't we call it a night?"

"Sure thing," Tradd replied. "I think I'll hang around for a few minutes, though, if that's all right with you. Maybe one day I can tell my two kids about all this."

Freeman thought about his own girls. "Okay, knock yourself out, Tradd."

"Thanks. I'll see you before I leave for the airport."

Freeman nodded and then walked off, retracing his steps along the dock and back up the path. The wind had shifted again, bringing with it more heavy fog. He shook off a cold shiver, yawned, and glanced at his watch. Going home to grab some shut-eye made no sense. He had a meeting scheduled with Leanne in less than three hours. The couch in his office would have to do.

As Freeman approached the top of the hill, a terrifying sound stopped him cold. It was followed by an earsplitting scream and hysterical cries, "Oh my God, oh my God, oh my God!" He spun around in time to see a mountainous wave sweep over Tradd, catapulting him against the canvas enclosure. He bounced off the shell like a circus performer shot from a cannon, his forward momentum launching him into the icy waters of the Sound.

Freeman paled, his knees buckled, and his entire body began to shake. He could not comprehend the messages his eyes were sending to his brain. There, less than two hundred feet away, a monstrous creature soared upward into the heavy mist, Tradd locked in its jaws. "Help me! Help me!" Tradd bellowed. "Oh, sweet Jesus, please help me!" For one brief, terrifying moment, man and beast hung there, suspended in midair, before crashing back to the surface. They hit with a thunderous boom that sounded like the roar of a giant avalanche...then disappeared into the depths.

An instant later, two guards came running over the berm of the hill, weapons drawn. They skidded to a stop, staring in wide-eyed disbelief. "What the hell..." the taller one gasped, a flash of fear streaking through his eyes. "Did you see the size of that goddamn thing?"

Freeman stood still as a statue, waves of nausea churning through his stomach. He was disoriented, his hands were shaking violently, and he could barely think. But he knew he must pull himself together, take charge of the situation. Walking purposefully toward the stunned guards, he shouted, "Listen, I'll deal with this. You two need to get out of here. Now! Do you understand?" His voice seemed distant somehow, like it was coming from some other person.

The guards didn't move at first, still paralyzed by the shock and horror of what they had just witnessed. Finally they looked at one another, did an about-face, and scrambled up the hill.

Freeman watched after them, disconnected from all sense of time and space. Seconds, maybe minutes passed, before he tentatively made his way back down to the spot where Tradd had been standing. He shuddered at the thought of retrieving the body, assuming there was anything *left* to retrieve.

Still, it seems like the good Christian thing to do.

Freeman's father was a non-practicing Jew, his mother, a devout Catholic who had dragged her son to mass twice a week as a kid. As an adult, he had never wavered from that routine and he could certainly use a touch of the Divine now. Stepping toward the water, an eerie quiet descended over everything, absolute, nerve-shattering quiet...and spooky as hell.

The first shock nearly stopped his heart – Tradd's legless, bloody torso popped to the surface, bobbing aimlessly on the water. "Good God!" Freeman gasped, the cold rush of air burning his throat and lungs like hellfire. His knees buckled. His stomach heaved. He felt lightheaded, thought for a second he would pass out.

Then the second shock – a gigantic dorsal fin, barely visible in the misty haze of the spotlights.

Before Freeman could move a muscle, a rush of water came crashing down with the force of a tidal wave. His next sensation was one of flight.

The impact sent him barreling head-first into the sea, wrapping him in the fiendish cold. Dizzy with fear, he clawed his way back to the surface, only to see the monster swimming full-bore toward him.

The speed was astonishing.

One hundred feet...fifty feet...then twenty-five.

Freeman gaped in horror, violent shivers coursing through his body. He said a silent prayer, held his breath, and waited for his life to flash before him.

It didn't...instead, the speeding beast veered right, heading on a collision course with the enclosed sea-pen. Its immense body then rocketed out of the raging waters like a ballistic missile, landing with earthquake intensity. Boom! The steel support trusses collapsed under the animal's enormous weight, causing the entire structure to implode. Chunks of debris came raining down from all directions at once. The screeching peel of twisted metal made a terrifying, unholy sound – and the pink, early morning sky became charged with electricity.

Amid the noise and chaos, Freeman managed to pull himself ashore, sickened by the acrid smell of smoke and smoldering canvas. An instant later, he caught flashes of the captured whale. Was he hallucinating? The giant creature had torn through the sluice gate, freeing its much smaller cousin from the rubble. Seconds later, they disappeared into the open sea. Then a second wall of water hit. Freeman felt a shock of cold, followed by a white hot explosion as it crashed down. His lungs screamed for air. His head felt like it had been crushed by a heavy stone. Stars exploded behind his eyes.

Sirens, he thought he heard sirens.

Then...nothing.

CHAPTER 38

4 April, 5:30 AM PDT
Kingdom of the Sea Oceanarium, Seattle, Washington

WITHIN MINUTES OF THE ATTACK, an awesome armada of emergency vehicles converged on the scene, light bars flashing, sirens howling. Police, fire, arson, and bomb squads were all there, followed by a parade of ambulances and a team of nervous-looking suits from the Department of Homeland Security. Next to arrive was the SWAT team. Then the K-9 unit, the bomb-sniffing dogs deployed to search the devastation for possible explosive devices. Finally, the stars and bars rolled in, led by the chief of police himself. A command post was immediately set up and a perimeter of yellow police tape cordoned off the entire area, banks of portable lights casting an eerie glow in the still lingering fog.

The place was pandemonium.

Cops were waving guns and shouting orders and heavy equipment was being hauled off trucks. The K-9 unit conducted a thorough search and only after officers declared the area free of explosives did the full contingent of emergency personnel move beyond the police line. In the middle of it all, the television vans showed up and soon the pink-hued morning sky was congested with media helicopters.

By 6:00 a.m. rumors were circulating that a Muslim extremist group based in British Columbia had orchestrated the attack. A reporter from *On the Scene*, a syndicated tabloid TV show, claimed the real target was the Space Needle, that KOS had been merely an elaborate decoy intended to distract the cops. The rumor had people all over Seattle in a panic, scrambling to get out of town before catastrophe struck. The mayor ordered all schools, businesses, and retail operations to close their doors. Even the airport shut down.

Detective Cloyd Steiger was informed by dispatch of the alleged terror plot as he rolled up to the chaotic scene, the first of his seven "Proverbs" spinning around in his mind: *We will solve no crime before overtime.* The investigation, interrogation of witnesses, and report writing could clock him as much as ten hours of OT. He flashed his creds to the officers at the outer perimeter and walked into a scene that reminded him of Dante's Inferno. It smelled of death and looked worse. He stood stoically for a long moment, surveying the floodlit carnage, barely able to hear himself think above the roar of the choppers.

The devastation was total and complete, the entire area rocked to its core. Steiger met briefly with his captain, received his marching orders, then proceeded down the hill toward the crime scene. As he moved past the administration building, he glanced at the police spokesperson setting up shop. He knew the drill. She was prepping for the first of what would surely be many press briefings, a job more about controlling information than disseminating it.

The machinery of spin is gearing up for an all-out media assault.

Nearing the water, Steiger could see a team of gloved-up crime scene techs going about their business, thoroughly and methodically, bagging and tagging as they went. They had fanned out from what appeared to be the torso of a body, making notes, taking measurements, checking the immediate area. A police photographer moved among both living and dead snapping photos.

The corpse, of course, was the responsibility of the body snatchers from the coroner's office. The detective's job was to work backward from the victim to the incident to the circumstances and finally, in the case of a homicide, to identifying the offender. At least that's the way it usually worked. But this case, Steiger knew, was hardly routine. He nodded at the other investigators, pulled a pair of latex gloves from his jacket pocket, and slipped them on. He then squatted down next to the torso. The victim had one arm, no legs, and eyes that were blank, bottomless, empty. Steiger gently closed the lids and lifted the man's chin, turning the head to one side. Deep gashes in the neck still oozed blood. His mouth was partially open, most of the teeth either gone or broken.

Hell of a way to go. I hope it was quick.

As Steiger stood up, he turned his back on a bracing wind and zipped his jacket. He was about to speak with one of the crime techs when another supervisor approached him from behind. He said he'd assigned two other detectives from the homicide unit as lead investigators. They were expected shortly. Steiger had no problem with that decision. During his long career, he had attended to countless scenes of violent death, each with its own particular kind of silence – and this one was especially unnerving.

Who needs this shit anyway!

Steiger called his partner, heading him off at the pass. He then headed back up the hill, his thoughts now shifting to Zora Flynn and their guarded conversation over lunch just three days earlier. He could not put his finger on exactly how her story tied to the turmoil surrounding him here, but he knew there had to be some kind of connection. As those thoughts swirled around in his head, he noticed an ambulance parked just beyond a vast pile of rubble. An EMT was attending to an injured man sitting inside the open back door, a man who looked ghostly pale, his eyes red and puffy. Even so, Steiger recognized him immediately.

Colby Freeman!

He seemed nervous and rattled, hardly the picture of confidence Steiger had observed on the KOS website. He'd checked it out immediately after his meeting with the boat captain – and came away impressed with Freeman's bio: business degree from Michigan State...family man...active in the local Kiwanis Club...big cheese in the theme park world. What light could he shed on this sordid affair?

As he approached the ambulance, Steiger flashed his badge, identified himself, and then asked, "You okay, Mr. Freeman?"

Freeman flinched, looked closely at the shield. "I'll live. What can I do for you, detective?"

"I'd like to ask you a few questions."

The EMT took a step back, turned to Steiger. "This man has suffered some serious trauma here. I need to get him to a hospital, stat."

Steiger's eyes lit up. "And *I* need a few minutes of his time."

"It's okay," Freeman said, his voice trembling. "I'm fine."

The EMT growled something incoherent, finished wrapping Freeman's wrist with an ace bandage, then disappeared around the side of the vehicle.

Steiger edged closer, tugged on his collar. "You know something, Mr. Freeman? I've worked double homicides, triple homicides, robbery, rape, and just about every other violent crime known to man. And I've never seen *anything* that compares to this. So why don't you tell me what the hell went down here?"

Freeman sighed. "To be honest with you, it's all kind of hazy. It happened so fast."

"Yeah, I hear that a lot, don't even write it into my reports anymore." Steiger reached into his pocket, pulled out a pad and pen. "Just do the best you can."

"Well, Samson Stadium is getting a complete makeover," Freeman said, his face dead-pan. "Bolder colors, better sight lines, a fresh new feel. Not to mention several state-of-the art safety devices. Anyway, see that big crater over there? Up until an hour or so ago it was a big steel and canvas structure that covered a large sea-pen – a home away from home for our star performer, Samson. We'd moved him there during the renovation. Anyway...my colleague had never seen an orca up close before, so we came outside, walked around to the viewing window."

"In the middle of the night?"

"We were working late. The project is running behind schedule and –"

Proverb number seven: Everybody lies.

"Okay, you and your colleague were working late. What happened next?"

"Samson was resting. In that state he slows down, becomes very quiet underwater, his dives highly irregular. It's how he sleeps."

Steiger scribbled a note. "Sleeping, you say?"

"Yes," Freeman replied, rubbing his temples. "Then everything went crazy." Over the next several minutes, Freeman described the terror he'd witnessed and experienced, pausing now and then to take a sip of bottled water. After he'd finished, he slumped against the side of the ambulance. "The size and power of those creatures...I'm telling you, detective, there just aren't any words."

"Yeah, so I've heard. Then what?"

"Well, I managed to scramble out of the water somehow. That's when I discovered my colleague over there, lying in that very spot. It was absolutely horrifying."

Steiger nodded. "I understand. Listen, does your colleague have a name?"

Freeman seemed paralyzed by the question. He looked off, continued to talk. "In hindsight, I suppose it was pretty stupid, right? I mean I knew he was a goner, no way *anybody* could've survived an attack like that. But in the heat of the moment, it never occurred to me that one of those creatures might come back. Obviously, I was wrong." He paused, sighing deeply again. "You know, detective, that structure was designed to withstand hurricane force winds. But look at it now, crushed like a piece of tinfoil."

"I can see that, Mr. Freeman," Steiger said, letting the other question slide for the moment "So what about that star performer of yours?"

"Samson? Why he escaped, of course."

"Escaped?"

"That's right. I still can't believe it."

"Well, now, isn't that convenient?" Steiger added, hiking an eyebrow. "Let's get back to that colleague of yours, okay? I need a name."

Freeman rallied a bit, sat up straight. "Oh, sorry, sure. It's Tradd, Preston Tradd. He works for a consulting firm we use here at the park from time to time."

"Which firm?"

"I'd rather not say."

"And why is that, sir?"

Now for the big one.

"It's confidential. I'm not at liberty to disclose anything beyond that right now."

"Listen, Mr. Freeman, we've got a dead guy down there. Deader than *hell*. And me and my colleagues need to figure out exactly what he was doing here, why he ended up in several pieces. So you might want to reconsider your answer."

"I'm sorry," Freeman said. "I think it best if I speak with our attorneys first."

"Then I'd be wasting my breath to ask about Dr. Katrina Kincaid?"

Freeman's face registered no reaction. "Yes, I heard about what happened to her. Another terrible tragedy. She'd been treating Samson, you know, doing a great job. He was –"

"Only now she's dead," Steiger interrupted, his words quiet but hard as steel. "And the whale's gone. Come to think of it, lawyering up may not be such a bad idea after all."

"What's that supposed to mean, detective?"

"You tell me, Mr. Freeman. You tell me."

CHAPTER 39

4 April, 6:15 AM PDT
Puget Sound, Washington

THE *NORTHERN STAR* steamed north at ten knots in light winds, running hard against the current. Zora's exhausted crew had bunked down soon after leaving the park in Seattle, all except Houdini. He sat motionless on the aft deck, his legs crossed, the backs of his hands resting on his thighs. Was he brooding? Meditating? Zora wasn't sure. She set the autopilot, stepped to the starboard side of the bridge, and leaned against the window-sill. The water was calm, deep blue, and the sun poked through wispy clouds with promises of a fine new day. She could feel its warmth, yet a cold chill crept up her spine.

She was thinking about all that had happened in the past week, how her endless adventures had brought her to this place that now seemed so dark and lonely. First, there was college, then her world travels, and finally, the biggest challenge of all, conquering the macho world of commercial fishing. Now, maybe it was time to recalibrate her priorities. She'd made money, sure, but not much of a difference. She would be thirty-seven in less than a month, had never married, never even experienced a satisfying, long-term relationship. There'd been no shortage of men along the way, yet she tended to go for the charming, dangerous types. "Bad boys" cut from the same cloth as her father, betrayal hardwired into their DNA. No future there, not after watching what it had done to her mother, unraveling her life piece by agonizing piece. It was late in the game for kids too – though not too late – and she sometimes imagined what it would be like to raise a rug-rat or two.

So...where to from here? Hell, she couldn't fish forever.

As she pondered that thought, the handsome face of Mickey Kincaid lodged in her mind. She wondered how he was holding up, how he was dealing with the loss of his sister, the pain, the sadness, the anger. Zora's thoughts then turned to her mother. She picked up the framed photo and clutched it to her chest.

I miss her. I miss her so much.

At that same moment, Zora heard stirring down below, caught a whiff of freshly brewed coffee wafting up from the galley. She stepped back to the wheel as Lapenda yanked open the pilothouse door. He was carrying two mugs in his left hand. "Hey, Skip, figured you could use some joe. High octane stuff, made it myself."

"Great, thanks, Rico."

"Hope you're hungry, too. Cassidy's cooking up a skillet of his famous disaster omelets. He threw everything in there this time, *including* the kitchen sink."

"Sounds good. I had a Pop Tart earlier, that's it."

They stood in silence staring out the window, sipping coffee. Zora felt like she'd hit a wall, everything exposed, raw. All she wanted now was to return Mack's boat, hop on a plane, get to Utah as soon as possible – and hold her mother's hand.

She was startled by the sound of her phone, surprised there was even a tower within range. She picked up. "This is Zora...yes, of course I remember you." As she listened, her bottom lip began to tremble, her face turned pale, and tears welled up in her eyes. "What do you mean she just walked out the door? Yes...yes...*what* man? In her room? What the hell are you talking about?" There was a minute or so of silence, then, "Oh my God. No!" The coffee mug slipped from her hand, crashed to the floor, shattering into a hundred pieces. "But how...how could you let her...never mind. I'll get there as fast as I can."

Zora dropped the phone on the chart table, staggered backwards, her face a horrid pallor.

Lapenda reached out with his free arm to steady her. "Skip, what is it?"

"My mother," Zora said, haltingly. "She's..."

"What?"

"She's dead."

"Dead!" Lapenda gasped. "How?"

Zora slumped against the pilot's seat, her mind numb. "She froze to death. An orderly found her a few minutes ago, lying on a bench inside the gazebo."

"On the property?"

"Yeah, next to a small lake. Mother loved that spot. We'd sit there and talk for hours when I visited. Sometimes she'd even remember who I was."

"But how does that happen? They lock up those places tighter than a drum, don't they?"

"Good question, Rico," Zora replied, her voice trembling. "That was the owner of the place. She's not exactly sure what happened. She said a janitor stepped outside to take a smoke break and left the back door unlocked. Next thing they know Mother's gone. Apparently she'd been complaining about a strange man in her room. Everyone thought she was hallucinating, though, or talking to ghosts again."

"The goon who took her picture," Lapenda said. "Has to be."

"Yeah. Anyway, the cops apparently looked everywhere except where she was. Jesus, I..."

Lapenda set his mug down, wrapped Zora in his arms. "I'm so sorry, Skip."

Zora buried her head in his chest, reached for her mother's picture again, a rage now burning deep inside her. She wanted to throw something, break something, lash out, anything but steer this boat. For a full minute, she stared at the photo without speaking. Then she took a step back, brushed away the tears, and screamed, "Mitchell fucking Chandler!" The loud shriek nearly caused Lapenda to jump out of his skin. An instant later, she dug into her pocket and found the DA's card. She grabbed her phone and drilled in the number he'd written on the back. Angrily rocking from one foot to the other, she waited for the other party to pick up.

Finally, after several rings, he did.

And Detective Cloyd Steiger got an earful.

CHAPTER 40

4 April, 6:45 AM PDT
Kingdom of the Sea Oceanarium, Seattle, Washington

AFTER CLICKING OFF, Steiger sat for a long moment in stunned silence. He then made a call of his own. He hadn't spoken with Jefferson County Prosecuting Attorney Scott Rosekrans since Rosekrans had been ordered by SIU to steer clear of the Katrina Kincaid investigation. Now, however, there were two more deaths connected to these seemingly interconnected cases of blackmail and murder – the mangled consultant, Tradd, and Zora's mother. He could no longer sit on the sidelines.

The conversation was brief.

Steiger told the DA it was imperative they meet, that important new information had come to light on both cases. He didn't elaborate. They agreed on a time – ten o'clock. Before leaving the chaotic scene at the park, however, Steiger briefed the captain on his conversation with Colby Freeman. He did not mention Zora Flynn or the disturbing phone call he'd had with her moments earlier. After hitting the road, he tuned in an all-news station broadcasting nonstop coverage of "an alleged terrorist plot at KOS-Seattle." Despite repeated denials from a police spokesperson, breathless reporters continued to push for any kind of statement that might suggest Armageddon.

Steiger soon tired of the endless drivel, punched off the radio, and drove on in blessed silence. Less than three hours later – after a lengthy delay at the Edmonds ferry dock – he rolled into Port Townsend. He slowed as he passed a collection of ornate Victorian mansions that dotted the craggy bluffs towering over Water Street, the town's main artery.

Moments later, he pulled into the driveway of a yellow charmer with a wraparound porch and million dollar views of Admiralty Inlet. Steiger and his wife had been eyeing the lovely three-bedroom gem since it had first come on the market. It needed some major work, which was reflected in the relatively modest price. They planned to retire here, a prospect that felt infinitely more real to him than it had just a few days earlier. During his long career as a cop, he'd gone off the grid too many times to count but never with the stakes this high, never with the governor's hacks lurking in the shadows.

He stepped out of the black Caprice, walked to the edge of the bluff, and sat down on a rickety wooden bench. From here he could see the thriving business district below, a charming three block area that carried on the Victorian theme of the stately homes above it. Steiger had been to this same spot once before, remembered clearing his head during the heat of a particularly baffling homicide investigation. Now the face of Captain Zora Flynn swam into focus and with it, the pieces of an even more disturbing puzzle – the computer printout that linked Dr. Kincaid to KOS-Seattle and perhaps Mitchell Chandler...the mind-bending assault on the park by the rogue whales...his interview with a harried Colby Freeman...and, finally, his most recent conversation with the captain. Steiger felt terrible about the death of her mother, but the revelation had also confirmed his hunch that Freeman was lying about his star performer. A whale had indeed escaped from the sea-pen, a whale that was clearly *not* Samson.

A few minutes before ten, Steiger arrived at the Courthouse. He parked in front of the building, hiked up to the third floor, and was ushered into the Prosecuting Attorney's office. Scott Rosekrans was standing behind his desk, his eyes drifting slowly over a stack of documents spread out in front of him. He looked up, the two men shook hands, and exchanged some small talk. Steiger didn't have to ask what the DA was working on. He could read the cover page of the preliminary investigation report himself:

Jefferson County Prosecutor's Office, Port Townsend, Washington.
Crime – Homicide.
Victims – 1 Katrina Eliza Kincaid, Age 35.
Location – Fort Worden State Park.

"Did Towers give you this file?" Steiger asked, hiking an eyebrow. "I better call Ripley's."

Rosekrans snickered. "Yes. He had no choice, really. If he *does* track down Dr. Kincaid's killer – and I'm not holding my breath – I'll be prosecuting the case. Not much to go on, though. And I've gone over this stuff nine ways from Sunday since you called."

Stepping closer, Steiger took the next few minutes to peruse the crime scene photos, lab results, autopsy report, and half a dozen aerial photographs of Fort Worden State Park taken from a TV helicopter. "Point taken, Scott. Not a damn thing here that can lead us to the killer – no fingerprints, footprints, hair, DNA residue, weapons, or anything else that might be mistaken for physical evidence."

"Which is precisely why I'm anxious to hear what you've got, Cloyd." Rosekrans was now perched on the edge of his desk.

Steiger pulled up a chair, took a deep breath, then launched into his narrative. Over the next twenty minutes, he sorted through the intermingled threads of the two cases exactly as they'd unfolded in his head during his brief reflections on the bluff a few moments earlier.

Rosekrans reacted with surprise and shock, taking some time to gather his own thoughts. "That's really tragic about Ms. Flynn's mother," he said. "But what about the rest of her story, disposing of Samson's body, capturing the other orca?"

"No reason to doubt any of it. This woman doesn't make shit up."

"Okay, let's back up then. Tell me about this Preston Tradd character. Presumably he's the blackmailer who showed up in Sitka?"

Steiger nodded. "There wasn't much left of him, but from my description over the phone, Flynn seemed certain it was the same guy."

"It's why Colby Freeman lawyered up when you pressed him for more information."

"Right. And why he lied about Samson's so-called *escape*."

"Listen, did you ask him if he knew Dr. Kincaid?" Rosekrans asked.

"Yeah. He said he felt bad about what happened to her and all, that she'd been treating the sick whale and making good progress. Then he clammed up."

Rosekrans sighed. "Obviously a lie, but a clever one when you think about it. He covers his tracks on phone calls and e-mails between them, admitting nothing beyond that. So it's his word against Ms. Flynn's."

"Exactly. Only now there's no proof she actually *captured* another whale. It's like trying to make a homicide case without the body. Which means there's no way to connect the man behind the curtain to *any* crime, let alone blackmail and murder."

"*Oz* being Mitchell Chandler."

"He's the reason you sent Zora Flynn to see me in the first place, right, Scott?" The answer was obvious, but Steiger had asked the question anyway. "You knew the history there, what went down with my ex-partner."

Rosekrans gazed around the room then looked back at his friend. "That's a big part of it, yes. Like I told you the other night, Cloyd, I got that call from Jake Towers not five minutes after I'd finished the prelim exam on Dr. Kincaid. He told me he was taking over the investigation – *hijack* would be a more accurate description. It just didn't pass the smell test. What, I'm supposed to believe he's clairvoyant? That he somehow *knew* her death was not an accident? Anyway, the next thing that popped into my head was the tormented face of that young rape victim over in Port Ludlow."

Steiger nodded. "The scumbag who destroyed her life made a mockery of the justice system, all courtesy of Towers and SIU."

"Exactly. So when Ms. Flynn told me about meeting with Dr. Kincaid shortly before she died, about Samson's prognosis, about the blackmail scheme involving the capture of another whale..."

"Déjà vu all over again," Steiger said. "Only this time there's an even *bigger* reptile."

Rosekrans sat quietly for several long moments, nervously tapping his fist into his hand. "Listen, I had a feeling this bubble was gonna break sooner than later, so I did some research." He explained that, according to his own inside sources, Mitchell Chandler had funneled millions of dollars into Governor Ryan's treasure chest through a group called the Evergreen Foundation, a nonprofit arm of Chandler Global Enterprises. All on the up-and-up, too. There was no legal requirement that the names of donors be disclosed and no limit on the size of donations.

Steiger knew about Chandler's cozy relationship with the governor, but not about the secret fund. "Crony capitalism at its best," he said.

"Sure is," Rosekrans replied. "Chandler and his fat-cat friends pony up a few hundred grand and walk away with millions in no-bid government contracts. But you know what, Cloyd? Nothing really surprises me anymore. I was still living in Houston when Enron's house of cards collapsed. Remember that?"

Steiger did, in fact, remember. All too well. Two corporate crooks named Ken Lay and Jeffrey Skilling had cooked the books, bamboozling everybody from Wall Street to Main Street. Steiger had invested some of his own hard-earned cash into the company soon after *Fortune Magazine* had crowned it, "Enron the Incredible." Like everyone else, his money had gone up in smoke.

Rosekrans continued. "The thing I can't figure in *this* deal, though, is what's in it for the governor? He can't be that desperate for cash." The DA paused, the ghost of a smile creasing his face. "Unless he pulled a page from the John Edwards/Schwarzenegger playbooks and has a love child out there somewhere."

"Might not be as far-fetched as you think, Scott."

"Ryan? No way, I don't see it."

"Not a mistress necessarily, but maybe some other little secret he's got squirreled away in the closet."

"You're saying he's gay?"

"No, I'm not saying that either," Steiger said. "I'm saying that maybe Towers has been dealing from the bottom of the deck. He found some dirt on the governor, something explosive, and sold the information to the highest bidder."

"Mitchell Chandler again."

"Bingo! It's why we need to find out what else is on the Kincaid woman's hard drive besides the e-mails. There's not enough there to make a case. Where's the computer now?"

"Still with Towers as far as I know," Rosekrans said. "He sent over a copy of the evidence file, that's as much as I know."

"Which actually tells you a *lot*, right?"

Rosekrans nodded, glanced at his watch. "Listen, give me a few minutes, okay? I need to speak with the Circuit Court judge before she leaves on vacation. Be right back."

After the DA left, Steiger pulled out his cell phone and exchanged calls with a colleague. They spoke for several minutes. He clicked off on the second conversation shortly after Rosekrans returned. "That was a friend of mine, Scott. He works in the forensics lab over at Washington State Patrol. I assumed that's where Towers had taken the hard drive. But no cigar. It's not there."

"Not there!" Rosekrans exclaimed, then frowning demanded, "Where is it?"

"Same question my friend asked. He's got a snitch inside the SIU offices in Olympia, one of the analysts. She told him the box had been sent to a private lab just outside Seattle, outfit called Data-Locke. And you'll never guess who owns it?"

"Something tells me I'm about to find out."

"The governor's brother-in-law." Steiger went on to explain that a report had been sent from Data-Locke to SIU the previous afternoon. According to the snitch, the document included a glut of scientific mumbo jumbo, but no mention of any hidden file.

"Any chance they could've missed it?"

"Highly unlikely, Scott. I'm told Data-Locke hires only the best and brightest, geeks who can find anything on a computer – hidden, disguised, deleted, whatever. I'm speculating here, but I'd bet even money they never *saw* the hard drive. Instead, the brother-in-law pulled an end around, dummied up a report, and then destroyed the drive."

"Figures." With a snort of disgust Rosekrans moved from his desk to the window and stared outside. "So we're back to square one. Without that hard drive, Chandler's untouchable."

"Unless we con the con, Scott."

Rosekrans instantly spun around, squared himself with Steiger. "What do you mean?"

"Look, it's a long shot, but this game's already rigged, so it might be our *only* shot. What we do is this. We get Chandler to come over here, meet with you. Let's see if we can jam him up a little, maybe get something we can use, some inside juice."

"Under what pretense? I mean –"

Steiger stopped him with a raised hand. "Tell him you know how badly he wants the Kincaid case solved. You say Towers is a fine investigator and all, but you hint that he's not getting the straight scoop from one of the park's employees."

"And who exactly do I say *that* is?"

"You don't. Tell him you promised to keep the person's name confidential. Stress to him it's information you're certain he'll want to know." Steiger took a deep breath. He knew he was lobbing a Hail Mary. He too had done some digging on Chandler and the man was obsessed with secrecy to the point of paranoia. His management style: rule-by-fear. And nobody in the organization talked out of school, not if they wanted to remain in his employ.

"But why on earth would he divulge *anything* to me?" Rosekrans asked. "Even if he takes the bait, which is one helluva big *if.*"

Steiger readily agreed. "Look, there are no guarantees here, but I can think of two good reasons why he'll bite. First, Towers might just be holding a hammer over Chandler's head, too, the proverbial double-cross. He's a conniving little twit, and I wouldn't put it past him. Second, you know Chandler's type as well as I do – arrogant SOBs who always think they're the smartest guys in the room."

"In his case, he probably is."

"Maybe so. But if the man's dirty, he'll want to know everything *you* know, which means he'll purposely interject himself into the investigation. Happens all the time. And don't forget about the other wild card here..." Steiger trailed off, letting his colleague fill in the blank.

"Zora Flynn!"

Steiger slowly nodded. "You would never accuse that woman of bringing a knife to a gunfight, Scott, and right now she's got Chandler square in her crosshairs. Hard to say what she might do. She damn near ripped me a new one on the phone. Personally, I'd pay to see a showdown between Flynn and Chandler. Professionally, I can't go there."

"No, we're a nation of law and order," Rosekrans agreed. "There are lines you just don't cross and legal avenues to settle scores. That said, we should probably bring *her* to the Courthouse, too, otherwise we've got a loose cannon on our hands. Where is she now?"

"Somewhere in Puget Sound, on her way back from Seattle."

Rosekrans shifted a bit and stared out the window again, as if looking for the boat. Turning back to Steiger he said, "Then make the call. As for Chandler, I read that he brings a team of bodyguards with him wherever he goes. So even if he *does* fall for our little ruse, having a bunch of armed commandos rolling into town, well, it's –"

"We can play that game, too, Scott. I'll put a SWAT team on standby. We do it all the time, and believe me nobody messes with these guys." Steiger thought back to his own days as a SWAT dog, remembering how the adrenaline started pumping the instant the phone rang. It would take a half hour or so to bring the unit together, but once assembled the officers could be airborne in under a minute.

"Okay, that works," Rosekrans said. "But meeting with Chandler still feels like a crap shoot to me. You know he'll bring along counsel, and it won't be some ham-and-egger street lawyer, either."

Steiger flashed a mischievous smile. "I don't think so, counselor. Only guilty men walk in with their attorneys."

CHAPTER 41

4 April, 12:30 PM PDT
Port Townsend, Washington

THE SLEEK EMBRAER PHENOM 100 dipped out of an azure sky and touched down softly on the tarmac at Jefferson County International Airport south of town. The Very Light Jet, or VLJ, carried six passengers, including a two-person crew, and was designed for takeoffs and landings at small, general aviation airports like this one. It consisted of little more than a single asphalt runway, a makeshift Customs building, the usual assortment of single-engine Cessnas, and a collection of sheet-metal hangars. The "international" scope of the operation was confined mostly to vacationers from north of the border who flew their own planes.

Chandler Global Enterprises owned a fleet of larger, faster jets but the company's CEO had no problem with this little beauty. And Mitchell Chandler was on board now. His driver, Rizzo, was a former Air Force ace. He sat in the co-pilot's chair. Chandler's security detail rounded out the passenger list, three buff, unsmiling men in their thirties with military buzz cuts. They were dressed completely in black, and had spoken only when spoken to during the short flight from the company's airfield in Olympia.

Two hours earlier, Chandler had been surveying the frenzied scene at KOS-Seattle when his office informed him that the Jefferson County DA had called. The reason, he'd been told, was that Rosekrans allegedly had new information pertaining to the Kincaid murder investigation. Chandler had promptly returned the call, only to learn that one of his employees may be withholding information on the case. He pressed for details, but got nowhere.

After considering his options, Chandler decided to call the DA's bluff, thinking a show of concern and cooperation – contrived or not – could be worth their weight. He'd then run through the possible suspects in his mind. Leanne Bucaro? She seemed like an unlikely candidate, considering her daughter's health issues. Colby Freeman? Also unlikely. Big Boy Medlin? Not a chance. Chandler had hired him when no one else would, then stuck by him through a blizzard of personal and professional storms. Loyalty mattered for something, right?

Predictably, Chandler's lawyers had rejected the plan as foolish and risky. But the boss was the boss and that was that. Besides, he'd reasoned, there wasn't a shred of evidence connecting him to any crime. Sure, the tragic accident that had taken Dr. Kincaid's life was regrettable. So too was Preston Tradd's horrific fate. And then there was the captain's mother – her death had to be the most puzzling of all. What in God's name had compelled an old woman to go wandering off alone on a bitter cold night anyway? He was not responsible for her bizarre behavior, or for the other unfortunate incidents either...and no court in the land would find otherwise.

Chandler pushed those thoughts into the recesses of his mind as the jet taxied to a stop next to the terminal building. It was a one-room frame structure badly in need of a paint job. In short order, everyone except the pilot had deplaned. Idling just steps away were two vehicles that had rolled in moments earlier from a rental agency across the bay. Rizzo took the wheel of a silver Mercedes. Chandler slipped in behind him. The muscle, hauling a cache of automatic weapons in three oversized duffel bags, piled into a black Chevy Tahoe. Their orders: form a perimeter some distance from the Courthouse to avoid an unwanted show of force.

If needed, of course, they could be on the scene in a matter of seconds.

And not one of them would hesitate to kill to protect the boss.

Four miles northwest of the airport, Zora maneuvered the *Northern Star* into the Port Townsend Boat Haven. The eight hour trip from Seattle had been slow and draining, the currents running against the big seiner most of the way. Minutes after the vessel docked, Lapenda, Cassidy, and McCabe piled into a cab and headed for the local hospital. McCabe's shattered wrist was badly in need of attention. Houdini remained behind, on the boat, making minor repairs to his kayak. Zora had asked him to focus on a very different mission, one that included a wild card over which neither of them had any control.

She thought about that now as she walked toward the moorage office to pay the slip rental fee. The shocking news of her mother's death had left her stone-cold numb, and every step seemed like a grind. Moving slowly along the dock, she flashed on the dark premonition that had crept into her head following her terrifying encounter with the man-eating sharks.

It doesn't get any darker than this – and bad things really do come in threes.

Despite feeling exhausted and overwhelmed, Zora knew she had to rally. She had to shake off these intense feelings of despair and make things happen. It's what she did, what she'd always done. It took every ounce of courage she could muster, but by the time she reached the office a hidden reserve of adrenaline had kicked in. She suddenly felt more wired than tired.

After paying the bill, Zora played back in her head a second phone conversation she'd had with Detective Steiger shortly before docking the boat. He had called to invite her to a meeting taking place at the Courthouse just moments from now, a meeting between the DA and Mitchell Chandler. Steiger said she could listen in on the entire exchange from a conference room down the hall. Zora had reluctantly agreed, knowing in her gut the scheme was doomed. Chandler might be a greedy bastard, but the man could never be played like that.

She'd then reached out to Mickey Kincaid, updating him on everything that had happened over the past twelve hours. It had taken him several minutes to digest it all, especially the tragic news involving her mother. But when Zora asked for his help, there'd been no hesitation whatsoever. She'd then provided sketchy details of the half-baked plan she and Houdini had hatched, a plan that was still very much a work in progress.

Mickey agreed to pick her up at the marina. He was waiting in the parking lot now.

Sliding into the cab of Mickey's truck, Zora felt like melting into his arms, falling asleep, and waking up on the other side of never. Maybe she would dream that perfect dream, the one where she was floating on a silvery cloud, surrounded by a million dazzling stars. Maybe then she would forget the insanity of the last seven days. Seven days that seemed like seven months. "Thanks for coming, Mickey," Zora said, forcing a smile. "It means a lot."

Mickey smiled back, reached over and gently squeezed her hand. He then pulled out of the gravel parking lot, turned right on Sims Way, and drove toward town.

"Your mother," Mickey said, struggling to find the right words. "I can't believe it. I'm really sorry."

Zora looked off, sighing. In the paralyzing minutes after taking the call from the nursing home, she'd asked herself a thousand times what she could have done differently. She thought back to her meeting with Detective Steiger in Seattle. Following lunch, he had proposed two different scenarios for rescuing her mother, both involving force. Too risky, she'd decided, thinking that if she captured and delivered the orca as planned, maybe all this would go away. Now, it all seemed so stupid and naïve. Worse, she could not shake the image of her beloved mother sitting in that gazebo: alone...confused...and freezing to death.

"Hey. You okay?" Mickey asked.

"Yeah, I'll be fine."

"Listen, if you'd rather not talk about it..."

"No, it's just that nobody seems to know what happened exactly." Zora explained about the strange man her mother said she'd seen in her room. "He must've snuck in, taken Mom's picture, and e-mailed it to that cockroach, Tradd. I hope the little twit burns in hell."

"No shit!" Mickey said. "Listen, for what it's worth, I'd put my money on a Mother's instinct. She must have figured out you were in danger somehow and went looking for the cops."

Zora nodded, a pained expression on her face. "Yeah, that would be just like her."

Mickey reached over and squeezed her hand again, holding it a few seconds longer this time.

After a long silence, Zora said, "So what about you, Mickey? How did it go?"

Mickey took several moments to collect his thoughts. He then spoke about an awkward moment he'd shared with his sister a few months earlier. He said Katrina had expressed a desire to be cremated if anything bad ever happened to her. "You know, I joked about it at the time," he added. "Never thought I'd actually have to deal with it, though. She was so young...so alive."

"I know. I'm so sorry, Mickey."

"Thanks. I can't imagine her not being around anymore. Kat was my best friend and one of the smartest people I've ever known. But hey, not all is lost. At least her spirit will be close by. I'm going to scatter her ashes over Discovery Bay. It was her favorite place in all the world."

"Any idea when?" Zora asked. "I want to be there, that is if things don't go all to hell over the next hour or so."

"They won't," Mickey said, with a confident tone Zora found comforting. "And I would like that, for you to come I mean. I'm thinking in maybe a week or so. Honestly, I had no idea Kat had so many friends. I'm getting calls from all over the place, people asking about a memorial service, or if a fund's been set up in her name. Honestly, it's –"

"Yeah, it's way too much right now." Zora closed her eyes, wanting to reach out to him, decided it wasn't the right time or place. "No reason to rush anything, Mickey."

Mickey nodded his agreement, and turned his attention back to the road. They were almost there. He made a soft left on Washington Street, then drove up the steep hill toward the Courthouse. "So what's with this meeting, Zora? These guys don't really think Chandler will sing, do they?"

"Nah, in fact Steiger called it 'a high-wire act without the net.' I'd say that about nails it too. But they saved me the trouble of tracking down Chandler's sorry ass, so I went along."

"And if the DA strikes out, we go with Plan B, right?"

"Uh-huh," Zora replied in a whispered tone.

"Okay then. I'll drop you off at the Courthouse and stay out of sight."

"Yeah, I'll holler if I need you."

Mickey put a hand on Zora's shoulder. "Listen, you sure you're okay with this?"

"Well, when everything is stolen from you, Mickey, there's nothing left to lose. So yeah, I'm more than okay with it. C'mon, let's nail this bastard."

CHAPTER 42

ZORA WAS USHERED into a conference room on the third floor of the Courthouse, a stark, sparsely furnished space two doors down from the DA's office. The walls were beige, the floors worn, and the only window looked out on a half-empty parking lot. The air was stale and smelled musty. Rosekrans and Steiger were seated at a marred-up oak table long past its prime. Frowning and grim-faced, they offered condolences for her loss, then got right down to business.

Rosekrans explained what Zora already knew, that the plan wasn't much of a plan at all. But it was worth a shot, he said, mostly because murder cases were often cleared by what amounted to pure chance. He would meet with Chandler, set the trap, and see if he took the bait.

Steiger then jumped in, making it clear there would be no Perry Mason moment. That kind of drama, he added, only happened on TV, or in the movies. Instead, their best hope was to mine some nugget of information from Chandler, or force a mistake, anything that might eventually connect the man to the crime.

Rosekrans studied both faces silently, and pushed a button on the phone sitting in front of him. "You'll be able to hear the entire conversation." He gathered together a few files, stood up, and walked confidently out of the room.

Zora watched after him, mentally preparing to set Plan B into motion. It too was a shot in the dark. She knew that. She also knew that every so often even the wildest ideas worked. She recalled a book she'd read as a child, when she was five or six. It was about a humble rabbit that used her razor-sharp teeth, lightning speed, and lucky charm to outwit a plundering fox.

Hell, maybe we'll get lucky, too.

Steiger seemed to sense Zora's unease. "You think this is a monumental waste of time."

Zora glanced into her bag, made sure her cell phone was within easy reach. "What I *think*, detective, is that guys like Mitchell Chandler don't make stupid mistakes. And even if he does fall into your little trap, he'll never see the inside of a prison cell. The rich and obnoxious never do, right?"

Steiger shrugged. "The straight answer, Ms. Flynn, is…yes! Truth is, we've got nothing in the way of forensics, and there's no way to make a circumstantial case stick, not with the goddamn CSI factor hanging over our heads."

"CSI factor?"

"The television series. Changed the public's perception of what modern technology can and can't do forever. Things have now become so distorted, we better hand the DA a 'smoking gun,' or forget going to trial. Jurors walk into courtrooms expecting to be dazzled by the science, to see conclusive evidence for every crime. Doesn't matter that a whole lot of what folks see on TV is crap, they think we can make a case by trapping shadows. And those of us in law enforcement are guilty too, by the way. We all push the margins of science."

Zora's mind churned through the possibilities, landing on the only logical question. "Which leaves us pretty much nowhere, then, right?"

"Not necessarily. Like I told you on the phone earlier, Chandler's curious or he wouldn't bother to show up. He's not sure what we've got and it's a solid bet he doesn't trust the guy over at SIU. Pure conjecture at this point, but we think Towers might be attempting a little blackmail scheme on his own. So we're playing the FTMS card."

Zora sat back, held his gaze. "Follow the money, Sparky."

Steiger chuckled at the new twist on an old standby. "Yeah, you got it."

A minute or so later, Rosekrans's voice crackled over the voice box. Mitchell Chandler had arrived. And just as Steiger had predicted, he was alone.

No entourage. No attorney.

Zora felt her heart beating as fast as the rabbit in that story. She cracked the door, set her jaw, and peered through the opening. Chandler soon appeared at the top of the stairs, got his bearings, and strode down the hall like he owned the place. He was dressed in a custom-fitted jacket, dark sweater, and khaki slacks. It took everything she had not to go off the rails, rush out of that room, and kneecap him. She wondered if the DA would answer the bell. He was on his home turf and had left the conference room wearing his game face, but there was a better than even chance he'd get his ass handed to him.

Zora and Steiger listened as Rosekrans quickly dispensed with the formalities and began sifting through the evidence in Katrina's case. He hinted at some grand revelation from a park employee whose name, he said, must remain off the record. It was a perfectly choreographed performance, folksy and direct, yet Chandler met every move with abject detachment. If he was feeling any distress, there was no indication in his voice. His indifference and impatience seemed to grow with each exchange. He was a rock. Zora closed her eyes and pictured him sitting in that room – cold, unflappable, a card shark refusing to tip his hand.

He knows the DA's firing blanks. And Steiger knows it too.

The stilted conversation lasted less than ten minutes. Then, in a steely voice, Chandler thanked Rosekrans for his concern, offered his continued support, and promptly exited the office. Steiger shot a disheartening glance at Zora, shifted in his seat, and slammed his heavy arms down on the table. "Game-set-match." A moment later he was out the door, all other thoughts left unspoken.

Zora sat without moving, staring mindlessly at the wall. She was riddled with guilt, grief, and a burning desire for revenge. The man responsible for her mother's death, for the murder of her friend, had proved to be a criminal on a grand scale. In the eyes of the law, however, he would be held accountable for nothing.

But there will be justice!

Shaking with rage, she grabbed her cell and punched in a number programmed into the speed dial. Mickey picked up on the first ring. "Go!" she screamed. Zora then dashed from the conference room, and sprinted down the hallway. She took the stairs three at a time, all cylinders firing now. After reaching the landing, she burst through the lobby doors shouting Chandler's name.

He wheeled around, gave her a brief sizing-up glance, and with annoying calm said, "And who might this lovely creature be?"

Zora marched toward him taking long, angry strides. There was a hint of madness in her eyes. "You know damn *well* who I am, Chandler. And I'm in a really fucking bad mood, thanks to you. See, you took away the most precious thing in my life. Now *your* number is up. And guess what, I just appointed myself judge, jury, and executioner."

Chandler stood his ground. "Is that so?" he replied, adding smugly, "You know, I'm reminded of something Plato once wrote – 'Spectacle is one of the basic elements of drama.' Seems to me you've taken his words to heart, young lady."

"Yeah, well, the Dalai Lama had a better line, Chandler. 'The enemy is a very good teacher.' So pay attention, you might just learn something here."

"Really. I doubt that. As for the rest of your little diatribe, I'm afraid I don't know what you're talking about. And I'm a busy man." He turned, dismissing Zora with a condescending wave. "Now if you'll excuse me, I –"

An angry fire ignited in Zora's eyes. "Liar!" she screamed. She lunged toward Chandler, grabbed his shoulder, and spun him around. She then buried the toe of her boot in his crotch. It wasn't the most elegant of martial arts moves, but effective nonetheless.

Chandler gasped, collapsed to his knees, writhing in pain.

Rizzo instantly bolted from the Mercedes, waving a Sig Sauer pistol in the air and shouting obscenities. He charged Zora like a blitzing linebacker. She spun around. Where the hell was Mickey? The thought had barely registered when he suddenly materialized, carrying a two-by-four the length of a baseball bat. With one mighty swing he cold-cocked the much bigger man. Rizzo's nose exploded. He clutched wildly at his bloodied face as the weapon flew from his hand. It bounced off the sidewalk, and skittered into the grass. Staggering backwards, he fell hard into a pile of overturned dirt.

Mickey glared at him for just a second, dropped the crude weapon, and rushed over to a still-writhing Chandler. In a series of rapid-fire moves, he yanked his arms behind his back and bound his wrists with a plastic zip tie. Mickey then pulled a roll of duct tape from his jacket pocket. He bit off an eight-inch strip, slapped it across Chandler's mouth. Zora scooped up the gun and together they dragged the big man to Mickey's pickup. They shoved him into the rear compartment and jumped in front. Moments later Mickey fired up the engine and slammed the gearshift into drive. The truck roared out of the parking lot, laying thirty feet of rubber as it fishtailed down Cass Street.

"You don't mess around, do you?" Zora said, clamping the buckle of her seat belt.

"What, the two-by-four, you mean?"

"Yeah, the two-by-four. A home run swing."

"Hey, do I look crazy enough to *fight* that dude?"

Zora had to agree. She managed a crooked smile.

"Okay, coach...where to?"

"North Beach," Zora said, emphatically.

"Why there?"

"Houdini."

"What about him?"

"You'll find out soon enough, Mickey."

Inside the Courthouse, a small crowd of onlookers stood dumbstruck, staring out tall banks of windows across the front lawn. Only after Mickey's truck had peeled around the corner and disappeared down the block did they react. Steiger and Rosekrans were huddled outside his office when a doughy woman wearing a flowery red dress came puffing down the hall. She was waving her arms frantically and chattering like a squirrel. It took stenographer Hazel Rafferty several moments to catch her breath, but when she finally calmed down she blurted out what had happened.

Most of it she got right.

After Hazel finished speaking, Steiger reached for his phone and punched in a number. The Commanding Officer of the SWAT unit in Seattle picked up on the second ring.

The team would be airborne in less than sixty seconds.

CHAPTER 43

4 April, 1:45 PM PDT
Port Townsend, Washington

ZORA DREW A QUICK BREATH as she poked her head around the corner of the 4-H building. It was one of several freestanding structures at the Jefferson County Fairgrounds. The expansive property sat on the north end of town, half a mile from the beach. The place was a ghost town most of the year, and it was deserted now. She and Mickey had decided to hide out here in hopes of shaking Chandler's security detail. His three bodyguards had roared into action within seconds of their boss's abduction, but lost the trail after Mickey rifled through Chandler's pockets. He'd found an iPhone with built-in tracking technology, and tossed it out the window.

Keeping low to the ground, Zora darted back to Mickey's truck. She knew there was no time to waste. She then placed a quick call to Houdini, a move that shifted their improbable plan into high gear. Moments later she spotted the SUV crawling past the entrance to the fairgrounds. The tinted windows were rolled down, three pairs of angry eyes scanning the whitewashed buildings. The vehicle inched along 49th Street and rounded the bend toward San Juan Avenue.

Stepping into the cab, Zora said, "They'll be back...and soon. Let's roll."

Mickey nodded, pulled the Sig Sauer from his belt. He turned and shoved the pistol under Chandler's chin. "We haven't met asshole. I'm Mickey Kincaid. Katrina was my kid sister."

Chandler squirmed in his seat, mumbled something incoherent.

"What's that, you useless prick?" Mickey said, gritting his teeth.

The man had no way of answering.

Mickey lowered the pistol, squared himself in his seat, and handed the gun to Zora. "Sig Sauer P220. Nice weapon. You can fire 10,000 rounds a day, every day, with this thing without a single failure. I'll bet you know how to use it, too?"

"Yeah. When you grow up around coyotes and mountain lions, you damn well *better* know how to shoot."

"Good. I prefer my trusty Beretta." He tapped the glove box.

Zora glanced at Chandler and then at Mickey. "Well, I have a feeling you might need it."

Mickey drove out of the fairgrounds, turned left on Kuhn Street, and headed toward North Beach. Less than a minute later, he skidded to a stop beside a small park. Looking north, the location offered dazzling views of the Strait of Juan de Fuca, Whidbey Island, and snow-peaked Mt. Baker. To the east, a narrow trail looped over a rolling field of high grass. It disappeared into a wall of fir trees on the edge of Fort Worden State Park.

Zora stepped from the cab of the truck and looked around. The wind was whipping off the Sound in all its glory and a gentle rain began to fall. The beach was deserted. "Stay with the truck, Mickey, okay? Keep our friends in the SUV occupied, if they show up. I prefer to handle this sack of shit by myself." She opened the back door and waved the pistol in Chandler's face. "Get out."

Chandler fixed her with an angry stare. Shaking his head, he slid awkwardly across the rear seat and out of the vehicle.

Zora placed her free hand on his shoulder and shoved him toward the boat ramp, a wide concrete slab that angled some thirty feet down to the water. Chandler stumbled, nearly fell, then staggered to stop ten feet from the rocky shoreline. When he turned around, Zora was inches from his face. She glared at him for an intense moment before reaching out and ripping the duct tape from his mouth.

"Are you out of your goddamn mind?" Chandler shouted, flexing his jaw back and forth. "This is kidnapping. I'll have you –"

Zora pointed the gun at his head. "You're breaking my heart here. Now shut the fuck up."

"Or what, you'll shoot me in cold blood? If you think you've got the horses for that, captain, bring it on."

"No, Chandler, a bullet to the head is too easy, too quick. A flash of pain and then it's over. So that's number one. Number two. You're going to come clean here. If you lie, I'll know. Number three. I talk, you listen.

And I'm not in the market for bullshit. Understood?"

Chandler shook his head defiantly.

"Good," Zora said, lowering the weapon. "And just for kicks, I'll be recording all this." She pulled a smartphone from her pocket, activated the voice recorder, and set it on the ground next to her. "First question: The dead guy at the park. He's the weasel you sent to Sitka, right?"

No response.

Zora raised the pistol again, her hands steady, elbows locked. Then she squeezed the trigger. The bullet tore through the air just inches from Chandler's right ear.

"Jesus," he screamed. "What the –"

"Start singing, Chandler, or the next one burns a hole in your forehead."

"Look, be reasonable here. We can make a deal, okay? I've got plenty of money, more than enough to set you up for life. I'll have the cash deposited in a Swiss bank account. Access it whenever you like. No strings. How does a million sound? Two?"

"I didn't want your goddamn money before, and I sure as hell don't want it now."

"C'mon, captain. Think of what you could do with that kind of cash."

Zora cut him dead, her voice taking on a dangerous tone. "I don't believe in third chances, so spare me the hat dance." She then moved the gun six inches to her right, squeezed the trigger again. This round zinged by his other ear.

Chandler took several quick breaths, his eyes a mix of rage and fear. "Yeah, okay, that's him. The name's Preston Tradd. He worked for a consulting firm we keep on retainer."

"So I heard," Zora replied. "You know what that fucking moron said to me, Chandler? He said, 'The people I represent do not play by the rules. They *are* the rules.' Sound familiar?"

Chandler shot Zora a contemptuous look. "The world's a tough place, okay? It's either hunt or be hunted. I prefer to be the hunter. Besides those were his words, not mine."

"Either way, it's sick. And look where it got *him*. I call that Karma. What about you?"

No answer, which was an answer itself.

Zora took another step closer, the pistol held high. "Now talk to me about my friend's sister."

"A terrible accident," Chandler whispered. "Most regrettable. I mean that."

Zora pounced, her gaze now bordering on murderous. "Regrettable! What about my mother? Is *her* death regrettable, too? She's dead, Chandler. Dead! You got that?"

Chandler shifted nervously and said, "Look, I –"

"You think the rules only apply to the little guy, don't you? You see right as wrong and wrong as right. When do the ends stop justifying the means, Chandler? How many fucking mansions do you need? How much goddamn *money* do you need? Twenty billion not enough? You need forty billion, a hundred? I just don't get you people."

"And you never will," Chandler said, a smug look creeping over his face. "It's not about the mansions, or the money, captain. It's about *respect*. It's about winning the game, beating the other guy, coming out on top. Nobody remembers who came in *second*, captain. Nobody!"

"Is that right? Yeah, well, if you listen real good, Chandler, you'll hear the Fat Lady singing because *this* game is over. I'm making up the rules now and I say it's payback time."

"C'mon, take it easy here."

Zora picked up the phone, dropped it in her jacket pocket. "And it's all right here on this tiny device. Does that nail it for you, Sherlock?"

"Yeah, I suppose it does," Chandler said sarcastically. "And I assume you got the part about holding a gun to my head, too. The authorities will love that. It's called a forced confession, captain, and it will *never* stand up in court."

Zora shot him a sharp look. "Well, damn, guess you got me there. So I'll tell you what, Chandler. Why don't we settle this thing the old fashioned way, just you and me?"

Chandler said nothing, his face a mask of confusion and contempt.

Zora moved slowly to Chandler's side then slipped in behind him, the gun still pointed at his head. "You are one-hundred-fucking-percent screwed." She then removed the zip tie, stuffed it in her jeans pocket. Backing away, she bent down and carefully set the gun on the ground.

Chandler wiped the sweat from his brow, steadied himself, and smiled. An instant later he made his move. He lunged at Zora, spun her around, and delivered a direct blow to the kidneys. A razor of pain sliced through her body.

She staggered backwards, stunned by the power and suddenness of the punch.

"Brown belt, tae kwon do. Pity nobody told you, captain."

Chandler lashed out again, this blow aimed at the bridge of her nose. Zora ducked, suddenly overcome with an uncontrollable rage. She didn't have to think about her next move. It was all instinct, the three fundamental points of counter-attack part of her muscle-memory: strike hard and fast; strike through the target; be prepared to strike more than once.

The ultimate goal: submission.

With dizzying speed, Zora tagged Chandler with a backhand chop to the neck. Next she delivered a lightning-quick stab to the ribs and two piston-like punches to the abdomen. He shrieked and keeled over.

She gazed down at him, breathing fire. "*Black* belt, Aiki-jujutsu. Pity nobody told *you*."

Chandler recovered quickly, dug in his heels. He countered with a surprisingly swift right cross. Zora saw it coming. She dropped to one knee, grabbed his wrist, and flipped him onto his side. She then pancaked on the ground, whipsawing in behind him. Before he could react, she wrapped her legs around his midsection in a scissor hold. Locking her wrists firmly under his chin, she squeezed tight, like a boa constrictor subduing its prey. Chandler lost consciousness less than fifteen seconds later. As soon as he went limp, Zora untangled her arms and legs. She slowly stood up and waited for the lifeless mass to move.

It took under a minute.

"What the hell just happened?" Chandler groaned, stirring slightly.

"Rear naked choke hold," Zora replied. She now held the gun again. "A little above your pay grade, I'd say."

Zora was about to shift into the next phase of her plan when something moved, something behind her. She spun around and froze.

Shit!

A black Chevy Tahoe came barreling over the hill with a burst of acceleration, moving so fast its wheels nearly left the road. Some thirty yards from the water, the big SUV bit hard on the gravel, did a one-hundred-eighty-degree spin, and skidded to a fierce halt.

The beef had arrived in full, splendid force.

Zora whipped back around, but Chandler had already made a run for it. She caught a glimpse of him crouching behind a stack of driftwood, his hands pressed hard against his face. Two seabirds streaked overhead, cursing at all the commotion, forcing her to drop to her knees.

"You're an idiot, captain," Chandler roared. "An idiot!"

"Fuck!" Zora shouted. She jumped to her feet, saw Mickey out of the corner of her eye. He was crouched behind the passenger side door of his truck, weapon in hand.

"Run, Zora, run," he hollered, holding his gaze on the three thugs who had scrambled out of the SUV. They were wearing bulletproof vests and armed with one of the most powerful submachine guns ever made: the Colt M4 Commando. Moving fast and sure, the goons took up positions at the rear of their vehicle.

Exposed and vulnerable, Zora dashed across thirty feet of no man's land, zigzagging as she ran, her boots crunching hard on the gravel. She dived past the front bumper of Mickey's truck and did a roll, coming up into the squat position. "Holy shit!" she shouted, gasping for air. "They're armed to the teeth."

"Yeah, enough goddamn firepower to blow us to Shanghai."

There was a rumble of distant thunder, the sky flashed white, and then the bullets started coming. They tore through the side of the truck in waves, shattering windows, sending glass flying everywhere. A few pinpoint shards ripped into Zora's cheek. She ducked instinctively, crouching low, blood dripping onto her torn jacket.

"Fuck them," Mickey roared, a murderous rage in his eyes. He came up firing, first at the tires then the windshield. He emptied the semiautomatic pistol, dropped back down, and slapped in a fresh mag.

The attackers answered with another shelling, the bullets so close Zora could feel them whiz over the top of her head. The noise was deafening. She wiped off the blood with her coat sleeve, pulled out her cell, and hammered 911 on the keypad. A calm female voice answered at the other end, but before Zora could speak the phone exploded, hit by a ricocheting shell. A burning pain tore up her arm. She cursed.

"You okay?" Mickey said.

Zora grabbed her wrist, seething. "Yeah, I think so. It's only a flesh wound."

He yanked a red bandana from his neck, wrapped it around her wrist and tied it off.

Abby flinched a little. "That works, thanks."

Mickey then leaned forward, fired off several more rounds. The report of the pistol was so close to Zora's head it knocked her backwards.

"How the hell did they find us?" she shouted.

"No idea," Mickey replied.

"What about ammo?"

"One more mag, that's it."

"Dammit, Mickey, I guess this would be a good time then."

He stared at her blankly. "For what?"

"The cavalry to show up."

CHAPTER 44

4 April, 2:25 PM PDT
Port Townsend, Washington

MINUTES AFTER WORD reached the Courthouse of a mob-style shootout at North Beach, Rosekrans and Steiger stepped out the front door of the historic old building. The parking lot was swarming with cops. Chandler's driver was slouched low in the back seat of a squad car, his wrists cuffed behind his back. His battered face looked like the face of a heavyweight fighter who'd gone the distance with the champ and lost every round. He was plastered with dirt.

The young paramedic attending to him kept glancing nervously over her shoulder, as if to say, *stuff like this isn't supposed to happen in places like Port Townsend.*

Steiger watched it all unfold with a certain level of detachment. There were lots of questions that needed answers, but at times like these tactical strategies trumped the investigative process. He wasn't officially involved in the case, of course, that's just how his mind worked. Even so, procedure called for him to notify Jake Towers at SIU. He'd decided against it, and convinced Rosekrans to hold off as well. Towers would find out soon enough. Instead, Steiger had asked the sergeant in charge of the SWAT team to pack an extra suit of body armor and have the chopper swing by the Courthouse to pick him up. It wasn't exactly SOP, but his buddy had agreed. He was old school, went to the mat for his men. He did the same for his friends.

The DA checked his watch for the umpteenth time, glanced up at the graying skies. "Over half hour since you called, Cloyd."

"They'll be here any minute."

"You sure this is a good idea for you to go? How many years since your SWAT days?"

"Too many to count, counselor. I piloted a chopper in my former life. Still do from time to time when they let me. We trained with the Army Rangers down in Ft. Lewis, south of Tacoma, mostly blew stuff up. There was a Bavarian village right on the grounds. We'd blast our way in with stun grenades then open up with Uzis, take down the bad guys and rescue hostages. We were ten feet tall and bullet proof."

"Sounds intense."

"It was, but I'm too old for that shit now. You better believe I'll let the big guns out first today."

"Smart move, Cloyd. Look, there could be a lot of lives on the line out there. Ever since those monster whales showed up, we've been bursting at the seams. Hotels and B&Bs are booked solid, lots of people camping out in the park, hordes of media. The sheriff has cleared the area and blocked all the roads coming in and out. But you never know. The last thing we need is some idiot playing cowboy and getting himself all shot up."

Steiger fidgeted with his badge. "No argument there, Scott. I'm more worried about Zora Flynn, to tell you the truth. I've dealt with some tough characters in my day, from gun-toting drug dealers to homicidal cop killers, and I was never afraid, not once. And you know why? Because I can read the streets, I know how the game is played out there. But I swear this woman's in a league by herself. And she scares the hell out of me."

"You think she plans to kill Chandler then?"

Steiger nodded. "Put it this way, Scott. If I'm in her shoes, lost my mother like that, I'd probably burn his ass, too. And I'm no momma's boy. So, the answer is...yes, I do."

Rosekrans thought about that. "You know something, Cloyd. I just don't get it. How does someone like Chandler, with all that money of his, get mixed up in a crazy blackmail scheme like this? Why not just admit the whale's dying, play the sympathy card, and ride out the storm? Instead, three people are dead and here we are wondering what the hell is going to happen next."

"Like I said before, Scott, guys like Mitchell Chandler don't think the same as you and me." Steiger remembered reading about Chandler's approach to business, his belief that investments were to be dominated, not owned. He wondered if any of that mattered to him now.

Then they heard it – the low rumble of a helicopter approaching from the south. The flying tank swept into view above Port Townsend's ferry dock. She was one mean machine, a battleship gray Bell UH-1. Its original designation, HU-1, had led to the popular nickname, *Huey*. The chopper landed softly on the front lawn of the Courthouse then revved down its turbines. Steiger hustled to the open doors, ducking low. In addition to the two-man crew, he could see the unit consisted of the sergeant and seven SWAT officers. They were all wearing heavy body armor and carrying an arsenal of weapons: submachine guns, assault rifles, breaching shotguns, stun grenades, and sniper rifles.

One of the officers jumped down, grabbed him by the arm. "Welcome aboard, sir. We'll get you suited up right away." Steiger was not surprised to hear a female voice. For most of its existence, Seattle's Special Weapons and Tactics Team had been an all-male bastion. The unit now included four women among its elite thirty-member force, half of them part of this mission. After helping him into the bulletproof gear, the officer motioned to an empty seat, then crouched down on the floor.

"What's our 10-20, sir?" she asked.

"North Beach," Steiger shouted. "The good guys are driving a black pickup."

"Roger that, sir."

Seconds later, the pilot pulled back on the control stick and the big Huey slowly lifted up, hovering about twenty feet above the lawn. He then dropped the nose five degrees and banked off over the Courthouse into a threatening sky.

Steiger stared out the open door. He was in the middle of a shitstorm and there was no turning back.

Jesus, I hope we're not too late.

CHAPTER 45

4 April, 2:40 PM PDT
Port Townsend, Washington

ZORA AND MICKEY had been pinned down for close to twenty minutes now, nearly out of ammo, and playing a dangerous waiting game. Their eyes beamed across sixty feet of bedlam with nowhere to go. That's when they heard the thundering roar of the helicopter, flying low and moving fast. The chopper swooped in from the east, dropping below the tree line over Fort Worden State Park. It hit the dirt in a military-style landing behind a grassy knoll a hundred yards from Mickey's truck, creating a powerful downdraft.

The SWAT unit rolled out loaded for war, weapons at the ready, taking heavy fire from Chandler's muscle-men. Using hand signals, the officers moved into position on the backside of the hill, careful not put Zora and Mickey between them and their adversaries.

Holy shit! Zora thought. *They're intimidating as hell just to look at.*

The officers hit with full automatic fire, riddling one of their targets with so many rounds he danced like a puppet. He was dead before he hit the ground. Everything was noise and confusion, the barrage relentless. The other two goons came up shooting and dove into the SUV. The big engine surged, spinning the vehicle around in a tire-ripping turn, spitting gravel thirty feet into the air. It then went careening down an embankment in a hail of bullets before crashing violently into a drainage ditch. The muscle staggered out, hands raised, soaked in blood.

The SWAT team moved in swiftly on full alert. Two officers flanked right, three took the center, and two flanked left. The sergeant shouted, "On the ground, now! Spread 'em. Hands behind your heads, fingers interlocked."

Zora watched in amazement, momentarily stunned. She then turned to Mickey and grabbed his arm. "Listen, I need your phone, okay? I don't have time to explain."

"Okay, sure." He pulled his cell from a jacket pocket, handed it to her.

Zora then leaped to her feet and ran full tilt for the beach. She skidded to a stop, her eyes darting in both directions. She spotted Chandler sprinting across a minefield of rocks and driftwood toward the lighthouse at Point Wilson. Zora screamed his name, fired a warning shot into the air, and tore off after him.

Chandler glanced back over his shoulder, hesitated for a brief moment, but kept on running.

The chase continued for another minute or so, then Zora heard the intense *whomp-whomp-whomping* of the chopper. She looked up and did a double-take. Steiger was at the controls, Mickey in the copilot's seat. The big bird circled out over the strait, banked hard, and soon landed on the shore about twenty yards from Chandler. He pulled up, frantically looking for an escape route that did not exist. There was water on his right, a soaring bluff on his left, and a menacing machine behind him.

Zora turned on the afterburners, running flat-out until she was nearly on top of him. She held the weapon six inches from his head. "Get on your knees, numb-nuts."

Chandler stood stone cold, breathing hard. He knelt down slowly, raising his arms in mock surrender. "Whatever you say, captain."

Steiger then came hustling along the beach toward them, Mickey at his side. "Okay, I need everybody to cool their jets here," Steiger said, spreading his hands apart. "We're gonna do this the right way."

"Who the hell are you?" Chandler shouted, craning his neck.

"Detective Cloyd Steiger, Seattle PD."

"It's about time. Listen, you need to –"

"Shut the fuck up," Zora barked before Steiger could respond. She waved the gun menacingly in Chandler's face.

"C'mon now, Ms. Flynn," Steiger said with a deadeye stare. "You need to turn him over to me. Right now. There'll be a full investigation, no more of this SIU bullshit. I promise you I'll nail this guy, send him away for a nice long stay in Walla Walla."

"I believe you mean it, too. But you know damn well he'll skate. You said so yourself."

"Look, I understand what you're doing here. If this lizard was responsible for killing my mother, I'd probably do the same thing. I wouldn't be wearing a badge, though, would I? So this needs to stop. Vigilante justice is not the answer."

"Well, I got news for you, detective," Zora snapped. "It is today." She pulled Mickey's phone from her pocket, and punched in a number she'd committed to memory.

A mile to the northeast, just beyond the Coast Guard complex, Houdini answered the call. He hadn't been able to discuss the plan with Zora in any detail, but he knew it was time to pull the trigger. Confirming his position, he snapped the phone shut and engaged the motor on the twelve foot Zodiac. After leaving the *Northern Star*, he had kayaked down to Kala Point where a trusted friend had loaned him the rugged, inflatable boat. He'd then come to this spot to wait for further instructions. He had them now. Picking up speed, Houdini maneuvered the craft through choppy seas, the shifting tides an ever-changing mosaic of new color schemes. He glanced up at the sky. Threatening dark clouds had moved on and the drizzle had stopped.

A good sign, he thought. *The weather is cooperating.*

From this vantage point, the rugged cliffs bordering the strait looked wild and unsettled. Houdini imagined this was how the land had looked four thousand years ago when his People first arrived on the shores of Neah Bay. Long before there was a United States of America. Long before the white man destroyed the Makah's way of life. As he motored on, his mind was a jumble of dark thoughts. He remembered his sad goodbye to Samson, and the cruel act of betrayal he'd been forced to deploy in capturing its replacement. But then his thoughts quickly shifted to the rogue whales. How glorious it must have been to see them free the captive orca from its temporary prison. He only wished he could've been there.

Houdini contemplated all of this, along with many unanswered questions. Where had the mighty rogues come from? Why were they here? And were they truly envoys of fate as the Old One had predicted? His words came to Houdini now: *There are forces at work in nature beyond our understanding, yet all of us are related to everything else, to the elements, to the earth and seas, to all animal life. It is the Native way. When the time is right, my son, you will know, through dreams and visions, powers all shamans receive from their ties with the spirit world.*

Near the lighthouse at Point Wilson, Houdini motored through a patch of calm water. He slowed the boat, and took the engine out of gear. On shore, just around the bend, he could see Zora and three men. Men he assumed to be Mickey Kincaid, the detective from Seattle, and Mitchell Chandler. The thought had barely registered when the wind picked up, gusting from the west, blowing ocean cold in his face. In that same moment he saw it, a glossy black dorsal fin, arched slightly forward, and rising slowly out of the water. It was massive, more than three stories high. An instant later, the pitch of the boat shifted and the whale disappeared.

Houdini peered over the side, searching the dark waters below. His breath was now coming in short bursts. He felt a sudden chill as the elegant body appeared again. This time the whale was some forty feet down, its ghostly image suspended in a liquid state of limbo.

Donning his distinctive red cloak and headpiece, Houdini reached for the rattle lying beside him in the rubber hull. He then began the familiar chant, channeling his ancestors as he'd done the day before. The clock was ticking, just as it had been then, and he felt a sharp sense of relief when the gigantic creature began its ascent. The sleek black shape slowly emerged in a swirling cloud of white foam, sending a plume of water fifty feet into the air. The spray cascaded down onto the boat with a loud, whooshing sound, like a cold mountain waterfall. Houdini shook off the deluge with a surge of adrenaline.

Seconds later, a series of disturbing images began slinging through his head like an art-house film in fast-forward – some in black and white, others in vibrant colors, all remarkably vivid. Houdini felt his entire body begin to shake, his senses heightened. It wasn't a feeling of fear, but rather a magnetic attraction fueled by wonder. He reached into the numbing water and gently stroked the whale's rubbery rostrum. The creature responded at once, rotating a quarter turn to reveal a fiery copper slash that ran half the length of its body. Shivering with energy, Houdini squeezed the rattle tightly and looked squarely into its penetrating black eye. He couldn't say for sure what he saw – recognition, acceptance, understanding – but he was certain of one thing: the colossal blackfish was staring back, with a great and mysterious intelligence.

As Houdini resumed the chant, something even more astounding happened, something so completely unexpected it shook him to the bone.

The whale began mimicking the sounds it had just heard.

And the replay was pitch perfect.

CHAPTER 46

4 April, 2:55 PM PDT
Port Townsend, Washington

BACK ON THE ROCKY SHORE, Zora and Steiger continued their standoff, staring at one another across a thirty foot expanse of sand, rocks, and boulders. Zora glanced out to sea, caught a glimpse of Houdini, then turned back to the detective. "Okay," she said. "It's showtime."

Steiger didn't budge. "I don't know what you've got in mind here, captain, but whatever it is it ain't gonna happen." His right hand drifted toward the weapon tucked into his shoulder holster.

"I would reconsider if I were you, detective," Zora said, her eyes flashing. "Besides, this is just the first act." She then threw Chandler a murderous glance, lowered the pistol...aimed...and fired. The bullet ripped through the leather toe of his shoe.

Chandler grabbed his foot with both hands, squealing like a wild pig. A few drops of blood trickled between his fingers. "What the fuck? The woman's insane, I tell you."

Steiger ignored the plea, lowered his hands. "Okay, okay...I'm standing down here."

Mickey inched closer to Zora, his intense eyes imploring her to do the same.

Zora had known all along that a coerced confession would never stand up in court, just like Chandler had said. But she still wanted the satisfaction of hearing him talk. "Tell my friends here what you told me."

"Look, I'm bleeding and –"

"It's your big fucking toe, get over it. I said talk!"

Chandler glared back at Zora. After a long hesitation, he rattled off a list of crimes committed in his name without taking responsibility for any of them. Then, without missing a beat, he shouted, "Now, call for a god-damn ambulance."

"Sorry, no can do," Zora said. "But I do have one more surprise for you."

Chandler protested fiercely. "Detective, you need to –"

Steiger didn't move.

Zora leveled the gun at Chandler's crotch, her gaze hard and steady. "Please, do something stupid."

"Jesus, what *now*?"

"See, there's this guy named Buck Brannaman. He talks to horses."

"Well good for him," Chandler snapped.

"They call him 'The Horse Whisperer.' You're a big movie mogul, Chandler, you must know the film."

"Sure, Robert Redford and Kristin Scott Thomas. What about it?"

"Turn around."

Chandler winced, shifted sideways, and craned his neck. Mickey and Steiger followed his gaze to the rolling, gray waters. Two hundred yards offshore, they spotted Houdini. He was at the helm of the Zodiac, moving slowly east to west, framed by the snow-capped peak of Mt. Baker. On any other day, it was the stuff of postcards. But not this day.

"The guy in the boat," Zora said calmly. "His name's Houdini, like the magician. He talks to animals too…whales…*killer* whales to be precise. And they listen to him. I've seen it."

"This woman's out her mind, detective. *Do* something."

Steiger studied their faces, again said nothing.

Several tense moments passed. Then Houdini roared in on the inflata-ble. He beached the craft and jumped onto the sand. His eyes were filled with wonder and anticipation.

"They came, right?" Zora asked, a bit wide-eyed herself. "How did you know?"

The wild card – a critical piece of their precarious plan – had turned out to be the ace of spades. Five aces to be exact.

Houdini shrugged "I didn't. They just *knew*."

Zora reached for Houdini's hand, but froze at the sound of the earth shattering noise. She looked past Steiger as the sea came alive, infused with energy. An immense dorsal fin burst through the surface, the water boiling up and streaming over its pointed edge in sweeping, silvery waves. Four more monsters soon erupted from the depths, tails lashing, their blows echoing in an ear-popping chorus of *Kawoofs!* The mighty creatures soared upward in a stirring, choreographed spy hop, hovering at the apex, their sleek black fins reflecting the brilliant sunshine. Then, as if by silent cue, they dropped back into the sea and out of sight. The impact of their collective mass was so powerful, however, it triggered a tsunami-like wave.

In the next instant, an enormous wall of water came hurtling toward land.

"Get down!" Zora screamed. She dove head-first into the deafening rush of water, her body pummeled by the snarling foam and jagged rocks. She came out of the darkness, only to be blindsided by another foaming torrent. Again, she fought her way to the surface, her lungs screaming for oxygen. Her head hurt, her neck hurt, a searing pain knifed through her chest. She tried standing in the swirling waters, but her aching legs would not cooperate. Finally she managed to pull herself up and survey the scene.

It looked like a war zone.

The chopper was teetering on its nose, the rotor blade a twisted hunk of metal. Mickey and Steiger had been swept to higher ground, driftwood scattered around them. They were conscious and did not appear to be seriously hurt. Chandler lay sprawled out on the beach, moaning loudly. He was covered with bull kelp and eelgrass, but he too seemed okay.

Next...Houdini popped up from behind a massive bolder. He had also avoided serious injury. Zora motioned with her hand, then she and Houdini slogged their way through debris and knee-deep water to the Zodiac. It had been tossed violently against the cliff, miraculously bouncing back to its original position. The small Honda outboard was askew but still firmly attached to the wooden transom.

"You think it'll work?" Zora asked.

"Yup, it should." Houdini tilted the propeller into the water, and made a few adjustments to the fittings on the mount. After checking to make sure it was in neutral gear, he yanked the pull cord. The engine sputtered and coughed. He pulled the cord a second time. No luck. On the third try the engine jumped to life.

"Good," Zora said, staring down at Chandler. He glared back, shouted a string of expletives, and started crab-crawling along the rocky shore. She reacted quickly to overtake him, the tempest inside her now raging at full force. After securing his arms behind his back, she pulled the zip tie from her pocket, looped it around his wrists, and pulled tight. Zora was running on empty now, not exactly sure what to do next. Then she looked up, and what she saw took her breath away. The rogue whales were knifing back and forth in wide sweeping arcs a hundred yards from shore, moving closer with each rotation.

Suddenly everything came into focus.

Sensing his fate, Chandler roared, "No! You can't... you won't."

On the sandy ridge, Mickey and Steiger tried to stand, but both men were too groggy to pull themselves up. "He's right," Steiger yelled in a hoarse voice. "Don't do it, captain."

"Sorry, detective," Zora hollered back. She and Houdini then hauled Chandler to his feet. He was a load, but they managed to drag him to the boat and shove him over the side. He landed with a heavy thud.

"You'll never get away with this," he screamed, his voice now frantic.

Zora leaned down inches from his face, the sweet countenance of her mother coalescing in her mind. "Ask me if I care, Chandler. Ask me if I *fucking* care."

In that moment, their eyes locked. Chandler's face was a mask of horror. Zora held his gaze, taking a mental snapshot of a desperate man, a man decisively beaten at his own game.

It's not enough, she thought, *not nearly enough.*

Even so, sentencing this man to his own death was not in her DNA. It didn't matter how justified that decision might be, or how irresistible the urge. Zora threw Chandler a final, piercing look and then stepped over to disengage the engine. As she reached for the lever, a volley of loud shouts rang out in the distance. Spinning around, she spotted a platoon of SWAT officers, sheriff's deputies, and Port Townsend's finest hustling along the beach. They were waving weapons in the air, their handheld radios squawking incessantly.

Zora's back was turned for only a few seconds, but time enough for Chandler to make his move. Scrambling to his knees, he made a wild dive for the gear shift, engaging the boat's engine. "You really *are* an idiot, captain," he shouted.

An instant later, the inflatable craft roared out to sea. After moving a safe distance away, Chandler attempted to maneuver the Zodiac back to shore.

Part way through the turn, however, a massive wave side-swiped the boat. It lurched hard to port, throwing Chandler backwards into the rubber hull.

Looking on, Zora's entire world suddenly shifted into hyper-slow motion. She heard more shouts from the approaching cops, but they were unintelligible, like the muffled, reverse-echo sound of a song played backwards on tape. A quarter-mile out to sea, the out-of-control Zodiac zigzagged wildly, motoring headlong into what was now a maelstrom of leviathans. Chandler held on for a few desperate moments before being tossed into the roiling sea. He came up for air, but his frantic screams were quickly choked off by the sharp, strident calls of the giant orcas. One creature pounced immediately, wrenching Chandler clean out of the water. The beast then flipped him upside down and flung him across fifty feet of swirling foam. A second beast snagged him in midair, spun him around like a top, and sent him flying in a different direction. Chandler's left leg was now gone, a shower of blood streaming from the stump.

"Jesus," Zora exclaimed. "What the –"

"It's how orcas teach their young to hunt and play," Houdini shouted. "And *kill*."

The other three creatures soon joined in, whipping their helpless prey from one gaping mouth to another, over and back, in a gruesome game of volleyball without the net. The speed and force were so great, Chandler's body nearly exploded. Seconds later, there was nothing left of him at all. The whales then let loose with a final train of bellowing roars, thrust their mighty tail flukes into the air, and disappeared beneath the surface.

Silent minutes passed.

The seas calmed.

An eerie quiet descended over North Beach.

On shore everyone stood frozen in place, too stunned to even move.

And for the longest time, no one did.

CHAPTER 47

THE FOLLOWING DAY, as the Courthouse clock chimed the hour, Detective Cloyd Steiger followed Jefferson County Prosecuting Attorney Scott Rosekrans out the front door of the grand old building and down the steps to a makeshift stage. They were joined there by the FBI Director, Washington State's attorney general, Port Townsend's mayor, the chief of police, and the local sheriff.

Steiger had a bit of a shiner, but otherwise the doctors had given him a clean bill of health. He stopped on the concrete landing for a few seconds, looking over a rolling sea of humanity. The press conference had been announced just two hours earlier in hopes of avoiding just such a spectacle, but social networking sites and frothing reporters had gone into overdrive. The three block area resembled a Bangkok market. So did the sights and sounds and smells, sharp and biting. As far as the eye could see, there were street performers, food vendors, activists, and thousands of curious onlookers, all jammed together in one big mash-up.

Of course the usual media suspects were out in full force – *Dateline, 60 Minutes, 48 Hours, CNN, Fox News, MSNBC,* along with the big dailies led by *The New York Times* and *Washington Post*. Internet news websites and major TV networks from around the globe also joined the circus. Off to one side, harried producers, camera crews, and a dozen cable windbags jockeyed for position behind barricades manned by a contingent of sheriff's deputies, most of them awestruck by the power of celebrity.

Jia-li Han, however, was not among the masses. She had been afforded the VIP treatment and was sitting in a roped-off section adjacent to the stage. A cadre of state politicians sat on either side of her, preening for the cameras.

One person, however, was conspicuously absent: Governor Spencer Ryan.

Steiger took in the Felliniesque scene with a strange sense of detachment, thinking it was a fitting sequel to the bizarre chain of events that had transpired the previous afternoon. The images played over and over in his head, locking on the moment Mitchell Chandler had fallen back into that boat, his fate sealed by his own hand. And therein lay the greatest irony of all because Zora Flynn had never intended for Chandler to die. She'd explained to Steiger that all along her plan had been to force a confession out of the man and then – assuming the rogue whales showed up – scare the bejesus out of him. It was a masterful performance, too.

If the woman ever decides to give up fishing, she's sure as hell got a future in Hollywood.

As for his own role in all this, Steiger had done what cops were supposed to do: enforce the law. The oath to serve and protect was one he'd always taken seriously, even if it meant shielding the likes of Mitchell Chandler. But that oath, at least as he interpreted it, allowed for a certain amount of "discretion." And so when it came to the assault and kidnapping charges hanging over the heads of the captain and her partners-in-crime – Mickey Kincaid and the shaman – Steiger had chosen to look the other way. And by doing so, he'd essentially absolved them of any pending charges. After all, he reasoned, they'd suffered enough already. What could possibly be gained by adding to their grief?

To help sell the story, Steiger had provided authorities with a somewhat "altered" version of events. He explained that Chandler had gone to North Beach willingly and that his security team had overreacted, forcing Seattle's SWAT unit into action. The tale was a whopper. He knew it and so did the DA. He looked sideways at him the entire time.

A veteran FBI agent called in on the case accused Steiger of "gaslighting." It was a tactic used back in the day by cowboy cops to manipulate facts and distort reality. The agent had no proof, of course, and he didn't press the matter. Then, there were the officers on the beach. To a person they said they couldn't be sure of what had happened. They recalled that seconds before Chandler's horrifying death, they'd seen him speed off in the Zodiac, waving his arms and screaming something unintelligible. But that was the extent of it.

Chandler's two surviving henchmen, under guard at the local hospital, predictably offered very different accounts of the entire affair. But their stories contradicted statements made by law enforcement and others, which left only the man himself – and Mitchell Chandler was deader than dead.

Steiger was thinking about all this as Rosekrans took the stage. He was dressed in a tailored, gray three-piece suit. Despite the chaos swirling around him, he appeared remarkably calm. He stepped to a tangle of microphones and digital recorders clipped to the lectern, cleared his throat, and motioned for quiet. It took the caffeine-fueled crowd some time to settle, but the din soon subsided.

"Ladies and gentlemen," the DA said. "Thank you for coming. I will be brief and answer a few questions afterward." He introduced himself and then paused, choosing his words carefully. "Let me begin by making one thing very clear. While we believe the events at the oceanarium in Seattle early yesterday morning are linked to what happened here in Port Townsend later in the day, the FBI has unequivocally ruled out terrorism as a motive in both instances."

"Old news," someone shouted. Indeed the Internet had been buzzing with reports about the rogue whales and the trail of destruction left in their wake.

Rosekrans continued. "Now, as most of you know my office is looking into a number of serious felonies related to these events, with the able assistance of local police, the FBI, and our state's attorney general. These crimes include blackmail, conspiracy, and manslaughter, along with the illegal capture of one of our region's most precious assets, the killer whale." The DA paused again, now seeming to find his rhythm. "Since this is an ongoing investigation, I am not at liberty to discuss specific facts relating to these cases at this time. However, I *can* tell you that we have identified two of the individuals we believe were involved, both of whom are now deceased – Preston Tradd, a consultant from Irvine, California, and Mitchell Chandler, owner of Kingdom of the Sea theme park in Seattle, among other entities. As additional information becomes available, we will pass it on to all of you as appropriate. Now, are there any questions?"

"What can you tell us about Chandler?" one reporter shouted out.

Another chimed in, "Yeah, how exactly did he die? And what about the shootout on the beach?"

Rosekrans adjusted the microphone, took a sip of water. "Again, not all the facts are in. But I *can* confirm what has already been reported on the news. At approximately 2:45 yesterday afternoon, there was a confrontation between Mr. Chandler and two other individuals at North Beach, just a few miles from here. We believe Mr. Chandler's security team misconstrued it as some kind of threat and responded with violence. Seattle homicide detective Cloyd Steiger, seated here to my right, had wisely put the brave men and women of his city's SWAT team on alert. And they interceded. Unfortunately, one man died at the scene and two others were arrested. When detective Steiger attempted to bring Mr. Chandler in for questioning, he refused. He chose instead to flee the scene in a motorized boat, at which time he met his demise."

"Who did Chandler confront at the beach?" blurted a chorus of voices.

"I can't disclose that information at this time," Rosekrans said, pointing to a local writer he recognized. She was immediately shouted down by Geraldo Rivera from Fox News.

"What about this boat you referred to?" Rivera asked in an acerbic tone. "Did it just magically drop out of the sky?"

"No, it did not – and we're looking into that."

CNN's Anderson Cooper grabbed the spotlight next. "I spoke with several eyewitnesses last evening," he said dispassionately. "They claim that Mr. Chandler was abducted right here on the front lawn of the Courthouse by an African-American male and a tall red-haired female. Are they the two other *individuals* you referred to?"

Steiger stiffened in his chair.

It was the one gaping hole in an otherwise airtight, if implausible, tale.

The eyewitnesses had indeed given statements to that effect, yet upon further questioning they'd told police they weren't exactly sure what they'd seen. The great debate around town quickly became, what was behind this collective change of heart? Was it because the five women and two men believed justice had been served? Were they sparing the taxpayers from an expensive trial? Or, was this simply a case of Port Townsend at its quirky best? The scuttlebutt among those in the know had it that at least four of the witnesses – enough for a quorum – were devoted fans of *Waking Ned Devine*. The movie was about an entire Irish village which entered into a pact of silence in order to claim a huge lottery prize. Steiger had seen the film years earlier and counted it among his favorites. It was funny, poignant, and entirely plausible. He chuckled at the thought of old Ned sitting in his chair in front of the TV clutching the "lucky" ticket in his cold, dead hands.

The scuttlebutt, Steiger happily concluded, had carried the day.

Rosekrans glanced over at him now, seemed to read his mind, then turned back to the silver-haired reporter. "No comment, Mr. Cooper."

Nancy Grace stepped forward, sneering her epic sneer. "I heard from reliable sources that the governor is involved? Is that true?"

"Again, I cannot disclose that information," Rosekrans remarked. "Next question?"

The DA faced a few other fastballs, hit a couple out of the park, then made a hasty retreat from the podium. He nodded to the dignitaries who followed him up the stairs and into the heavily-guarded Courthouse. The questions were still coming at him in machine-gun volleys.

Steiger trailed a few feet behind the others, holding the door open for Jia-li Han. Immediately after they entered the building, she pulled him aside and asked for a minute of his time. They made their way to an open office down the hall, away from the thunderous mob.

Jia-li smiled an all-knowing smile and said, "Listen, detective, forget what those eyewitnesses said, we both know what *really* happened to Chandler on the front lawn. Frankly, I don't care about any of that. What I *am* curious about, though, is what went down at the beach?"

"It's all there in my report, Ms. Han," Steiger said with a straight face. "Signed, sealed, and delivered."

"Right. And I'll see it eventually. But something tells me there's a lot *more* to the story."

"Then I guess you'll just have to wait for the results of the investigations. There'll be two, you know. A criminal investigation conducted by local cops – and an officer-involved shooting investigation involving the SWAT team. My homicide colleagues back in Seattle will handle that one."

"I'll be sure to follow up on those. In the meantime, I intend to keep digging."

"As it should be," Steiger said. "Only you can scratch me from your list of contacts, Ms. Han."

"Yeah, why is that?"

"Well, after I gave my statement yesterday, I hightailed it back to Seattle, had a long talk with the wife. We both decided it was time. So this morning, I turned in my badge and gun."

"Wow! You retired?"

"Yeah, I had a great run and finally got justice for Eddie."

"Eddie?"

"My former partner. Long story. Maybe someday I'll tell you about it over a few Coronas. Let's just say he's at peace now. And so am I."

"Sounds good, detective," Jia-li said. "So what are you going to do with yourself? Somehow I don't see you sitting around on the front porch strumming an old guitar."

Steiger walked Jia-li to the window, pointed to a shiny motorcycle parked in a barricaded lot next to the Courthouse. The big iron horse was the V-Rod Harley-Davidson, 100th Anniversary edition, everything black and chrome. "You know what they say, 'For Every Soul, There's a Harley.' She's packed up and ready to roll. By the time you get back to the TV station, I'll be in the wind. Somewhere between here and nowhere."

"That's so cool." Jia-li looked so happy for him, Steiger thought she might just plant one on his cheek. "Listen, you remember my fiancé, right?"

"Jason? Sure. How's he doing?"

"He's great, thanks. Making a big change, too, as a matter of fact. He kissed the tort world goodbye last week, which sure didn't break this girl's heart. Dance with the devil long enough and you grow horns and a tail. Anyway, he just opened a free legal clinic in Belltown."

"Good for him."

"He's out there in that mob somewhere, but he asked me to say hi."

"I appreciate that. Give him my best."

"Sure thing," Jia-li said. She stepped closer, wrapping her arms around Steiger's waist. "You're a good man, Detective Cloyd Steiger. A *really* good man."

"And you're a class act, young lady. Now go knock 'em dead."

"I will. You ride safely and well, okay?"

Steiger winked, broke into that broad Irish grin, and then marched out the door.

CHAPTER 48

9 April, 11:15 AM PDT
Discovery Bay, Washington

FOUR DAYS AFTER the press conference, investigators were still trying to figure out exactly what had happened during those chaotic few hours at KOS-Seattle and later the same afternoon in Port Townsend. Media coverage also continued unabated. Reporters from around the globe scrambled to find any new tidbits of information, bleary-eyed from mining the same old territory. Adding to their frustration, there had been no further sightings of the rogue whales, perhaps because the creatures had returned "to the source of all things" in a giant spaceship. At least that's what Captain Cody and his Cosmic Commandos believed. The Captain claimed to have photographic evidence of the celestial phenomenon, but so far he had not produced it.

The real story, of course, was much more down to earth...and it would change everything.

Twenty minutes and a million miles from the hysteria at North Beach, Zora and Houdini stepped aboard the *Sockdolager*, Mickey's scrappy twenty-four-foot sailboat. It was docked outside his home on Discovery Bay. Mickey had arrived a few moments earlier to prepare for what would surely be an emotional day. After greeting his guests, he took the helm while Houdini and Zora cast off the mooring lines. The breeze quickly picked up and the boat was soon running under sail in a northerly direction along the eastern shore of the bay.

A mile or so up the coast, Mickey tacked to starboard, catching a gust of wind that carried them into a sheltered cove off Protection Island – a national wildlife refuge frequented by gulls, puffins, and harbor seals, each noisily striving to outperform the others. After lowering the main sail and drifter, Mickey allowed the boat to drift a bit closer to land before dropping anchor. Houdini took a seat next to Zora on the lee side of the cockpit. Mickey stepped into the companionway hatch, his elbows resting on the coaming. He explained that it was here, on this spectacular stretch of water, that Katrina had experienced her first up-close encounter with an orca. An experience that forever changed the course of her young life.

And today she was coming home.

For Zora it was the second solemn occasion in three days. Forty-eight hours earlier, she'd laid her beloved mother to rest on family-owned property near the Idaho ranch that had been *her* home for so many years. The quiet site was shaded by a stately oak tree that stood tall on a rolling hill overlooking the Snake River. A long-time family acquaintance – a grizzly-bearded river-runner turned Holy Man – had presided over a private memorial service attended by close friends and neighbors.

Now Zora had come to say farewell to a dear friend, perhaps offer a bit of comfort to her grieving brother. "What about your parents?" she asked.

Mickey sighed and said, "I finally reached them, two or three days ago now. I've lost track of time. Anyway, they got back as soon as they could. It's been really hard on them, hard on all of us. They couldn't handle coming out here, so I went over to the house early this morning. They said their goodbyes then."

"I understand," Zora said. "Give them my best."

"I will, thanks."

Mickey took a deep breath, and punched play on a portable DVD player. He then picked up a brass urn sitting on the deck. After several long moments of contemplation, he emptied the contents in a slow, deliberate sweeping motion. A light wind carried Katrina's ashes over calm seas to whispered prayers and a haunting Celtic melody from her favorite artist: Loreena McKennitt. Blinking away tears, Mickey turned to Zora and Houdini and whispered, "Thanks, both of you. This really means a lot to me. It's what Kat would have wanted."

"We're all going to miss her," Zora said, fighting her own tears, but with no more success than Mickey.

The song soon ended, followed by a long silence. The wind sweeping softly over the waves was now the only sound. Moments later, fifty yards off the port bow, the dorsal fin of a resident orca cut the surface. Then, in a gesture so subtle it might have been imagined, the whale lifted out of the water, seeming to offer a prayer of its own. It was an image none of them would ever forget.

For a long time no one spoke, listening to the lapping water in quiet reflection.

Then...Katrina's cat, Vera, appeared at the top of the cabin stairs. She stretched regally, moseyed over to Houdini, and with great fanfare hopped onto his lap. A second or two later, she was curled up in a tight ball, purring contentedly.

Her presence immediately lightened the mood.

Zora leaned over, scratched Vera's ears. "So glad you found her, Mickey. Where was she?"

"Ah, just hangin' out," he said. "She knows something's up with Kat for sure...but good to see she's found a new friend."

Houdini gently stroked the cat's neck, staring off into the bay, seemingly lost in thought.

"What is it?" Zora asked.

There was a long pause, then he whispered, "The rogue whales. I know why they've come."

"You do?" Zora exclaimed, shooting a curious glance at Mickey.

Houdini nodded, shifted in his seat, and began to talk. Like pages ripped from a diary, he walked them through his recent conversations with the Old One. He described the Old One's friendship with Chief Raven Claw and their previous encounters with the mighty blackfish. In spare, halting words he went on to explain about the violent, disturbing visions he'd experienced before the rogue whales surfaced at North Beach – and the incredible sense of calm he'd then felt in their presence.

As the story unfolded, Zora and Mickey listened with a growing sense of awe, but neither of them spoke.

Continuing, Houdini said, "I didn't say anything because it was all a big blur, everything scattered and disjointed. Then the images slowly started coming together. They morphed into a series of three short *films* I guess you'd call them. The first included flashes of melting icebergs, blazing forests, raging rivers, warring armies, starving children, and the like."

"Global warming," Zora said matter-of-factly. She remembered something Katrina had once told her. Research, she'd said, indicated that hundred-year climate events were now happening every five to ten years. Events that were real, one way, and directly caused by humans.

Houdini nodded his agreement, adding, "And if I'm right, the oceans are in much worse shape than anyone thought. So is the rest of the planet. What that means is, many of the cataclysmic events scientists are predicting forty, fifty years from now are coming at us a whole lot sooner."

"How *much* sooner?" Zora asked.

"I had no idea at first. So many of the pieces just didn't fit. So I went online, did some research, ran a bunch of numbers. First I looked at Chief Raven Claw's encounter with the rogue whales. It happened a few years before he died, which meant sometime in the late 1920s. The visions I had from that period were made up of angry speeches, screaming crowds, death squads."

"The rise of the Nazi party," Mickey said. "Has to be."

"Yup. Hitler became Chancellor in '33. The Gestapo began their assault on the Jews six years later. Then came the horrors of the concentration camps and death chambers. All of that suffering could have been stopped, *should* have been stopped. And Chief Raven Claw tried, but no one listened."

"What about the Old One's encounter?" Zora asked.

"It happened over six decades later. He too was an old man by then. And the visions that came to me from that era were much different than the others – secret hideouts, hooded gunmen, exploding buildings, those kinds of things."

"*Terrorists.*" Zora and Mickey said it together.

Houdini nodded again. He explained that the real trouble had started in the early 90s following Desert Storm. It was then that Osama bin Laden had fled from Saudi Arabia, hid out in Sudan, and began building his terror network. Then in '98 he issued a public fatwa declaring holy war, or jihad, against the West and Israel. "He signed it as head of al Qaeda," Houdini added. "Three years later, we got sucker-punched."

A long pause, then Zora said, "Okay, so you're saying the rogue whales warned us about Hitler and bin Laden. I get that, or at least I think I do. But how does *Mitchell Chandler* fit into all this. He's hardly in their league."

"I agree," Houdini said. "But it's not about any one individual, Zora. It's about the perverse movements they lead. In Chandler's case, it's about pure greed – and the hell with the environment or anything else. Think of what's happened over the years, the loss of all those lives, the human suffering, trillions of dollars up in smoke." He then filled them in on the Old One's trip to Washington, D.C., and his meeting with a senior government official there. The Old One, he said, had warned them about 9/11, but he was ignored by higher ups. "They weren't listening *then*, they're not listening *now*. So this isn't about thousands or even millions of lives being on the line. It's about *billions* of lives."

Zora nodded. It made sense to her now. And the symbolism gave her chills, mostly because of something else Katrina had said, that the largest predator known to mankind had shown up amid wild weather patterns occurring with increasing frequency all over the globe. *Dirty* weather as it was being called in some circles.

Zora's voice pulled tight, ready to crack. "So, what's the verdict?"

"Actually it's not that tough to figure out," Houdini said. "The Holocaust happened less than ten years after Chief Raven Claw's encounter with the rogue whales. There's a similar timeline in play with the Old One and 9/11."

Mickey interjected, "So, if that pattern holds true, we're looking at major seismic events happening all over the world, what, sometime during the next decade?"

"Jesus," Zora said. "That's really frightening."

"Damn right it is," Mickey added.

Houdini shook his head. "Problem is, I don't see anyone listening to me *either*. I mean, what exactly do I say? My name is Houdini. I'm a shaman. And guess what folks, those colossal creatures you saw on TV spoke to me in a vision. They told me the planet was headed for oblivion. Sounds crazier than the nut jobs who claim the sky is falling every twenty years or so. I can hear the howls of laughter now."

Just then, the cat stood up, stretched languorously, jumped back onto the deck, and disappeared down the hatch.

"See," Houdini said, a smile creeping across his face. "Even Vera doesn't buy it."

The mood shifted again.

Mickey said, "Look, I agree. It *does* sound crazy. You're implying that these rogue whales not only foretell the future, they communicate it too."

Houdini nodded. "I'm not *implying* anything, Mickey. I'm saying it's going to happen, just like the Holocaust and 9/11 happened. Look, some truths can never be proven true. The mystical connection that exists between the Great Spirit and the animal world is one of them. This connection is very powerful, especially with the eagle, the wolf, and the great orca." Houdini paused, lowered his head. "We Indians know it is so. But that won't help us here. If anything, it hurts our case. "

"Hold on a sec," Zora said. "It's different this time."

"*What's* different?" Houdini asked.

"The rogue whales. People have *seen* them, know they really exist. They've witnessed their intelligence firsthand. How else do you explain what happened to that family on the speedboat, or the reporter from Seattle? The whales knew they were *all* in trouble and saved their lives."

"The reporter," Mickey added. "Of course. Who better to..."

"Exactly," Zora interjected, smiling her first genuine smile in what seemed like a very long time. "I'll call her as soon as we get back."

CHAPTER 49

10 April, 1:15 PM PDT
Port Townsend, Washington

THE NEXT DAY, Mickey, Houdini, and Zora gathered around the lone picnic table in the tidy little park at North Beach, scene of the explosive fireworks just six days earlier. Other than an elderly woman walking her Lab along the shore, the area was deserted. The sky rumbled and the air smelled like rain, but so far the showers had stayed away. A mile offshore, three Navy cruisers steamed into view, a sleek black submarine wedged between the second and third ships.

Mickey explained that the convoy was headed to a major munitions handling facility located on Indian Island across Port Townsend Bay. "Makes you wonder, though, doesn't it?" he said.

"What's that?" Houdini asked.

"The Trident's a nuclear-powered gunslinger, carries enough ballistic missiles to wipe out a small country. So, why the escort?"

"Yeah, good question," Zora said. She leaned back, glancing over her shoulder at a late model Volvo that had just pulled in to the parking lot.

Jia-li Han stepped out of the vehicle, a resolute look on her face. She walked over, introduced herself, and sat down. After a few moments of small talk, she removed a notepad and pen from her bag. Smiling, she said, "Thank you for confiding in me, all of you. I promise to do your stories justice."

Zora nodded. "We're counting on that." She had called the reporter immediately after stepping ashore the previous afternoon. They had agreed there would be no camera crews or recordings here today, but that Jia-li was free to take notes.

"Listen," Jia-li said, looking at Zora. "I just got word that the two-hour special I mentioned to you on the phone airs next week...on NBC...with a global feed. Network execs assigned a team of senior producers, writers, and researchers to help me pull everything together." She wrote down the date and time on her notepad, ripped off the page, and handed it to Zora. "Now," she added. "I can't wait to hear your stories."

And over the next hour, she did.

Zora and Mickey went first, tag-teaming as they walked Jia-li through the brazen blackmail scheme involving Samson and the captured whale. Then, piece-by-piece, they presented the evidence they'd uncovered in the deaths of Zora's mother and Mickey's sister. When asked about the demise of Preston Tradd, Zora expressed her regrets, especially for his family. Even someone as deeply flawed as him, she said, deserved some measure of sympathy. She conveyed none of the same sentiments for Mitchell Chandler, whose fate had already been well documented in the media, even if the reports weren't entirely accurate.

As their story unfolded, Jia-li took copious notes and asked a lot of questions.

Then Houdini told *his* incredible tale, beginning with detailed narratives of the spiritual encounters between the Old One, Chief Raven Claw, and the rogue whales. Next he vividly described his own remarkable encounter and what he believed the whales' message to be. When he stopped talking, Jia-li held his gaze, making no attempt to hide her amazement.

Zora understood. Hearing all this a second time hit her even harder.

Finally, after several moments of silence, Jia-li set down her pen. "Can I just say that this is the most extraordinary story I've ever heard. Nothing else even comes close. It's going to rock the world. I can't thank you enough."

Houdini eyed her a bit skeptically. "So you plan to hold nothing back?"

"Not a thing!" Jia-li said, glancing around the table. "Maybe it will help if I tell you a little story of my own. Other than my fiancé, I haven't told this to another living soul. So please bear with me." She then recounted her own life-altering experience with one of the giant orcas, just minutes after she and Jason had been saved from certain death at the hands of the pirates. When Jia-li finished speaking, she added, thoughtfully, "You know, I've had the privilege of interviewing some of the most brilliant minds on the planet, but the wisdom and intelligence I saw in that animal was truly something special. I know you speak the truth, Houdini. And soon the world will know it, too."

One week later, the heavily promoted, two-hour special entitled *Rogue Justice* aired live in prime time in the U.S. It was seen by nearly three billion people around the globe, the most watched television show in history. Millions more watched on handheld devices.

The story hit with explosive force, its impact immediate and profound, both at home and abroad. At noon the following day, Governor Spencer Ryan of Washington resigned in the wake of evidence so meticulously researched and documented, he was left with no other choice. Criminal charges were pending. Ryan's brother-in-law – along with one of his lieutenants at Data-Locke Corporation – was promptly arrested for destroying evidence material to a homicide investigation. An hour after that, Jake Towers was indicted on multiple counts of fraud and conspiracy. The entire SIU unit was immediately suspended, pending further review by the woman who had taken over the state's top job: the lieutenant governor.

That same afternoon, Colby Freeman and Robert Dean – a.k.a. Iago – were also arrested and taken into custody by authorities. So was Darnell Atwater, identified by Zora as the gun-toting thug who had accosted her outside Mickey's place. Each of the men faced prison time for their roles in the Samson cover-up, the illegal capture of an orca, and the deaths of Katrina Kincaid and Stella Flynn. But the DA promptly dismissed the involuntary manslaughter charges against all three suspects. Rosekrans had explained to Zora and Mickey that the charges would be tough, if not impossible, to prove in the absence of any hard evidence. Neither of them took issue with the decision, applauded it in fact. The real villain, they said, had paid the ultimate price.

Leanne Bucaro and Big Boy Medlin were not implicated in any crime, leaving Savannah Sokolov as the only wild card. And Savannah immediately came forward, confessing everything she knew. She told the truth, the whole truth, and nothing but the truth and Rosekrans believed her. He decided not to file conspiracy charges, recommending instead probation and community service for her role in the cover-up.

The following day, a memorial service was held inside a private club not far from the Capitol Building in Olympia. Despite Mitchell Chandler's inglorious fall from grace, a large contingent of colleagues and employees gathered to pay their respects. The eulogy, delivered by the company's CFO, began with these words, *"When Mitchell walked into a room, he didn't ask a question, he made a statement... "* It was a somber affair as these things tended to be, yet the only tears shed were those of a stunning woman dressed in designer black.

Savannah Sokolov arrived alone and left alone.

Five days later, it was announced that Savannah had been named CEO at Chandler Global Enterprises, as specified in the living trust of the man she'd loved and lost. Her first order of business was to gather together all KOS employees worldwide, via teleconference. At that time, she introduced sweeping changes to be implemented at each of the company's fifteen theme parks. The changes, she said, had been discussed with Mitchell Chandler prior to his death. The fact that he'd only alluded to them in a general sense didn't really matter. The overall reaction among the rank and file was upbeat and positive. In Seattle, Big Boy told everyone who would listen every word of it was true.

The press release issued from the new CEO's office read, in part:

> *I am happy to announce that beginning today we are implementing a number of new initiatives designed to revolutionize our Aquatic Theme Parks Division.*
>
> *First, killer whale performances at every KOS park worldwide will cease immediately.*
>
> *Second, all breeding programs involving orcas have been permanently suspended.*
>
> *Third, killer whales currently in captivity and able to survive on their own will be released into the wild, pending examination by a team of seasoned veterinarians.*
>
> *Fourth, animals with serious health problems, or otherwise unreleasable, will be retired to large, netted sea-pens located in coves or bays with floating docks, facilitating close observation and expert medical care. In these instances, each whale will be teamed with at least one other companion, allowing them to live out their lives in a more natural, less stressful environment.*

Fifth, a whale-adoption program will be implemented to further enhance the emotional and educational benefits, and to help drive and sustain the momentum.

Sixth, an Oscar-winning team of documentary filmmakers has been retained to track, via satellite, the movements of those whales returned to the wild. This will be accomplished by mounting tiny, unobtrusive HD cameras at the base of the dorsal fins. This ground-breaking program will enable people the world over to travel with the orcas, hear what they hear, see what they see, all the while providing scientists with invaluable research data.

And finally, all Samson Stadiums will be systematically converted into IMAX 3D Dome Theatres to showcase films created from the footage captured by our documentary team, along with other productions featuring some of our most treasured cold-weather and deep-water species, including polar bears, dolphins, and sharks.

Activists and animal lovers everywhere rejoiced at the news. Some expressed skepticism, but most agreed the new CEO's commitment was genuine and sincere. It was one final announcement, however, that put all doubts to rest. Following an emotional meeting with Zora, Houdini, Mickey, and leading environmentalists, Savannah unveiled the "Kincaid Initiative," a series of ambitious research projects funded by KOS to "better conserve and manage the resources of the oceans by deepening knowledge through advanced scientific studies."

As exciting as all that proved to be, even more heat was generated by Houdini's astounding "prophecies." During the TV special, Jia-li Han had recounted them virtually word for word as described to her at North Beach. The following day, two skeptical pundits nearly burst into flames defending their "doubt and denial" campaigns against global warming. They summarily accused Jia-li and network executives of "reckless reporting and shameful exploitation by promoting a bunch of Indian hocus-pocus."

But, as severe weather continued to hammer the globe – and dire predictions mounted – many of the most obstinate critics threw their support behind stronger measures to protect the environment. And for the majority of scientists already on board, the truth, scope, scale, and full impact of the climate crisis had been dramatically and convincingly reaffirmed.

The debate, they proclaimed, was finally over.

There was, however, one sobering footnote to the extraordinary hub-bub. Just days after the television special aired, one of Jia-li's producers surreptitiously obtained copies of Top Secret government documents pertaining to the Old One's meeting in the nation's capital in October, 1999. The transcripts revealed that he had predicted a series of four catastrophic events occurring on the east coast on the same sun-drenched, summer's day early in the new Millennium. The attacks, he'd said, would come from the skies.

In late August, 2001, the documents resurfaced.

Few Washington bureaucrats took the ominous warnings seriously.

The counter-terrorism czar was one of them.

The president was not.

CHAPTER 50

23 April, 8:15 PM PDT
Port Townsend, Washington

IT WAS RAINING OUTSIDE and chilly inside, though the warmth of the blazing fire in the open stone fireplace had begun to take the edge off. Zora relaxed on the sofa in Mickey's cozy den, staring into the dancing flames. The sounds and scents were about as soothing as anything she could think of right now. She was dressed in a cotton sweater and corduroy jeans and wore no makeup. Her hair was still damp from the long, luxurious shower she'd just taken. She leaned down and scratched Vera's chin. The elegant gray tabby was splayed out in full regal manner, fast asleep, on the soft edge of a colorful, hand woven area rug.

Mickey walked in from the kitchen moments later, a bottle of red wine in one hand, two glasses in the other. He was barefoot, wearing blue jeans and a black T-shirt. "Vera has the run of the joint as if you couldn't tell."

"No kidding. She's a real charmer, isn't she?"

"Yeah, that she is." Mickey said, easing down next to Zora. "And what about you, Zora? You doing okay?"

"Yeah, fine, just a little tired is all."

"Sure you're not hungry? I can whip something up if –"

"No, the wine's perfect, Mickey. And the fire. I so love the smell of burning wood."

He nodded, popped the cork, and poured the wine. For a long moment they sat quietly, without saying a word. It had been nearly two weeks since they'd met with Jia-li Han at North Beach. Mickey had done his best to convince Zora to stick around after that, if only for a few days. He said he would take her camping into the meadows and mountains of the

Olympic Peninsula, a world away from the camera crews and reporters still lurking about in the area.

Zora had wanted to stay too, torn between her head and her heart. In the end she'd said, "No," and reluctantly Mickey had driven her to the airport. They spoke little during that drive to Seattle and embraced awkwardly outside the terminal, unable to look each other in the eyes. Back home in Sitka, local cops cordoned off Zora's street, keeping a pack of still-hungry reporters in check. And for the next several days, she avoided everyone except a trusted neighbor. The only television she watched was the blockbuster special, after which she'd called Jia-li Han to congratulate her on a powerful and refreshingly honest report – a Pulitzer Prize-winning piece of journalism if ever there was one. The announcements from KOS that followed were a bonus. Zora liked that woman – Savannah Sokolov – imagined her as the older sister she never had. Maybe one day they could be friends?

But nothing seemed to placate the hollowing sadness Zora felt over the loss of her mother.

Then toward the end of the week, as she sank deeper into despair, something extraordinary happened. Zora dismissed the first night as a fluke. She did the same on the second night. But at 4:00 a.m. on the third night, she awakened a surprised Mickey out of a dead sleep, asking him if his invitation to escape into the wild was still on the table.

Despite the ungodly hour, his answer was an enthusiastic, "*Yes.*"

Late that morning – *this* morning – she'd taken an Alaska Airlines flight back to Sea-Tac wearing her trademark baseball cap and sunglasses. Only this time, she'd added a blond wig to the get-up. It was part of a Marilyn Monroe costume she'd once worn on Halloween. She felt ridiculous, but it worked. No one had bothered her during the flight. Mickey met her at the airport sporting a killer smile and two dozen yellow roses. He made no attempt to push any of her personal buttons on the drive north. She liked that. He seemed to know instinctively what mattered and what didn't. For once in her life, she felt like she could let her guard down.

Now, some eight hours after leaving home, Zora sat quietly by Mickey's side listening to the steady rhythm of the rain, feeling the warmth of the fire. He poured more wine and offered a toast, "To new beginnings," he said.

They clinked glasses.

Several minutes went by then he added, "So, do you feel like talking about your eureka moment?"

"Yeah, I think so. But I'm not very good at this stuff, Mickey, so hang with me, okay?"

"I've got all the time in the world."

Zora shifted position on the sofa, curled one long leg under her, and took a deep breath. "Okay, you remember me mentioning my friend, Callie, right?"

"The terrible accident with the horses, sure"

"And the screams, Mickey, the awful screams."

He nodded.

"Nearly every night for thirty years I fought the same dragons, over and over. Then three nights ago it all stopped."

"You're kidding. Just like that?"

"Yeah, just like that."

Mickey thought for a long moment before responding. "Well, I'm no shrink but you've been through a hell of a lot over the past few weeks, Zora. Maybe what came down in the end with Chandler triggered some kind of catharsis. You wiped the slate clean, so to speak. You squared things with your friend, Callie. You got justice for your mother." He paused for another long moment. "And for Kat, too. I can't thank you enough for that."

Zora took a deep breath, her radiant green eyes changing color in the crackling firelight. "I don't know, Mickey, I hope you're right about Callie and Katrina. As for Chandler, I like to think it was his arrogance that got him killed. God knows I couldn't have gone through with it, much as I despised the man. Hell, I do that and I'm no better than him, probably worse."

Mickey took Zora's hand in his. "Look, there's no right way to lose people you love, not like we did. And facing the truth is never black and white. So yeah, Chandler got what he deserved. I believe that and so do the people who matter. Let it go, Zora. You deserve that."

"You really think so?"

"I know so," Mickey said. He set his wine glass on the table, pulled her close, ran his hands through her thick red hair. Zora melted into his arms and, for several long moments, they rocked gently back and forth.

"Thank you for that," she whispered.

Mickey traced the outline of her lips with his fingers. "You're the most incredible woman I've ever met, you know that?"

Zora felt a giddy flight of adrenaline, smacked him on the arm. "Ah, c'mon, I bet you say that to all the girls."

"No, I mean it."

"But you don't know me, not really."

"I know this, Zora. I'm a better *me* when I'm with *you*. I've never felt that way before."

"Oh, Jesus, Mickey…"

Mickey drew her back into his arms, softly, tenderly. She could smell him, practically taste him, his flesh warm and comforting. It seemed like forever since she'd felt wanted and protected. She wrapped his hand in her long, supple fingers and pressed the callused palm to her mouth, kissing it gently. "But my father, he made it so hard for me to trust…"

"I'm not your father, Zora. I'll be there for you. I promise."

She looked longingly into his eyes and in them saw truth. There was no yesterday, but Mickey had promised her tomorrow if only she would trust him now.

Zora kissed him fiercely.

Then the world went silent.

Epilogue

AT DAWN THE NEXT MORNING, high above the Strait of Juan de Fuca, the Old One stood ramrod still on a narrow, jagged ridge etched eons ago from solid granite. His eyes were fixed on the restless waters a hundred feet below. The swells slammed so hard against the craggy rocks, the noise sounded like thunder. Yet he did not flinch.

Neither did Houdini. He was standing at his mentor's side, an arm's length away. He'd spent the past hour recounting all that had happened since their last meeting, his delivery as crisp and clear as the early morning sky. In summary, he said, "The captain and the carpenter, Old One, they are very special people."

"Indeed they are."

"You are not troubled by our deceptive actions then?"

"You did what needed to be done, my son. Sometimes it is the best way, the *only* way. And you learned many lessons from the great blackfish, is that not so?"

"Yes. We *all* learned many lessons."

The Old One nodded, staring out to sea. "How strange it is for a species that lives its life without sun to lift the soul, to teach it how to soar, to send light into the darkness of people's hearts. Nature in her wildness has so much to teach us. We must never turn away from that wisdom, or be afraid of things we don't understand. There is such deep intelligence there, a mysterious force that connects all people and all things to Gaia, Mother Earth. We must use her knowledge wisely. Anything less and we shame the Great Spirit."

"You speak great truths as always, Old One."

The revered sage then turned slowly and placed his right hand over Houdini's heart. In his left hand, he held the distinctive feather of an eagle. "I am an old man and the time is long past for me to relinquish this sacred honor. An honor bestowed on me by Chief Raven Claw many moons ago as his forefathers had done with him. And so, with this symbol, I ask the Great Spirit to bless you and guide you on your journey. It is now in your hands."

"I am honored, Old One, but I am not worthy."

"Oh, but you are, my son, you are *most* worthy."

Houdini took the feather, clutched it to his body.

No words were needed. None were said.

They stood quietly after that, listening to the waves crashing on the rocks below, smelling the fresh salt air. More than three weeks had passed since the last sighting of the rogue whales, yet Houdini felt their presence now. He sensed the Old One did, too. And sure enough, in that sacred moment, five creatures burst from the gray swells, together as one, in an enormous breach. An instant later, they cleared the surface, climbing ever higher, their wild calls like a distant echo from some far-off time, silencing every creature on land and over sea. The breathtaking show of power and grace lasted only a few seconds, a final tribute it seemed to a kindred spirit. And then they were gone, moving with the ancient, endless currents toward the vast Pacific Ocean.

Houdini felt humbled and small. "Will we ever see them again, Old One?"

"I may not, but you surely will. You see, the mighty blackfish have come to call us back from the edge, to fire our imaginations, to rekindle our sense of awe. They have come to remind us that we are not nature's master, we are all one. All things are connected. It is their gift to the world."

A long pause, then Houdini said, thoughtfully, "Ancient minds that hold timeless lessons."

"Yes, my son," the Old One replied in a low, calm voice. "And we must listen and learn. We must learn what they know."

Acknowledgements

The author gratefully acknowledges the help and support of many individuals who contributed to this work. They include Leanne Bucaro, Howard Garrett, Denise Guerrero, Art Insana, Peter Jaycock, David and Jane Lambkin, Linda Langton, Alan McLaren, Jason Neal, Rick Oltman, Nina Paules, Peter and Anna Quinn, Real Robles, Scott Rosekrans, David Samuels, David Sellars, Linda Silva, Detective Cloyd Steiger, Karen Sullivan, Bob Walthers, and June Williams. Many thanks to all. With special thanks to a wonderful friend and editor, Olivia Rupprecht – and to my rock, Michele Wolpe, for being there, always.

WILLIAM NEAL has worked in televison for more than twenty years, primarily as a writer and producer, with over 400 hours of prime time credits to his name. For three years, he served as Executive Producer of the award-winning TV series *E! True Hollywood Story*.

A former college and professional hockey coach, Bill lives in Southern California. *Rogue Justice* is his second book and first novel.

For more information, please visit the author's website:
www.william-neal.com